UNSPEAKABLE: THE KILLING SCHOOL

ALSO BY HART RIVERS

THE MURDER ON THE MEKONG SERIES

UNBREAKABLE

UNKNOWABLE

UNSPEAKABLE

UNSPEAKABLE: THE KILLING SCHOOL

MURDER ON THE MEKONG, BOOK THREE

HART RIVERS

Book and cover design by eBook Prep
www.ebookprep.com

June 2022
ISBN: 978-1-64457-320-4

ePublishing Works!
644 Shrewsbury Commons Ave
Ste 249
Shrewsbury PA 17361
United States of America

www.epublishingworks.com
Phone: 866-846-5123

For the ones who hold us close
When the darkness is deep

One does not become enlightened by imagining figures of light, but by making the darkness conscious.

— CARL JUNG, THE PHILOSOPHICAL TREE, 1945

NIGHTBIRD

The Nightbird flits from tree to tree, following the chase through the sultry jungle. The moon is full and bright here along the Mekong River and there is the glistening of dark arterial blood on the leaves.
Fear and death perfume the dank air. It mingles with the sound of labored breath and pounding boot-clad feet. A young Vietnamese soldier cries out:
"Người lính ma!"
Ghost Soldier.
"Người lính ma! Người lính ma! Bao—"
Bao, his commander's name, is the last word he speaks.
Bao, leading the way forward, whirls around just in time to see the boy drop. A too-young recruit picked-off on his watch. But his other men, they are hardened jungle warfare killers and in quick succession he sees first one neck, then two, then all but his own neck snap side-ways, raised weapons falling just before their bodies begin to resemble beached squid with their collective limbs going flop, flop, flop.
He has seen so much horror in this war, but never has he seen anything like this. His men, his entire squad, must be the victims of some insidiously poisoned darts aimed with deadly precision from a well-hidden enemy. For whatever reason he has been spared, and not for a minute does he believe it is from the amulet his grandmother placed around his neck for protection.

Ghost soldier.

He remembers his grandmother's warning to beware of *Con quỷ*—a demon that only exists in the minds of those who believe in the supernatural, which Bao does not.

Still, he feels his heart slamming against the amulet; a shiver of foreboding snakes up his spine.

"Bao," calls a voice he's never heard before, from what direction he cannot tell. "Tôi đang đến, Bao! Sẵn sàng hay không ở đây tôi đến!"

I am coming, Bao! Ready or not, here I come!

This is not the same game of hide and seek he once played with his twin brother as he crouched, quietly snickering, in the hidey hole of a familiar, fallen tree. No, it's not like that at all with the sweat slick on the back he plasters against the spiny bark of a huge palm where he tries to blend into the waving fronds and debates: Prepare to fight, to die, to flee?

The dagger strapped to his chest, pried from an enemy's rigor mortis grip with GERBER USA etched into the blade, is more reassuring than a mother's milk laden breast. And the AK-47, clenched in his sweaty palms, will now and forever be his most cherished possession.

For all the good the same weapons did his men, all of them eliminated by some wraith-like creatures—*surely not just one*—still waiting for him.

Ghost soldier.

"Ready not, here *I* come," Bao whispers in broken English just as he leaps from his hiding place and sprays the surrounding area with a fresh round. He saves a single bullet for himself, just in case.

And then it is eerily quiet. Only the sound of a lone bird calls from a branch overhead.

Bao glances up.

A figure that belongs in some super-human cartoon streaks down.

And then Bao is on his back, knife drawn from the sheath bandoliered at his chest, blade tipped into the hollow at his throat.

"Gotcha," says the human-creature with a grin. "Time to go to the Fun House."

"Kill me."

"Sorry, buddy, but you're not getting off that easy."

"*Con quỷ.*"

"Oh, I've been called much worse, trust me. Sticks and stones and all that."

"*Người lính ma!*"

The Nightbird cocks its head and takes flight with the sound of dark laughter beneath its wings.

CHAPTER 1

The Republic of Vietnam
Undisclosed Location
Summer, 1969

The last time Jerry Prince closed his eyes he was in full psycho ward restraints stripped down buck naked on a stretcher. When his eyes slid slightly open he could see stars in the sky outside the chopper he had been boarded onto. Given his latest killing spree that the Army brass needed to keep hush-hush, he was pretty sure their best course of action was to toss him out over the South China Sea to become just another poor GI MIA never to be seen or heard from again.

Which meant if he was still alive what they had planned was going to be worse than death. Like ending up in a padded cell deep in the bowels of the military version of a facility for the criminally insane where he could expect to be living out the rest of his miserable life.

Moving his fingers and muscles like a reptilian Houdini, his stretching brought to life the extraordinary Irezumi tattoo of the mythical Nightbird across his chest, its head sweeping up to his neck in blue-black detail. The wingspread slightly rippled as he weighed the odds of taking out the Special Forces guards—one at his head, two at his feet—before overtaking the pilot.

Although he was careful to appear still sedated, over the loud bleat of chopper blades a familiar viper-like voice whispered into his ear, "Going somewhere? I don't think so. Why don't we poke out the bad birdie's eye?"

Jerry felt the plunge of a needle go straight into his neck.

The last thing he heard was the mocking, dark laughter of Agent J.D. Mikel.

∼

THE NEXT TIME Jerry Prince opened his eyes he was alone. He thought.

He let enough time pass to determine there was no one else breathing within range of his highly attuned ears before blinking…then blinking again, rapidly, to fully wake up because clearly nothing he was seeing, feeling, was real.

He tested his arms, his legs. No restraints. He did the old cliché and pinched himself and…okay. He was actually awake and in a room with a cream colored ceiling. A white fan turned overhead. Beneath his back was a very comfortable mattress on a real bed with real sheets and a nice cushy pillow under his head. He heard the tropical calls of birds. The soothing trickle of a fountain. Wind chimes tinkling.

This was all wrong.

There was some good quality rattan furniture with batik style cushions and a nice rattan desk with an Oriental lamp. Next to the desk was a carved teak chair with some inviting clothes draped over it.

If he didn't know better, he'd think he was back on R&R in Thailand.

Jerry got up, put on a white tee-shirt that covered his tattoo, followed by black VC style pajamas, and slip-on sandals. They fit.

He suspiciously eyed a screened door. Tested it. Unlocked. This was all very nice. Too nice. *What kind of crazy mind game was this?*

Intending to find out he stepped onto a palatial veranda filled with vases of white jasmine and red geraniums. A fine table covered in white linen was set for two with a large silver domed tray in the middle.

Might there be a claymore mine hiding under the silver, just waiting for his lift of the dome to take him out permanently while Mikel laughed from his hiding place?

But, no, that wasn't Mikel's style. He would look you in the eyes while he killed you.

Of course, that was half the fun.

A sweep of his gaze beyond the veranda only heightened Jerry's certainty that someone was fucking with him big time:

In the midst of a beautiful garden that looked like it belonged in a LIFE magazine was a man in a real cowboy hat with an authentic looking rattlesnake band around it. He was wearing a very white, precisely pressed doctor's lab coat over a fancy blue rodeo shirt, the kind with pearl buttons. A large silver and turquoise buckle rode the center of his faded, old jeans. The cowboy was pruning a gardenia bush.

The guy gave him a wave and Jerry noticed the feet approaching sported a pair of highly polished snakeskin boots tipped in silver.

"Howdy, pardner!" he called in a deep, Texas accent, and as he stopped, nearly toe-to-toe, Jerry noticed he was as tall as himself—well over six feet—and a little older, say early 30's. He reminded Jerry of Rowdy Yates on Rawhide, kind of Eastwood handsome and tough. Longish chestnut colored hair, steely blue eyes. All Tex needed was a horse to go along with his polite invitation.

"Join me for breakfast? I can brief you on your first assignment."

Jerry hesitated. *It's always better to escape as soon as possible, here's your chance to cut and run. This guy looks easy to kill if he tries to get in the way.*

"Now Jerry," said Tex with a big, friendly smile like he was a mind reader, "Don't run. Hear me out. C'mon now, at least have a nice breakfast before you go. Besides, Old Hoss, I got snipers up in the trees in four directions aiming right at you, right now."

Jerry smiled back. "Okay, why not?"

Once seated across from each other, Tex poured the dark brew from a silver carafe and pushed forward a crystal container filled with condensed milk.

"I believe you like it with two heaping spoonfuls? Hope you don't mind I took the liberty of ordering up your favorite bacon omelet. Here, the croissants are excellent, especially with some of this fresh mango jam."

Jerry raised a brow.

"Now you don't think I'd go to all this trouble just to poison you, do you?" Tex guffawed like a good old boy and took a forkful of Jerry's omelet before washing it down with his own coffee that had come from the same carafe.

Smell test passed—and it did smell delicious—Jerry put his own fork to good use.

"I'm afraid you have me at a disadvantage," he said between bites. "Just who the hell are you, if you don't mind me asking."

"Doctor Ronald Miles, MD, PhD—but don't call me Doctor-Doctor, just call me Miles—Director of the Institute for the Study of International Conflict. In Spook speak that's ISIC, or the joke of course is `I SICK.' Everybody here though just calls it The Killing School."

~

MILES TOOK off the cowboy hat, finger brushed his hair back, and studied the predator relishing breakfast across from him. So much energy pulsed from each lift of his fork and gulp of coffee that Miles could easily envision this killer of all killers suddenly planting the cutlery into his own very fine brain.

Jerry Prince was easily capable of far more than that. Which was exactly the reason the mastermind behind this whole operation—The Ambassador, Phillip Jordan—had ultimately agreed to have the infamous Ghost Soldier sent here.

The sense of pulsing energy that could easily turn fatal had Miles darting his gaze to the tree tops where his snipers were stationed. His pupils weren't liking the sun and the energy waves felt like they were creeping under his skin. Possibly a consequence of his usual Monday morning 1ml micro hit of Lysergic Diethylamide Acid.

He took his favorite Ran-Bans out and put them on. Much better.

Miles fleetingly wondered if Jerry Prince had any affection for the drug himself. Unlikely for a full-time predator, though such stats weren't included on the psych report Miles's freakish eidetic image photographic memory pulled up. He could see it as if the report were sitting right in front of him and zoomed in on the most essential details:

NAME: Jerry Prince aka Milton Kastanski aka David Smith aka multiple other aliases
VITALS: U.S. Army Captain, Special Forces. 6'2" 188 pounds. Age 26. Right handed. Martial arts expert.
PERTINENT HISTORY: Prince is the product of a rather cruel childhood followed by mostly punishing foster homes. He was a murderer at the age of 15. The resulting personality combined with a high intelligence and gifted physical attributes presents a unique package of killing ability. Indeed, his Lethality Index is a remarkable 9.5 out of 10. Hand-eye coordination and speed are superior. Pain threshold very high. Capacity to inflict pain and suffering high to the point of indifference though the

psycho-sexual sadism response is actually quite low. His empathy responses are acute in the way of a highly sociopathic character disorder. **HIGHLY CLASSIFIED:** Prince initially joined the Army in 1964 and quickly displayed unique abilities that escalated his advancement until 1966 when a consensus was formed he was responsible for the serial murders of soldiers under his command. To avoid public scrutiny he was quietly transferred to Madigan General Hospital's locked ward (see Attachment A) where he managed to escape in 1967. Under the alias of (redacted) he again enlisted under the assumed identity of a college graduate with ROTC credentials and then quickly rose in the Army's ranks as a highly valued Special Forces military asset. The details of his tenure, and especially the storied and infamous Ghost Soldier escapades in 1968 through 1969 necessitating the CIA to bring in their best hunter assassin to finally capture Prince, insured his (1) being rendered to ISIC for researching and exploiting his established assets and (2) training and harvesting of any untapped abilities. (see Attachment B).

As Miles continued to mentally flip through well over 200 pages of documentation while honing in on the most tasty and relevant bits, his anticipation rose to elation at the prospect of working with such an anomaly of nature.

One of the great things that Jerry Prince had going for the purposes of The School was that he was really not impaired at all in the way most would consider him to be on the evidence of his history. He was not a wacko-psycho or clinically incapacitated crazy. No, in fact, he was wired in a way that allowed him to be rather skilled at reading other people's needs and wants, of being charming and disarming, sensing vulnerabilities, being manipulative, being very likable when he chose.

He was exactly what Miles was looking for. This creature could quite possibly be highly functional and productive in the right milieu. That milieu would involve giving him challenging, productive work in a challenging environment which, Miles knew, was how Jerry liked it. As one of the top predators on the planet he would be mostly content with his tracking, capture and killing assignments. Of course, he was driven by the usual blend of revenge, resentment, and "pathological narcissism," as his fellow shrinks liked to call it.

"Such a rare and exotic animal you are," Miles mused aloud. "Invaluable for the work."

The fork paused. "And just what is this work, might I ask?"

A nod at the butter knife his companion picked up, presumably to sample the mango jam, and Miles asked, "I imagine you've heard of the Phoenix Program?"

"One of the CIA's better ideas. Nothing like out-terrorizing the terrorists when it comes to interrogation and assassination—with a little help from our Australian and RVN friends."

"Take 'er up a notch. Make it ten."

A dark eyebrow rose. "Go on."

"Well, pardner, essentially what we've got here is a top secret research and teaching institution that could benefit from your particular expertise: Killing. Torture. Psyops. Political mayhem. More coffee?"

"No thanks. Please proceed."

"You, Jerry, have singular abilities and skills that your government considers to be extremely useful—that is, if those abilities and skills can be focused and directed in a more positive way than you've directed them before. Let's be frank with each other. You screwed up. You got caught. And why? Because you lacked focus. You lacked direction. You weren't able to harness the wild horse inside and got bucked off. Big time. I can help you learn to harness that horse and realize your true potential."

"Oh, really?" The predator leaned back in his chair, crossed his arms. "And just how would you go about doing that?"

"I am a neuroscientist and a clinical psychologist. But in your case what's most important is that next to research, I like to teach. Only if I have a motivated student, mind you, who is driven to succeed." Miles lingered over a sip of his own coffee, letting that sit between them before he laid down his aces. "The thing is, though, how much can anyone enjoy their success when they have to go around constantly pretending to be someone they're not because society doesn't appreciate what they do best, or who they really are? What I'm offering you is something you've probably always wanted but gave up on having a long time ago: You can do your thing and not be locked up for it forever. You won't have to hide who you are or what you are. Far from it, my friend. You'll be rewarded for it, handsomely, and you can live freely."

The lithe and powerful arms that had been crossed slowly uncrossed. An elbow that could easily knock out a windpipe came to rest on the table while a deadly thumb and forefinger thoughtfully stroked a ridiculously chiseled chin.

"Seriously?"

"Seriously," Miles confirmed.

"You know, from my experience, anything that sounds too good to be true, usually is."

"That's exactly what I thought when I first heard about you. Upon doing my research, I came to a very different conclusion. The CIA—or more specifically ISIC—believes you have the potential to be the ultimate model for our Future Elite Modern Warrior. As Director of the Institute, you could even say that I've staked my reputation on it."

As Jerry remained silent, pretending to consider—because, really, what was there to consider when he'd just been handed the keys to the kingdom vs life in the dungeon of a locked ward—Miles could feel his senses sharpening. Expanding. His earlier 1ml micro dose of LSD was kicking in, and so was an idea that got him to wondering what might happen if he did a little sideways experimentation with this Future Elite Modern Warrior... if that elitism might be sped along with a little help from the God of Drugs.

"So...?" Miles prompted.

Jerry's answer was a sharp salute, before he extended a palm across the table.

"Yaaa-*hooo!*" Miles whooped and pumped Jerry's hand until he realized that only one of them was still doing the shaking and it wasn't his prized recruit. "Now, how about a little tour of our school before it gets too warm? You are welcome to bring the cutlery with you, but I did salvage this if you'd rather have it instead."

He placed Jerry's personal combat knife between them.

"A tour sounds good." Jerry took the knife. Handed Miles his hat. "Lead the way. Pardner.'"

CHAPTER 2

T he "tour" promptly proceeded with "just call me Miles" going into all kinds of detail about the flowered landscaped gardens he said were spread throughout the ISIC facility—which the doctor clearly took great pride in as well, gushing, "It is a beautiful campus!"

As he swept a lab-coated arm to encompass the French colonial style quarters where they had done their deal on the veranda, Jerry could only think: *Holy fuck!* Had he actually died and gone to heaven? There had to be a catch somewhere because it was too good to be true… but then again, he did have exceptional talents and skills, and sure, like the doc said they could run a little wild sometimes, get out of control, but… *what if?*

"Now adjacent to this fine dining room—told ya, you'd like that omelet!—if you go a little ways down that path, we have a luxury theater and an excellent drinking club. Anything and everything you want, all top shelf. What's your pleasure, Jerry? No, don't tell me…Jack! Got a case of it waiting for you after our little tour. Now let's go check out the rec area."

From one winding cobblestone path to another they moved on until arriving at a first-rate workout room and full-on gymnasium with gleaming hardwood. The nicest locker room he'd ever seen emptied out to a tennis court that looked like it belonged at Wimbledon. Nearby was a plot of white sand with a volleyball net, which led to an Olympic sized swimming pool, surrounded by a tropical landscape filled with bird of paradise and an explosion of exotic flowers that climbed over a tall stretch of formidable fencing. No doubt to keep the VC out and whoever wanted to get out, in. Though, at this point, Jerry couldn't imagine ever wanting to leave.

"The School is obviously not hurting for funds," he noted.

"Wait till you see the rest, it only gets better! C'mon!" The doc kept up his running patter until they reached a very modern, highly equipped clinic, complete with a surgical procedure area and recovery unit with seven hospital beds.

All of the beds were occupied. None of the patients looked particularly good with various appendages missing, faces either disfigured or wrapped in gauze, and either appearing comatose or groaning in misery.

"Just think of it," sighed Miles, almost dreamily. "Think of how much information is in each and every one of these brains, in all of our brains—obviously some of us have more in them than others—but with just the right techniques, which we're still perfecting...wait. Wait. I have something even better to show you. This way."

Into an adjacent dental clinic—"also used for research"—they went.

Several chairs were occupied. Each of the "patients" had an attending "doctor."

Miles, clearly in charge, shooed one of them away.

"Now, Jerry, I know you just got here but given your aptitude for such things I think you'll find this as fascinating as I do. It's amazing, absolutely amazing, how cooperative people become with their mouth clamped wide open..." As the wide open mouth he pointed to gagged out a plea for help, Miles launched into a demo of "how just a little water poured down a clamped open mouth can physiologically trigger the choking reflex because, you know, it's an extraordinarily powerful vulnerability. Remarkable, really, just watch how this tiny bit of water overpowers the brain no matter what..." and as the body in the chair responded as if electrodes had been placed into his head and an electrical switch thrown, Miles exclaimed, "See? POW! BOOM! There goes that choke reflex and your body believes, absolutely believes it is dying. You're not of course—see, he's not really dying—but you *are* drowning as far as your brain is concerned and that is all that matters. Amazing isn't it?"

Apparently, the doc was equally amazed at teeth drilling and how, "It takes really very little actual drilling for nerves once that mouth is clamped open again to get someone saying just about any secret you would want to hear from them. Just think of it..."

The guy kept saying "just think of it" and damn if you didn't just "think of it" even if you did not want to. Even for Jerry it seemed kind of creepy, and for anyone half normal of course it would be VERY creepy, but the way the doc delivered it you did start to think about it because it sounded kind of scientifically interesting, and if you showed any interest at all he launched into way too many descriptive details that even the famed Ghost Soldier finally needed a break from.

"Thanks, doc, but mind if we move on?" he prompted when Miles started for another chair.

"Oh, sorry! I'm afraid I get carried away sometimes. Once I'm in `The Zone' I forget that not everyone shares my enthusiasm for my particular area of expertise."

Given the doc's motor mouth, Jerry wasn't sure if he should ask. He did anyway.

"I'm not really into torture." The assertion was so absurd that Jerry covered his mouth and pretended to cough. "It's true," he insisted. "While it might appear otherwise, torture....no, let's call that persuasion, such a kinder word... is simply a means to an end." Gone was the Texas twang and so was the cowboy in a lab coat. The Doctor-Doctor was IN. "My expertise, Mr. Prince, is mind control. While interrogation techniques are in the upper echelon of funding and research by the CIA for security purposes, it is, shall we say..." his voice dipped low, confidential, "the meat and potatoes of ISIC, but rather bereft of true intelligence, creativity, and ambition. They can do much better than the silly little demonstrations I tired you with just now. That's why they hired me. My professional qualifications are quite extensive and I am happy to provide you with a CV, but for now suffice it to say that given your own unique qualifications, we could be quite the Dream Team. That's what the CIA is banking on—and you can see how heavily that banking is in every direction you look, so...shall we proceed?"

Well. If this didn't just get more and more interesting. Jerry tipped a pretend hat and affected the Texas twang the doctor had dropped. "Aftah you, doc."

THE DOC WAS ENJOYING the tour so much Jerry had to wonder how often he got outside company. Not that a school created for perfecting mind control and torture techniques was the sort of place that issued an engraved Open House invitation unless you worked there or were one of the poor saps being worked on.

"About those guys in the beds and dental chairs," he interjected when the doc paused for a breath, "How did they draw the lucky straws?"

"Primarily they are VC, and any other kind of political opposition to the present regime as you may have ascertained from—"

"But a couple looked, you know, like they could be from other countries."

"And indeed, they are. Our government's enemies aren't restricted to the North Vietnamese." Miles slid him a sly grin. "You know."

Jerry chuckled. At least the guy had a sense of humor.

"Makes me wonder who decided I should be put on the payroll instead of being strapped into one of those chairs."

"It came from the top. The Ambassador. Phillip Jordan." Stopping at the edge of what looked like a little town square, Miles hastened to add, "But of course I lobbied aggressively on your behalf. After reviewing your records, I helped convince him that you could be invaluable to The School. And Jerry, I truly believe it."

A spark of something, so deep down he really didn't know where it came from, maybe from something good that happened in his shitty freakshow of a childhood, felt like a strange little flutter. It was like…like he didn't want to let the doc down?

At least he didn't want to kill him. And he did sort of like the place. Even the little village off the town square with more cobblestone streets and tidy white bungalows with red tiled roofs for "staff living quarters" was kind of homey and cute. Certainly, compared to a life of institutions, foster homes and barracks.

"But you won't live here, of course," Miles advised him. "This is where the lesser personnel live. Not that they aren't important. Everyone selected to be a part of The School is important. Like family, just with different roles to play."

"I'm sure you all get together to play Scrabble on Friday nights."

Miles guffawed and slapped Jerry on the back. "We always do a head count. You never want to risk being missed!"

From there they veered off in a south-bound direction that eventually led to a jungle path, carefully camouflaged to the naked eye. Gone were the cobblestone streets and walkways. The jungle path ended in a circular clearing that literally reeked of squalor.

"And here we have our lovely Dungeon area. This is where they—they being the hunters and gatherers you will be supervising—initially bring most of the poor souls procured from the Phoenix Program. As you said, one of the CIA's more effective capture and interrogation programs with their waterboarding and such, but obviously falling short of certain desired outcomes, which isn't all bad since that is why we have The School. It is like a rather tropical Dickens setting, wouldn't you say?" He paused just long enough for any personnel within hearing distance to nod. "I am sure that to some degree the prisoners are happy, or let's say grateful, to be sent to our nice, clean hospital facility if it means leaving the filth and hunger here..." A sniff. Another sniff. "Not to mention the stench! Actually, I am glad to be showing you around as I have not been down here in some time and now that I see how they have let this place go... Yes. I am now, RIGHT NOW, officially declaring this a clean and sanitary dungeon. You—Lieutenant!"

"Sir, yes, sir!"

The 2nd LT that had been summoned gave a sharp salute to the Director of ISIC who had probably never worn a uniform outside of a lab coat.

True to form the doc went into way too much detail about how clean he wanted the place to be by this time tomorrow. Apparently, the dental chair business was common knowledge because the LT blanched and started calling out guys who looked like a crazy anthill of cleaners.

Jerry busied himself with a little tiger cage-to-tiger cage investigation. He was familiar with tiger cages having once visited ugly Con Son Island during his Special Forces training. Most of these were that style with the small concrete trenches and bars on top, typically a regulation 5 feet wide, 6 feet long and 6 feet deep. And, typically, they housed five to seven prisoners that would be poked and prodded and beaten with sticks or rifle butts through the upper grate. Typically.

Some of these weren't your typical tiger cages. They were smaller, constructed out of bamboo, and looked like they really were built for containing one four-legged animal. The four- legged animal would be able to stand up and lie down. A two-legged human would not ever be able to stand up or ever stretch out lying down. They lay cramped and constricted in their own filth covered in flies. He counted twenty.

Pausing in front of one to get a better look at the emaciated creature in the mud and excrement, the pitiful mewing inside the cramped space was joined by a heavy sigh behind him.

Company. Guess who?

"This is what is left of an evidently brutal interrogation before arriving here. And they expect me to work on this? Ridiculous," grumbled Miles. "From now on, I'll be counting on you to bring me much healthier subjects. Especially the intelligent ones. You know, the teachers, lawyers, activists, Buddhists, politicos. That is what we want to work on. You *will* be much better at this than your predecessor, won't you?" He actually winked when Jerry frowned. "No, no, no just joking! This poor thing was not your predecessor. Ha-ha got you with that one!"

It kept on like that until Jerry's head felt like a 33 record spinning on 45. He had a certain feeling, one he hoped was right, that him and the doc would not end up being huge buds, and therefore not hanging out a lot together except for business... at least he hoped so. This place reminded him of a severe grown up version of the worst kind of foster home, where you had to live with the kind of people nobody ever liked to be around and didn't want at their house, but you're stuck living together anyway. Sure, you could feel a little bad for some of them, but there were just too many with bad habits, particularly the mean, bullying kind. Just throw that group together running a prison facility in a boring, scary place like this and you had so much potential ugliness right away.

Eventually the endless tour backtracked to where the jungle path began. As if there were a fork in the road determining if you were heading straight to Hell or receiving a heavenly pardon, a north-bound path meandered through a bamboo grove where they crossed a small footbridge and entered another lovely garden, much older than anything they had previously seen. Sited perfectly within the garden was a large marble fountain with cascading water that found its way to a koi pond filled with exquisite koi and inviting, nearby benches. Perhaps fifty feet from the pond was a tall stucco fence with a scrolling iron gate.

"Just so you know, past that gate is another road, a bit rough and only wide enough for a jeep, but it cuts over to the dungeon area, maybe a five minute ride. Close enough to get there quick if need be and far enough away not to hear or smell anything unpleasant. Tell you what, I'll show you the library and classrooms tomorrow, they are really something, but we'll wind this up with an introduction to someone who's looking forward to meeting you."

Miles swept his hand toward a gleaming-white vintage French Colonial villa with a wide and welcoming veranda. As Jerry took the short flight of broad stairs leading to the expansive porch, he felt an acute sense of anticipation. A large rattan bladed ceiling fan circled slowly over a nearby table with an embroidered tablecloth. Seated at the table was a man of military bearing, smoking an unfiltered, aromatic cigarette, a French Gauloises. Long black hair slicked back, he had an impressive mustache and very white teeth when he smiled, stood, rested the cigarette in a crystal ashtray, and reached over to shake Jerry's hand.

The man's grip was very, very strong and firm.

Jerry met him eye-to-eye. Returned his grip with an equal pressure. Smiled back.

"Jerry Prince, this here is Monsieur Hugo Goulet." The Texas twang that had disappeared sometime between drilling teeth and delivering marching orders to an LT now scrubbing a host of filthy tiger cages, was back. "Commandant Goulet runs the camp here and we all answer to him. And now Commandant Goulet, it is surely my pleasure to present to you the highly anticipated addition to our team, Jerry Prince. As you know he will act as my new Officer in Charge of Long Range Security and we will see how quickly he rises from there. At any rate, we are fortunate to have someone of his abilities and aptitudes, and I anticipate the two of you will enjoy a good, long, and profitable relationship here at The Killing School."

Jerry watched Goulet arch an eyebrow, ever so slightly. It had a strange kind of hypnotic effect. Or maybe it was just that he'd never met anyone, woman or man, whose features were so perfectly stunning it was hard to look at them at the same time you couldn't help but stare.

"Please, Doctor," replied Goulet in a voice to match his almost other-worldly looks as he released his grip but not the eye contact. "Won't you join us as I was just sampling my newest arrival of absinthe?"

"Well, pardner," drawled the Doc, "I would love nothing better than spending what's left of the day enjoying the absinthe and discussing that most interesting obscure Marquis de Sade book you have uncovered but...I have a surgery. I need steady nerves there and concentration, so I'll leave the two of you together and make amends when we next meet."

From his peripheral vision Jerry saw Miles wave his hat like the Cisco Kid, heard him call, "Happy Trails!" as he sauntered down the path they had arrived on.

"Absinthe?" politely inquired his host.

Jerry had never cared for the pale green, licorice infused libation, hated it actually.

"Sounds great," he replied.

CHAPTER 3

It was officially Jerry's Day #2 at The Killing School, now TKS for short. He had never kept track of the days the way Army draftees did, counting down from 365 and a Wake-Up to when they returned home, lucky enough not to be sent back sooner in a body bag. He, however, had never had a real home to return to. But when he had awoken in his nice room again with a bacon omelet and coffee waiting on the veranda, there was something different from all of his other mornings before: A sense of acceptance. Support. Purpose.

The Commandant, who had insisted he call him Hugo, had a lot to do with that.

And, he supposed, so did Miles, who was stepping into the additional role of Professor as of today. Besides more TKS Orientation Miles would be administering some tests in furthering his hypothesis that he, Jerry Prince, could indeed become the prototype of the Future Elite Modern Warrior.

Miles had even granted him his own new nickname: FEW.

Jerry could only hope their breakfasts together would bear the same distinction.

"So, pardner, how did your visit go with Commandant Goulet after I left yesterday? More juice?"

Before Jerry could answer, another round of freshly squeezed OJ was in his glass.

"Commandant Goulet is a very impressive individual," Jerry took a sip of the juice, leaving it at that.

"He's even more impressive than he looks, and he is quite something to behold, isn't he?"

"He probably doesn't have any trouble picking up the ladies."

Miles guffawed. "Aw, c'mon now, Old Hoss! It was downright unnerving, wasn't it? Always a lot of fun to see anyone encounter him for the first time. Including you."

It was true. The Commandant was not simply handsome. He was without doubt the most beautiful human being Jerry had ever encountered. Like Greek god statue beautiful. He himself was tall, athletic, smart and in most circumstances outside of a pool party at Rock Hudson's house, would be considered the best-looking guy in any room. But, The Commandant was on another magnitude. If you could make a thoroughbred out of Gregory Peck, Cary Grant *and* Rock Hudson this would be the dazzling result. Perfect skin, perfect hair, perfect face, perfect physique, a remarkable voice, but... something more.

"Okay, I'll admit that I was a bit taken aback at first." It was a reluctant admission, but he was curious about that something more. "And then you add in that he's charming, sophisticated, a great conversationalist and really deep thinker and—better stop there before I start sounding like a fag, but... There's something else about him that goes beyond all that."

"Gestalt."

"Gestalt?"

"It means the whole forms more than the sum of its parts. The Commandant is a rare creation of nature—a lot like you that way. Not quite mortal. Watch him and learn, Jerry. He has weaponized this aspect of himself and can exploit it ruthlessly." Miles leaned in. "I actually helped him hone that a bit." He put a fraction of an inch between thumb and forefinger. "Not much but sometimes that little extra can be what puts you over the top."

"Little extra...what?" *My, professor, what big pupils you have.*

"Focus. Training your mind. I've got all sorts of exercises for us to work on with that. And..." Suddenly he blinked and out came the Ray-Bans. "There are other assists for us to discuss. Later. Now the day's a'waistin' and we have work to do, so chow down, Old Hoss!"

Jerry wished he'd quit calling him that.

Nonetheless, he dug into his bacon omelet and tried not to think of how he could take out the doc if he got too grating. And no, he wasn't

16

going to think about disappearing over the flower-wrapped fence after arrowing his combat knife—that Miles had given back to him, had to remember that—and planting it straight into the sniper's heart.

There was only one sniper. A surreptitious glance had informed him the others had not been summoned this second morning.

Jerry wondered if there would come a time that he lost count of the days he was here, or if he would keep count like some people did their blessings. Imagining such things was dangerous, and how well he did know that, because he had lived a life of disappointment and disappointment made him angry and when he got angry, he had a tendency to take it out on those who didn't necessarily deserve it.

Maybe Miles would work with him on that, too.

JERRY WOKE UP ON DAY #3 feeling pretty confident about how orientation and the tests had gone, so he wasn't prepared to see Miles eating breakfast alone without the anticipated morning beverages and a nice bacon omelet waiting.

For him.

Was the honeymoon over already? Had he screwed something up? Were they planning to get rid of him despite all the promises that had been made?

Sucker.

That's when Miles raised his solo glass of OJ in a salute and announced, "Seems you have an invitation from none other than Commandant Goulet to join him for breakfast. While I'm sure you'd much rather share coffee and conversation with me, he is the commanding officer, so *buenos días* and *adios*! Oh, and Jerry? Outstanding work yesterday. Congratulations on both achievements."

"Both?"

"Such invitations from Commandant Goulet are even more rare than exceeding my expectations, which were already quite high. Enjoy your breakfast."

Jerry gave him a cursory salute and practiced grin, then turned his back before Miles could see the melting to something closer to actual emotion. It made him feel kind of queasy, because unless he got angry, his emotions ran quite cool, untouched by most anything so called "normal people" were affected by. Things like death, pain, love. But this weird sensation inside was akin to a rubber band stretched taut, with an alien ray of waking hope on one end, the black abyss that was home on the other—only for their comingling to snap him in the direction of another veranda where it turned out absinthe wasn't half bad in the right company.

Such a disconcerting start to this fine tropical morning as he made his way to his summons, still some coolness in the air. A slight breeze moved the palm leaves overhead; the heat and humidity of the Delta would arrive soon. But in the moment was a stillness as the wheels in Jerry's brain replayed everything over and over while he wondered if the whole grand deal he'd been offered was a special delivery from Hell—given to him just so it could be taken back—and that's where he really was, not in a waking dream.

Jerry palmed the combat knife in his black silk trousers.

In a flash, blood beaded across his forearm. Huh. Must not be dead after all.

The black silk tunic matching his pants was part of the fine wardrobe he'd been given. Unlike his arm, he hesitated before slicing off a strip from the tunic's bottom to efficiently bind the wound.

Physical pain rarely bothered him, could even be pleasant since it made him feel some sensation... sometimes. No wonder a part of him had wondered why his once foster mom had screamed bloody murder when he took an axe to her to commit just that.

The axe was bound to fall on him, too. Every day that went by that he bought into this extravagant fantasy brought him that much closer to the whole charade falling apart. He *had* to remember that. Story of his life.

Stopping in the shade near a cluster of gardenia bushes with wide, white fragrant blooms, he took in the inviting veranda, with whirling, cooling rattan fans above a table covered with a sun-flowered tablecloth, set for two. His host hailed him.

"*Mon ami!* Please, come join me."

The too-good-to-be-true moment extended from another firm hand-shake, to a seat at the finely dressed table, to the aroma of fresh coffee. "South American style," explained his host while the houseboy poured heated milk simultaneously with the dark, rich fragrant brew.

"Delicious."

"Grown in the Highlands at my farm," said Hugo while Jerry sipped his coffee and prepared for the usual bullshit briefing to put him in his place since that would be more of the usual than whatever crazy shit was going on around here. But no, as the other man turned his otherworldly gaze full upon him, as if seeing him for what he had the capacity to become, not for what he was, Hugo said simply, "Jerry, you have some aptitude for warring."

Given his military credentials—if you left out the part about doing his own guys to get his fix—his warring aptitude spoke for itself.

"Uh... thanks?" Since that didn't sound respectful enough, he followed up with, "I mean, thank you, sir."

Silence. A gesture and the houseboy disappeared.

Then, "I have read over your file and reports from Dr. Miles. You have had your, let us say, 'problems.'"

Jerry did not like squirming but under the man's incisive gaze and anticipating what was probably coming, he did squirm. The combat knife in his trousers, he glanced at the silver gracing the table, just in case.

"Non, non," came Hugo's firm warning. "Do not entertain such thoughts. Not with me. I can easily kill you first but that is not my desire. You are too valuable to this grand enterprise to lose. Particularly once you and I strike our own grand bargain."

"A bargain?"

"*Oui*," he confirmed. "I wish to be your mentor, and you, my protégé. But this cannot happen without the right soil in which to plant our true beginnings, from which the rest will grow."

"What kind of soil?"

"The kind you have not had before, Jerry. We have no trust, do we? Between us there is no trust. So, we cannot put down our guard. Yes?"

Yes. No. He didn't know how to answer him beyond an honest, "You are correct. There is no trust."

"Then we must correct this." Hugo left the table and lifted from the veranda a young lychee tree in a bright blue pot. He sat it in the middle of the table, right in front of Jerry. "This is for you...and for me. We must find a place that is good for it in the garden and we will dig and plant it. We will both be responsible for it. It needs light, water, food to survive, and to thrive it needs care. Then it grows and thrives and flowers and bears fruit."

"You mean that you want us to plant this thing, so we can...grow and thrive and flower together?"

"*Exactement.* You will bring the plant. I will meet you with a shovel." Hugo pointed to a perfectly groomed expanse of yard, punctuated by the exquisite old fountain, swimming koi, and surrounded by artful gardens resembling flowered leis around a floating island of verdant green.

It was surprisingly relaxed and yet almost ritualistic the way they met, him with the plant, Hugo with a shovel, as they roamed about the grounds until Jerry abruptly stopped, deliberately gave his back to the nearest garden where a perfect planting space kept company with a profusion of other plants.

"How about here?" he asked, standing in the middle of the pristine lawn.

"Splendid."

And as Hugo handed Jerry the shovel, while Jerry handed over the plant, his new mentor, The Commandant of ISIC, explained, "Jerry, *mon ami*, this tree is our trust. We plant it together. It will grow between us, fresh and new, uncrowded by what has already been planted in our pasts. When we do what we say we will do, then the other can believe in the other. It is something that grows like a plant because trust is a living thing between all people, friends, lovers, family, not words."

No other words were spoken as they put the small lychee tree into the ground together, heaped the fresh turned earth upon it, and Hugo said something in French that sounded like a blessing before clapping Jerry on the shoulder and pronouncing, "So, let us go back for some breakfast, more coffee, and discuss goals before we plan your first mission."

CHAPTER 4

One week bled into two, then three, and before Jerry knew it, he had been in Paradise for a full month. Paradise mostly being time with Hugo, who was teaching him all sorts of things about language, the world, gardening, strategies, the fine art of assassination vs crude killing.

While he would never put time spent with Hugo in the same category as that with Miles, he had to admit that Professor Miles was an excellent lecturer. And boy, did he like to lecture once he got into The Zone. Which was always, no matter what was on tap for the day.

Take history, for example:

"We, at The Killing School, are even more secret than the Phoenix dark ops program. The Phoenix Program is buried under layers of bureaucracy above us called CORDS. It all goes back a long way but let's say 1963 when CIA station chief Peer DeSilva realized that the Vietcong were way ahead of him in terms of torture and murder. DeSilva took on this challenge in a big way. He centralized the intelligence operation under Saigon's Central Intelligence Organization at the National Interrogation Center and started hands-on training of the Vietnamese. He knew how to organize, this DeSilva. In just a year he had a Provincial Inter-rogation Centre in every province. He imported CIA experts who had worked on Russian defectors. They had advanced techniques over the old school methods of rape, electric shock, hanging and beating. While those are still favored for the terrorism effect, when the goal is simply extracting information, suffice it to say

that new is better. Now, Jerry, be sure you're taking good notes because there will be a quiz on this."

Scribble, scribble. Scribbling as fast as possible, until—he laid down his pen.

"I learn better by listening."

"I see, an auditory learner. Then forget the pen, and if you'd rather, we can test verbally, though I have seen some of your earlier writings and they are quite remarkable."

Jerry knew those were his journal writings from the Madigan General lock down ward documenting his childhood, his first kill, all his secret thoughts. It made him feel exposed, vulnerable. He did not like that.

"Now, Jerry..."

If he had to hear "Now, Jerry" One. More. Time...

"C'mon, pardner. I can see those hot wheels rolling, rolling, rolling! Remember what we practiced? How you take a breath when you feel some agitation coming on..."

Shit. This was always so hard. Making that choice to let all that Red Color of hot rage come through—or he could go with Blue Color, the cool color. He would choose... *"Blue,"* he breathed, followed by seven deep blue, cool, cleansing breaths, all the while doing the tapping of thumb to middle finger, and there went the red going down and away while the blue filled him with calm, cool clarity, and direction. It worked for rage, for anxiety too. Allowing him to "get centered." He could do this now in all sorts of stressful situations because the key was perseverance and he had a gift for that on top of lots of practice.

"Very good, Jerry. Now, by 1965 William Colby assembled all these new tech-niques into the Counter Terror program whose aim was to create various teams of operatives that could use assassination, abuses, kidnappings, intimidation and torture against the Viet Cong leadership. And, of course, against absolutely any one that the Americans deemed a threat to their puppet government. Anyone. It expanded hugely just a couple of years ago, in 1967, when our esteemed Ambas-sador, Phillip Jordan, who by the way is a very dear friend of The Comman-dant's, started moving dark moneys into it and helped create CORDS. You gotta love our USA acronyms...Civil Operations and Rural Development Support, sounds like we are all just simply helping farmers have a better life, doesn't it? Ha-ha, fooled them! CORDS took a stick and beat all hell out of the Vietcong's lower tech interrogation techniques—but you already knew that and sorry to bore you. The main point, Jerry, is that the real battle for mind control is right here and WE are the true core that is being counted on to win that war. With you, as

an intrinsic part of our team, we WILL perfect our ability to bend, shape, and extract whatever we need from a brain. Any brain. And that, my friend, is a weapon more powerful and far reaching than any nuclear bomb in the world."

Jerry aced the test. He aced them all. And as the months sped by, he learned how much he did not know, and he learned how much there was to learn. He realized he was IGNORANT and emotionally unintelligent. But emotional intelligence could be learned, and he had a high capacity for learning beyond the physical feats and tests of endurance that had always come so easily when he'd been a prized asset to the military.

And still was, just in a much bigger, more secretive way.

He was a teacher/trainer in his own right: a stellar understudy of Miles while Hugo continued refining his devoted protégé. Plus, there was Jerry's "day job" of capturing, detaining and transporting alleged enemy insurgents, any perceived political enemies of the Republic of Vietnam, and spies. Such spies did not yet extend to the likes of J.D. Mikel, or even Doctors Israel Moskowitz and Gregg Kelly, Mikel's little sidekicks that Jerry knew quite well. Izzy and Gregg were the head docs—as in, shrinks —Mikel had brought in to help track down a psychopathic killer. The one they thought was permanently put away even as he was being secretly delivered to The Killing School.

Had it been a year ago already?

So much had changed since, sometimes Jerry hardly recognized himself.

"Better take a good, last look!" Miles threw over his shoulder while he finished scrubbing up to assist for the big surgery.

Their ISIC surgical facility saw plenty of use, though not typically with one of the Agency's superior plastic surgeons flown in. Jerry still pinched himself every morning, but he should be black and blue from this one. Having one of the top surgeons specializing in facial reconstruction IN THE WORLD sent specifically to work on HIM was yet another reassurance of how deeply he was valued by those who saw him for who and what he was, not some fake, two-faced pariah of society.

Even knowing just how deceiving appearances could be, Jerry had to admit the guy staring back in the hand mirror was damn good looking. One last wink at his image and he laid the mirror on the stretcher where he had already been prepped.

"Ready, pardner?" Miles asked as he adjusted the drip running through the IV in Jerry's arm.

"I was born ready. Let's do it."

As the sedative began to kick in, which felt a lot different from the psychoactive drug therapy the doc had recently begun to administer, and certainly a switch from the absinthe that... Hugo... The Commandant... his mentor....

And that was where his mind began to drift, back and back, to shortly after they had planted their lychee trust tree. He was at the table again with Hugo, the rattan fan circling slowly overhead and Hugo was saying, *"You are a soldier, are you not, mon ami? We soldiers fight other soldiers to win hearts and minds, and now we are in a war together to gain control of the minds that would oppose us. The CORDS people will give us lists of names. They are all to be disposed of eventually, but we will bring most of them here for our little experiments. The abductions will be your new responsibility... Another drink? How do you like the absinthe, our lovely la fee verte? You know the little green fairy. She is magic, no? The old French soldiers they liked to think she protected them from malaria. Malaria, certainly not; but boredom, yes. It is known to have special psychoactive qualities...especially the one here, we add a bit of le docteur's concoction et voila!"* The green shining drink appearing luminous, Hugo saying, *"We will become good friends you and I...You will learn to speak French, tchin, tchin!"* Glasses clinking. *"Not so much for me. Though that will be appreciated, you will learn for your work. The procurements will begin, as you Americans say, small potatoes? But as you advance they will most come from the educated Vietnamese class and they will speak French. Tomorrow we will begin our classes. French. War. More gardening."*

Classes... so many classes.... And as The Commandant's beautiful face shape-shifted into the hard planes of Rowdy Yates, his voice became a blend of Texas twang and a lecturing tone, saying, "Our curriculum may appear to be focused on terror, interrogation, and torture, but it goes much deeper than that. It's like theories. Theories aren't just ideas, they are put forth to be able to explain and predict. A sort of way of knowing about the way, the when, and the how of stuff that happens. Torture, for example, has a lot of what we'll call 'beliefs' built up about it, about how it works and how it should be done and how effective it is in interrogation and intelligence gathering. One of our primary goals here, Jerry, is finding out how to interrogate individuals in order to extract...?"

"AIQP: ACCURATE INFORMATION as QUICKLY as POSSIBLE."

"Damn straight, Pardner!" Thump that desk. "And this, of course, is very different than torture for punishment, revenge, or simply for purposes of terror. Now, give me an example."

"Example: If you leave a body that's been skinned alive outside a village, it has a big impact on residents in the village with regard to not wanting to have the same thing done to them. Or their loved ones. Protecting others can be a highly motivating factor. On the other hand, it also can work the other way and highly motivate some individuals towards wanting to do the same thing back and worse to whoever they believe committed the atrocity. And that brings us to Revenge."

"Yes." Miles tapping fingers, ever so pleased. "Your paper on revenge was excellent. I am giving it 5 Stars. You may have the paper back since I committed it to memory. And, I made an extra copy to personally keep."

Five big GOLD stars all circling around the title of his essay proudly extended to his hands and dancing before his eyes:

REVENGE

It has been my observation that REVENGE is a part of human nature that is actually extremely satisfying. It really does make you feel better. You, as in Everyone. Anybody with a sibling pretty much knows that if your brother or sister slaps you, you feel a lot better after slapping them back....getting even. Even is good, not being even feels bad. The old Eye for an Eye/Tooth for a Tooth may sound like a trite ancient saying, but it is grounded in the truth of tens if not hundreds of thousands of years of human experience. Revenge, getting even, does not of course make everything better, but compared to nothing, "I suffer, you suffer equally or as close as possible" feels good, feels even. It always has. It always will.

A broken finger for an eye does not feel good or even. It seems obvious to me now that I spent a great deal of my youth doing everything I could to get even. And, unfortunately, not usually with whom I felt aggrieved. Sure, killing my stepdad felt really good when I did it, but it did not make us even. I wish he could have spent a good, long time here at The Killing School as a subject of an experiment. He would have made an excellent subject.

Allow me to further expound: Just as theories are

needed in order to explain and predict, experiments are needed for science. And, for experiments, you need subjects. In my present capacity as Officer in Charge of Long Range Security I procure subjects for this purpose, and it is my responsibility to see that they arrive healthy enough for the experiments. Due to the number of procurements, I also oversee a detail of "hunters" who I have personally trained to track, capture, and when necessary, kill. It is very similar to my previous job in the Army but taken to a higher level. The Commandant, in turn, has over-seen much of my training.

And what, might you ask, do Training and Revenge have in common?

More than meets An Eye for An Eye.

To maximize their effectiveness, they both take planning. Discipline. Coordination. And when they achieve the desired outcome, both Training and Revenge feel G-O-O-D.

Sometimes Training and Revenge even cross paths. For Example:

I am always early for any meeting or appointment and I try to impress the importance of that upon my trainees. But one day last week I was going to be late for class, where I was expected to help assist. The reason for my tardiness was that I had been cleaning up messes all morning that a certain trainee had not seen to—had even contributed to. His name was Salvador. I had stopped in the "dungeon" area, god what a stench, and crouched down to look at the mess of a human being in Tiger Cage #12. Keeping in mind I had impressed upon Salvador the importance of delivering healthy subjects, you can imagine that I was furious when I first thought the subject in #12 was dead. Just when I was going to signal to a guard for the usual disposal, I saw a slight movement.

"Put the body on a stretcher and take it up to the

Library," I instructed. "Leave it outside the door. Not too close, it's too smelly."

So, after I issued my orders to have the body delivered EXACTLY 5 minutes after my own arrival for class (being held in the Library) I began to PLAN my REVENGE.

The thing about new interns is that you always seem to get some new recruit who is too enthusiastic and tends to go too far with their initial lessons. OK, the first time is understandable; they like to show you their enthusiasm. But this guy. Salvador. He had been warned, twice actually, and so this nearly dead subject number 3 was strike 3 for Salvador as far as this instructor was concerned. It's great to like your job but not when liking it too much means you ruined the job. Like other interns, many also from police academies and military schools in Central America, he was here to learn about interrogation and procuring Intel—NOT just have his fun brutalizing someone. Well. Salvador was in for a lesson. And it just so happened I knew he was at the class I was no longer hurrying to get to.

While it was very tempting to race to the Library and make a mess out of Salvador, I practiced DISCI-PLINE by meditating on my REVENGE. I took deep cleansing breaths, yes to get the stench out of my nostrils, but mostly to get calm and "centered" as the professor has taught me. When I got to the Library, I had achieved that sometimes difficult objective.

The Library is a very beautiful room with deep leather chairs, beautiful teak desks, gleaming teak floors, and mahogany wall paneling. There are rows and rows of books, manuscripts. Even scrolls. One of my favorite areas is a little museum corner with a real display of interrogation instruments from ancient Asia to the Nazis in WW2. The resource materials which have come from the very top of the CIA and NSA, and I have studied extensively, deserve their own paper.

Now, Doctor-Professor Miles was giving a lecture on Japanese Unit 731, about the chemical and biological experiments that he said made even his psyche feel shredded after reading about what they did on anybody, and that included women, children and babies, even fetuses.

I looked at my watch. The body would be delivered in exactly 2 minutes.

As I turned my attention to the matter of COORDI-NATION, I gave Professor Miles a small signal, that little movement of my thumb to indicate we have trouble that needs addressing, and I gave a slight nod to the trouble who was slouched in the corner and not really paying much attention with that kind of, "I'm too cool for school" sort of look.

Professor Miles raised his eyebrows. He smiled and said, "OK, class. A demonstration is often much better than words, especially for people with us who are having trouble listening."

And just as the body was delivered outside the door, he called, "Salvador?"

"JERRY? C'mon, pardner. Time to wake up." Miles lightly tapped the arm in restraints. Couldn't take any chances that his most highly prized experiment—his Future Elite Modern Warrior—might act on instinct before the anesthesia wore off. The gauze masked almost the entirety of his face and Miles felt like a kid in mid-December already champing at the bit to tear into his Christmas morning presents. He'd never had a chance to completely alter someone's facial structure before—okay, he'd only assisted, but thanks to his eidetic memory and hands on experience, surely he could duplicate the results! Maybe give Jerry an identical twin one day.

Too eager to wait for the drum-rolling moment of surgical unveiling, Miles opened the box just in from Texas.

After plopping the finest Stetson money could buy atop Jerry's mummified head, Miles guffawed. Quietly. He'd give Sleeping Beauty a little while longer in La-la Land since he was behind on his notes documenting a transformation so remarkable that Jung and Freud and yes, *you*, Dr. Carl Rogers, would hail him as a Master, deserving of their collective ranks.

THE PROFESSOR'S NOTEBOOK

There is much to cover since my last entry. First, I will tackle the usual business of progress made with our experimental subjects.

As always, the following research was held to my impeccable, rigorous, and highest standards of experimental design. Experimental Subjects #1-10 had equivalent Control Group subjects to be compared to (as best as could be obtained re: age and physical and mental characteristics). Essentially the overall goal was—and continues to be—to find the most efficient method of mind control. Efficient being cost effective in terms of time, money, personnel and especially with regard to results. My goals are as follows:

1. Procure in a timely manner any strategic information through interrogation.
2. Ideally control and manipulate behavior short term and long term. I am hoping for over a lifetime.
3. Eventually initiate long term mind control over all chosen military personnel.

#3 is the MOST important, and more on that shortly.

This first round in the Control Subjects Group received the old, standard interrogation techniques including: Escalated beatings, whippings, scourges, excision of fingernails and toenails, the infliction of ever more increasing levels of physical suffering, etc. All of this occurred on a regular daily schedule for the Control Group.

The Experimental Group Subjects, on the other hand, were stripped, isolated in a private cell and blindfolded. They were subjected to noise, endless sonic levels of heavy metal music or jingle bells and kept sleepless for hours and hours and then allowed to sleep and then quickly woken again. The disorientation took place right away. They did not know where they were or how long they had been there or whether it was day or night. They were trapped inside their own minds, minds quickly unravelling. Unravelling because of the disorientation; unravelling because of sleep deprivation; unravelling most of all, in my opinion, from not what was being done to them like the Control Group, but because of what they were doing to themselves.

I will further explore this theory with new Control/Experimental Groups.

In addition to this I have been working extensively with hypnosis, which brings us to my favorite subject: Jerry Prince. Future Elite Modern Warrior.

In my extensive work with Jerry I've had to tread a very fine line—and I'll get to that. But first a concern regarding his attachment to The Commandant, Hugo Goulet. His long experience in the French Foreign Legion is something Jerry highly admires, no doubt from seeing too many TV movies growing up and becoming indoctrinated into thinking that someone in the FFL has a certain movie star appeal—and Goulet certainly qualifies for that on many levels. But, as a result, he seems to be what Jerry would like to "grow up to be." I have helped Jerry understand in our ongoing sessions that the "attachment" he has formed has caused him to project ideas of idealism onto Goulet and as a result he must be careful since Goulet is not perfect, he is just a man, and should Jerry feel that his idol has let him down or he becomes disappointed with Goulet, then he could just turn all that positive feeling into negative and then want to destroy, that is kill, his idol. Therefore, he must keep ahead of his emotions and combine thinking and emotions to keep his "clarity." This has been a hard and difficult kind of therapy and for most people not always that effective. I was able to convince Jerry that deep change demands deep work, and the deepest work involves a combination of

hypnosis and psychedelics. We have proceeded nicely with both Psilocybin and LSD, but that is where the fine line has emerged.

It has been essential to keep the lethality alive in Jerry while developing
an ability to maintain good judgement and sense of consequence. The
psychedelic sessions have enabled him to do deep work in integration and
also provide healing for the trauma of his early childhood and the
wounds of his years in foster homes and, consequently, allow him to
recover some of his humanity. This does not yet extend to empathy, the
ability to cry, or other highly developed prosocial responses from the
ACC region of the brain. I am unsure if even I can completely transform
him, particularly since it would entail his integration of complex
emotional qualities that I myself do not possess, nor would I wish to, but
the challenge is nonetheless irresistible.

Clearly, this fascinating evolution should further secure my future stature
in the science community. Presently, however, we are still faced with
many contradictions to treat as delicately as land minds since, while we
are doing all this redemptive work on Jerry's humanity, he must remain
able to do the necessary wickedly dark work. In our hypnosis sessions I
have layered in the deep belief that all the bad stuff we have to do is to the
"enemy" which makes it acceptable, even mandatory, with the rationale
being that we are preventing even worse stuff from happening which
makes it all good in the end. Jerry is an agent for the "greater good" and
sometimes we have to do bad things to preserve the greater good.

In conjunction with all of this is the most remarkable achievement of my
work thus far at ISIC—indeed, my most ambitious goal in a truly remarkable career! The hypnosis/psychedelic sessions have also, at their deepest
level, begun to build the "Code Purple Jerry." While still an engrossing
work-in-progress, Code Purple Jerry is the assassin I can soon trigger
into operation with just those words: "Code Purple Jerry." Let me be clear
that this is a whole other level of consciousness that is under *my* control
and not Jerry's conscious control. Let me also be clear that the assassin I
am building is not the same killer who arrived at ISIC a year ago and has
flourished under my tutelage.

I have to say I do feel a bit like Dr. Frankenstein, creating my own entity
inside of Jerry's psyche so a portion of his mind belongs to me, and can be
controlled only by me. Already I have had him do things, simple things,
like drop two glasses of juice at breakfast, then go back to his room, take
off his tee-shirt to admire that extravagant Japanese tattoo of some mythical bird on his chest, then cover it back up and return to the table. Two

minutes later, Jerry is back, latching a last button on his shirt and looking at the broken glasses beside his chair, the spilled juice, and demanding, "Who did this?" (To which I took the blame for swatting at a bee and calling for cleanup). When the simple commands worked, I took it up a level and suggested that this notebook was invisible. It was amusing to ask him if he had seen my notebook anywhere and to watch him look all over and not see it right on the table in front of him. I do have to say that particular experiment gave me some peace of mind since this notebook is the LAST thing in the world I would want him to read, but what is of tantamount importance, is that Jerry does not remember ANY of this. As far as his mind is concerned, nothing he said, nothing he did, ever happened. To wield this much control over anyone, particularly an elite warrior I foresee as the prototype for this and future wars—highly skilled killers following commands without question, or remembrance of their actions—is mind blowing even to me.

I will continue to record our sessions on tape to further dissect and document Code Purple Jerry's evolution. Meanwhile, we will see how the physical transformation impacts his perception of the outside world. He has not been allowed out much due to concerns he could possibly be recognized. Of course, our primary concern has been to ensure he has ample control over himself—and, most importantly, that *we* have control over him.

CHAPTER 5

Saigon, RVN
Fall, 1970

For Jerry, accompanying Hugo to the Presidential Palace in Saigon for a glamorous social event was truly a coming out party. In addition to wearing tailored evening clothes for the first time in his life, he was wearing his brand-new face. After having his ears, nose, jaw and cheekbones worked on by a reconstructive master, Miles had seen to the finishing touches with blue contacts and blonde hair in a longish surfer cut look. He'd always been considered handsome but with the new overall effect and the clothes he could easily pass for a blonde Tarzan in the Lord Greystoke mode.

When the bandages had first come off there was still swelling and bruising but the plastic surgeon had been thrilled with the results. Miles went full-on cowboy with his *yee-haws* and *yah-hoos*. And now, even several months later, he was still a bit startled to see his own reflection. Not to see who you had looked like all your life in the mirror took some getting used to.

So did the advantages that came with no further concerns that he could possibly be recognized—and the advancement in ISIC to Spook that came along with it. That's right, a whole new level for a whole new job. For someone who'd basically grown up in foster homes, being groomed in the arts of espionage to attend an affair at a palace was like sleeping in a field of poppies en route to Oz.

"Champagne?" Hugo offered from across the seat of the long black Cadillac limousine ferrying them to the gala.

"*Merci mais non*," was his polite "thank you but no" response to his teacher of French. Gardening. And far more than the social graces, protocols, and manners necessary to mingle with the elite.

"You will do splendidly, *mon ami*," Hugo assured him, tapping out an unfiltered French Gauloises from the engraved silver case Jerry knew he dearly prized—a parting gift from his regiment in the French Indochina War. Lighting up in that elegant way that was uniquely Hugo, on a stream of white he blew out, "Trust me."

Jerry thought of their trust tree, its planting enshrined in his memory as an event more momentous than a first kiss, a first car. A first kill. It was a comforting memory he turned to when things took an uneasy turn.

That wouldn't happen tonight. The setting and those attending this big Republic of Vietnam Fine Arts Awards Gala may be "A brand-new rodeo" as Miles would say, but the work was straight-up in the wheelhouse Jerry proudly ran with military precision: procuring and disappearing a now deemed undesirable politico.

"We should be there soon. I will exit the car first. You have your instructions."

"Yes... *Oui*," Jerry self-corrected. "You will engage The Ambassador but I am not to approach or speak to him since he will be accompanied by his companion."

"Ah, the lovely Kate Morningside, always a pleasure."

"She sure as hell wouldn't think that about me given our history."

"It was in another lifetime, *mon ami*, but yes. An unfortunate earlier encounter. She should not recognize you, but…"

"Don't worry. I'll be aware of where they are and stay out of their lines of sight. While you mix and mingle, I'll track the target. Then once you give the signal, it will all go down as planned. Piece of cake." That's right, easy as Hugo asking for a private word with the target, maneuvering him into range, Jerry stabbing said target with the prepared injection, a quick hustle out the exit and into a waiting vehicle while Hugo returned to the gala, then all of them reuniting to make their clandestine return to The School via the chopper on ready.

As he patted the syringe in his dress coat pocket the limo rolled to a stop. Hugo snuffed his Gauloises and with a champagne flute salute, bade him, "Please. Have some fun. As the French would say, `If a man has money to buy two loaves of bread, he should buy one loaf and spend the rest on flowers. Bread will feed a body, but flowers are food for the soul.' The job is important, Jerry. But there is nothing wrong with gardening when the opportunity presents, no?"

The door opened. Hugo emerged from the limo, crystal and Cristal poised to work the crowd in well-manicured hands.

Jerry had always prided himself on his nerves of steel, but as he tooled around the block in the back of a limo that looked like most of the others pulling up for the gala, he couldn't deny that being in the middle of a fire fight or worse would have him less nervous than walking in on a red carpet.

Fortunately, the crowd and number of flashing cameras had slightly dispersed by the time the limo crept up to the red carpet a second time.

Jerry got out. The flashes were only half-blinding. With the political situation the security was extreme and with the censoring of so much of the local press, the press that was there were all government flacks or foreign correspondents. So, why sheets of paper were suddenly being thrust at him along with ready pens, he wasn't sure. They hadn't rehearsed such a potential response to his movie-star entrance, abetted by his marquee idol looks.

They had, however, provided him with another identity, along with the necessary photo ID in his wallet to prove it.

Jerry scribbled unintelligible autographs. Flashed his new smile for the cameras. Helped a young woman up who appeared to momentarily faint. And then finally, mercifully, he was inside the grandest interior entrance he'd ever seen—and that included each and every LIFE magazine he had hungrily consumed in his heretofore life.

While navigating his way from the voluminous entrance, impeccably dressed staff rushed to refill glasses, serve canapes, and see to every need of the opulent crowd speaking mostly French and English. There was little Vietnamese to be heard in this grandest of all venues in Saigon, where Jerry immediately made a visual sighting of his target, got him on his radar. Next, he located Hugo, who was conveniently engaging The Ambassador, Phillip Jordan, along with Jordan's rumored fiancé, in an animated conversation.

The fiancé, Kate Morningside, had to still hate his guts even if she believed the Ghost Soldier as dead as The Ambassador had reported to Command. The stately salt-and-pepper diplomat and bombshell blonde made a striking couple. No matter they were something of a May-December romance, they were apparently well suited in more important ways.

Having seen to his responsibilities first, as he always did, Jerry wondered if he dared take a little self-indulgent break as Hugo had encouraged, and drift to a corner near the bar. Maybe order something up that wasn't absinthe with an LSD chaser for a change but still elegant enough to blend in better than his favored Jack, two fingers, neat.

"Could you make that two *Soixante Quinzes, s'il vous plait?*"

His order, echoed by a sultry feminine voice, intruded on Jerry's intent to have a rare moment that didn't involve a target or anything else to do with The School.

She smiled, knocked him dead with her conspirator's grin.

He knew her face, such an unforgettable face, even if she no longer recognized his. He hoped. Surely she couldn't. As for his voice? Fortunately, they had barely spoken. And that had been nearly three years ago, back in early '68.

"Mademoiselle Chene." He took the liberty of kissing her extended hand. Her skin smelled like jasmine and just for a moment, he wondered if she would taste the same. *"Enchante."*

"You know me?" she replied in English.

"But of course," he returned, dropping the French and not missing a beat—unless he counted that strange little skip directly beneath the tailored coat pocket that housed a syringe filled with one of Miles's special concoctions. "Like many here, I am a fan of your work. Congratulations on the award. It is well deserved."

"I'm nervous." Her whispered confession was accompanied by a little duck of her head, as if she could hide the stunning Eurasian features that belonged on the cover of Vogue while her gritty war photography splashed across the pages of LIFE and TIME. "It's why I hoped I could hide over here in the corner with you and have a breather, not to mention a drink. Do you mind?"

"Are you kidding? I'm delighted!" Too late he realized his smooth moves had been hijacked by honest to god excitement. Ever since Isabelle Chene had arrived with her camera to capture the reality of a day for troops in the long bloody nightmare that had been the Siege of Hue, he had been almost obsessed with her work. Okay, completely obsessed. And he definitely was not the kind of guy any woman wanted obsessing over her, work or otherwise. But she wouldn't know that. No more than she could be aware that he had appeared in one of her award-winning photographs, or that he had accumulated a collection of her magazine glossies that had been confiscated with his other trophies.

But that was a different time and he was a different man. One who didn't have time to waste if he was going to put his newly acquired gardening skills to work.

Before she could respond with more than a demure, "Oh please, you're too kind," a server appeared with a linen draped tray bearing their *Soixante Quinzes*—a heady mixture of gin and lemon and sugar topped with champagne, otherwise known as a French 75.

Jerry didn't wait for the formal presentation of the cocktails and swept both up from the tray with a *"Merci"* to the server before personally offering Isabelle her sparkling libation.

As blue eyes met slightly tilted browns, framed by long sooty lashes, Jerry suavely recouped with a sincere, "May Dame Fortune ever smile upon you, but never her daughter Miss Fortune."

They tapped, sipped, and Isabelle offered, "Here's to blue skies and green lights!"

Tap, sip. His turn: "May your luck ever spread. Like jelly on bread."

"Oh god, I can't top that one!" Her laughter sounded like wind chimes and the neck she arched commanded the attention he was pretty sure should be elsewhere. Knew damn well should be elsewhere. Like on the target he should be tracking while appearing to aimlessly roam about, all the while staying out of Kate Morningside's sight.

A quick assessment of the bar assured him she wasn't anywhere near. As for the target, Vuong Quan, the anti-government playwright, he was approaching their secluded table.

"Isabelle!" called Quan. "I've been looking for you. And your parents. Are they here?"

"Regretfully, no. Other obligations, you understand?" In a hushed voice, she said, "They were afraid to come tonight, as I thought you would be."

His response was a look of defiance, followed by an innocuous, "Most unfortunate, but please give them my best when you next see them." He turned to Jerry as Isabelle's laughter faded and her easy smile appeared strained. "The two of you seemed to be having so much fun. My apologies for intruding."

"No apologies needed," Jerry assured him. And though resent it he did, he graciously insisted, "Please, join us."

"Yes, of course!" Isabelle echoed. "Vuong Quan I would like you to meet...?" Now she tilted her head and the way the light caught the sweet slope of her jaw, the tilt of her eyes, Jerry found himself wondering if the bartender had slipped something he'd never had before into his drink.

"Troy," Jerry supplied, grateful for all the rehearsals that had accompanied the sham ID. "Troy Hunter."

"And here I thought you were Troy Donahue. Or maybe Tab Hunter." Isabelle laughed that great laugh of hers again. "Oops! Got them both wrong. Quan, shall we move on?"

"I can be Troy Donahue for the night." As he doubled down on his quick assurance with a signature pose, someone tapped Quan on the shoulder.

After a brief exchange he excused himself, saying, "It seems someone on the committee wishes to speak with me. See you on stage, Isabelle. And Mr. Donahue, I hope to have the pleasure of meeting again."

"I have no doubt that we will," was Jerry's droll reply.

The technique the professor had taught him—that 7 count centering tap of middle finger and thumb—came in handy in a way that Jerry had never anticipated as Isabelle leaned closer and suggested, "So, Troy, would you be game in scouting out a new location before we have more company? The bar's getting crowded and just between us I have a little problem with social anxiety. It seems there's always someone wanting to know, `How did you get that shot?' or `How can you stand it?' when all I want to do is hide behind my camera and be as incognito as possible." She laughed softly. "You must think I'm silly."

"No." He shook his head. "What I think is that you're an observer of the world who prizes her privacy and I get that. I also think you couldn't be incognito if you tried. And, there's one other thing."

"Yes?"

"I think we need to get out of here." Jerry hailed the server who had managed to be close as a raised fingertip without appearing to actually be hovering, placed his order, and exactly two minutes later—no need for a watch, he could time it precisely in his head—he and Isabelle were making their escape from the bar.

Like a couple of teenagers sneaking out after curfew and hoping they wouldn't be caught, up a somewhat hidden staircase they raced—only to be stopped by a severely frowning guard.

Isabelle showed him a VIP pass, flipped her long, silky black hair over a shoulder covered in a tasteful peek-a-boo number, and said, "He's with me."

The guard nodded, stepped back with a sharp salute.

Jerry thought he had seen it all by now, but the sheer over-the-top opulence of the restored palace was not to be believed as his partner in crime took his hand, slipped through a deserted room, and then, there they were. The two of them. On a balcony. Covered in moonlight.

She raised her crystal flute to his so the perfect curlicues of lemon peel tickling the rims touched. The sparkling bubbles had nothing on the evanescence going on between their locked gazes.

He thought he might kiss her and was about to lean in when she asked, "Special Forces?"

"Excuse me?"

"Let's be honest. We're all playing roles whether we want to or not these days. The way you hold yourself, move, walk, look around, see everything. It reminds me of those guys. I've spent a lot of quality time with them, though not so much lately. I can't explain it, because I'm quite sure we've never met before…trust me, I would remember if we had…but there's something about you that's familiar. I only mean that in the best of ways."

The urge to kiss her intensified to something distinctly foreign. Maybe it was owed to all those sessions with Miles. Or maybe it was that they didn't get out a lot at The School unless it involved their usual hunt and capture routine. Whatever the case, he hadn't seen this coming.

As he weighed his next move, Jerry heard voices.

There was Kate Morningside laughing, saying, "Phillip, Hugo, I'll meet you downstairs. Please don't take long. I'll be ever so bored in your absence."

"As Phillip and I will no doubt bore each other senseless without you to keep us on our toes."

"Agreed, my dear." The Ambassador's rich baritone, to Hugo's elegant tenor. "We will see to our boring business and join you shortly."

And that's when Hugo and The Ambassador decided to plant them-selves not ten feet away from the balcony where he and Isabelle were hiding with the moon smiling down on their just right moment to steal a kiss.

Jerry swiftly calculated his options. He had three—no, just two since kissing her until the principals of The Killing School were gone and hoping all she would hear were fireworks did not even qualify for consideration. That left him with either making their presence known asap—which he really did not want to do—or taking a chance that Isabelle would overhear critical, top secret information, that perhaps even he was not supposed to be privy. And if that happened? His duty would be to permanently silence her as immediately as possible.

A quick glance over the balcony confirmed it would be a killing distance; it was a dark, private area beneath; the sound of revelry in the background would mute any last screams while she fell—if he didn't strangle her first.

But he did not want to do that. Actually, he wasn't sure if he could. That was... disconcerting. He'd never had trouble killing when necessary before. Even when it wasn't necessary. *What was wrong with him?* Had Miles messed with something critical to his performance in one of their sessions, even if he hadn't meant to?

He'd think about that later.

Jerry raised his glass along with his voice, proclaiming, *"La nuit est exquise mais pale en comparison de vous!"* And because he knew the night was exquisite but could never compare to her, and because he knew he would probably never see her again, and that he would never forgive himself if he didn't, he laid a quick, urgent kiss against her surprised open mouth, gripped her elbow, and marched them both into the room.

"Oh, pardon us!" He stopped cold, as if startled to have encountered what had to be the two smoothest guys in the world who looked at him without recognition and collectively turned their attention to Isabelle.

"Mademoiselle!" they both exclaimed, greeting her effusively and kissing her cheeks in that French way.

"Congratulations on your award, my dear." This, from The Ambassador.

"Indeed, ma chère," echoed Hugo. "And oh, what lucky man is this, your handsome escort for the evening?"

It was like having Cary Grant and Sean Connery play a scene.

As Isabelle laughed delightedly Jerry could still taste her.

"Ah, this man? He is the famous American actor, Troy Donahue." She gave them both an exaggerated wink, only to turn a smile on him that could have melted a polar icecap. "I was just showing him the stunning view from the veranda." The way she touched her fingertips to her lips felt like an extended intimacy between them, when a soft breeze had blown through her hair and brought the scent of frangipani from the quiet, dark garden below. No sounds of war, only shared breath. "Mr.

Troy Donahue, I would like you to meet the honored Ambassador Phillip Jordan. And, the renowned Hugo Goulet, who you never want to play cards with."

"So nice to meet you, Mr. Donahue," said Hugo with a short bow.

"A pleasure, certainly," concurred The Ambassador. He extended his hand.

Jerry detected an ever-so-slight hesitation in the gesture. Phillip Jordan knew just who and what he was. What he had been. What he was capable of now. Just because Jordan's pet dark ops program could only flourish with the likes of him and Miles—aka Mr. Boogeyman of Death and Dr. Pain—did not mean he desired to share company with the hired help.

But then again, their esteemed employer could have politely avoided actual contact with a perfectly acceptable bow rather than the handshake he was offering now. Particularly since his little finger appeared to have been severely injured at some point, crooking awkwardly on an other-wise well-manicured hand.

It was not an extended handshake as he and Hugo had first shared on his veranda. And while The Ambassador's grip was firm and assured, it lacked the same man-to-man connection that military brothers in arms instinctively understood. This was a diplomat. Not a soldier. They could do business together and respect their disparate roles because it served both of their purposes. Make no mistake though, it was crystal clear who had the control and power, who gave the orders and who was to follow them, and who moved in a whole other level of the world.

All of that became understood in one brief handshake.

The four of them made all the right noises to politely part company with the two men offering to leave first, but as Jerry and Isabelle passed the guard who had granted them entry and took their time descending down the stairs they had raced up before, he was acutely aware of how rare the moment was. Like a life so rich and full of promise, only to be snuffed out in the mere seconds it took for a bomb to blow. Or, for an assassin to make his intended hit.

"You know those gentlemen," was his casual comment.

"Yes. Ambassador Jordan and I have met a few times before due to his interest in the arts, particularly photography, and even more particularly photography associated with this horrific war. He called me personally about the award and... just between us, I've wondered if he had anything to do with the selection. I know my work is good, but there are other photographers I would consider more deserving."

"I beg to disagree. But we'll let that go for now since I'm curious. The other man who seemed to know you... I believe you introduced him as `The renowned Hugo Goulet' that you'd never want to play cards with?"

"Oh, Hugo! I've known him forever. His family owns the plantation next to ours—at least they did. He sold to foreign investors upon coming into his inheritance. My parents were approached but they were not interested, even though Hugo encouraged them to be more forward thinking." She shook her head, her hair moving like a dark waterfall a man could drown in. "Given the way this war is going, they should have listened. They think with their hearts, not with their heads."

"An understandable human condition but with a potentially unfortunate outcome."

"Exactly. You understand."

Far better than he wished. It was one thing to pass yourself off as a fellow human being with the expected responses. It was quite another to actually feel something and struggle with the right thing to say.

And so he said nothing while trying not to wonder what might have happened if they hadn't been interrupted... especially if his chest had pressed too close and the weapon he would soon be using had been detected before he could abduct her friend, the troublesome playwright, whose defiance had led him too easily into a lethal trap.

There would be time later to consider such questions, moot as they would be.

He slid her a smile. It was a smile for a spy movie.

She laughed, more like a romantic caper, as if she knew that watching Beach Blanket Bingo and the Elvis movies with ingénues frolicking in the sand were his guilty pleasures, best enjoyed alone in the dark.

They reached the end of the staircase. They reached the end of what he was 99.9% certain would commemorate their final moments together.

"Would you mind if we tried that last kiss again?" he asked. "I'm afraid it was a bit rushed. I can do better."

Her response was the wrap of her arms around his neck, the urging of his mouth to hers. And when they connected...

It felt like an explosion of a fleet of B-52's going off in his head while an implosion gravitated lower, then lower still when she whispered into his ear, "Meet you back at the bar once the awards are over and we'll pick things up from there?"

Jerry nodded. He watched her go. Put his palm over a heart unaccustomed to this strange racing—only to encounter the slight bump of a syringe intended for one of her friends.

Hugo descended the stairs, caught his eye. Gave him a sly smile.

Jerry stole a last, longing glance at Isabelle's retreating back.

He returned his attention to Hugo, paused in his descent. There was a question in the subtle lift of his eyebrow.

Hesitating, but only slightly, as had Ambassador Jordan before offering his hand, Jerry patted his pocket.

They were good to go.

STILL DRESSED in their evening attire, Jerry sat across from Hugo and wished they were just arriving in the limousine for what had been an unforgettable night, rather than lifting off in the black ops chopper with their prey.

Vuong Quan was still zonked out and trussed up for good measure, which seemed a fairly ridiculous precaution given his most lethal moves were contained to the strike of typewriter keys. Nonetheless, in case he woke up during the short hop to ISIC, Jerry wanted extra insurance that Quan couldn't throw himself overboard into the Mekong River, which would be a far kinder fate than what awaited him at The School.

"Well done, *mon ami*." Hugo's long draw on his Gauloises accompanied the curious arch of a sculpted eyebrow. "You could have stayed, why did you not?"

It was true. Hugo had offered to trade places, allow Jerry to return to the gala while he took care of Quan's transport alone, and have another chopper waiting for Jerry on solo at dawn.

"That was a grand gesture, Hugo," he evasively responded, tapping the spot where the syringe had been, and where he had felt that strange earlier racing. "*Merci, beaucoup.*"

A glance at Quan, stirring slightly, and, oddly, Jerry found himself hoping Miles would go easy on the guy. Or, at least, Miles wouldn't ask for assistance once the delivery was made. Sometimes the doc liked him to do demonstrations for the students because he did have a gift for AIQP, amongst other things.

"You did not answer me. What is troubling you?"

"Nothing."

44

"You know you can trust me." Hugo leaned forward, smiled. "Especially when it comes to gardening."

Jerry thought back to his earlier assumption in the limo that he would have no need to pull out the memory that was his comforting go-to when things took an uneasy turn…

As they had tonight.

He had come a long, long way in a relatively short time, thanks to Hugo's shaping and refining of a protégé, transforming what had once been crude with the skill and eye of a master sculptor. As Michelangelo had said: *The sculpture is already complete within the marble block, before I start my work… I just have to chisel away the superfluous material.*

Yes, Hugo had even instructed him in philosophy, the arts, enough to get by with those whose elbows he might need to rub. But it was gardening that had altered the trajectory of a relationship he prized above all others and had provided the foundation on which they now stood.

Which was why, when Hugo pressed, "What is troubling you?" Jerry ignored the slight groaning noise coming from the trussed-up Quan and didn't worry about him hearing. Like he would be repeating anything overheard, anyway.

"I liked her," he confessed.

"But of course," said Hugo. "Isabelle is a lovely young woman. What is there not to like?"

There was a strange little voice far in the back of Jerry's head that whispered if Hugo was as fond of Isabelle as she seemed to be of him, he would have some concerns about his protégé getting anywhere near her.

"I liked her too much," he admitted. Then remembering the trust that had been embodied by a young plant that had taken root and was flourishing both in the garden and out, Jerry confessed, "Enough to remove myself from her presence."

Unfortunately there can be no doubt that man is, on the whole, less good than he imagines himself or wants to be.
Everyone carries a shadow, and the less it is embodied in the individual's conscious life, the blacker and denser it is.

— CARL JUNG *PSYCHOLOGY AND RELIGION* (1938)
COLLECTED WORKS 11 P.131

FISH SAUCE

Republic of Vietnam
March, 1975

Nguyen Liem, tank Commander for the People's Army of North Vietnam, sat on the front of his T-54 tank, dubbed The Flying Pig by his crew. Out of habit and prudence his war-weary gaze searched left, swung right, then darted skyward for any sign of threat. And yet, as they streamed down a ravaged road out of Ban Me Thout, the major city of the Central Highlands the PAVN had attacked and captured in *only two days*, it seemed like there was nothing left to resist them. Nothing left to fear. *They* would be what was feared now. They and the army flowing behind them, inexorably heading for Saigon.

Jubilant shouts of *"Chiến thắng! Chiến thắng!"* filled his ears as his men on board relished the sweet taste of *Victory! Victory!* The four of them had survived together longer than any other crew he'd had. They were like family and all of them had given each other food related nicknames, probably because so often they had been hungry.

On board with him was "Porkrib"—a joke because his ribs stood out— and slapping Porkrib on the back was "Noodlesoup"—no one could slurp up a bowl faster or louder—and then there was "Chopsticks." Chopsticks was at it again, drumming the controls with the same steel chopsticks that had pierced an enemy heart before turning them to a precious goat's liver.

Once, while they all prepared to die in a tunnel with bombs raining down, Chopsticks had secretly confessed that sometimes he dreamed of playing drums in something the filthy Americans called a "band."

As for Nguyen Liem, they called him "Nuoc Mam"...Fish Sauce. He was never without it. Even in the hardest times, when they had eaten leaves and roots and bamboo shoots, he had always had his bottle of Nuoc Mam, for it would make the most meager meal have at least a taste of home for his crew.

It was dangerous, if not stupid, at this early stage of the North's ambitious offensive plan to retake the South, but Fish Sauce stood up on the front of the tank like a big hood ornament and held up his hands to scream along with his men, *"Chiến thắng! Chiến thắng!"*

The joy, the absolute joy of recovering his country, taking it back from the invaders that had subjugated his people for over a century, was sheer ecstasy. *This* was liberation. *This* was for his grandfather enslaved by the French on a rubber tree plantation who had fought and died, and it was for his father and both uncles and little sister who had fought and died. *This* was for all the nights and days of his grandfather's slavery, for the nights of terror from the B52s dropping more bombs on them than all of WWII, for all of the children burned alive by Yankee napalm.

Right now, in this very moment of bliss, they were heroes cruising down Route 7. Villagers were lined up on all sides cheering as they passed, many throwing flowers at the tank he commanded.

Fish Sauce caught a pink peony. He sniffed it.

He gave a short bow to the peony—no flower had ever smelled so sweet—then tossed it back to the cheering multitude.

An elderly, stooped woman who had surely seen more sorrow than joy until this day, caught the creamy white bloom, flushed with pink at its tips, and held it gently as a newborn against her bosom.

The black tunic covering her chest shook. She was openly weeping.

A scan of the crowd assured him that many others were weeping along with her. Many with joy, but no doubt others with fear.

Those would be wondering if they would be found out now that the Americans they had sided with were abandoning them. Those would be the RVN traitors who knew they were finished.

How many had already stripped and thrown away their uniforms? After all, a tsunami of liberation was coming and, in its wake, would be a tsunami of vengeance for a hundred years of oppression and cruelty and humiliation.

"Nuoc Mam," yelled Chopsticks, flipping one of his prized steel posses-sions to Nguyen Liem. *"BẠN là anh hùng CỦA CHÚNG TÔI!!"*

Although he glowed inside, and wanted to believe it true, *"Fish Sauce. YOU are OUR hero!!"* was too much praise to accept for a man who would be nothing without his crew whose uniforms were soiled from diesel oil and battle, that were ill-fitting from lack of nourishment no matter how much sauce he laid on.

Now he would see to it that they had clean uniforms befitting their stature. They would be well-rewarded with a feast fit for the greatest hero of all—Ho Chi Minh himself.

And once his military duties were officially over? He would find what was left of his family, no matter how extended they might be. That would include Isabelle, the plantation owner's daughter who had befriended the twin sons of a servant. His mother had been the servant. And once the world was restored to its proper order, perhaps their positions would be reversed and Isabelle would be the one in need of a friend.

That could be as early as sometime next year. Maybe. Hopefully.

Time was always a nebulous thing in war, and his greatest fear was that it would not be on his side with the additional mission he had muscled in on.

His dear twin brother Nguyen Bao had been captured. Bao's superior officer believed him taken to a secret death camp of the American monster known as the CIA.

Fish Sauce's grimace softened as he recalled an American movie, spoken in French, that he and his twin had once watched with Isabelle. It was called "Tarzan."

Beating his chest, he let out a blood-curdling yell of victory—*"Chiến thắng! Chiến thắng!*— once more…

But it would be the cry of an excruciating death he would extract should he indeed find his brother at the death camp Bao's superior had called *trường giết người.*

"Trường giết người," he whispered. Fish Sauce's English was not very good but this darkness he could translate: "The Killing School."

He had convinced Command that no one would be more motivated to do anything and everything necessary than a proven officer desperate to save his brother. And yet, as personal as this mission was, there was much more at stake than rescuing Bao from a place so successfully hidden the closest coordinates thus far were only in a jungle somewhere south of Saigon.

There were no guarantees he would be the first to arrive and successfully retrieve documentation of the CIA's monstrous experiments while recovering any other prisoners and capturing any of the war criminals still present. Perhaps more intel would emerge and the mission would become a higher priority that leapfrogged over him while he and his crew continued to grind ever forward from Ban Me Thout, their easy victory behind them, with those ahead bound to be far more challenging...

And yet, within a week, Fish Sauce stared in disbelief at the Thach Han River, its narrow stream considered the dividing line between North and South Vietnam since the Peace Accords two years before.

Quang Tri, sitting on the southern bank, had endured fierce battles, many against the formidable U.S. Marines. But now, all that greeted them were ghosts and the mist drifting from the river they crossed without so much as a whisper of resistance.

It was only in a whisper that Chopsticks declared, *"Chiến thắng. Chiến thắng,"* as if a shout might shatter what had to be a collective illusion.

Unbelievable. Quang Tri—seized without a fight!

Thrilled as he was, Fish Sauce was a realist. Hue, Da Nang, Qui Nhon, and the home of his childhood, Nha Trang, over 400 miles to the south, would surely not be so easy to topple en route to the grand prize:

SAIGON.

The fall of Saigon would mean the ultimate collapse of the puppet RVN government.

At the rate they were going, dare he hope all their grand objectives might be accomplished by the end of this year? Could December, 1975 bring a far more significant celebration than the holiday called Christmas that Isabelle's Catholic family would celebrate, with her always giving him a special gift and cakes, even though he was raised Buddhist?

Fish Sauce laughed softly to himself. Maybe he was more a wishful thinker than a realist after all. It was only March 19 and they had a very long way still to go.

With a whistle he ordered Porkrib, Noodlesoup, and Chopsticks back into The Flying Pig.

Saigon and The Killing School were waiting.

CHAPTER 6

Peace Mission Hospital
Nha Trang, RVN
March, 1975

"Izzy didn't return your call? Again? That's three times in as many months."

"Yeah. And he hasn't written back twice now, either." Dr. Gregg Kelly accepted the icy cold G&T his wife Shirley extended. Yet again he wondered what sort of intriguing genetic cocktail they had made with her fair skin and coppery colored ponytail, next to his surfer's tan and sun bleached hair. Patting the space beside him on a plush cushioned rattan porch swing, the only furniture left on the wide sweeping veranda of a house that could have belonged to Matisse, his thoughts returned to his best friend, Israel Moskowitz.

The fact that Izzy, who had served as his Best Man just a few years ago, had been so silent was cause for concern. Sure, Izzy was a beyond brilliant psychiatrist and had landed a plum position at Columbia University in his home town of New York. But. Gregg knew, all too well, that physicians could heal others far easier than they could heal themselves, particularly when it came to the psychic wounds war could inflict. Especially this one. Vietnam. What a crock of shit. What a mind fuck. And Izzy had really gone through some terrors.

Gregg took a deep breath and sighed. So many lives and minds lost, and for what? Nothing.

As Shirley nuzzled close, her brown-gold eyes tilting to meet his bluer than blues, Gregg had to amend that last part. Were it not for his being drafted straight out of USC with his shiny new Ph.D. in clinical psychology seven years ago, he wouldn't be rocking steady on the home front with his child in Shirley's slightly rounded belly, while the South China Sea sang a lullaby and the world as they knew it fell apart around them.

At least the mission should be relatively safe for the short time they had left before everything would likely, too quickly, crumble and collapse. It had been a painful but necessary decision to move the mission hospital to Thailand. The risk was simply too great to stay and hope for a peaceful resolution to this long, long war. The end game of civil wars was never nice and usually exceptionally bloody, and neither side was going to be happy with Americans.

"I can understand Izzy preferring to stay in the States while the rest of this awful drama plays out, but I had hoped he would find a way to come visit us, just once more, before we pack up what little is left." Shirley slid her husband a private smile. "Then he could swing up to the new hospital with us and, oh! What do you know? Margie just happens to be helping us out while she's on `vacation.'"

"Let's see... stay in Hawaii with all her well-earned Army perks. Or: Take some leave for Thailand while its next door neighbor implodes just to work a pediatric burn unit on `vacation' and possibly run into the ex who dumped you." G&T in one hand, empty palm up on the other, he pretended to weigh Major Margie Kennedy's imagined options. "Eh. Close but no cigar. But I should be sending her one in..." Never had day counting been so sweet. "Just four more months!"

Shirley gave him a playful smack on the leg. "You know she would come in a heartbeat if she thought the two of them still had a chance. Or, even if she could find out what in the world went wrong when everything seemed so right. At least, to her. And to the rest of us."

Gregg could only shake his head. The hell if he knew. He and Izzy were each other's most trusted friends...at least he'd always thought so. But Izzy's refusal to talk about why he'd abruptly broken things off with Margie shortly after being released from active duty, his increasing evasiveness over the years, and now, radio silence...

"I hate to say this, but I've actually been thinking maybe I should get in touch with JD."

"That's a switch. Usually it's JD getting in touch with you."

Not for the first time Gregg held his silence about the whys and wherefores of that. There were some things that even Shirley, the one person he held most dear, who had surely saved his sanity, if not his life, could never, never know.

Only Izzy knew. They shared secrets that bound them as close as brothers. Secrets that could get them killed, or worse, if they told. *Dead men tell no tales.* General Claymore had made that "Sir, yes sir!" clear.

Wait. No, no. *Surely not.*

As the G&T lodged in his throat, Gregg urgently reminded himself that he and Izzy were highly insured. JD had seen to it—though of course if it weren't for JD, they never would have had their necks on the chopping block to begin with.

Gregg let that go along with the breath he'd been holding, told his paranoia to take a long hike off a short cliff, and made his decision.

"Let's make a little trip to Saigon."

"Okay, but...why?"

"Well, we've been on our sabbatical here to say goodbye to all our good friends heading in other directions themselves. Saying our long goodbye to this place that's meant so much to us, and so many others. And, since we have just ten days before we leave for the new hospital, this is definitely going to be our last chance to say goodbye to Saigon. There's no telling when it'll be safe for us to come back and visit again once the city falls. Which, it inevitably will."

Shirley slowly nodded, only to call him on his own bullshit. "Something tells me there is a certain someone you'd rather meet there than here, don't ask me why, and you don't want to leave me alone, so I should throw a few things into an overnight bag and plan on an early flight. Then once we're there you'll suggest I go shopping, not too far from where we're staying, mind you, while you go about whatever business you would rather me not be privy to with that certain someone."

She cocked her head in such a way that the lowering sun rays spiked a golden crown around her, reminding him of a glowing Madonna by Raphael...with a Gil Elvgrin pin-up twist.

"You know I have a thing for really smart girls." At Shirley's speculative raise of an eyebrow he quantified with, "But just the one with a heart to match."

Shirley's giggle as he goosed her only emphasized where she ranked next to Kate Morningside. The torch he'd once carried for his California girl was deader than dead, and so was Shirley's close friendship with the fellow nurse who once actually cared about saving lives instead of snuffing them out and caring about no one but herself.

Kate. He had known her all his life and then, *justlikethat,* he didn't know her at all. It was as if a body double had taken her place while some mad scientist took over her mind and turned her into the Bride of Frankenstein. Actually, that was pretty much right on the money, given that she had married that sleazy snake of a diplomat, Phillip Jordan, after she'd left JD for dead.

"Okay, I'll go pack while you make whatever call I'm not supposed to hear, and tomorrow I'll go shopping in Saigon while you do some clandestine meeting with JD." Shirley put a finger to her delectable lips. "*Shhh.*"

And then she put her lips to his. A quick little kiss, followed by a wink, and all Gregg could think was that he had to be the luckiest guy in the world.

Except for this genuine concern about Izzy. He'd lost so many people he cared about, but to ever lose Izzy would be the next most horrible thing to losing Shirley.

JD, amazingly, just might come in as a not so distant third.

As he sipped at the remains of his Tanqueray and Tonic, Gregg took stock of what they had built here, what they had to look forward to:

The new place on the Andaman Sea in the very south of Thailand was already up and operating. It was beautiful; they had recreated the mission gardens Shirley had lovingly established here. The new mission house proper was modeled on this one, too, but with more bedrooms.

Thanks to their very generous benefactor, they could afford it. And, it certainly didn't hurt that they were taking their reputation with them as the finest pediatric war trauma treatment center in Southeast Asia. All of the children, the nursing school students, teaching staff and residents were already there, and there at least they wouldn't have the horrific memories of something even worse than war:

The Ghost Soldier, who had brutally murdered Shirley's first husband, Dr. David Donnelly, in this very house, and nearly killed the two of them along with a host of friends, including Margie, and a much kinder, better version of Kate.

A soft, cooling breeze came off the bay and wafted across the garden.

The scent of jasmine and the sound of small waves breaking on the sand, the rustling leaves of the coco palms above the veranda, worked their soothing magic. He was grateful for all the lovely memories that they had created here to cover over the ugly ones.

It was almost enough to make him forget the killer who was, thank God, safely consigned to the bowels of a high security military lock down ward for the criminally insane. And yet, despite the expanse of time and continental distance, he could still hear his voice, the sound of his laughter, as if they were sharing another beer at a local beach party.

Not for the first time Gregg wondered where the top-secret facility was, and if he could pull the right strings for clearance, would it provide some healing benefit to visit what he could only describe as a psychopath's psychopath? So engaging, so seemingly normal. *So twisted.* That might help with the occasional and deeply disturbing intrusive thoughts that a monster, who he had once considered a friend, had managed to escape, and was walking freely amongst an unsuspecting public.

Just the thought made him feel like a cadaver was breathing down his neck while an icy fingernail slid up his spine.

Jerry Prince. That was the monster's name. And the grisly deeds he had done, what he could still do if set loose, was unspeakable.

IT HAD BEEN a while since Jerry had been in Saigon, which suited him fine since every time he stepped foot in the city he thought of Isabelle, of that one magic night that still haunted him even after four years and counting. He had never seen her again. Just as she had never again seen her playwright friend.

Quan was long dead. Actually, Jerry had been the one to kill him. It was, at that point, an act of mercy that Quan had begged for.

At least so Miles had told him, and he had no reason to doubt the doc about what had been an odd experience: One minute he was listening to Quan gurgle for it all to be over and feeling sorry for him, and the next there Quan was with his throat slit open from a scalpel Jerry didn't remember picking up from a nearby surgical tray. But sure enough, there was the scalpel with the number 10 blade, dripping blood, right there in his hand.

What had bothered him most, and did to this day, wasn't so much that he had put poor Quan out of his misery. It was that he didn't remember doing it. And he had a very good memory.

Now Jerry, Miles had said, patting him on the shoulder, *don't let this bother you, pardner. It's just a result of some of the deep work we've been doing with the pharmaceuticals to help you recover some of that humanity you lost because of that evil stepdad of yours. What you see in your hand is the evidence that your subconscious is stepping up to the plate on behalf of your better nature, and the old part of you that went around doing folks in for no good reason is blocking out what was meant as a good deed. That's all. But you are winning, and I am very proud of you. You should be proud of yourself. Now let's end class early, call someone over to clean this up and we'll go pay a visit to Hugo, have ourselves an early Happy Hour.*

The incident had bothered him enough to tell Miles he wanted to put their sessions on hold. After winning a reluctant agreement, he had a sense that his new status of Spook had been altered. Not that Miles had said so, or that Hugo had called him in to make it official, but there had been no further red-carpet galas. Then again, much of that could be owed to so many fewer events, especially after the so called "Peace Accord" that everybody knew was just a pathetic, bullshit escape clause for the US to hide behind because their war in Vietnam was lost.

ISIC was another matter. If anything, they had put the pedal to the metal, and he had the hours, not to mention the official title of Assistant Director, to prove it. Interesting, though, that the new title was granted shortly after he agreed to pick the deep work LSD sessions back up... But. Then again, he had earned the distinction of the promotion, which included much of the responsibility in getting their entire, complex operation moved. It was still a transition in progress, without anyone knowing exactly when all the shit would hit the fan in this doomed country, but inevitably they would be closing shop and picking business right back up at their new top-secret location in Thailand as their head of command had decreed.

Namely, Ambassador Phillip Jordan. And when he said jump, you didn't ask how high before grabbing a pole vault and going for a world record.

Which brought Jerry to his present assignment here in Saigon. Something quite bad had happened the week before: One of their journalist detainees, Tran Phan, had somehow managed to escape.

This was particularly concerning since it had been on his watch and nobody, NOBODY, had ever escaped from the ISIC compound before.

The fact that however the hell Phan had gotten out of his tiger cage unde-tected was somewhat counterbalanced by the certainty he would not have the skills to make it out of the surrounding jungle alive. And yet, he had gotten out, not a trace left behind, so Jerry had the very worrisome snake in his head that someone very, very good, like J.D. Mikel supernaturally good, might have paid them a visit to check the place out.

Whatever the circumstances, it was enough to make him sweat and that was even before The Ambassador had blown up. The word that had come down from Jordan to Hugo, who apologetically repeated the order verbatim was:

I don't give a good goddam if Phan was eaten by a tiger. Find the tiger and tear its entrails out if necessary, but bring me proof that the journalist is dead.

On the heels of that, murmurs began to ripple through the intelligence community that a high-profile journalist had made his way into a well-guarded Saigon compound. And then just yesterday a rumor emerged that the Americans had a secret facility where the journalist had been taken after being kidnapped, put in a cage, and tortured.

This is my fuck-up, he told Hugo. *Just get me a chopper, any intel on the location, and I've got this.*

It did not matter that most of the American troops were gone and the contractors with any sense at all were getting out yesterday with any money or family that they had, or that there wasn't much American money to be had anymore anyway. What mattered was that ISIC could be internationally exposed to conjecture, inspection, and something far worse than embarrassment to the United States:

Embarrassment was a Lt. William Calley facing a court martial, and cameras, for personally taking out 22 unarmed South Vietnamese civil-ians in the My Lai Massacre. Hardly an isolated incident, but slaughtering a village of 500 mostly women, kids and old men, while inciting plenty of public outrage, didn't make the whole Army look bad when it could be blamed on a rogue platoon.

But ISIC? Their highly orchestrated, dark money government funded project made Lt. Calley look like a Boy Scout hoping to make Eagle. And despite the layers upon layers of secrecy to protect the school's godfather, if the true nature of their work and his association with it got out?

A highly regarded US diplomat who worked deals on the world stage and, according to Hugo, not only got along famously with Kissinger but exchanged Christmas cards with several Presidents...alas, Kennedy was dead...Well. There you had it.

It was imperative that he find the journalist before any further damage was done. Present Tran Phan's fingers, tongue, and even feet if he had to in a big gold box with a fat red bow, to reassure Jordan that his reputation was safe and any forthcoming rumors or probing would not be due to some inexplicable lapse by a loyal employee whose hand he had shaken exactly once, at what had been the very last Republic of Vietnam Fine Arts Award Gala.

As Jerry tried to put that unforgettable night behind him yet again and focus on the destination at hand, he picked up his pace along the bustling sidewalk. The sooner this was done, the sooner he could get back to his kitten Panther. He just loved that little kitten. Loved it so much that in his rush to make sure Panther was fed and had plenty to eat in his absence, he'd totally forgotten to wolf something down himself.

The rumbling of his stomach joined a moving carnival of cars, jeeps, bicycles and Vespas blaring horns on the street to his left. To the right was an endless line of glass fronted shops showcasing everything from Seiko watches and Teac tape decks to vibrant bolts of raw silk and cigarettes. The smell of pho and weed everywhere filled his nostrils.

Pausing to take a sniff of the fragrant broth wafting from an open café door didn't seem too overly-indulgent, but just as he turned to hurry on his way, another pedestrian bumped into him. Or maybe it was the other way around.

"Sorry," Jerry said automatically, then corrected himself with a quick, *"Excusez-moi."*

"No, my fault," the guy said back. "Should've been watching where I was going."

Another American. But… he knew that voice. Nobody had a voice like that except…

What the hell was Gregg Kelly doing here?? He should've been deployed back to the states over five years ago, draftee time up so he could go back to surfing on his California waves, doing more shrink work on head jobs, or teaching, or…

A split second of eye-contact and Jerry instinctively pulled the neck of his tee higher, put his head down, moved on.

But in his peripheral vision, reflected in the café window, he saw Dr. Gregg Kelly still standing there, still looking like he belonged in a Coppertone ad, except with his mouth almost comically open, as if he'd just seen a ghost.

After a quick half block, a sharp turn down an alley, then a zig-zag cross between two other busy streets, Jerry stopped in front of a bakery. His 20/10 vision assured him that Dr. Gregg Kelly was nowhere in sight.

Pretending to study the array of exquisite French pastries in the storefront window, he assessed his reflection in the glass. The distinctive tattoo that reached his neck was effectively hidden. There was absolutely no way that Kelly could have physically recognized him. Most days he still hardly recognized himself. Only…

"Sorry…Excusez-moi."

"No, my fault… Should've been watching where I was going."

He had recognized Kelly's voice before registering the startled look on his face.

Doc Kelly was a good shrink. Shrinks actively listened to voices all the time. Even with the major plastic surgery job and all these years apart, it was entirely possible Kelly had made the ID with a muttered: *"Sorry… Excusez-moi."*

Never had he needed that centering seven count finger tap more. Especially since Kelly had been like J.D. Mikel's third nut in a jock strap.

Returning with evidence of Phan no longer being a threat was immediately relegated to a lower position on the Cover Your Ass laundry list. The ankle-deep shit he and his cohorts at TKS had been in this morning had just gotten neck high if J.D. Mikel entered the picture…

If he hadn't already.

CHAPTER 7

"What?" Ex-CIA agent, J.D. Mikel, thought he'd seen and heard it all. Apparently not. "You have to be kidding me."

"Do I look like I'm kidding?"

JD watched Gregg toss back another shot of Jack in the corner booth of a dark bar where they had rendezvoused to discuss a mutual friend gone MIA in NYC.

That friend would not be Jerry Prince.

"But you're not 100 percent certain," JD pressed, as if it mattered, when even a niggling suspicion was enough to warrant an agency-wide emergency alert—if he still worked for the CIA.

"Like I said, the face was different but the voice? I couldn't forget it if I tried, and believe me, I *have* tried. Not only that, he did this quick pull at the neck of his tee-shirt, like a reflex to hide something—and okay, maybe that was nothing, but the way he moved was as telling as any tattoo. I may not be a Kung Fu monk-star like you, but I grew up on a surfboard and can tell who's on a wave and surfing it with their own way of moving 300 yards out." Gregg shivered, which told JD as much as the words coming out of one of his best friend's mouth. "What I know, and so do you, JD, is that how someone moves is as distinct and unique as a signature. And I am telling you that everything about that guy had JERRY PRINCE written all over him."

"I believe you." JD stroked the scar racing down his cheek. Sometimes he covered it up with makeup. Other times, when the job called for it, or rather had in his previous life, he wore facial prosthetics, contacts, wigs. No one knew better than he how deceiving an outward appearance could be. Anyone with the know-how could completely revise their features, even permanently with surgery, but only the true masters of deception took it all the way with a change of voice, intonation, pitch; and just as importantly, movement. Frequently he had been a hunchback, or severely pigeon-toed with a halting gait, even seemingly one-armed, or a portion of his leg missing with his pants tied just beneath the knee and foot strapped against his upper thigh.

So yes, it was entirely possible that Gregg had bumped into the man—if you could call a human butcher that—who he had personally put on a chopper in full restraints, and with three Special Forces guards for backup, delivered him to…

"Shit." JD groaned as the chances of Gregg's siting horrifically skyrocketed. "Phillip. That sonofabitch."

"Other than an apt character reference, what about him?"

"You and Izzy were with me when we got Jerry loaded onto the chopper."

"Right. Then you took off with him to make sure he was properly handed off to… no. Don't tell me."

"Exactly. We landed after dark in Dalat, and Phillip was there with General Claymore. My plan was to escort our special delivery all the way to the States and see him personally behind bars in a straitjacket, but Phillip intercepted me while we were transferring our precious cargo from the chopper to the plane that was waiting—said they needed me right away on this urgent other mission, and he and Claymore would take things from there. I had no reason at the time to doubt that's exactly what they would do. After all, Phillip was the one who assigned me to the Ghost Soldier case to begin with."

"Shit," Gregg whispered. "Shit!" And then he rubbed at his temples, the way Izzy would push up his black horn rimmed glasses, when deep in thought. "I'm trying to remember that time I actually met Ambassador Jordan face-to-face. At the 99KO's headquarters, when it was still in Nha Trang, and Claymore was there, making some not so veiled threats to me and Izzy if we ever opened our mouths about the fact Jerry Prince ever existed. But while Claymore seemed most concerned about wiping the Army clean of a psycho before they had a public relations nightmare on their hands, Jordan was asking questions."

"What kind of questions?"

"They were psychological in nature. He inferred that the military could use more killers like Prince, if they could just find a way to keep them from crossing the wrong lines. Then he wanted to know how a mind like Jerry Prince's worked. Said the information could be useful. Meanwhile, Izzy and I were given a file to examine that had those incredibly disturbing journal entries Jerry wrote before he escaped Madigan General and found his way to Nam. I'm sure you saw everything before we did, including that last entry: NOTES FROM HELL."

"I did. Most disturbing. I thought the one he titled KITTENS was the worst. Jesus."

"Yeah," Gregg agreed. "They were all horrific, but that one was like the worst thing I've ever read or heard of, ever, ever. And as a shrink, you know I've heard some really awful stuff."

As they let that sit between them for a long moment, JD wondered if he had been too hasty, or too selfish, in the personal choices he had made since dragging a couple of drafted shrinks from one near death experience and straight into another. The last one, though. It had been a death of sorts. For him.

He had pretended immunity, but not for a second did he think that Gregg or Izzy had bought it. Especially after he resigned as the CIA's go-to assassin and went to lick his wounds on the pretext of training a new generation of assassins at the place where he had been raised—a school that was hundreds of untold years old, carved out in the Highlands jungle, where an order of monks were even deadlier and more secretive than the Shaolin Temple. He had been a mere boy, an unwanted son of a hateful American power broker and a French mother as exquisite as she was suicidal, when the monks had embraced him as one of their own.

"How's school?" Gregg suddenly asked, as if needing as much distance as possible from butchered kitty cats and Notes from Hell. "Still the most popular monk, or are you gunning for the old Abbot's top job?"

"Man, you're good." Grateful for the laugh, JD gave him the Cliff's Notes. "I turned in my robe last week and my hair's growing out again, if you didn't notice, while I've been debating between an early retirement on my little island, or maybe doing something with my family's old tea plantation—expanding the Dragonwell production—or, I've been thinking about looking ahead instead of back, maybe invest in something called 'personal computers.' There's this new US company called Microsoft that some kids named Gates and Allen just launched, virtually yesterday, so I guess my investigative skills aren't completely washed up. Since I know a bit about technology, I'm thinking about approaching them and—"

"JD." Gregg leaned forward, looked him square into the eyes until Gregg's sky blues probed beneath JD's 7-UP green bottle surface. "What are you doing?"

Such a simple question. And yet, so loaded with ramifications, especially if he was honest with himself. What Kate had done to him, or really, specifically, what he had allowed her to do to him, was break his heart so completely that he had hidden, taken refuge at the monastery where he continued to live with a kind of living wound. It had been like this contorted emotion that kept crawling across glass shards of memories that exquisitely cut and renewed the wounding that only got deeper because it was riddled with betrayal, with the knowing he had been fooled. What had emerged was a disgusting kind of self-pity and loathing, mixed with a grinding, depressing, craving, longing for...

Kate.

His dreams at night would find him drowning while Kate stood above him, watching him sink into the dark, choking depths of the Mekong. That's when he always awoke, wheezing, hardly able to catch his breath. Indeed, he had his own private Notes From Hell. Most of them compliments of Kate Morningside who had climbed up the Agency's ladder while wallowing in bed with the bastard he had once revered.

"What am I doing?" JD repeated. "Honestly, Gregg, I'm no longer sure. I wouldn't say that to anyone but you. Or Izzy. As close as I am to Zhang, I don't think my step-brother would quite get it, so I wouldn't even tell him. But, when you reached out to set up this meeting because you couldn't get hold of Izzy, a part of me felt excited in a way that I haven't felt for a long, long time. I'm not sure if that's pitiful given who I used to be, or more like a little sick considering there could be a legitimate cause for concern regarding the wellbeing of someone I would give my life for —and who has more than once, risked his for me. Same as you."

JD leaned his left elbow on the table so the silver Montagnard bracelet circling his wrist glimmered in a stream of dim lighting. Gregg did the same, his own matching bracelet, ceremoniously presented years before, exactly where JD had placed it.

"Listen, pal, and I want you to hear me good. What you just said is anything but pitiful or sick. It makes more sense than just about anything you've said or done in years, at least from this side of the chair. I'm not denigrating your decision to leave the spook business cold, or to retreat into a monastery even the CIA wouldn't want to breach, if they could find it, while you've sought your own source of healing and meaning beyond a job that you defined, more than it defined you. But JD, meditating, fasting, teaching the fine art of maiming and murder when you're not painting, while all fine and good…" Gregg shook his head. "It's been an escape, not a cure. No one is better at what you do, than you. You left at the top of your game. Perhaps you lost your appetite for it for a while, got burned out not to mention getting burned badly, but hanging it up in your mid-thirties?" Another head shake. "Or expanding a tea business in a country that's on the verge of collapse, if you don't retire to an island in the same collapsing country?" Another shake. "Even if you have plenty of friends from the incoming North, not to mention your brother Zhang, you're not cut out to be a tea tycoon… any more than you are to getting in on some ground floor opportunity that may or may not take off in a country you've visited exactly twice and couldn't leave fast enough. As American as you may appear when you want to, as much a legal citizen as you are, and even with as many years of serving in a very dark capacity at the US government's behest, you are no more American than a koi is a whale. No matter how much of the world you travel, Southeast Asia is embedded into the very marrow of your bones. It's your touchstone. Your true home. The profession you walked away from is much the same. You may have left it, but it never left you. Of course, you felt excited about needing to find Izzy. Of course, you got a much needed shot of adrenaline in the process. You've been away a long time. Too long."

"Are you saying…?"

Gregg nodded. "Agent Mikel, you may never work for the CIA again but you can still write your own ticket wherever else you want. It's time to dust off your cloak and dagger, now that you've put away the robe."

While that was still soaking in, coming from Gregg Kelly of all people, actually urging him to get back into the business of assassinations, the good doctor reached over, tapped JD in the middle of his chest.

"Now to the heart of the matter," Gregg went on. "You got to drop the Kate baggage."

"I'm sure I don't know what you mean." He really did NOT want to talk about this.

"See? Here you go again, avoiding the real issue." Tap, tap. Middle of the chest again. "Who fooled you, JD? Who fooled you right here?" Tap. Tap.

JD answered him with a stony silence, not liking the turn the conversation was taking.

"Who fooled the world's smartest, toughest, scariest cloak and dagger man?" came the question again, a little more sideways before taking a direct hit. "Say her name."

"Kate," JD muttered, hoping that would appease Gregg so they could just move on.

"Who?" Gregg cupped his ear. "I couldn't hear you."

"Fine." But it wasn't fine. He wasn't fine, and hadn't been for a long time, they both knew it. Giving in ungraciously, he snapped, "Kate. Kate fooled me. Happy?"

"Yeah. I am. Because until you confront what she did, what she took from you—and you know exactly what she took—you will not have what you need to put yourself 100 percent into anything, or anyone else, again. So, let's just go ahead and put it out there. What did she take from you, JD? Besides your trust, when she fooled you, what did Kate take? True story."

JD gave Gregg a hard stare—the way he used to. They had started as almost opposing forces, rivals, before forming an unlikely friendship. But deep as that friendship went, it had never quite crossed into Gregg's professional territory. JD felt like a highly reluctant patient having his feet held to the emotional truth flame. He'd liked it a lot better when he was the one in charge because finding Ghost Soldiers and protecting Poppy Kings were his professional realm. Or, had been.

Tap, tap. Middle of the chest. "JD? True story."

The persistence and the tapping were starting to piss him off a little. It actually felt good, certainly better than the depression, the withdrawn sort of flat-line state he'd kept himself comfortably numb in.

"She took my heart." JD pushed Gregg's forefinger away and slapped himself square in the chest that he had guarded so closely. Guarding, guarding, always holding back, ever since he'd been that little boy who lost his mother and got sent to a monastery. Until... "I let her in and she lied to me, she took my goddam heart and treated it like trash. True story."

"Okay. That's good. But here's the deal, JD. That's not the end of the story. You still have a heart. Kate only took a piece of it. Don't let that keep you from going out into the world again, full hearted, at everything." He extended his hand.

JD met his grip. And in that connection swirled a convergence of things that felt too important not to catalog, and take out later for a more careful examination: A rush of relief, as if he had been holding his breath and hadn't realized it, which was insane since he was constantly focused on breathing. Coupled with that was a sense that he had been waiting for something that felt like granted permission that he had been withholding from himself.

A strange sensation of escalating excitement mixed with a terrible sense of unease. It reminded him of his first mission when he was twelve, posing as a shoeshine boy in order to eviscerate a very bad man of political stature whose pants were down for a "special shine" in a luxury suite at the Raffles Hotel in Singapore. How odd that now, 25 years later, he could demonstrate to his students the unrivaled power of the mind's ability to override even a normal sense of fear: Going into such a deep meditative state that a bullet fired beside his ear did not register with his steady pulse. And yet, Gregg's urging him to return to the spycraft he had indeed left at the pinnacle of his career made the once formidable Agent J.D. Mikel undeniably a little…nervous?

"What are you thinking?" Gregg asked.

"That I convinced myself I had lost my edge. You know that essential driving force to be the best, be the most lethal, be craftier and smarter and faster than whatever, or whoever, is your target or opponent or objective, with the clear intention to achieve, to seduce, or kill."

Gregg nodded. "But the true story?

JD took a deep breath. He had left out one very critical detail that went beyond Kate, even as she remained intrinsic to that ultimate wounding. But he knew. So did Phillip.

"True story," JD slowly responded, and this much to Gregg he would confess. "It wasn't ever the edge that I lost. It was…" Releasing their extended handshake, JD patted the spot that housed more than an anatomical organ upon which the body depended in order to truly live. "And from the bottom of mine, Dr. Kelly, I thank you. Please know that I do prize your insights, professional wisdom, and the loyalty we share."

"Promise you'll take everything I've said under consideration."

"Absolutely." One of Izzy's favorite words. Even if precipitate for a whole new cloak and dagger wardrobe, at least he had a personally important mission to focus on, to investigate, to fix. "Now I have some advice for you in exchange. Neither of us can be certain that you literally bumped into Jerry Prince on the sidewalk today. But even if there is .0001 percentage of a chance that you did, I strongly suggest that you immediately check out of the hotel with Shirley and take yourselves just as immediately to the new mission hospital in Thailand. By the way, Zhang sends his best along with another donation that's being wired into the campus expansion funds."

"He's too good to us."

"Not at all. He can never repay you and Izzy for all that you did to help save his people and the poppy fields that support them. And Gregg, neither can I."

"Thanks, JD. But if you really want to pay me back—"

"I know. I know." JD held up his hands in mock surrender. "And you in turn will—"

"Go back to the hotel and inform Shirley that we need to be on the next plane, train, or bus heading to Thailand. Do not pass Go! Do not collect $200! Or risk going directly to J.D. Mikel's jail."

"Precisely. The old mission's not that far from my island and I can pack anything she doesn't want to leave behind, bring it to the new place." And with that, JD went about the business of setting priorities: "After I look into what's going on with Izzy."

CHAPTER 8

La Colombe d' Or
St. Paul de Vence
South of France

Wearing cat-eyed sunglasses, a silk scarf cinched around chic blonde hair blowing in a sea salt breeze, Kate decided she felt more like Grace Kelly than the other actress she was most frequently compared to—Catherine Deneuve. Especially while driving down a curving road in Phillipe's luxurious MBZ Cabriolet, the top down, and a glorious French Riviera spread out below with the Mediterranean sparkling in the late afternoon light.

Kate wondered if such acclaimed actresses ever had stage fright, even after multiple performances and glowing reviews. She kept thinking the newness would wear off and the nervous excitement of her own performances would dissipate, but even going on five years, such was not the case. Perhaps because her roles were more dangerous and she had to get them right the first time.

The drive over much too soon, Kate hooked her arm companionably through Phillip's and they walked along the cobblestones that wound down the steep curving path of the lovely village of St. Paul de Vence. A wonderful, magical place, with a series of lovely shops and small art galleries, it sat in its medieval lost-in-time grandeur a mere few miles above Nice in the south of France. Being just down the hill from the hotel where they were staying—Phillip's beloved Chateau St. Martin in the ancient village of Vence—their ultimate destination was a favorite place for him. No wonder she was so eagerly anticipating her first visit to the remarkable and famous La Colombe d'Or, even though they were going for business, not strictly for pleasure.

That they would save for later at their Chateau St. Martin suite.

The entrance to the fabled place that was the La Colombe d'Or, where Picasso and Matisse had once gathered with other artists, was as fairy-tale like as Phillip's gallant opening of a weathered, old wood door that lead to...

Somewhere beyond extraordinary. An exquisite wrinkle in time.

Inside, they stood next to a sculptured fountain as Phillip was greeted effusively by an elderly waiter dressed in a crisp white shirt, black tie and trousers.

"Ambassador!"

"Gaspard." Phillip returned his greeting in the French way, then introduced him with real affection. "Kate, this is a very fine old friend I've known since my student days. My father thought a great deal of Gaspard, as do I." A slight inclination of his stately head her way. "And this is my lovely wife, Kate."

"*Enchanté*, Madam." Gaspard's smile was warm and genuine, as though she was the original and unique ingénue and not likely the 100th young woman to be brought to this place and introduced. Unlike Phillip's others, however, she had managed the distinction of "wife."

"Is my favorite table available?" Phillip asked.

"But of course, Mr. Ambassador. I received word that you were coming."

"And that special company will be joining us?"

Gaspard's slightly raised brow was met with Phillip's subtle nod.

"But, of course. All will be made ready for your company's arrival."

But of course. In hers and Phillip's world a dinner was rarely just a dinner. A private getaway was anything but. And their newly acquired eyebrow raising status as husband and wife had far more gray lines than the black or whites that most couples considered acceptable to cross.

Old but spry, Gaspard took them immediately across paved stones where white clothed tables, set with old silver and crystal, led past an aged fig tree and ultimately to a green oasis where a corner table, perhaps perennially reserved for Phillip, afforded them a leafy, flowery bower of privacy while providing a grand vista looking down to the blue Mediter-ranean Sea.

Upon reaching the table, Phillip gave Gaspard another meaningful nod, to which the elderly waiter said, "Ambassador, shall I bring the champagne you prefer… after I show Madam some paintings?"

"*Trés bien et merci*." To Kate then: "By the time you return, all the business will be finished… except for yours."

As Kate followed Gaspard she glanced over her shoulder. The man being clearly led to Phillip's private table was of military bearing and matched the photo in the file she had been given. He was from Singapore, "a rising star in the opposition to my friend whose family is presently ruling" Phillip had explained. "Amazing that he's managed to get so far, he must have incredible cunning and balls."

Be that as it may, he was a walking dead man right now. Singapore was too important just the way it was; there would be no changes at all. It was becoming the Switzerland of Asia. Maybe even more efficiently organized and controlled than Switzerland because one man had essentially created and ran it: Phillip's friend.

The enemy of Phillip's friend was married, had children, a large extended family. He also had a weakness for attractive women other than his wife. And that's where she came in.

Out of the shaded garden and into the brightly tiled sunny space of the bar, Gaspard led her, until he nodded to a corner seat.

"The place of Picasso. His flowers are inside. Come." And then they were in a darkened hallway and Gaspard was saying, "Matisse was the first artist here, but soon his friends, too."

He pointed to the Chagall painting, just casually there, as though it always had belonged with the Miro and Picasso's flowers. The old fashioned country inn's casual elegance combined with masterpieces allowed her to forget the real purpose of this distraction, just for a moment, and so she laughed gaily, "*Mon dieu*, what delight!"

The elder man turned to her, smiling. "Oui, it is delightful. As are you, Madam Kate. Phillip's father would approve. You are a real companion for him I see, not a dalliance. Now, if you wish to sit there while I see to the Krug"—he gestured to an old, plump brocade covered chair—"No one should bother you here. We will return to the table when you are ready."

It was a lovely, secluded spot to innocuously check the contents of her Hermes clutch: lipstick, a compact with embedded code, a small silk embroidered bag. She was rarely without the Beretta in her purse, and today was no exception in the unlikely event that their luncheon companion had his own agenda. But it was the tiny vial within the bag that was the real murder weapon intended for the Singapore man: a slow acting but inevitably lethal poison. He would enjoy this champagne with her and Phillip, then his meal, and then have an increasingly uncomfortable night followed by catastrophic renal failure by this time tomorrow.

As she returned to the table, Gaspard not far behind her with the Krug she would personally add a little something special to for their guest while she engaged him in a sparkling conversation, she wondered: How much intrigue had the old waiter been witness to through all the wars? How many meals served to walking dead men?

She waited for the perfect moment to tilt the politics of Singapore back into the favor of the existing regime, and once her job was done, Kate made a toast to such a glorious day and to their fortuitous meeting.

The adrenaline high she rode added an extra sparkle to her eyes, but it was the memory of the lovely Picasso flowers that tilted her lips into a luminous smile as the French Riviera's Mediterranean glistened gem-like beneath them...and Agent Katherine Lynn Morningside-Jordan allowed their ill-fated Singapore man the pleasure of lighting her after-dinner Gauloises.

~

Chateau St. Martin Hotel
Vence
A few hours later

THE CALMING SURROUNDINGS of his personal suite, in what he considered the finest hotel in the world, were exactly what Phillip Jordan needed. The bedroom, at the top of the old tower, had a different kind of art on display from the masters at La Colombe d'Or that, to his highly discerning eye, was equally spectacular.

He gazed at her now, his delectable companion in bed, blonde hair strewn over a pillow, plump pink lips slightly parted as she slept beside him in the nude.

Of course, the sex had been, as Richard Burton once exclaimed about Elizabeth Taylor, "nearly pornographic." It was always thus with Kate following a murder. Killing, like combat, created a biological aphrodisiac cocktail far beyond everyday life. Sex and war had always partnered, been

71

conjoined for our kind of apes. It took Katherine to a very different place. Her rapture carried him along too, at least for that all too brief time.

He eyed her gold cigarette case and wished that he still smoked. It had been years since he had given it up as a personal choice... and now, he would make another choice. A Gauloises would not only complete the look with the sleek black smoking jacket he donned, it might help soothe the agitation that had him padding down the winding staircase into the palatial living room, a single unlit cigarette and engraved lighter residing in the jacket whose purpose it was meant to serve.

The living area was softly lit and warmly appointed, lightly fluttering drapes revealing a peek-a-boo twilight outside open balcony doors. The ambiance was such that it stirred a sense of nostalgia. He had been here, in this very city, when the idea had first come to him. And what had begun as an idea was to become his dearest political baby and favorite brainchild: ISIC.

From its inception he had believed in the school's potential for developing cadres of international students who could return home to their respective countries and do what they were trained to do: Destabilize a government. Maintain order through intimidation, torture, and extermination of any kind of resistance or alternative to the regime the USA wanted to rule. Critical to its success was ensuring that ISIC be operated outside of formal oversight. It just would not look good to the world at large to discover the USA, the "beacon of light for the world," had a place that researched mayhem and violence on human bodies and minds.

It especially would not look good for anyone of his stature to be involved. Which was why his rare visits, which he relished, required some planning. He always had to create a very visible meeting somewhere far away like here, in France, where a body double was photographed going in and out of hotels and restaurants and meetings, then the photographs would be "leaked" to "Hello" and "Life" and "Paris Match" and "Der Spiegel" news.

But now. Of all times, NOW, what could be a final visit before the entire operation was completely dismantled and the move to Thailand complete, he might need to put all those precautions aside and make a show of being at such a fine research facility.

He could almost laugh at the irony of it—using the media to beat an escaped journalist at his own game.

Phillip's sly smile turned to a grimace at the intrusive ring of a phone.

Exactly four people would know where to reach him and he really did not want to talk to any of them at the moment.

"Bonjour." He glanced in the framed mirror above the console where the phone had remained thankfully silent until now.

"Phillip, mon ami, I fear we may have a problem."

"Of course, we have a problem." Taking what comfort he could in deciding he still looked good, fit, his hair graying but in the distinguished way that his father's had, Phillip kept his voice low. "It's called an escaped journalist who just leaked a story about ISIC to the BBC. It seems the State Department would like to speak to me about it. However, I would like to speak to you first about an idea I have to circumvent his credibility and intervene before this mess gets any worse."

"Oui, a most unfortunate event, and I wish to hear your idea. But that is not the first problem we need to discuss. We have a new situation."

Wonderful. One shit show was apparently not enough.

"Very well, Hugo. Speak."

"It is about Jerry."

"What about Prince? Has he declined those important sessions again, or exhibited any behaviors counter to our intent? I certainly hope not since it would be a shame to destroy him after everything we have invested." Examining the bump on his nose, Phillip scowled. He had thought to utilize the plastic surgeon that had performed such a splendid job on their prototype elite warrior, but had decided to keep the bump as a visual reminder of the score he had yet to settle.

As for the permanently impaired finger not even the best surgeon could fix, he was lucky it hadn't been amputated.

"Jerry is trés conscientious," Hugo quickly assured him. "Trés loyal. We have no need to dispose of him... even if he may have been recognized while on the hunt for the journalist in Saigon."

"Impossible. Prince's unrecognizable remains were presented to Command five years ago. The only ones who could make a positive ID before we took care of the visual issue are you, me, and our highly indispensable, even if highly annoying, Dr. Strangelove." An apt code name for Miles, given the tweaking he had done on Kate for more than her husband's own benefit.

"It is another doctor he thinks could make trouble. It is one you know. A psychologist. Docteur Gregg—"

"Kelly? What the hell! He and that missionary woman Kate used to be friends with should have already left." Of course, he knew Kelly had returned to the RVN, stepped into the #2 position to run the Nha Trang mission hospital Prince had nearly wiped out with an impressive body count. That had been the summer of '69, and of course he'd kept tabs on JD's pet shrinks ever since. While Kelly had married the missionary, the other one, that Moskowitz psychiatrist, was a medical research specialist at Columbia University Medical School. He typically worked six days a week, 12 or more hours a day, walked home from work to an apartment in Central Park North that he had inherited from his aunt, rarely kept company, no longer went to synagogue, and ate every meal alone in the same restaurants, day after day. Routine, orderly, colorless. Just reading his annual report was enough to put an insomniac to sleep.

Once a year had seemed sufficient when he'd ordered the routine surveillance on Kelly and Moskowitz. Even after their unwitting contributions to that Poppy King fiasco with JD and the step-brother ruining his finger and dislocating his previously perfect nose, the shrinks were ultimately just drafted academics who weren't important enough to bear more than a cursory watch.

"There is more," Hugo continued. "Jerry said that he re-traced his steps in hopes of tracking Kelly back down and bringing him here. While our *magnifique* hunter did locate his quarry, he made the decision to return immediately home instead... without the docteur. Or the company that Kelly met outside the bar Jerry deemed unwise to enter."

A premonitory prickle raised the precisely clipped hair on Phillip's nape. His body tensed remembering, the pain surely, but more the pain of humiliation. His still perfect complexion, reflected in the mirror, flushed at the memory that never failed to elicit a terrible, visceral response. One that underscored why there could be vendettas played out across lives and lifetimes because a thirst for revenge ran so deep that only the head of your enemy on a stake and their blood in a goblet could quench it.

"Are you telling me that he's no longer in retreat?"

"Oui. He did not try to disguise himself, although a portion of his head is still shaved."

Unable to stand the sight of the veins bulging out on his unlined forehead, or the crimson stain that had spread from his cheeks all the way down his neck, Phillip commanded himself to stay calm. Yes, he had to stay calm. This was far too important to bungle with a rash decision. No doubt JD had periodically emerged from the monastery and roamed about at will in disguise since their last atrociously violent encounter—so violent he had shat his pants before JD heaped on the ridicule that was even worse than broken bones and a bloodied face. *Win the game? You're nothing but a piece of the game yourself, you delusional cretin, not the master of it.*

Now, finally, if what he had just heard was true, his grinding unmet need, one as basic as the first man's instinctive dictate to ensure his genetic material lived on, was possibly within reach...

As close as the abduction of Dr. Gregg Kelly. Sweetening the lure with a double kidnapping was tempting. The brilliant but ever-so-predictable Israel Moskowitz could be easily obtained and rendered to ISIC for extra insurance. He could even give an order now and have Moskowitz ensconced in a tiger cage in less than two days. Not killed, of course, since he would be no good to him dead. That would only incite JD to retaliate, when the objective was to lure him in and teach him a lesson he would never forget:

He was the pawn, along with his high and mighty step-brother, Zhang. They would see who the true cretins were, and that Ambassador Phillip Jordan was the undisputed master of The Game.

"Phillip," called his awakened bride from upstairs. "What is keeping you? I'm waiting. More you and more champagne. Not to mention my favorite lighter."

"A moment, darling," he called back. Then, to Hugo, puffing on the other end, he made his intentions known. "We need to act swiftly. My first intervention idea has now expanded to two. Not to worry, Hugo. Your boy Jerry is safe. He is, in fact, highly intrinsic to accomplishing both coups I have in mind, so we will be keeping him quite busy."

After what sounded like *"dieu merci,"* Phillip had to wonder if Hugo was a bit precipitate in thanking the god of a master plan that did seem inspired even to the hasty maker of it.

Fishing the single Gauloises out of his silk lined jacket, Phillip put the first cigarette he'd had in twenty years to his lips.

"I will immediately have the whereabouts of Dr. Kelly ascertained for a well-timed extraction," he informed Hugo. "After Kelly is remaindered to ISIC, our dear Mr. Prince will be dispatched on his second most important assignment."

With the flick of a 24K gold lighter he'd had especially commissioned for a first anniversary present to his deliciously young wife of three years now, Phillip glanced at the inscription: *You light up my life.*

And with that, he inhaled. Deep.

CHAPTER 9

U pon leaving the point of rendezvous with Gregg, JD moved with the flow of sidewalk traffic while having his radar attuned to anyone who moved or even remotely smelled like Jerry Prince. Given the severing of his ties with Phillip, most of his old associates were also of the passé variety. Fortunately, he had maintained contact with certain key individuals who had already come in handy.

This included a certain Air America pilot who greeted him at a private area near the Tan Son Nhut airport, a swift LOH chopper on ready to take two hops and then land at what once had been the 8th Field Hospital, where he had first helped himself to two freshly minted young doctor draftees assigned to the Army's psychiatric unit known as the 99KO.

The 99KO was long gone now, relocated to Da Nang, way back in 1970. But for some reason he felt an odd yearning to walk the grounds the US military had abandoned, only to be immediately taken over by the spread of poor Vietnamese from the shack town surrounding the hospital. Cat tracks, sandbags and bunkers, various buildings—mess halls, barracks, hospital units, headquarters, what had been a Red Cross refuge —it was all still here, and bulging with refugees fleeing from the North and growing by the day, if not the minute, from the PAVN's escalating momentum of a hungry vulture swooping down to devour any prey on its path.

JD wasn't sure what he had been looking for, but he did not find it in these sad surroundings. Nor as he roamed the downtown area of Nha Trang, also filled with frantic refugees, where memories teased him of a dinner party and dancing a first dance with Kate. Of driving a group from the 99KO that he wanted for friends, while all too aware that for a Company man like him friends were a luxury he could not afford. It had been the summer of '69, all of them in their summery finest, riding in his '57 turquois Chevy, white ragtop accordianed down with the smell of jasmine and a salt sea breeze making the war that brought them together feel like an odd blessing.

Now the city resembled a hollowed-out version of its former self, with anyone with foresight and the means to do so having already sold or abandoned their shops and businesses. The pawn shops and gold exchanges were thriving in contrast, with jostling lines outside as desperate-to-leave people were selling whatever treasures they had to escape.

While the Peace Hospital Mission was protected to a certain point due to their policy of "turning no one away," no matter what political affiliation throughout the duration of this long and senseless war, JD was relieved that Gregg and Shirley should be on their way to the relative safety of Thailand, if not tonight then surely by tomorrow. They really should have left before now but he knew how extraordinarily difficult it could be to let go of something, someplace, or someone you loved so dearly that you could justify just about anything to stay, even to your own detriment.

There was no temptation for him to linger in this once refined, cultured city, and so JD hailed a cyclo, who dropped him off in the harbor area. As expected, this was more bedlam with at least half the population trying to be somewhere else. Anyone with a boat to their name was quickly making a fortune. Luckily for him, his own destination would not be considered far away enough by the desperate.

Spotting an island fisherman in a familiar fishing boat, he quickly arranged for a ride to the nearby island he sometimes called home. It was one of several off the shores of Nha Trang, that might as well be a thousand miles and a thousand years away, where life passed in the same slow movement of seasons as it always had before the Americans and before the French. Whether the islanders would still be here after the North arrived and took over could very well be another story.

The Headman, who was like the elder or mayor of the little fishing village, greeted JD. He assured him that the small cottage JD had purchased from the family, with a generous stipend for them to watch after it during his absences, was just as he had left it.

After politely declining a cup of tea, JD made his way to the simple thatched structure that looked like any of the others on the outside. He had always taken precautions to keep his little hideaway secret except from a select, trusted few and was pleased to see it was as untouched as the Headman had said. Inside, just as he had left it, were a radio and communications setup and a Teak stereo with a tape system that ran off a generator.

It worked.

There was a rattan bookcase, a traveling typewriter and desk, a box of painting supplies, and a rattan rocking chair. He had a tatami mat in what passed as a "bedroom" but the hammock in the trees outside was where he liked to read in the breeze that came off the sea, and that's where he'd typically slept... until he brought Kate here where they had not done much sleeping.

Despite who she was sleeping with now, at least she had kept this much to herself. Otherwise, Phillip would have torn the place apart, knowing a booby trap would be detected and incur no more injury than a good laugh at his expense.

Changing into a bathing suit, JD took his mask and snorkel and fins off the wall pegs, picked up his sling spear. He walked down to the fine sandy beach and then entered the water, headed out to the reef. The diving here was extraordinary; the reef very healthy and alive with every kind of tropical fish. There were the yellow Tangs in golden clouds and then he passed by a big blue rainbow hued Parrot fish and ribbons of white mouthed eels. He took a deep breath and dove lower. He wasn't really hunting for fish, he just felt calm here in the quiet blue deep. A different world with different rules where the soft, warm water caressed him, reminding him of how her skin once felt on his hands, how she touched his own neck, how her lips—

Stop it. It's over. She practically killed you. Worse, you know who she chose.

Diving deeper still, JD willed the water to wash him free of her, free of the past, free of everything but some singular essence of purpose. Then maybe he could be free of all the questions he still had and stick to the answers he could provide.

Thus far they would not include Izzy's exact whereabouts. The call he had made from Nha Trang to Izzy's residence—3 pm in RVN, 2 am NYC —had gone directly to an answering service that picked up for emergencies. Deciding it prudent to disguise his voice and keep the message cryptic, he affected a Bob Dylan accent and said, "Please tell Dr. Moskowitz this is Mr. Jones and something is happening but I don't know what it is. No need to leave my number, he has it already and I do anticipate the courtesy of a call as soon as he gets this."

It was all veiled in subtext, references made to the night Izzy got Dear Johned by his hippy girlfriend who called him Dr. Jones while she went to Woodstock. It had taken some strong weed, Jack, and good friends to pull him out of his funk. Margie had helped more in that direction than their entire unholy trinity.

JD watched a nearby octopus change color and become virtually invisible as it entered a cavity of the reef. Waited…stealthily reached out. Then, with a stunning speed and ferocity, snatched its unsuspecting prey.

There were teachers everywhere:

Izzy now had exactly eight hours to respond.

Peace Mission Hospital
Nha Trang
The next morning

"Shirley, I do not like this." Reluctantly following Shirley up the familiar veranda stairs, Gregg's usually appreciative gaze on her backside darted in every other direction. "I told you JD would come and get anything you didn't want to leave behind."

"I know. You've told me at least ten times, but there are some things that can't be replaced if he can't find them. Just let me get my grandmother's wedding ring and our personal papers and, oh, the family Bible my parents gave us and—"

"And I'll give you ten minutes. That's it. I'll have the car running."

"But we were fine before we left." Holding a key to the bright red front door that had welcomed so many inside, she insisted, "And we should be fine spending one last night."

"No." The crimson paint, framed by big pots of red and white geraniums, was a sudden reminder of all the red that had been splashed in the house they were about to enter. He should have put his foot down before they left Saigon. He should have just told her.

"What is the matter with you, Gregg? Ever since you saw JD—"

"Shhh. Keep your voice down." Catching her wrist before she could insert the key and turn the ornate gold knob, he struggled to use his calming voice, the one that had talked many a GI pushed over the edge out of his M16 and into a mental ward. "He wasn't the only one I saw—or, who saw me."

"What are you talking about," she demanded, "And why are we whispering? For heaven's sake, it's broad daylight!"

She did have a point. Maybe he was overreacting. Splitting the difference between Shirley's insistence on returning to the mission, then immediately acting on JD's insistence that they leave, had seemed a reasonable approach since Shirley had been led to believe the infamous Ghost Soldier was dead, and for reasons of national security—and her own safety—it was better that she remain ignorant.

At least so he had thought, until the short flight was over and the uneasy sensation roiling through his stomach increased with each mile closer to the mission, until it felt like the weight of ten grenades had made their way into the pit of his belly.

"I'm sorry."

"For what?" she wanted to know.

"For not telling you what happened yesterday. Something disturbing. I didn't want to upset you. But, now that we're here... in retrospect, I should have. I'm sorry, Shirley."

"Don't." She placed her palm over his heart and he wondered if she could feel it racing. "Don't apologize. Just tell me."

"I think there's a very good chance I bumped into..." Deep breath. "Someone we thought was our friend... until he murdered Dr. Donnelly and massacred half of the staff here."

Shirley's mouth moved but nothing emerged. She turned ghostly pale, swayed against him while she shook her head, just shook it and shook it, muttering, "No, no, no, no. He's dead. Dead. The Army said so, they told you and you told me and..."

Gregg held her against him, hating his utter stupidity in putting them at even a small risk. Though, if Jordan was involved and wanted to silence them, or use him somehow to get to Zhang or JD, not even Mars would be far enough away. Certainly not Thailand. Or, New York.

"You can never tell a soul, Shirley. Promise me you will never tell." He gave her a small shake to drive it home. "There are powerful people involved, people without a conscience, who would not hesitate to hurt us —or, our child. We can talk about it later, in private. I only tell you now so you understand the importance of getting the things we came for and leaving as quickly as possible."

Thanks to JD he had a working knowledge of tampering, of traps, taps, and wires. Upon determining it was safe to enter, he immediately went for the gun he kept hidden near the entrance and had actually learned how to shoot. No evidence of anyone hiding inside, or having been there while they were not. Phone lines still intact— though it wouldn't take an intruder to shut down service once the city fell, with Da Nang no doubt going first.

Without a word they gathered their few irreplaceable treasures and left the rest behind for the Northern wave that would eventually come or for vandals or possibly those who might seek a borrowed refuge. When he started to automatically lock the front door, which was ridiculous considering, Shirley stilled his hand and placed a gentle, departing kiss to the red door's center with the benediction: "Thank you dear house for all you have given us. Now care for the needy, protect the innocent, and continue to heal the sick in our absence."

"Amen," was all Gregg could say while a thick emotional lump in his throat played see-saw with the belly grenades that felt ready to explode any second.

"Yes, so be it." The softness of Shirley's whisper was a sharp contrast to the hard line of her grimace, the slice of her gaze across the gardens she had tended as lovingly as she had their patients. "I just pray that anyone who comes here to kill again is stricken down the moment they step foot on this porch and burns in hell for good measure. Fry, bastard, fry."

God did he love this woman. Whoever thought missionaries were made out of sugar did not know his wife. Hooking a protective arm around her, he kept the pistol lowered to his other side until they reached the car. Although it was the same nondescript sedan they had left near the airport and driven back to the mission maybe fifteen minutes before, Gregg looked under the chases—fine—glanced into the backseat—fine too—and made Shirley take cover a safe distance away while he opened the passenger door. Nothing went BOOM.

They got in. He put the pistol into the glovebox, conveniently close but prudently out of sight. Took a breath and with a silent prayer for their safety, turned the key.

Click.

Tried again.

Click.

The stomach grenade took on the tic-toc-ticking of a bomb.

"It must be the battery," he tried to reason.

"The battery was fine when we got here."

I know, I know, he wanted to snap while his eyes felt like they were doing somersaults into the back of his head and a bevy of bees sounded between his ears.

"There has to be an explanation," he managed to calmly say. "No reason to panic. You stay here while I get out and check under the hood."

As he reached for the door handle, she gripped his arm. "Don't."

"We can't just sit here."

"Something doesn't feel right. I don't want you opening the hood."

"Then what do you suggest?"

"The phone still works. Can you reach JD?"

"I can try." No, he was not too proud to go running to JD. He could only hope that JD was sitting by his SAT phone and had reception.

"Then maybe we should just get out of the car and go inside and you call JD."

The car was very quiet as Gregg weighed their lack of options.

The sound of a lone bird called from somewhere overhead.

And then came the unmistakable crackling of a radio, transmitting the low sound of a familiar chuckle from beneath the front seat. Gregg immediately wanted to throw himself over his wife, their child, protect them however he could, but... in that moment he was paralyzed. He couldn't even exhale as he sat, immobile, listening to the voice he had recognized on a crowded Saigon street.

"You should listen to your wife, Gregg. Now both of you get out. Shirley, I see you there on the passenger's side; Gregg, leave the gun in the glovebox, and nobody gets hurt. See you both on the veranda to tidy up any other details."

Looking up to the space they had minutes ago departed, there he was. The Ghost Soldier. Jerry Prince. Rocking on their swing with a big, friendly smile—and an M60 machine gun pointed straight at the windshield.

CHAPTER 10

Columbia University Medical School
New York, USA

Dr. Israel Moskowitz, Professor of Clinical Psychiatry and Neurology and Co-Director of the Child and Adolescent Division of Psychiatry, sat in the deep chair at the far end corner of the big table around which sat fifteen other academics of the Faculty Senate committee on ethics. He pretended to listen to an associate droning on while he pretended to sip thoughtfully at his coffee and further pretended to scratch a few notes, all the while he pretended not to be a fake and a fraud.

Come on now, he wanted to say out loud, *A show of hands of who is with me, who else here is a fake and a fraud—and just how ethical does that make us?*

No one at the table knew he had served in Vietnam. He had buried that as deep as the Army fatigues that had found their resting place in an alleyway burn barrel. The stigma of his service was clear when even the homeless guy in ratty clothes waved away an offer of the nearly new fatigues and helped chuck them into the barrel.

Things had deteriorated from there. The unspeakable thing he had done, that no one knew about, not even Gregg or JD, and god not Margie, was not as easily disposed of as a uniform responsible for more blood spilled than any scalpel he had ever wielded in surgery.

A surreptitious glance at the message he'd been handed upon arrival that morning had Izzy eyeing the door again. Not only in case he needed to make a mad dash before he puked all over the Vice Provost sitting beside him, but with JD, you never knew. The message could have been a tip off that he'd walk through the door any minute innocuously pushing a coffee cart and delivering pastries, only to slip his comrade in absence a little something special, and this time tomorrow, no telling where they'd both be.

"And what say you to the Committee's proposal that more thorough background checks should be implemented in our future hiring practices, Dr. Moskowitz?"

Izzy took another pretend sip of his coffee, coughed discreetly, said, "My apologies, I seem to have something stuck in my throat. Of course, I concur with the committee majority. And now, if you will excuse me, I have a pressing matter to see to that came to my attention just prior to this meeting. I'll review any further notes sent to my office and respond accordingly."

With a pleasant enough expression—he hoped—Izzy gathered his papers and felt every eye in the room follow his back as he made his exit.

He took a quick turn to the nearest Men's room, fortunately vacant, and ducked into a stall. There, he vomited up the lox and cream cheese bagel he'd had for breakfast before receiving the note, and heave-hoed the meeting's coffee along with it. Reluctantly emerging, he swished his mouth with the little bottle of Listerine he always kept handy, thoroughly washed his hands, twice as had become his habit, and did a quick check of his reflection in the mirror.

Izzy did not like what he saw, hadn't for quite a while. His complexion was pasty. The solitude he kept with too much comfort food for safe company showed in his face, his waistline. Good thing he was over 6 feet, which helped distribute the pudge, but he still Looked Like Shit.

Would Margie want to kiss him now? If he were her, no way. And after the way he'd dumped her, she'd have to be a masochist to want to get anywhere near him.

The bathroom door opened. Izzy immediately exited, pretending to check the note he pulled from his pocket to avoid eye contact. Eye contact had become increasingly difficult; not such a good thing for a psychiatrist trying to connect with a patient. Fortunately, he never saw patients anymore, especially not kids, and primarily focused on brain research.

Acknowledging greetings when necessary while his stomach churned bile, Izzy traversed the campus, pretending what normalcy he could, all the while wishing he had eyes in the back of his head to better detect anyone who might be following him—though even if he didn't see JD, that didn't mean he wasn't lurking somewhere near.

Great, came the intrusive thought. *Just add paranoia to your OCD and that not-so-little list of phobias.*

Izzy checked the Rolex he had inherited from his father, the Seiko he'd bought in Vietnam having gone the way of a donation.

He was due to conduct a neurology lab in 20 minutes.

Shoulders hunched, he went through his regular routine at an assigned locker. Remove his streetwear. Remove his watch. Peek into his wallet. *Wince.* Quickly put it away with the rest. Pause to remind himself that the sound to come was only a metal locker locking and not a gun going….

Click.

Next came his surgical scrubbing, gowning, and gloving until an assistant called, "Dr. Moskowitz, two minutes!"

Two minutes to opening curtain. A cadaver was waiting in the theater over which he was to preside.

As he took his place beside the draped cadaver, a flash of memory took him back to the 8th Field Hospital where he had lead a sodium pentothal procedure on a catatonic LT who could not bear the guilt of mistakenly calling fire in on his own men. It had been a bare basics Army surgical room with a small group gathered to observe. And here he was, five years later, 8,765 miles away, in an elaborate high-tech theater, where the deceased and he, its anatomical examiner, were sharing center stage with a large audience craning for a better view as he announced:

"A big welcome to the gallery. For a better view please turn your attention to the screen overhead"—he gestured to the cinema-sized one behind him, gave an appreciative nod to the nearby cameraman, gestured to a surgical assistant standing on ready beside a surgical tray filled with instruments—"And without further ado, let us proceed with the examination, and dissection, of our generous body donor, beginning with his brain. Please note that first we will score the calvarium—the vault of the skull holding the brain—with a saw."

The assistant held up two small saws. Izzy took the electric one, explaining, "I have chosen the vibrating saw for its efficiency; however, the hand saw works as well."

A bad déjà vu flash of Sgt. Washington discreetly covering his shaking hand during the sodium pentothal procedure tripped into something even worse: A slight tremor he could feel snaking through his nerve ends. His hands had not trembled in years. Was it the note that was setting him off? The overhead lights obscuring his view of the audience and an absolute fear, warranted or not, that someone who shouldn't be there, was?

Whatever the cause, he was desperate to buy some time and just as desperate to get this over and escape.

"Walking you slightly ahead," he continued in a freakishly conversational voice, "after I apply the saw, a chisel will be used to ever so gently separate the top of the calvarium from the lower skull in order to expose the brain and its coverings known as…"

Izzy did not realize he had paused until an eager student called out, "The meninges!"

While Izzy nodded, muttered, "That is correct," he forgot that he no longer believed in God long enough to pray that no one could see the fresh white sheet trembling as he pulled it off in what felt like slow motion while his eyes locked on a pale, exposed, and very dead forehead.

In its center was a small black tattoo, so fresh the ink still shined on refrigerated flesh: **99KO**

~

"Has the doctor been delivered to the school yet?" Phillip tapped out another Gauloises and wondered why he ever gave up smoking.

"Jerry has sent word that they are en route. I wish we could have done this another way, but it is too late now. Are you sure you wish to go through with the other plan?"

"Of course, I'm sure. Otherwise, I wouldn't have gone to such pains to orchestrate it all to begin with."

"But…" The sound of Hugo inhaling on the other end of the phone had Phillip going for his new lighter. "Do you not think it better to direct Jerry to take the docteur to the new facility and just hold him there? ISIC will be moving soon enough anyway, and—"

"And you know that while I appreciate your input, I really don't like to be second guessed. No. It all plays out according to my original plan. We'll move everything and everyone worth moving to the new location soon enough, but that doesn't include old baggage, grievances, public suspicion, or anything else better handled at the existing compound. I have an aversion to moving garbage; all it does is stink up new construction."

"Very well."

The way Hugo sighed indicated his disapproval, which Phillip truly did not appreciate. Even if he considered Hugo a friend of long standing and an excellent strategist, lately The Frenchman as he was known in certain circles, had been more cautious, a little too protective of his protégé, even discreetly raising questions about the fuzzy edges of their higher purpose—which the esteemed Monsieur Hugo Goulet had himself been instrumental in shaping.

They covered a few more immediate bases, only for Hugo to be the first to say *Au revoir*. Phillip didn't like that either. He was the one in charge. Barring any President past or present, *he* was always the one to hang up first. A minor power play but everyone knew it was an acknowledgment of hierarchy not to be ignored. The slight maneuver gave him to wonder if Hugo was dropping a hint that their paths were no longer so aligned and he would be edging away from their shared ISIC orbit.

Phillip blew a smoke ring, shook his head. He could not believe Hugo, with his vast experience in the trenches and familiarity with the world stage, would be so naïve as to believe such a thing possible.

HUGO SIGHED AGAIN as he looked at the cradled phone, then went to find what peace he could in the garden he already dreaded leaving. He had spent much of his adolescence and most of his adult life in what he still thought of as French Indochina. Where could he go? Not back to France. The villa near Vence that had belonged to his father's parents and remained in the family was still there, but no one was going to invite him home.

Non.

He knew how these things worked:

Men like him were courted and bid for in time of war but when the war ended and the dead were tallied and fingers began to point, and blame and recrimination began, then he was at risk.

In most of the western world, if the extent of his deeds were exposed, he would be wanted as a war criminal, and so, outside a self-imposed exile where he could never be found, his only country was by default The Shadowlands. Those places where law and order had been lost to chaos and the rule of power. There were always plenty of those to choose from, anywhere there was a war or ongoing conflict was always good for someone with his skill set, experience and contacts. Want to purchase hard to get weapons? Call The Frenchman. Want a political opponent disappeared? Call The Frenchman. Want to develop a death squad? The Frenchman was the man and had been for two decades.

But now. Now the all-powerful USA was going to lose a war and the fallout would be huge. He had been invaluable to the US after the French Army had fallen. When Dulles, handpicked by Eisenhower as CIA director, had personally asked for a meeting, it was clear that the pockets were deep and that they were even a little desperate, so he had asked for everything. Remarkably and almost immediately he got everything he wanted. It had been a long and lucrative war. Phillip and he had ultimately created this "school," and at the time of its inception he had thought, "why not?" Why not take everything they had learned about succeeding at war and formalize it, create a cadre of instructors, then a network of acolytes in the USA's empire of vassal states? He had no doubts he was still needed. What he knew and what he did was the way of the world, the world in shadow, but still the way the world worked.

Ah, well.

Pausing at the lychee tree that he and Jerry had planted, he ran a palm over the smooth gray bark, plucked a red orb of its precious fruit. Like the tree, his relationship with Jerry had grown strong and he wished that he could take both of them with him. So too the garden pond, where he sat on a weathered bench to better watch the koi lazily swim while the sun settled into a vibrant pink dusk. Some of the fish were older than he was, and they meant more to him than any of the people left here except for Jerry.

Hugo tapped a Gauloises out of the engraved silver case. He had a few mementos and this was one of them. A gift from his regiment from the French Indo China war. So many men lost, and yet he had smoked more cigarettes from the case than all the good men he'd buried, including those who had died from the necessary decisions he had made. He was good at difficult decisions. That was a part of being a commander and a warrior. Life and death decisions were usually difficult and too often had to be done quickly with limited information, therefore experience and instinct were crucial.

He had enough information on top of the rest to have already made his decision.

The Americans had lost their war. The Vietnamese had worn them down politically, psychologically, and militarily just as they had his own mighty French army. Now there was just the sad bloody ending to play out. There certainly was not going to be a peace. There was not to be a border. Sooner than the Americans thought, there was not going to be a South Vietnam. There was just going to be one country and for a time it was going to be a very ugly, dangerous country for anyone at all associated with the United States of America.

Hence, their ISIC operations basically being duplicated at the new dark site in progress, just across the Gulf of Thailand on the Adamant Sea and accessible to Bangkok yet remote from the eyes of the world. It was where Phillip expected him to be joining Miles and the rest of the essential staff that could not be easily replaced. Of course, the research "subjects/prisoners" would need to be disposed of, which would now include the American doctor who should be arriving shortly and would not deserve his inescapable fate. Why Phillip was acting like an *enfant terrible* who wanted everything done NOW, mixing and matching multiple schemes under increasingly dire circumstances instead of parceling things out to address them separately in the most beneficial settings...

Ah, well.

Perhaps the rumor mill that needed to be squashed thanks to an escaped journalist couldn't wait. Their original ISIC needed to be closed with a clean record to avoid any further speculation while their new location went undetected. That much Hugo could understand. But this other craziness of dispatching Jerry to bring the doctor *here*, that had nothing to do with a legitimate concern that his protégé had been recognized. Non, non. This was all about *revenge*, a vendetta that Hugo personally found deeply troubling.

Troubling or not, revenge could wait. It was Phillip's hubris that determined it couldn't. He thought himself immune to the laws of nature and of war and of man, above them all. He could do anything! Everything! And no one would be so bold as to try to stop him.

Mostly Phillip was right—few things touched him the way they did mere mortals who did not direct the affairs of the world. This did not make him immune, however, to the world making some decisions without his permission, especially if his own were ill-timed, foolish, or put personal vendettas above simple good judgement.

"I will take you with me" he told his favorite white and gold koi, "Somehow I will find a way, you will see. Now I must check on Jerry's kitten."

Just then the *whoop-whoop-whoop* of chopper blades overhead announced company. The wheels that had been set into motion would now play out as Phillip had decreed.

Ah, well.

CHAPTER 11

As the chopper began its descent and Jerry made sure the trussed up cargo he was carrying was still unconscious, he continued to wonder just what in god's name had gotten into him. *Why* had he lowered the M60 the moment Shirley got out of the car and he realized she was pregnant? *Why* had he felt compelled to make that apology for slitting her late husband's throat? *Why* had he gone so easy on Gregg when he stupidly tried to hide his little pistol and fire off a shot that shattered a leaded glass window instead of hitting the intended target—him, the once infamous Ghost Soldier? He could have snapped Gregg's arm like a twig for trying something like that but no, all he did was send the puny weapon sailing into Shirley's gardens like a long triple into the outfield grass.

All of that in a matter of minutes. He remembered it all, unlike the lapses of time when things happened that he couldn't remember... though, maybe he wouldn't remember any of this when he woke up tomorrow. There was definitely a part of him that wished he wouldn't.

After all, then he wouldn't remember how Shirley got down on her knees and begged him not to take her husband away, wasn't one enough? And he wouldn't have to remember the terror in her eyes, spiked with downright hatred, when he gave Gregg a good push that was mostly for show, over to the phone where Gregg dialed up JD who must have been babysitting his SAT on the other end. The conversation didn't take long after opening his palm to take over the details he had to deliver:

Him: Bonjour, JD. How's life been treating you since we parted ways?

JD: Fine. How are Gregg and Shirley?

Him: Fine. As long as you follow orders.

JD: I'm listening.

Him: I'll be taking your buddy to an undisclosed location, and leaving a little something here for you in exchange to consider. You will soon receive coordinates regarding the point of incarceration, should you wish to save him.

JD: Okay. Given that we've got enough going on with the North inhaling everything in its path, I suggest we dispense with the bullshit and cut to the chase. Phillip doesn't want Gregg, he's just using an innocent party to get to me. Let him go and Phillip can have me in exchange. Are you at the mission? I can be there in—

Him: Sorry, pal, but we both know who's calling the shots here and it's not us. However, since you, me, and our favorite shrinks go back a ways, here's a little insider intel on the QT. Further insurance is being procured from the US to make sure you play along. Just between us, I'm actually looking forward to seeing Izzy again.

JD: And I'm looking forward to making Phillip pay in some very painful ways for this latest scheme he's constructed. You deliver that message to the Asshole-In-Charge.

Jerry knew that was one message he would not be delivering, just as he knew that he did not doubt JD would willingly trade himself for Gregg Kelly—no funny business at the mission, just probably lots of dead people, with The Ambassador going first, if JD was delivered to The School minus leverage. Which brought Jerry to that complete lapse in predator judgement by tipping his hand with the whole Izzy on the QT thing, followed by telling Shirley not to look while he jabbed a needle into the side of Gregg's throat, then advised her to high tail it to Thailand

ASAP, and, "oh, Shirley, be sure to take the gun with you for protection on the road."

Somehow, he did not think Phillip Jordan would approve of his Future Elite Warrior's delicate handling of this particular kidnapping. Miles… hard to say; he could be unpredictable.

But then there was Hugo.

Hugo was the only one Jerry could entrust with just about everything. Even the equally disturbing situation that had occurred last month, shortly after he had gotten Panther and had second thoughts about bringing in an NVA officer named Nguyen Bao who might be working for the wrong team but seemed pretty decent when it came to upholding certain principals that Jerry had come to value.

While he had been noticing incremental changes for a period of time, it really was a lot like that Bowie song when he looked in the mirror and turned to face the strange. And on that particularly strange day last month, right after the Bao incident, and before this whole Kelly mess got started, he was in a small village for a routine pickup of two men the RVN had declared dissidents which made them ISIC material.

His team easily overwhelmed the first of the men from the List.

"Go back to camp," he instructed them. "I'll stick around for the other one to show up."

But just as they were leaving, out raced a small boy from his hiding place. He threw his arms around the legs of the man being marched away, crying, "Bô! Bô!" which meant "Daddy! Daddy!" and begging him not to go.

As one of his ISIC team raised the barrel of his M-16 to bash the kid in the head, Jerry barked, "No! Stand down," while the father extricated the child and told him not to worry, that he would return soon.

Obviously, this was one daddy who was never coming back but the boy must have believed him because he almost immediately made up a song about Bô´coming soon, which he repeated and repeated, like the counting you do in Hide and Go Seek, until he gave up on the song and switched to another activity to vent his frustration. Jerry watched him pile up some sticks, then kick them down, pile them up, kick them down, harder and harder, until they broke and that's when the kid began to cry. Like little shoulders shaking, nose running, inconsolable weeping, with no one there to comfort him because everyone else was hiding and afraid to come out.

Just thinking back on it made Jerry's throat tighten up all over again, had him feeling that unexpected stab of an emotion that took him back to his own long history of abandonment. He had been a little boy once, longing for a daddy who would never desert him, and there he was over twenty years later, an adult in a position of authority who could make a difference that wasn't granted to him.

Forget this shit, he decided, then held out his hand and said, "Let's find your dad."

He was well acquainted with looks of raw terror, had often taken real pleasure in being the cause of it. But when the father saw who had custody of his child, when the father's knees hit the ground and pleas for mercy rushed from his mouth, Jerry was aware of feeling something not good.

And then he fixed it.

He said, "Go home. Take your son and go home."

"Go home," Jerry repeated softly to himself, relishing yet again how liberating it had felt to step outside his usual procurement duties to make an independent, unprecedented decision based on a feeling he thought was called...compassion?

Not that a drop of it was wasted on the men he sliced with a glare and the warning: "We will return with our quota but if anyone speaks of this, I will cut out your tongue and shove it down your throat while you sleep."

Thus far he had not had any tongue cutting or shoving to make good on.

As he felt the chopper's familiar decent into the ISIC compound, his troubled gaze on a heavily sedated Gregg who would never meet his own child, two things were uppermost in Jerry's mind:

How was Panther, did his little kitty miss him?

And: Whatever the hell was going on with his head, his decisions, his memory lapses...

WHY?

THE PROFESSOR'S NOTEBOOK

ENTRY #330

As always there is much to cover since my last entry. And, as always, the following research was held to my impeccable, rigorous, and highest standards of experimental design. Unlike the usual Control Group experiments, however, this particular documentation goes into in a very special notebook, and is primarily intended for transfer to the ISIC REPORT I will be personally handing to Ambassador Jordan when he arrives so we may better discuss my brilliant progress with Code Purple Jerry (CPJ).

Now, before I proceed with the clinical material, a few notes on the critical importance of The Drug for the experiment under discussion. Tweaking the chemistry of the drug seems like a bit of a crapshoot as well as an art. I sometimes think of myself as a kind of shaman or ancient alchemist with my potions. It has become clear to me that it is not just the drug chemistry itself, but the bio chemistry of the different brains that the drug chemicals are interacting with, then you top that off with the individual history, culture, and even family background and that means you have an endless list of variables to account for.

A prime example is working with a predator like Jerry who was indelibly shaped in his formative years by systemic abuse until he became the one to fear. In contrast is Katheryn Morningside-Jordan who had a stable childhood and continues to exhibit original personality traits of willfulness, but has been systemically shaped by deep hypnosis and the administration of the aforementioned alchemies which began five years ago—March, 1970. Although she has no memory of the drugs administered or codes implanted periodically since, the outcomes are indisputable with her rise as a top CIA operative and Ambassador Jordan's continued appreciation for my contributions to his marriage.

Per the illustration above regarding subject histories, personalities, and differentials beyond my control, the one significant control I DO have is creating and tweaking the chemistry of The Drug for individualized outcomes. Thus far my quest has been to find that magic ratio of chemicals that have the reliability of ketamine, the deeply profound effects of LSD and psilocybin, while maintaining the emotional accessibility of MDMA.

This is particularly crucial for Jerry and my objectives that are admittedly not just professional in nature (more on that later).

The success of the following session with Jerry is largely due to the exact dosages and formulae mixture kept in my private files, which will remain private to ensure no one else can duplicate what I have worked so hard to achieve—and that includes my iron clad control over CPJ, which further ensures I stay invaluable to ISIC. While this does not bear mention in the ISIC REPORT, these dictated notes most certainly do:

Top Security Clearance Only

Progress Report on Phoenix Project X (CPJ/Jerry Prince)

Session #149 0900 hours February 2, 1975

Place: ISIC, South Vietnam

Setting: Psychedelic Psychotherapy room. This is a pleasant and calm room. The lighting is subdued. There are hardwood floors with soft rugs. The room has French doors which look out upon a lovely garden. The room and garden are very quiet. There is soft music (Hovhaness's Mysterious Mountain) in the background which the subject has previously identified as soothing and pleasant. There is water, fresh juice and sliced fruit available as needed. Controlling the environment and all sensory input is critical in psychedelic work. Everyone from Hoffman through Aldous Huxley to Timothy Leary has emphasized this.

RX: This dosage of medication is a special mixture of MDMA and MKUltra LSD introduced via injection at 0905 hours. The subject is reclining on a comfortable couch. There are soft pillows and an eye shade if needed.

Set: 'Set' is short for the mindset during a trip. It includes the preparation and expectations of the voyager and guide before embarking on a psychedelic experience. (Fadiman, J.)

Intention for the session: I want to go back to a critical time in the subject's childhood which I believe to be a turning point in his psychological development as a child and crucial to him becoming a psychopathic killer. According to his own personal writings during his internment at Madigan General's lock down unit, he had a very important bonding and emotional experience with a cat. In our previous session he described in detail the secret relationship with the cat, how he had hidden its existence from his sadistic and brutal step-father, and how, when the cat had kittens, and his pilfering of food for the animals had been discovered, he was subjected to a horribly traumatizing episode in which he was forced to kill the animals by his step-father.

0920: There is some slight sweating and flushing noticeable as well as the usual teeth clenching and grinding as the physical effects of the drug manifests.

Jerry (smiling): "So great, so great, this is the best, such a wonderful feeling. You have been so good to me, Miles. My god the music is flying me. You know I love it here. You and Hugo know it's my first home, ever, really."

This is what the drug does. It drops emotional defenses, literally melts them like ice and opens the subject emotionally towards a connection. I allow him to enjoy this emotional euphoria until 0945 hours.

0945: I glance at a glass mirror where a single witness is visually observing, without audio access, and waiting for my signal. I nod. Moments later the therapy room door opens and two kittens of rare beauty are pushed inside. One is a solid, sleek black, the other a fluffy calico; they are very young, just taken from their mother. Jerry has not yet seen the kittens. His eyes are closed, in a rhapsody with the music.

Very softly I whisper: "Jerry, you remember what we talked about last time?"

A look of pain passes over his face.

"Jerry," I softly instruct, "I want you to take a deep breath and know that it's okay, whatever you are feeling."

Even with the drug coursing through him now, I observe a steely resolve drop like a mask over Jerry's face.

"Now, Jerry. I have a special present for you. Open your eyes. Here is a peacock feather."

He obeys and says, "It's beautiful, wow it's very beautiful, the colors are flowing."

"It's a present, but it's to play with the real gift. Look over by the door, see what's coming over."

I am watching intently with no idea of what will happen and hoping the camera I have running is getting this. Will he kill the kittens? In order to keep his mask and defense system intact, will he kill them?

I watch as Jerry's enhanced perceptions take in what is happening. I watch as his face literally shudders. There is an involuntary gasp, a yowling dry sob. He rolls off the couch and crawls slowly toward one of the kittens. *What is he going to do?* He sits up and the black kitten prances towards him while the calico darts under the couch. He reaches out with the peacock feather and shakes it in front of the approaching kitten which clumsily pounces. Jerry flicks the feather again, the black kitten pounces again. The man who first arrived here as a brutal predator, inured to all feeling but the joy of killing and the release it brought him, begins to giggle until he's laughing uncontrollably.

"It is your kitty," I tell him, then prompt, "Can you say that, Jerry? I want to hear you say it out loud."

"It's my..." For a moment, he tenses. The steel curtain is still there, or is it not?

The black kitten comes up to Jerry's hand and licks him with its tiny rough tongue.

"It's my kitty," says the predator, gently, gently touching.

"That's right, Jerry, it's your kitty," I assure him, but to myself I am thinking it is actually his human heart *that I have captured.* I note the time of this extraordinary accomplishment. It is 1015 hours and I have broken through.

The session ended there. I allowed Jerry the rest of the day to bond with the kitten and take it to his private cottage where I checked in on him several times. He did not leave his quarters until the next afternoon when he promptly returned to the Psychedelic Psychotherapy Room at the appointed time for his follow up session with the kitten.

Session #150 1300 hours February 3, 1975

Before administering the prescribed special mixture of MDMA and tweaked the MKUltra LSD that worked so remarkably well the day before, I asked Jerry how he was feeling. His response is as follows:

"I'm not sure. Maybe a little weird, off balance. Except when I play with Panther. That's my kitten's name now. And it's *mine*. Wherever I go, Panther follows me. He likes to play games."

"What kind of games?"

"I snaked a sock around and he kept pouncing on it until I rolled some foil into a ball so he could chase it down. He's such a smart cat! Before I knew it he was fetching the foil and bringing it back to me to throw it again! I laughed so hard… I…"

"Yes?"

"I… actually, I kind of choked up, I was so happy."

"That's good," I told him. "That's good."

At 1315 hours I again administered my special mixture of MDMA and MKUltra LSD and advised him that it was a special dose, a little bigger than usual. He leaned back and the black kitten was on his chest purring while I monitored signs that the medicine was kicking in. If he noticed the calico kitten being let back into the room, shyly approaching the couch, he did not display signs of interest while he continued to stroke the one he named Panther.

"It is movie day," I told Jerry. "We are going to watch some films. The first one is a very special old movie called *Old Yeller* from 1957. Do you remember seeing that movie?'

"No."

"Good, then you will be surprised and after *Old Yeller*, we are going to watch another old film called *Black Beauty* and then a real old classic called *Bambi*."

Collectively the films run right at four hours making this an extended and very long session with film footage being taken of Jerry's responses while he watched the movies. Several times his eyes appeared to well up while he stroked his kitten. After the first round of films we took a short break so he could feed his kitten (the calico remained hidden under the couch and could not be coaxed out) and more light snacks were brought in.

At 1745 hours a booster shot was administered before we began the films all over again.

At precisely 2055 hours when Bambi races to the den for cover and a shot rings out killing his mother, Jerry rolled from the couch onto the floor and held himself in the fetal position. He was visibly trembling. The black kitten he had carefully released touched his hand and made a little mewing sound. The calico emerged from under the couch and began to mew while cautiously tapping at Jerry's shaking chest.

While Bambi began to call for his mother, I slightly reduced the volume and gently instructed, "Jerry, I want you to make a sound like the kittens. Can you mew like the kittens for me?"

The sound he made was brief and hoarse, but at least he had tried which was yet another breakthrough in this second phase of the experiment.

I praised his effort and encouraged him further, saying, "Again, Jerry, like the kitten, it's okay to make that little sound. It's okay to cry. Try again."

Jerry squeaked another sound, and then another, then suddenly he made a noise like a sob, followed by more sobs that were quite amazing to hear.

Guiding him to the ultimately desired results, I urged:

"Now say their names, Jerry. You remember your little kitties when you were a boy. Say their names again now."

"Butter and Jade and Tiger, and—and oh no, Friend, dear sweet Friend and Panda and—and..." With an agonized sob he choked out, "Panther" while his new kitten licked at his tears.

I patted his back in reassurance and concluded the session thus:

"Take all the time you need right now with this, pardner, just remember it all and let the feelings out while you cry, while you let yourself hurt. In a while we will get you some more snacks and I will start reading you a wonderful long story about some rabbits ...it's called *Watership Down*."

I noted the time.

At officially 2100 hours a man who had been more monster than human had learned how to cry, and I, Dr. Ronald Miles, Neurologist, Clinical Psychologist, and Director of ISIC had been the one to teach him.

This accomplishment cannot be underestimated. It is enormously significant that through a highly individualized, pharmaceutically induced process, I was able to gain unprecedented access to the very cradle of a human psyche (some may even say a "soul") that had been unreachable to even the occupant of it. My hypothesis going forward is that by breaking down all resistance and cracking into the equivalent of a hermetically sealed genie's bottle, while the genie has for now been set free, I was the one who released it and therefore its bottle, and fate, belong to me.

∽

Miles sat back with a euphoric sigh in his specially designed swivel chair covered in ostrich skin. It matched his favorite boots, replicas of what his Uncle Billy had worn. Boots propped up on his custom teak desk with a spread of real steer horns bolted to the front, he basked in the vista of his certificates, diplomas, and awards, all prominently displayed on the walls of his private office.

While he had recently had cause for concern about the genie he'd let loose, by no means would he let that spoil his moment of elation upon reviewing the notes he still needed to judiciously transfer to his big ISIC REPORT.

Clearly there were things that were personal in nature that would not be recorded. Things like wishing he could shove it all into Dr. Carl Rogers' face, along with all those adoring Rogers acolytes, bowing down as if he were second only to Freud. None of *them* were prodigies. None of *them* had been offered full rides from Harvard and Yale. And yet Rogers didn't want *him* in the UW psych department in freezing cold Madison because he thought the future Doctor Ronald Miles, M.D., Ph.D., wasn't suited for humanistic work? Not suited. Not suited?! Just look at what he'd done with Jerry!

So, he would leave out his grudge against Rogers and how he'd proven him wrong. Just as he would leave out the part about wanting to make Jerry cry because his own experience was severely limited—exactly once had he cried, when Uncle Billy died, and he had not been able to replicate the response since. Hence, he wanted to test the possibility of a proxy transfer of experience from subject to researcher (result: negative).

No, no. None of those things would bear mention in the ISIC REPORT that was going to the top to be evaluated and would influence his funding for projects, anticipated promotion, and status at the new facility in Thailand. This kind of documentation was very important for him since any connections/support he had only went so far to compensate for the social/emotional skills he was well aware were not going to win any prizes or move him ahead in the world.

The walls in his office were testimony that such skills were overblown and certainly not necessary to one's self-knowledge. Truly, he considered himself to be kind of a spiritual son of the great Nazi Hans Asperger with many of the great man's traits; without a doubt he had been deeply influenced by Asperger's philosophy and works, including his own willingness to "get his hands dirty for patriotism" as The Ambassador had noted.

What he had accomplished with Jerry was remarkable but now he was about to get his hands very dirty indeed upon the delivery of an actual fellow psychologist, a Dr. Gregg Kelly, along with an equally desirable associate being procured from New York, a Dr. Israel Moskowitz. They would be invaluable for experimental purposes! The work he could do with them—and on them!

The potential results might even be of Nobel quality.

"Just think of it," Miles dreamily mused.

Now whoa there, pardner, stop getting ahead of yourself again, just like you do when you envision that whole Army of Code Purple Jerrys with embedded brain chips and you're the only one with the remote control. Maybe you need to pull back on some of that micro-dosing of yours.

It took all of two seconds to decide: "Nah."

Quickly refocusing his attention on what would be his definitive Review, he debated on including the journal entry that had accompanied Jerry's file when he was first delivered to The School. Although it would be supportive rather than new material, there was something about looking at Jerry's typed pages from an old manual that never failed to speak to him. It had, in fact, proven the inspiration for his last phase of the experiment with the calico kitten.

Pulling the precious pages from a specially marked folder, Miles scanned the black type on onion skin he could recite by heart.

KITTENS

Maybe my stepfather should not have been too surprised when the gun went off. When I was younger, about 7, he rented an old broken-down house. It was in town but was kind of isolated next to an old abandoned estate. The estate house had burned down a long time ago leaving a burnt brick chimney, but there was a sagging garage still there with lots of old crap. Other kids would have thought it too spooky and dark and full of spiders and ghosts but not me. For a kid with no friends it was a pirate cave filled with trunks of treasure. There really were old chests of drawers and little boxes of costume jewelry. But then something better. A friend came. She was pretty scruffy and skittish but she was my friend. I took a hairbrush from my mom's room and I stole and scrounged food from the kitchen for my new friend and in about a week she was Beautiful.
I did not know she was pregnant, I just thought she seemed kind of chubby. She was so afraid of people but that was good because she never followed me home. Pretty soon I had a little nest for her with one of my old blankets and a broken cup for her food and water and with my care and feeding she looked beautiful to

me even with her scars and chewed ears from all of her scraps before I took her in. Then one day there was a huge surprise. Usually, whenever I got close to the garage she made her little sound, kind of a mewing squeak but today was silent and I was anxious and rushed in and there she was in her nest with 5 little kittens. Of course their eyes were shut and they just looked like little mice. They all grew so fast. They looked so different that I thought that they must have all been different kinds of cats. There was a fuzzy yellow one "Butter," and a sleek black one "Panther," and a big furry black with bright green eyes "Jade," and a striped "Tiger" and my favorite, a black and white "Panda." All of these little guys were soon great fun. They would swoosh around chasing each other and tumble each other over and over and for me it was about the best time and the most friends I had ever had. In the late afternoons in the fall I would bundle up and take my own nap in the nest with them all snuggled in with me.

One day I rushed home from school. It was just after Thanksgiving and I remember because I had been taking leftovers out of the fridge for all my "friends." I decided that I would take the drumstick. Stupid, because that is easy to notice missing, but I thought nobody likes drumsticks in this family and anyway I got to the old garage with the drumstick and came running in calling out "Panda," "Butter," "Jade," "Panther," "Tiger" and they were all so happy eating the drumstick and playing with it that I did not hear a thing until a low laugh came from the shadows.

And there was my stepfather. He was holding Friend, the mother cat, and stroking her. I was really happy for a minute because I thought he must like her, I mean how could anybody not and she was purring and I thought maybe he will want them to move to our house and they could sleep in my room and... he twisted her head and broke her neck and threw her so hard her head blew up in a red blob on the wall.

"So the little man has his own little kitties."

"I... I...I only feed them my food, I'm sorry."

"You are sorry," he said, "and it is not your food, it is my food, you have been stealing my food and now you are going to pay for it...."

I was already crying about Friend... I was so used to his beatings that I just got ready for it right there....

"NO, it is not going to be that easy," he said. "Go get the shovel."

I came back with the shovel resigned to thinking I would have to dig the grave for Friend.

"I'm sorry," I begged, "please, don't hurt the kittens, it's my fault, don't hurt them..."

"I am not going to hurt the kittens, you little idiot... you are. You did this, you *stole from me and you are going to fix it. You are going to kill every one of them with the shovel, the fast way with the sharp end or the slow way with smashing them, it's your choice..." he took out his Zippo lighter, lit a cigarette, and then left the lighter going, "or I am going to burn them alive, you got it little man? Kill them fast or watch them burn. Here I'll help you... kill the one you love the most first, the others will be easier...."*

Maybe he was right, but I did not know that then. My hands were shaking, I was crying too hard begging for their lives that I made a mess of every one of them, one after another, after another... I killed Panda last.

As Miles laid the onion skin pages down with a sigh, the faint *whoop-whoop-whoop* of blades from an incoming helicopter bleated in the near distance. In two shakes flat he was out of his ostrich skin chair and heading for the door. There, he paused for a last admiring glance at the various piles of pages neatly organized across the expanse of teak where his impressive ISIC REPORT by Doctor Ronald Miles, M.D., Ph.D., had been joined by an old typewritten journal entry he was most definitely going to include.

Taking it in its deepest sense, the shadow is the invisible saurian tail that man still drags behind him. Carefully amputated, it becomes the healing serpent of the mysteries. Only monkeys parade with it.

— CARL JUNG *THE INTEGRATION OF THE PERSONALITY* 1939

FISH SAUCE

March 25, 1975
Hue, RVN

It was one of the most beautiful sights that Fish Sauce had ever beheld: North Vietnam flags waving through the smoky, late night air, cheering crowds, the music of rifles firing triumphantly from a cache of seized M-16's.

"Chiến thắng! Chiến thắng!" shouted Chopsticks as he jubilantly danced around the Flying Pig with Porkrib and Noodlesoup and a swell of matching uniforms amidst more cheers of *"Victory! Victory!"*

Fish Sauce called his encouragement to dance even harder, for surely they had earned every celebratory step.

While Chopsticks waved for him to join them, Fish Sauce shook his head, and with a hearty laugh, declined. "Quá chóng mặt!"

Indeed, he was too dizzy from it all to join the throng of PAVN and VC soldiers claiming their latest victory and the second major city to fall: The old Imperial City of Hue.

Deciding to indulge in a little tour of their spoils of war, Fish Sauce strode past the remaining temples and gates and gardens that had not been destroyed after the TET Offensive in 1968, when the PAVN and VC had temporarily occupied the city. He had heard the Americans were at first reluctant to bomb such beautiful, historic structures, but that did not stop them from it. Of 160 original buildings, only ten complexes remained. The North did not think highly of the imperial era so who knew if the city would ever be restored.

Such a shame, he thought. He had visited here in his youth and the city had been a breathtaking sight. What remained seemed to be gasping for dear life while the city residents rushed past him in their flight to the east, or more likely south, having been caught off guard by a turn of events even he couldn't believe.

In just the past few days the People's Army of Vietnam had surrounded the Phu Bai Air Base and cut off the main corridor into Hue from the south. And from the north VC regiments went after a quickly retreating South Vietnamese Marine and Ranger group. Within a day—just yesterday—they, the PAVN, had captured the airbase and the VC had DESTROYED the last elements of the 147th Marine Brigade and 15th Ranger Group, devastating any hope of escape to the Navy vessels waiting off shore.

And this very night the PAVN had officially secured Hue.

Amazing. *Amazing.* What had begun in early March as Campaign 275 to capture the Central Highlands had been officially changed to the Ho Chi Minh Campaign as of yesterday. It seemed his fanciful dreaming of capturing the entire country by year's end wasn't completely delusional after all!

Fish Sauce surveyed the vast stores of weaponry he had helped seize after he and his comrades had completely surrounded and humiliated the South Vietnamese units with a swift and absolute defeat.

He counted, then counted again to be sure, 140 tanks and armored vehicles.

Even seeing it all with his own eyes he could hardly grasp the magnitude of their war chest! As for the offer to take whatever tank he wanted from the fleet that was now theirs, *all theirs,* Fish Sauce waved it aside and returned to his still cheering crew.

If he could have his pick of any tank in the entire world, Fish Sauce knew he would not trade their war weary Flying Pig for it, not even for an entire fleet of tanks at his command. So said his heart; Practice Wisdom concurred.

Practice Wisdom, perhaps his greatest asset as a commander, was a combination of a special kind of intelligence, instinct, and finely honed judgement that could be counted on, and was especially essential in difficult situations.

Liem, you are so smart, I think you will speak ten languages and build skyscrapers and even be famous some day!

Isabelle, so unaware in her protected bubble and innocence, didn't seem to realize the son of a maid in a shackled country would not have her same opportunities, no matter how much French or English she wanted to teach him and Bao, or how generous her praise when he showed her his marks from a much different school than her own.

In another time and another cultural socio-political place Fish Sauce didn't doubt he could have gone on to be an accomplished engineer or excelled in some other profession requiring a keen intellect. But his time and his place had dictated his path and he had become a tank commander and a very deadly one with a remarkable amount of Practice Wisdom.

Practice Wisdom had much to do with Chopsticks and the rest of his crew dancing in the moonlight as they shouted *"Chiến thắng! Chiến thắng!"* It was Practice Wisdom that had saved them many times over by his ability to decide faster than their opponents the best of bad choices, ensuring that they had lived when others had died. And so many, so terribly many, had died. They were a generation that had been harvested by the Americans, sometimes picked off one by one, other times just mowed down or blown up in mass quantities.

The Americans.

Fish Sauce stopped grinning at the dancing spectacle long enough to spit into the street, careful not to mar their precious Flying Pig with such consuming disgust. The Americans had managed to bomb their country with more hell fire than the horrendous amount of bombs in all of World War II. Just look at this city! Why the Americans thought the sheer amount of carnage and sacrifice from bombing after bombing after bombing would force his people to just give up was beyond his comprehension. Such a gross misjudgment by the swaggering Americans who thought the Vietnamese did not love their own freedom, that they would actually be willing to bow down to a culture whose mentality was to try eliminating them all, that they would somehow willingly join or be vassals of that kind of a monster mind.

How the tables had turned. Now the Americans were the ones being pounded, abandoning their allies here in the South. But the Americans were proud, not a forgiving kind, and on their way out they would inflict what further damage they could.

Was Bao still alive? Had he somehow survived whatever was being done to him at the Yankee death camp, The Killing School? Would this unsurpassed victory being claimed even now only encourage the evil doers to dispose of his twin more quickly if they had not killed him already?

Da Nang would be the next to fall. It was inevitable. But even as Fish Sauce joined Chopsticks for a last dance before they pushed on, he was aware of every tic-toc of the clock, the need to grind ahead of his comrades as they continued to reclaim their southern soil.

He had his orders.

His mission was clear.

And Practice Wisdom would pave his path to *"Chiến thắng! Chiến thắng!"*

CHAPTER 12

La Colombe d' Or
South of France

"Mademoiselle, Chene? This way, s'il vous plait."

As she followed the elderly waiter who had introduced himself as Gaspard, Isabelle could not imagine a starker contrast from the sheer madness she had left in Nha Trang, to the inviting serenity of her surroundings where delicate aromas of flowers, salt air, and culinary delights infused her senses.

The impromptu invitation she had personally received from Ambassador Phillip Jordan to join him and his delightful wife, Kate, for lunch, had been too intriguing to resist. Especially when coupled with a quickly arranged flight out of Cam Ranh Bay. It was almost impossible to get a ticket out and she could hardly afford one anyway with her once prosperous family in dire need of any funds she could pull from her own dwindling resources. For obvious reasons most people equated fame, awards, prizes and professional recognition with financial success, but that simply was not always true. Particularly when it came to media, the arts, journalism. Photography. Income was often feast or famine and increasingly more famine than feast.

"Isabelle!" effusively called Kate from a private table that was dressed in white and silver, with an exquisite Riviera view of the sparkling Mediterranean below.

"Kate, so lovely to see you again." And it was true. They shared a la bise —the French kiss-kiss greeting of cheeks—and genuine smiles that said "we-could-be-real-friends." Isabelle did not doubt it. They were the same age, mid-thirties, had both studied in Paris, navigated political circles without being overtly political, along with many other commonalities the two had discovered during their first, and only, meeting four years and five months before...

At the final Republic of Vietnam Fine Arts Awards Gala. She knew exactly how long it had been. A girl didn't meet and immediately fall for an amazing guy named Troy Hunter every day—only to be ditched while a good friend disappeared, and end up spending the rest of the evening with a sympathetic new acquaintance as they bonded over *Soixante Quinzes.*

She and Kate had agreed to stay in touch but predictably had not, their paths never directly crossing again.

"I believe congratulations are in order to the both of you since we last met."

"All the congratulations belong to me, I can assure you, with condolences no doubt in order for Katherine." Forgoing any kisses, one of the most elegant men in existence took her hands and gave a short bow. "Thank you so much for agreeing to meet with us here, Isabelle. Particularly under the circumstances."

"Particularly under the circumstances it is frankly a relief to be here."

"That is saying quite a lot, given that one of your favorite places has historically been in the trenches." The Ambassador pulled out a chair for her, while the lingering Gaspard did the same for Kate before parting with a promise to shortly return with the Krug.

The breadsticks and olives and triple crème brie already gracing the table with little plates reminded Isabelle all over again of why she had fallen in love with France during her days as an undergrad at the Sorbonne, where Kate had spent a semester as an exchange student. She had been uncommonly open with Kate after the Gala, but really did not like to talk about herself, found interviews horribly invasive, and much preferred the anonymity of a remarkable photo with nothing but a by-line for credit—along with whatever money was being paid for print replication.

Yes, money mattered. For validation. For shelter and food. And it

especially mattered now while her once proud, well-to-do, rubber plantation owning family struggled to transition in neighboring Thailand. They
really should have fled to France instead, but all of her mother's side had
frantically moved en masse this past month, once the PAVN, along with
the VC, began to aggressively plow south with barely a hint of American
concern.

"You must be wondering why I asked you here. Clearly not just for
lunch."

"I suppose over 6000 miles and a full day of travel is a bit of a ways to
go just for lunch, even to share it with you, Ambassador." With a little
wink to Kate she added, "But worth the trip to extend my condolences to
your wife."

"A trip is exactly what we'd like to discuss." Kate leaned forward, her
voice lowering. "It's with regard to a matter that Phillip deemed too delicate to discuss over the phone."

"Yes, well, the phone service is a bit iffy in certain areas, and bound to
get iffier at the rate things are going." Even as she said it, it struck Isabelle
as odd that The Ambassador was having his wife take the lead in whatever conversation they were wanting with a freelancer who had spent the
last ten years documenting a war that was down to its last gasps.

As if intuiting the train of her thoughts, The Ambassador said, "Before
we get down to business, if you don't mind my asking, Isabelle, what are
your plans for the future?"

"A very good question. Because I'm half Vietnamese and consider
Vietnam my home, this war has been very personal for me, something I've
known virtually my whole life in one form or another. But now that
everything is changing with the withdrawal of the US… while it's all very
dramatic now, it won't be long and the US media will have little interest
in my present work. It will only be a reminder to an already disinterested
and mostly disgusted public that their country exploited then deserted
my own. I'm sorry if that offends you, Ambassador, but—"

He held up a well-manicured hand, far more pampered than hers.
Good war photography meant you got your hands and much of the rest
of you dirty, and that's the way she liked it.

"Never apologize for simply speaking the truth. I appreciate your
candor. And I'm quite curious as to where you will go and what you will
do once this whole ugly mess will no longer support your talent."

"With all due respect, Ambassador Jordan—"

"Please, call me Phillip."

"Very well...Phillip. While war photography is my specialty—specifically this war as you just pointed out—I do have other credentials, including coverage of your Civil Rights marches in America."

"Yes, excellent work early in your career. I believe those photos were taken with a Leica?"

"You know your cameras."

"I know your work. And, I do know enough about cameras to recognize a Leica look when I see one."

Low depth-of-field image. Sections out of focus. It was her signature shot. The old Leica, now a classic, was her favorite camera, a gift from her parents when she went to study botany at the Sorbonne, only for that parting gift to ironically lead to her profession. She still kept the Leica carefully stored with the rest of her gear. The weathered canvas duffel had looked out of place in the luxury suite she would be returning to just for the night, having declined her hosts' gracious offer for a more extended stay.

"So Isabelle," continued Kate, "Where else has your camera taken you?"

"Generally, wherever there is conflict. Africa, Chile, the Yom Kippur War in Israel. Paris, of course. I was at the Peace Accords. Actually, I believe that was the last time I saw, um, Phillip."

"He gave me your best wishes, thank you." Kate's glorious mane of blonde hair shimmered as she shook her head, gave a wistful sigh. "January of '73. I can't believe how fast the time has flown... Nor, how fast the present situation is escalating."

"Yes," he concurred, "just last month my internal sources projected the North could overtake the country by next year, but in the past two weeks alone..." His grey-blue eyes searched the sky, calm and warless above them. "My God. First, Ban Me Thout, then Quang Tri, and now Hue is being overtaken even as we speak. I realize Nha Trang is fortunately another 400 miles away, but what of your family, Isabelle? Have they taken measures to leave?"

"They have." Two grandmothers, a mother and father, three siblings, seven nieces and nephews, plus over thirty aunts, uncles, cousins and assorted other mostly dear relatives to be exact. And she had to help them however she could—which would not be by joining them.

"And now what will you do? Or... let me rephrase that: What do you *want* to do?"

And there they were, back to his original question regarding her future plans. What *was* this about?

Interestingly, though, since he had pressed, she was emerging with an answer she had found elusive while being too focused on immediate concerns, events, and yes, what opportunities might unexpectedly present themselves—that was how the lens worked, how the best shots were captured, it was always the unexpected, not the contrived, staged, or posed.

"What do I want? What I've always wanted. To capture the truth. To tell other people's stories as objectively as possible while creating a visceral dialog between my viewer and subject." There was much more to it than that but her relationship with the camera was too personal, too private. The photographs that she took were an intimate dance with war and death, pain and destruction. She was a conduit who had to be so close that she could share breath, make others smell and taste what she did, hear the crying, feel the shudders, smell the blood, and yes, share the addictive blast of adrenaline. Soon, very soon, she would have to find her fix elsewhere.

Leaning forward, she confided, "I want the story of a lifetime. Something important. Risky. Controversial. I want the subject to excite me and keep viewers awake at night."

There was an exchanged glance between Kate and... Phillip. The discreet lift of a perfectly sculpted feminine eyebrow, followed by the slight lift an aristocratic male finger from their table and Gaspard suddenly resurfaced, bearing a champagne bucket filled with ice along with his apologies for his slight delay in delivering the Krug Grande Cuvee.

Crystal flutes filled, Isabelle felt an instinctive little chill, something of a sixth sense she relied on that had saved her more than once, tickle her spine as Kate handed her the first glass.

Kate then raised her own as Phillip did the same and—

"May I propose a toast to the story of a lifetime that we're here to offer you today. Something important. Risky. Controversial. Most definitely exciting..."

"And for a freelancer, highly lucrative," concluded Kate.

As the flutes were held aloft and a small silence had her name on it, Isabelle was too taken aback to say more than, "Could you please repeat that?"

"Perhaps it is better explained while we enjoy our champagne," suggested Kate.

"Tchin-tchin," Phillip followed up with a tap to the other two rims.

"Cheers," Isabelle added while her mind rebelliously darted to that unforgettable night when a mystery man had toasted, "May your luck ever spread, like jelly on bread," only to knock her senseless with a quick, hot kiss on a balcony while the moon shined down and the scent of frangipani from the garden wafted up... just before their magic moment was cut short by the arrival of Hugo and The Ambassador.

"We have a situation regarding a matter of national import," he was saying, "and I have been handed the responsibility of correcting what could needlessly become a public relations nightmare for the US. In exchange for your assistance, I am authorized to offer you whatever compensation you require... along with the distinct possibility of future assignments involving crucial matters on the world stage if this particular one goes well."

While she took a sip of some excellent champagne indeed, and that prickling sensation again whispered up her spine, Isabelle discreetly pinched herself under the table. In her time of greatest financial need while the future was much too fuzzy and she needed some significant new direction to go, here it all was, being handed to her literally from a silver platter where her favorite dish of mussels and frites was accompanied by the official State Department envelope Phillip extended across the small table after he and Kate had been similarly served.

It was all simply too good to be true. That had to be the cause for this instinctive alarm. One had to be cautious in where they went and who they followed for the sake of documenting a story. Just look at all the journalists and photojournalists she had known, or known of, now dead, or worse than dead, in the pursuit of an up close view so they could share it with the public:

Dickey Chapelle, killed on patrol with a US Marine Corp unit during Operation Black Ferret in '65 when a landmine fragment severed her carotid artery.

Sam Castan, working for LOOK magazine when he was killed by mortar fire with a unit of the 1st Calvary Division the following year.

Claude Arpin, writing for Newsweek, captured by the VC with a large group of other French and Japanese journalists while they were driving down HWY 1. All still missing since 1970 and god only knew what they had been subjected to if still alive.

That same April on that same HWY 1, Sean Flynn with TIME magazine and Dana Stone for CBS News, captured while riding motorcycles and believed to have been executed by the Khmer Rouge after being held captive for a year.

Those were just a few of her fellow story chasers. The list went on and on. She'd had enough close calls to feel lucky to be alive. It wasn't the sort of occupation that lent itself to things like marriage or having a family, but lately she had been wondering if once it was too late to reconsider priorities, at least with children, she might have any regrets.

"Please feel free to examine the contents of the envelope," Phillip continued casually after a bite of coq au vin, as if he were accustomed to brokering deals of a lifetime on a daily basis.

Which he no doubt did.

As much as she wanted to tear into the envelope and shout an immediate, "Yes! YES! When do I start?!" she pretended to enjoy a frite, what Americans called French fries, dipped into the savory juices of garlic, butter, and wine in the large bowl filled with beautiful mussels and...

"Thank you, but I would like to know a little more first about the assignment. By the way, this is delicious! How did you know it's one of my favorite dishes?"

She noticed how the recently married couple shared a glance before Kate gave her a warm smile and said, "You told me that night after the gala when we were, shall we say, maybe one cocktail ahead of ourselves."

Smiling back, Isabelle hoped she hadn't appeared suspicious before admitting, "Then your memory after that third one is better than mine."

"Just probably more practice," Kate laughed with a tip of her flute to pink glossed lips.

Isabelle collegially joined her in both laughter and a healthy sip while trying to keep a cool head about it all. She knew from experience there were different levels of danger, which was an inherent part of any risk one took. Whatever danger she was sensing here, however, was not the usual kind.

"I'm very curious now about this situation of potential embarrassment to the US—and just how you think I can help you."

"Here is the situation." With Phillip again stepping in, it struck Isabelle that he and Kate had a rare interaction, almost like a professional dance team. "You're well connected to the media, including the BBC, correct?"

"Yes."

"Then perhaps you've heard of a journalist who purportedly escaped recently from what he described as a horrific torture compound headed by the CIA in Vietnam?"

"Of course. Most disturbing."

"Even more disturbing, is that whatever he was subjected to, no doubt involved some brain washing by the Communists to cast as much of a dark shadow as possible upon a facility that, yes, has been considered a top secret government project for reasons I'll get to, but is completely legitimate and innocent of any nefarious activity. I can assure you of this because the project has been under my direction since its inception years ago. For one disturbed individual—who no doubt went through something horrific somewhere else and deserves nothing but compassion for such an experience—to create this despicable impression that places us under scrutiny in the international community..." More aristocratic head shaking. "It is truly unacceptable. We will be bringing the project to a close rather than move the facility prior to the American Embassy shutting down in Saigon, as it inevitably will. But what we cannot have is for rumor and accusations of crimes against humanity to taint our legacy, and by association that of the United States of America. I have assured the president himself that the entire fiasco will be effectively handled and put to rest prior to our leaving."

Leaning closer, his eyes locked on hers, he finished with, "And Isabelle, I have no doubt that, with your help, the truth will prevail."

THEIR MEETING CONCLUDED and Krug consumed along with lunch, Isabelle gave a last, parting wave to their table as she exited the legendary La Colombe d' Or.

Once certain she was gone, Phillip nodded approvingly at Kate.

"Well done. I could not be more pleased with the outcome."

"Are you kidding me? Phillip, you let her walk out before signing the agreement!"

"Of course I did. And, of course, she will." Explaining himself was something he never liked to do, but for Kate he would tell her what she needed to hear, even if only partially true. "We have some time. All of these sudden moves from the North are diluting the noise of everything else here, ISIC rumors included. A few weeks from now is perfectly reasonable and prudent to have Isabelle on board to bring her camera and stay as many days as she wishes, while we seemingly give her free rein to explore our compound, and walk away with an exclusive that should squash any suspicions and exonerate us in the eyes of the public." And that would suffice. Other intelligence agencies of the world wouldn't buy it, not for a minute, but who cared? Britain's SIS/M16, the DGSE in France, Australia's ASIS, the Ruskie's KGB, etcetera, etcetera, were not going to call attention to themselves by casting stones at their shadowy brethren.

"I was surprised you mentioned Hugo. As well as the documents you offered to let her review in advance. Really, Phillip. Top Secret?"

"Why, Katherine, surely you know how helpful the provision of information can be as long as you're the one supplying it. As for Hugo, given their long acquaintance, having him affiliated and present can only work to our benefit. Actually, there is someone else who might play nicely into the entire orchestration of it all. A pleasant diversion to distract our lovely Mademoiselle Chene, whether his presence proves necessary or not."

The way Kate's eyebrow perfectly arched still entranced him. The slight scrunch of her nose as if sniffing for something that could turn foul amused him still. And that keen intelligence that had attracted him as much as her rapacious sexual appetite from the beginning, none of that had dimmed.

It was her growing attitude of them being equals, which they were not, nor would they ever be, that had begun to creep under his skin. Perhaps he should speak to Dr. Strangelove about that, see if there was some other embedded code he could invoke when Katherine got a little too full of herself—as she most definitely was now.

"I think it best to simply let her come in, take her pictures, spread whatever propaganda you feed her, and be done with it. The more players, the more room for unexpected outcomes, diversionary or not."

"I can have as many players as I want," he informed her, knowing full well how upset she would be by the particular players he had queued up to deal with and dispense of before Isabelle Chene was formally ushered into the compound with an engraved invitation. "When the time is right for her arrival, I promise you will be one of my major players."

"Of course."

Phillip didn't like the sarcasm any more than the rest of his wife's attitude, but handled the situation the way no one else did it better:

"Timing is everything," he diplomatically responded, "And the timing of it all will be no less than impeccable." Leaning in, he murmured persuasively, "Trust me, darling."

CHAPTER 13

Undisclosed Location
Somewhere in the Mekong Delta

It wasn't far from the international airport at Tan Son Nhut to the old Chinese trading town of Cholon. And it was not far from Cholon to a small island in the Delta where it was a long distance back in time to an old Taoist temple rising from the center of a well-tended garden.

JD could see the temple from where he and Zhang stood on an open porch. A cobblestone walkway wound past various buildings in the compound, and he was grateful for the small shelter where they had stopped with their cargo before proceeding to the Temple proper.

Though the day to day rituals of the Temple had been the same for hundreds of years, the electronics and communication center in the Abbot's inner rooms were state of the art thanks to Zhang. The communications center networked all over the globe to coordinate not only Zhang's opium operations but the even more clandestine espionage operations of the home monastery. Although the entire place was in the process of evacuation in anticipation of the oncoming North, everything they needed was still operational and it was the best choice of location and proximity to ISIC to prepare for their rescue mission.

While he did not yet have exact coordinates, he had a substantial amount of Intel gleaned from various sources—the film footage left behind at the mission, an old BBC contact with access to a certain escaped journalist, a disgruntled fellow agent with some dirt...

But it was the cargo that would give them some much needed leverage.

The first raindrop hit, and then another, soon pounding upon the tile roof, the palms lining the walkway to the Temple. Yes, it was good to have a respite after the marathon of the past two days, which would be nothing compared to the mission awaiting.

As the rain continued its song and dance, JD left the porch to check on their cargo.

IZZY HAD FORGOTTEN Southeast Asia rains. Forgotten the musical percussion it makes on rooftops and palm tree leaves. Forgotten the all at once full on silvery deluge, the temperature drop and the deep scent of the damp foliage.

All of that exquisite detail had been pushed down deep, along with how the scent triggered memory—memory after memory after mostly unwanted memory—now reminded him of how frightened he was of the shadows out in the foliage.

Was he dreaming? Must be. Only in a dream would he see a blur of reaching palm trees instead of skyscrapers in the near distance, or feel his back cushioned by silken bedding as he listened to the musical percussion overhead blend with the soothing trickle of a fountain. Were he awake there would be the never ending cacophony of blaring horns on congested Manhattan streets where a smorgasbord of competing scents would range from gourmet to gutters to the even worse stench of fear rolling out of his pores at the sight of a cadaver with a **99KO** tattoo on its forehead—

Izzy' eyes popped fully open. His back came ruler straight off the bed of silk. And as a gasp that qualified for last-breath agonal ratcheted up his throat, JD's unmistakable voice, saying, "Welcome back, Izzy," erased any possibility that Dr. Israel Moskowitz was waking the fuck up in New York City.

The black horn rims that JD promptly perched on Izzy's nose brought into crystal focus that the tattooed cadaver had only been the beginning of whatever nightmare he'd been spun into, and he was staring at the man responsible.

"Damn you, JD, what have you done to me *this* time?" His hoarse demand sounded as if sandpaper lined his windpipe. Clearly, he'd been knocked out, but for how long? And just what in god's name had he been subjected to since somehow excusing himself from the autopsy theater, frantically changing out of his scrubs, wheezing his way outside where he barely managed not to break into a dead run, and then...

That's when everything went black.

"Well?" he croaked, and tried not to care that the scar racing down JD's right cheek was evidence of his loyalty to a certain doctor who would have been dead five years ago if JD hadn't worked a deal with a sadistic madman: His life in exchange for Izzy's.

"What have I done to you this time?" JD repeated with a short laugh. "Saved your ass, that's what. But I can't take all the credit." A short nod toward the open porch where rain dripped off the roof and there stood Zhang, JD's step-brother, dressed in the embroidered yellow silk robes of an Emperor and looking for all the world like the Poppy King he was.

As he approached on eerily silent feet, the draping robe could not disguise the sinewy athleticism of perhaps the world's most unknown and most lethal predator, ultimate martial arts sensei and the man Bruce Lee had clandestinely journeyed to study with until his recent death. Izzy also knew that as Asia's mightiest drug lord, Zhang kept thousands of Vietnamese natives gainfully employed in the cultivation of poppies from seed to the distribution of a rare #4 grade heroine that made its way around the globe. The CIA had gone after a piece of that action to fund their darker activities without oversight, but that was a whole other story Izzy had pushed down further than the rains he had willfully forgotten.

Zhang moved closer until he stood beside JD, so the two brothers loomed slightly above him. Zhang's gaze fixed on Izzy. A fierce intelligence and hint of warmth was all that gentled the intensity of eyes that Izzy had only seen in a tiger at the Bronx zoo when he was a child. No wonder Zhang was the subject of legend and, according to JD, there were those who wondered if he was completely human.

"You were fortunate my brother and I have an associate in what you Americans call New Jersey." Zhang, so near, the scent of lemongrass and ginger on his breath fanned Izzy's face. "Uncle Louie agreed to return a favor since we could not get to you in time."

"You mean you had a mob boss abduct me." It wasn't even a question. If there was anything left JD could do to shock him, Izzy did not know what it was. "Since I'm not able to recall what happened, would you happen to have any details—such as, would there presently be more than a tattooed cadaver creating a stir at the Columbia University Medical School?"

The brothers exchanged glances.

"Uncle Louie from New Jersey promised to be discreet," offered Zhang. "He said that his men waited until you were near their car, then quickly pulled you in and covered your face."

"I don't remember any of that."

"Because they had some of their personal doctors in the backseat ready with some pharmaceuticals to knock you out and keep you that way as long as needed." JD looked genuinely apologetic. "Sorry, Izzy. We couldn't take any chances. We only did what was necessary to ensure your delivery to us wasn't detected or intercepted—which was a very real concern. The important thing is that it worked."

"*What* worked?"

"Everything," Zhang replied with a satisfied smile. "The timing with your exit. The abduction. The sedation in what Uncle Louie called a hearse—"

"Hearse? HEARSE?"

"I think that's enough detail for now, my brother. Let's help Izzy up and get him moving again."

It was only as JD urged his nearest leg over a polished wood edge, elevated several feet off the floor, that Izzy fully comprehended his mode of transportation.

"A COFFIN?! YOU HAD ME DELIVERED IN A FUCKING COFFIN?!"

Zhang shrugged. "You would not fit into an urn."

"Phillip has eyes, intelligence, muscle everywhere," JD put in. "We couldn't risk you being spotted."

"BUT YOU KNOW I'M CLAUSTROPHOBIC!" So much for his raw throat, he couldn't seem to lower his voice below a horrified roar. With supreme effort Izzy took it down a notch. "What. If. I. Had. WOKEN UP?"

"There were holes drilled into the sides so you would not suffocate," Zhang assured him, as if that made "everything" all right. "And once you were on the private jet and in the air, the doctors were mandated to keep the top open to monitor your sedation, until the plane landed."

"For extra insurance we had some highly trusted associates pick you up at the airport. They assured us they had not been followed when we met at the point of rendezvous, and from there Zhang and I brought you by boat to this compound. That's the CliffsNotes."

Izzy did not ask who "they" were. Given Zhang's and JD's connections, such associates could run the gamut from deadly Buddhist monks overseeing a secretive, centuries-old assassin school where JD and Zhang had been trained, to Saigon's Cholon District pirates that were on a par with New Jersey mob bosses, just a little closer to doing business on the South China Seas.

Fueled by righteous rage, Izzy waved away any assistance and got out of the coffin on his own steam—only for his legs to buckle and his knees to hit ground, which pissed him off even more. While he let loose a stream of profanities, a dark little urchin within took some sick pleasure in actually feeling something other than the unending numbness of emotional confinement he had relegated himself to, mockingly laughed at his indignation.

See, no matter where you go, there you are. And you're still a fake and a fraud.

Did JD see him for who he really was, for what he had become? Did Zhang?

Holding on to what rage he could, Izzy chanced a meeting of eyes and was not sure what he saw in exchange, but the two men extending hands to help him up were virtually incapable of being fakes or frauds.

It made him feel small in their shadows.

Great. More self-loathing. Just what you need.

"You need to eat. Gather your strength for what is ahead of us." Zhang turned on his sandaled heel and moved with a panther-like grace to the open porch, threw over his departing shoulder, "I will see to our meal."

And then it was just him and JD, his hand still extended, eyes a *7-up* bottle green holding steady on Izzy's very Jewish deep chocolate browns.

Reluctantly, Izzy took the assist, sacrificing his pride for something rare he had let go of, just as he had Margie: the comradery he had once shared with JD and Gregg.

JD's grip felt like a life-line, pulling him up from his self-imposed exile that had been as isolating as the coffin that had delivered him from his comfortable, erudite, empty life in New York to the steamy hellhole of stinking Vietnam at the vicious dirty end of the war.

"Thanks," Izzy said curtly and tried to assemble the facial mask he most often wore.

"You can thank me by explaining why you lacked the courtesy to return Gregg's repeated calls, which instigated my own, and you also ignored—at the expense of your own safety I might add. That's not like you, Izzy. What's going on?"

What's going on? What's going on? The strains of Marvin Gaye filled his ears while an earlier time with Gregg and JD reminded him of bombs raining down, of strung out GI's needing their help, of heads decapitated by slicing blades of shrapnel while he and Gregg and JD barely escaped with their lives… of the subsequent damage he had done to other lives and could never undo.

"I've been busy."

"Bullshit. C'mon, bro. You can do better than that."

Izzy hesitated. JD would call him on any lie. "Look, I'm going through some personal issues that I don't want to discuss, okay?"

"Huh. Worse than a Dear John?"

A curt nod was all Izzy would give him, and it was more than he'd shared with anyone else. Even Gregg.

Gregg.

Izzy's fury, defenses, everything evaporated, except for a prescient chill at the back of his nape. What had he been thinking—that this entire craziness of bringing him here had been for giggles and shits?

"Something bad happened to Gregg, didn't it? That's why you smuggled me in."

"That, and so what happened to Gregg didn't happen to you, too."

"What about Shirley, the baby?"

"Oh, so you know about the baby."

"Absolutely. Gregg sent me a letter a few months ago when they first found out and…" He hadn't written back. Hadn't returned Gregg's calls.

"Shirley's safe for now. She just reached Thailand yesterday. I saw her at the old mission right before she left with an escort provided by Zhang. It is good to have friends in the shadows in certain times of need." A pause. The meaningful lift of a dark eyebrow. "Including Uncle Louie. You may want to write him a thank you note at some point."

Izzy glanced at the coffin. Shuddered. He suspected his raw throat was compliments of intubation—having a tube run down his throat and to his lungs for use with a ventilator—essential for general anesthesia, which paralyzed the body's muscles, including the diaphragm, thus making it impossible to breathe… or to scream, which he would have if even half-conscious, had anyone tried to get him into such a confined space. It took almost 20 hours to fly from New York to Nha Trang or Saigon, and it was rare to keep anyone under for even close to eight hours. Whoever the doctors were would have supplemented the general with other anesthetics that went beyond a simple injection.

For the first time Izzy took note of the clothes he had on. A dark suit, dress shirt, tie, wingtips. Someone had changed him out of his campus attire and into a formal, funeral-ready ensemble. He bent his right arm. A nice cushy bump of gauze indicated an IV had come along for the ride.

As the gravitas of the measures that had been taken sank in—possibly since the anesthesia was continuing to wear off—Izzy felt both violated and disturbed by JD's assertion that he should be grateful to a mob boss for any and all violations.

"They had to get clearance out of JFK. We were very lucky that Phillip didn't get to you first—"

"Ambassador Jordan?"

"Of course." JD's perfect mimicry of the man Izzy had met exactly once, followed by a well-placed death threat from a general if he or Gregg ever opened their mouths about a certain psychopath the Army wanted erased, did something unpleasant to Izzy's stomach. "In the event he was monitoring all outgoing flights and passengers, even possibly policing all cargo, we had to be certain if the casket was opened for inspection— whether in New York or upon landing at Tan Son Nhut—you would not only appear to be genuinely deceased, but unrecognizable."

"Oh. God." He'd never thought himself vain, but perhaps he was, searching his face with anxious fingertips. "Did they disfigure me?"

"Not exactly. Here, let me." With several quick yanks that smarted like hell, JD ripped off two bushy silver eyebrows, a Salvador Dali thin silver mustache, some nose putty, and after a light rub of his palm over what felt like a completely bare scalp, he gave a *ping* to the side of Izzy's left ear. "The gold hoop was a nice touch. If you laid off the doughnuts and did a few more pushups you could be a body double for Mr. Clean."

Izzy inwardly flinched. He knew he'd let himself go, seeking comfort in food, not caring if he was fit, sometimes on weekends and alone, not even caring if he was clean. Depression was an insidious thing, and he certainly knew more about it that most, but his trouble was rooted in something deeper than the disease. The fact JD's comment bothered him, that his own concern over Gregg far outweighed any concerns over his personal inner demons, was encouraging. The dark matter he struggled with had not completely robbed him of the ability to care.

"Enough about me. Please tell me Gregg isn't dead."

"Highly unlikely. Phillip would lose his leverage, especially if he doesn't have you for backup. I offered myself in exchange since I'm who he really wants, but Phillip wants to play his game. Gather the pieces. Move the pawns. Construct the rules then bend them at will. It amuses him. Feeds his ego. He will not be happy to learn we outmaneuvered him with your abduction. All the more reason to find Gregg on our own terms and not wait for whatever instructions or coordinates I'm supposed to receive that could be for Phillip's entertainment while he has Gregg punished as pay back."

"Do you have any idea where he is?"

"Yes and no. I have something to show you." JD hooked a thumb past the open porch where rain continued its percussion on the roof overhead and dripping palm trees bowed over a winding street leading to a temple. "This way."

As THEY MADE their way to the viewing room, JD could only wonder what was going through Izzy's mind, what had happened since he'd last seen him. It had been at Gregg's wedding several years before. While Izzy had seemed unusually quiet and the whole Margie thing was a big mystery, he was still the same Izzy when they had a little bachelor party for Gregg with a cookout on the beach, laughing over old times, turning up some Credence Clearwater on the 8-track, and getting decently smashed with some Jack and weed.

This Izzy was someone else. JD knew he'd done a lot of changing too, hopefully for the better in some ways, while holed up at the monastery. Hiding, really, as Gregg had pointed out. But Izzy, walking beside him in a funeral suit, his head shaved and lowered, belly round, skin sallow, remotely detached, bore little resemblance to the young psychiatrist he had plucked from the 99KO front line psych unit, mentored and learned from in return, fought with and fought for, while becoming true friends. The kind that no matter how much time passes between visits or chats, the bond is made of unbreakable stuff and will always remain solid.

Izzy was no longer wearing the silver Montagnard bracelet JD had presented to both him and Gregg five years before. The bracelets were a symbol of Zhang's respect for their courage and gratitude for their humanitarian service to others. But beneath those words, as he bowed to them on behalf of Zhang, was his own pledge of loyalty, symbolized by the bracelets that matched his own, pronouncing them brothers bound by more than blood.

How could Izzy possibly discard something like that? It made him wonder if Izzy kept it stored somewhere, if he would have put it on had there been some forewarning of his unexpected trip. Well. They had a journey ahead and would need to rely on each other as well as their wits, just as they had before. There was an important difference, though, other than the missing bracelet: Izzy was no longer in good shape. He was too soft. And it would be dangerous to them all if Izzy wasn't sharp, present, focused, on top of his best game.

Maybe they should leave him behind, well-guarded, with some kind of contingency Plan B if neither he or Zhang made it back.

"I'm not sure you'll be hungry after you see what I have to show you, Izzy. Maybe you'd rather eat first."

"So I can throw it back up?"

JD thought he saw a glimmer of the old Izzy in his sheepish half smile.

"Good point. Would you at least like to get out of those clothes and change into something more local? Zhang prepared a room for you, wardrobe included."

Izzy patted his expanded middle. "I'm not sure they'll fit."

JD feigned a punch that Izzy instinctively blocked, the way JD had taught him many moons ago.

"If they don't fit now, they will soon enough. Good block. You've still got it."

Typically he would have slapped Izzy some skin, but this was not a typical reunion. And what awaited them in the viewing room Zhang had tricked out, was hardly anything to High Five about.

They were the only ones in the small theater where a projector stood on ready to play the film he had watched multiple times in search of any minute clue to determine the whereabouts of Phillip's monstrous brain-child. But if Izzy could handle it, there was something he could provide that was not in JD's own professional wheelhouse.

Helming the projector, he dimmed the lights from a control board, though not completely. Even he preferred to watch this particular footage without it being pitch dark.

"Before I start the film, you need to be prepared for some really messed up shit. I can only compare it to watching those long ago films from Dachau or footage from Nanking. If you'd rather not have this burned into your brain, I can fill you in and we can skip the film.

However, it is highly instructive, and it would put you in a much better position to form a personality profile on the major star of this show."

"Is Gregg in it?"

"Thank God, no."

"Then turn it on."

Maybe Izzy hadn't gotten too soft after all.

The black and white film footage was a bit grainy but professional and clear, the light good and the sound unfortunately very good, as a Texas twang began with, "Howdy, pardners! And welcome to your first history class at what we affectionately call The Killing School. Today we are going to discuss a wide range of topics, such as Jung writings about alchemy and sorcerers, about mind and consciousness, deep stuff that is all right here—" The cowboy in a lab coat made a grand gesture to indicate all the books and reports filling museum quality bookshelves. "And here is where you will discover the Map, or Guidebook if you will, for finding out all the answers, at least all the answers so far. But with our research we are moving ahead, we are on the edge of the wave here, at The Killing School, that is the FUTURE of mind control!"

A short pause until clapping could be heard in the background.

"Yes, indeed, the future is here, but we want to be familiar with all that has come before, because they knew what they were doing way back when, and maybe it can connect with our new material in a new way, always remember that ....invention and discovery is all about making new associations, that is truly what invention and innovation is. Now, we got the Sorcerers diaries, all the old stuff, look at that Malleus Maleficarum there"—more grand gesturing—"The Witches Hammer by those old Heinrich Kramer boys. Yep, it's an old one, 1487 first published, and the very first format for cross examination and interrogation to find people guilty of anything and everything, especially witchcraft. An excellent guidebook for getting confessions of guilt. Make no mistake: Interrogation is art and science. It's not the dumb guy in the cartoons with the red-hot poker, though there are plenty like that. Are you taking notes? There will be a quiz on this. Now, gathering Intel is nothing new. Throughout history Intel could be life or death information—as in, your life and your death—and that information needed to be extracted out of the subject or prisoner as quickly as possible. And who would be brought in to get that information? The smart people. The ones who knew conjuring, hypnosis, every aspect of the mind game, plus the chemistry, the shaman knowledge of plants and minerals and animals and how they all interact with body and mind. These old folks, way back old folks, pardners, we are talking Egyptians, Abyssinians, Tang Dynasty, Aztecs, Incas and even before them, their interrogation was first class…"

JD glanced at Izzy. He was intently leaning forward, head cocked as the lecturer paced around, gestured dramatically, held up books, and went into extensive detail on Soviet hypnosis and drugs, the old Nazi experimental archives of the Angel of Death Mengele, the deep dark horror show of Japanese Unit 731 chemical and biological experiments on women, children and babies.

And then the camera followed the Lab Coat Cowboy into what looked like a hospital ward where he stood in front of a curtain. With a quick *whoosh* he slid the curtain away to reveal a group of ten people all sitting in chairs, naked, moaning in absolute agonies of pain.

Izzy looked to JD, uncomprehending. "What?"

"Look closer. They aren't just sitting on chairs."

As the camera panned out to momentarily capture a large group of spectators—"students"—sitting in rows of chairs, all wearing matching military uniforms while taking notes, the Texas twang continued, "Please note how any small movement will cause further pain…"

The camera swung back for a close up of the naked subjects, impaled on stakes securing them to their chairs.

"Now, what you will discover, is that pain is one thing, but the horror of disfigurement is another thing completely even for these poor souls." Lifting a surgical scalpel, he approached a moaning subject, whose moans became shrieks with the announcement: "And so, as you will see, peeling and stripping the face from this man while the others watch will bring almost any information they might have, very good information, very quickly. Watch."

Izzy leaned over and vomited. JD paused the film and handed him a waiting towel.

"Here, have some water, too."

"Where did you get this?"

"From an altogether suitable resource who left it for me at the mission when he took Gregg." Pointing to the frozen frame where a remarkably handsome assistant in fatigues and a lab coat held a surgical tray, JD concluded, "Our very own Ghost Soldier. Jerry Prince."

CHAPTER 14

Meanwhile, Back at ISIC

Gregg woke up from whatever he had been drugged with strapped into a chair. Sitting across from him was a man in Ray-Bans about his own age wearing a lab coat over a turquoise cowboy shirt with a matching bolo tie. He had on blue jeans with a fancy rodeo style belt and what looked to be a pair of custom cowboy boots with embossed designs and silver Conchos propped on a desk. Steer horns, spread across the front, pointed Gregg's way.

"Who are you?"

"Well, pardner, you may think I'm Vlad the Impaler pretty soon, but actually I am Doctor Miles—just call me Miles—Director of this fine research facility. Given some similar credentials, there was a time we might have been colleagues. I have read your bios, your professional papers. Impressive. Your work with traumatized children and soldiers, brilliant. I believe your theory of childhood trauma and its effect on the developing brain being analogous to combat fatigue or PTSD is quite perceptive. And, your work with animals, particularly dogs and horses as therapeutic adjuncts is unusually compassionate, creative and effective… again brilliant. I have to say, it's almost like we are two sides of a coin."

Gregg wondered if he was hallucinating. He struggled to think back and—

"Where is my wife? Do you have my wife?"

"Hmm... well..."

He tried to surge out of his chair, intent on grabbing the bastard by the throat to strangle Shirley's whereabouts right out of him, only to tip over and feel his cheekbone smash against a polished wood floor, his entire body quaking and held fast by the restraints.

The sound of boots scraping across hard teak was followed by the cowboy's lowered face filling his sideways vision.

"Now, Dr. Kelly, was that really necessary? All you managed to do was risk injuring yourself and possibly provoking me, neither of which would gain you an answer. Considering how badly you want that answer, I will give it to you..." A pregnant pause. "After we deal with the business that brought you here. Lieutenant!"

"Yes, sir!"

Moments later, sitting upright again, his cheek feeling like a bowling ball and not for a second did he care, Gregg demanded, "Is Jerry here?"

"Sorry, pardner, but he is on another assignment. Can I offer you something to drink? Coffee, tea, Pepsi? I'd offer you some Jack, but probably contraindicated with the rest of the pharmaceutical cocktail on ready."

"What you can offer me is a call to the embassy in Saigon. I am a US citizen. A psychologist for an American NGO and—"

"And you are a spy."

"A *what?*"

"I have the paperwork right here." Some official looking papers waved across the steer horned desk. "You have been clearly identified by the CIA and the US government as a spy, and thus rendered here for interrogation. Upon receiving your confession—and lots and lots of Intel to go with it—you will likely go to prison." He smiled. "Sadly, Doctor, if I do not get all the information I want from you"—he paused dramatically —"as far as spies go, it looks like your dear wife is next up on the suspects list. In fact, could be she's the real traitor we are looking for, mmm, what do you think? You could just give her up and get out of here, mmmm?"

Gregg could feel his jaw working, grinding nails.

"Unfortunately, we only have limited time to get this matter settled and your confession in order, so we'll need to get started right away. Sure you don't want something to drink before we get relocated to the lab and hook you up with a little psychoactive RX?"

"I am not a spy, and to even suggest Shirley is, that's—that's preposterous! She is a missionary!"

"Oh, come on, you all say that... though, I do have to admit that this missionary business is a great cover. Haven't heard that one before!"

Where was Shirley? Where was Shirley? Frantic, Gregg tried a different angle. "Listen, you said we had similar credentials. Can't we discuss this as fellow professionals? Tell me about your own work, publications. You must have an impressive CV to hold such an elevated position at... what did you say the name of this research facility is?"

"I did not say. But, my, you are good at this, aren't you?" Some mental calculations seemed to be going on behind the Ray-Bans while steepled fingertips tapped lightly and Gregg struggled to control his breathing, the race of his wild thoughts. Suddenly, his keeper leaned forward, grinning. "I must admit, Dr. Kelly, it is refreshing to have the likes of you around here. A fellow clinical psychologist who can speak the lingo and even get lively with some academic debate. I have my job to do, but as a professional courtesy I will walk you through everything as we go. In exchange I would very much appreciate your feedback for a report I am working on. May not be a perfect trade-off, but since we have to work with each other anyway, some scientific benefit would certainly make the outcome more worthwhile. What do you say?" A turquois cuff with silver spur cufflinks came across the desk before its owner guffawed, "Oh, sorry, forgot we had your arms tied up there for a moment! Tell you what, if we can reach a gentlemen's agreement, I'll have those taken off as long as you promise" —wag of a finger—"no funny business!"

Gregg pretended to consider while knowing any attempt on his end to lurch and strangle would come to a quick halt with a single shout of "Lieutenant!" The best he could do was to play along, being fully cognizant that his counterpart would know when he was being played... although, what appeared to be some narcissist tendencies had bought this conversation and an offer to have at least the arm restraints removed. Maybe he could negotiate the leg restraints next.

"If I agree to provide feedback, will you tell me if my wife is okay?"

"I will... once we finish with the experiment."

"Experiment? I thought your intent was interrogation, which won't go very far since what Intel I have could fit into a thimble and I'm no more a spy than you are." Opening his eyes wider to connect better with those behind the Ray-Bans, he asked, "Or, are you?"

"Yee-haw!" A slap to the official papers on the desk came with a whoop. "You are a joker and then some, aren'tcha? Bet you like Willie Nelson, too."

"Gotta love Willie," Gregg assured him. "He looks pretty straight but, between you and me, I bet he smokes dope." Even as he forced a grin, Gregg wondered just what kind of "psychoactive RX" he was going to be hooked up to, robbing him of whatever facilities he was presently struggling to maintain. "That good old red headed boy might even want to trade places."

"Oh, I don't think so." This Miles guy actually looked a little regretful. Strangely, so had Jerry before stabbing him in the neck with a syringe... yes, that part was coming back to him now. "Lieutenant! Would you please come remove Dr. Kelly's arm restraints?"

An immediate "Yes, sir!" Boot steps. Then the arm restraints were gone.

"I appreciate that." Shaking out tingles of recirculation, Gregg seized on their "gentleman's agreement," to what other advantage he could. "And, I would also appreciate a list of the pharmaceuticals you intend to be using on me."

"Well, for starters an I.V. of saline with a chaser of 3, 4-Methylene-dioxy-methamphetamine."

"I see. You intend to rev me up and magnify whatever I am experiencing."

"Exactly. It is so good to talk with someone who understands these things."

"Anything else?"

"Absolutely. You'll have something a little later like nice ice baths and bright lights and loud music to make sure you do not sleep. `No rest for the wicked' as they used to say back home!"

"And where is home, Miles?" Interrogation. Experimentation. Sleep deprivation. He was in some kind of CIA torture facility *and what had they done with Shirley?* "For some reason I'm guessing Texas."

Gregg was not expecting the slight frown as Miles swiveled his chair around and rose to his feet, stretching.

"Well, pardner, I think the better question is, what do you think of the Brady experiments?"

"You mean with all those poor little Executive Monkeys who died back in the late 50's?"

"One in the same. A very famous bit of research back then, but still on monkeys. I have a variation on that which has proven highly effective in eliciting information, particularly when I use family members."

Just as Gregg's bowels turned to water and a bevy of bees jammed between his ears, Miles gave him a cagey grin.

"Now, if I can have your agreement to fully cooperate with this experiment and provide professional notes on your experience as a subject, I will tell you what you are dying by inches to know... once we are in the lab."

"No. You tell me now."

"I do not think you are in a position to be calling any of the shots here, pardner."

"If you want my agreement and clinical notes, you will tell me: *WHERE IS MY WIFE?*"

Miles allowed himself a moment to debate. He had orders all the way down from the top to give this "spy" the full on breakdown treatment, but no kill. In fact, it was made very clear that if Kelly died during interrogation Miles was in some very deep shit, not that he would ever consider wasting such excellent material anyway. This man was a professional clinical psychologist with outstanding academic training, a former collegiate athlete and someone who had been through at least two perilous military missions. A formidable and resilient mind. Great material to test. Getting the spy confession obviously had to be top priority... but he had ten days for that, which gave him plenty of wiggle room to use the spy charge for an even higher purpose.

"My, but you do drive a hard bargain," Miles gave him. "Your wife is not presently technically accused of spy activities and as such she was not brought in with you." The relief flooding the other man's face was so palpable Miles almost felt happy for him. Happier still, though, that what he had sacrificed in upper hand negotiations had only increased his leverage. "That said, her close association with you makes her an obvious suspect, thus we will continue to closely monitor her whereabouts and daily activities so she can be immediately apprehended if necessary. Please do keep that in mind as we proceed, for should you become uncooperative, or difficult, we will have to pursue her own potential involvement in anti-government activities."

"Bastard."

"Now, now. No name calling. Speaking of, mind if we drop the formalities and I just call you Gregg?

"Call me whatever you want, just stay away from my wife."

"I'm afraid that decision will ultimately lie with you and just how cooperative you are. Much as the fate of your very own monkey. You, of course, will be the Executive. Congratulations on the superior position! Though I'm sure you're aware of the downsides such a responsibility carries." Ready to get this show on the road, Miles gestured to the LT standing on ready. "Remove the leg restraints." Then, to his newest and most highly prized subject yet, he cordially extended a hand to the door that would lead to a well-appointed library, which in turn would lead to the superb lab facilities he himself had designed, and would be put to their best possible use. "Shall we?"

Now that he was somewhat reassured that Shirley was safe for the moment, Gregg followed "just call me Miles" to whatever lay in store. Unfortunately, he had a good idea of just what that was. But mostly he was grateful for Shirley's immediate safety, if such an assurance was to be believed.

The last thing he remembered now was calling JD, then Jerry taking over the phone, and no, he did not believe Jerry brought her here. Something was different about him beyond his completely changed face, while his movements, his voice, were completely and unforgettably the same.

As he tried to memorize the various hallways and rooms they passed in what appeared to be a highly sophisticated and well-appointed teaching/medical facility, Gregg told himself that JD would have immediately gone to the mission to help Shirley. And Zhang would be his first go-to for assistance. Even now they were no doubt trying to find him at whatever this CIA dark ops interrogation center was... and what about Izzy? Shit, he'd almost forgotten about Izzy!

"Have you had any other American `spies' brought in recently?" The casual tone he'd tried to strike sounded strident in his own ears. "Or, am I the only one who drew the lucky straw?"

"Sorry, pardner, but I'm not at liberty to say."

What if there was some sort of sick surprise waiting in the lab, like Izzy being brought in to act as his "monkey" while he was appointed his "Executive?"

Any card-carrying shrink would be familiar with the Brady experiments, but after publishing a paper on the ethical/moral questions surrounding the trials, he knew as much or more than most. 1958: Eight paired rhesus monkeys strapped in chairs. All pairs receiving an electrical shock every 20 seconds unless a conditioned monkey—the Executive Monkey—pulled a lever. Six hours on/six hours off shifts. All four pairs of conditioned "Executive" monkeys died within 9 to 48 days from perforated ulcers they developed from the stress while their partners, the "yoked" monkeys who suffered the shocks if the lever wasn't pulled, did not die. The researchers had further found that the Executive monkeys suffered the most damage during the six hours off when their sympathetic nervous systems were allowed to process the stress they had been subjected to as the responsible party for the pain inflicted upon their partner.

"And here we are," Miles announced with an unmistakable note of pride upon reaching their destination.

Gregg took stock of what was a typical two way mirror observation setup which basically looked into a small room on the other side with white washed walls and a sloping tile floor with a drain. In the small room were two facing chairs bolted into the floor. One chair was occupied by a young distraught woman who was strapped, hands and feet, to the chair. She had electrical nodes attached to her wrists, ankles and one wire snaking up into, he presumed, her vaginal area.

Miles took off his Ray-Bans. Pupils somewhat dilated, steely gray blue irises matched his eager smile. "We've got video feed—LIVE!—and if you'll look real close there"—he pointed to a large video monitor—"There is your very own Monkey. The first but not likely the last VC compatriot spy you will be responsible for, and keep in mind that could soon be Shirley."

"I don't know her." Gregg's rush of relief that it was not Izzy was quickly followed by a sinking sensation that what awaited would be no less horrid. "Look, I'm not a spy, and for all I know, neither is she."

Miles pushed a button on the control deck. The young woman jerked spasmodically, screaming, screaming.

"Stop that!" yelled Gregg.

"Are you a spy?" asked Miles.

"No!"

Miles pushed the button again.

More screaming.

"Okay, Gregg, I think you have a good idea of how this is going to work. I have lots of these young people to work with, by the way. Now, after we get you hooked up with that special pharmaceutical cocktail to enhance the experience, we'll get you comfortable in that chair facing your spy associate. I want her to be so close that you can really see, hear and smell, how in every sense that you, that's right, *you*, my dear Executive Monkey, are hurting this poor young woman by not telling me the truth. Please be aware that we are not just limited to the old lever and shock routine." Raising an eyebrow, Miles asked him, "Ever heard of waterboarding?"

CHAPTER 15

NIGHT #1

As with the Brady experiments, the sessions lasted for six hours on, six hours off. The experience too horrific to process from his mind to the page, his "lack of cooperation" in writing a report resulted in where he had just been landed for his second "off time" break.

Gregg nearly collapsed in the cage he was assigned to: #9 according to the tag on the door. The moon illuminated the clearing so that he could make out numerous other bamboo cages like his where there was not enough room for their occupants to stand up or lie down. His nostrils were assaulted by the smell of excrement and he could feel something crawling leech-like up his ankles, while his bare feet balanced on bamboo covered by a pool of wetness that could have been urine mixed with filthy water.

His body craved water. After the horror of the waterboarding and what had seemed an eternity of drowning you would think he would not be constantly craving water. And yet as torturous as the waterboarding had been, it had provided the most relief he'd had throughout it all since he had been allowed to take the place of his poor tortured partner.

"Please, take me. Take me instead this time."

"Are you begging?"

"If you want, I will beg."

"Good enough. Just be sure to pay close attention to the experience so you can write down what is happening to you internally that the observer cannot necessarily see."

"I will. I promise."

And then he had not been able to follow through on his promise.

Moans and whispers and eerie silences emanated from the various cages as the guard who had thrust him into **#9** disappeared into the surrounding woods he had marched Gregg through after exiting what looked like a Club Med campus.

"How long have you been here?" he whispered in Vietnamese to the nearest cage to his right.

"Time does not exist here," came the halting reply. "We call each other ghosts because we are already dead. You are one of us now."

"There has been only one escape," drifted a whisper from his left. "But he is surely dead too. The Hunting Dogs went after him. Those are the soldiers that are released for hunting practice upon anyone attempting to escape. I cling to hope that my brother—"

An ear-piercing siren sounded. Strobe lights blasted them with light while blasts of discordant music accompanied the blinding lights.

Then suddenly, complete blackness. No sounds except for the suffering around him.

Gregg shifted his tortured, aching back. His eyes were still seeing spots from the strobes and his ears were still ringing when he asked his fellow prisoners, "How often does this happen?"

"Intermittently, so you will never know." The reply, coming from behind the cage, was in English. It belonged to a voice he never thought he'd be grateful to hear.

"Jerry." If only he could turn around, see if a gun was trained on him or a knife was on ready to slit his throat. "Jerry, please confirm that Shirley is safe."

"Safer than you, I can tell you that. Lean your head back and open your mouth."

Gregg did as instructed. When a stream of water poured into his mouth instead of acid or pee or the dangling head of a snake, he could have wept his gratitude. Instead, once the trickling stopped, he beseeched the disembodied voice, "Please give some to the other men. I'm sure they're desperate for water, too."

There was no answer. No movement, no sound. Jerry Prince was gone, leaving Gregg with the moans of those who called themselves ghosts because they were already dead.

NIGHT #2

Gregg wondered if the psychedelic drug was wearing off or just continuing. He would not even have known it was his second night if he had not marked his cage. He worried that maybe he had forgotten a notch, that it was actually night #3, and that he already was so disoriented he might not find his way back. His mind was everything, it was who he was, what he did, all his memories, his personality. He knew what they wanted was to take it from him, they wanted find what it took to break his mind, bend his will, take it and control it. It was terrifying to him. The pain, the torture, the torments were terrible but the insidious grinding pressure on his mind and will and the erosion of both were what was most horrible and the way they were doing it by making him responsible for the pain and suffering of the other prisoner, unbearable.

The cage to his right was empty.

The cage to his left whispered in Vietnamese, *"Liem, Liem. My brother, where are you?"*

JD was like his brother. Izzy, too. *Where were they?*

"Open your mouth."

Gregg did. He gulped. He tried to ask for water for the other caged men but all that emerged was a croak. Then he heard gulping in the cage to his left.

A siren sounded. Strobe lights blasted. Discordant music blared.

Maybe he was already dead, too, and this was Hell.

DAY #4

Miles had a good feeling about this morning's session. He had recently been examining some records the CIA had obtained for him of the mind control work the Chinese and North Koreans had been doing back during the Korean War. Top notch stuff really. A real shift away from the primitive medieval torture chamber model and moving scientifically towards a modern psychological and neurological emphasis on working with disorientation, drugs, stressing, impairing and distorting perception and cognitive functioning. This just confirmed all his work here. Between his own interrogations work and Jerry's cognitive restructuring, he felt well on the way to being able to control a super soldier and squeezing most any mind of everything he wanted at will. This recent work with Dr. Gregg Kelly was just a godsend. He still couldn't believe his good fortune of having his very own trained clinical psychologist to break down and analyze!

Oh, yes, he was truly developing a new and improved "Psycho-Analysis" that would make him the most famous mind doctor since Freud, and Dr. Carl Rogers could stick that up his pompous ass.

"Top of the morning, pardner!" he greeted the poor wretch shuffling into the lab who barely resembled the fine physical specimen he had been just a few days before. Enough of the tiger cage, Miles decided. By the end of the day, a bath and a nice, cozy bed would be in order. Even a pitcher of the fresh squeezed juice he temptingly poured into a glass. "I could share a glass of this with you, but you know the rules. First you have to sign the confession, which does not exonerate your wife should we have cause to determine she has aided and abetted your spy activities. However, by signing the confession, you can spare your partner further distress and get her an immediate glass of orange juice there in the monkey chair. Don't you think she would appreciate that so much more than what you are doing to her?"

Gregg's leech scarred legs could barely hold him up. He had automatically reassumed what was referred to as a stress position—a crouch like he was surfing with his arms extended. Miles had taken his chair away in the last session, so every time he dropped his arms from pain and exhaustion or tried to stand his monkey partner was delivered a shock. Like dominoes the shock would cause his monkey to scream and beg Gregg to make it stop, to please sign the paper so he could have some water. You didn't need to speak Vietnamese to know what she was saying.

One shock. Two shocks. Three. On the fourth the monkey collapsed, sobbing.

"Okay, a little break," said Miles. He nodded and a soldier came in with a small desk and chair. "Have a seat, Gregg," he invited. "You can see there is a yellow pad there and a pen. I would like to know what your observations are at this point."

Even as he barely made it into the chair, his legs giving way just as he reached it, his defiance was astounding. "MY observations, you sadist asshole, are that you are a monster, you are not a scientist, or a doctor or a professor. You are a nobody nothing locked away in the jungle as much as I am. You are a war criminal doing criminal things."

"Please, Gregg, calm down. All this hostility is doing no one any good, especially your associate there. Poor Ang, I think she may well die today thanks to you if you continue on this way. As you are aware, we have to increase the voltage a percentage every time you refuse. If you are not willing to sign the confession then bad things happen, you know that. Still, I would appreciate during this little break that you write down your perceptions, observations of your will, resilience, any thoughts of how you are rationalizing your behavior. You know the drill, Dr. Clinical Psychologist. Give me some clinical insights into just what is happening to you. I promise if you cooperate and meet my expectations Ang gets a glass of orange juice. Think of what that would mean to her, the liquid, the nourishment and the vitamin C. It could keep her alive. Poor Ang, she needs your help. Isn't it your creed to cause no harm—and yet here you are, causing all this pain. It could have all been avoided but this is what you chose, and so frankly, it is all your fault."

Miles could see the pen trembling in Gregg's hand. But then he clutched it in a certain way, like a knife, and with some unseen force of will surged from the chair.

He had taken one halting, aggressive step in Miles' direction, and *SLAM* went the lever. *SLAM, SLAM, SLAM.*

Ang flopped and twitched and convulsed with the current.

"Stop! Stop!" cried Gregg.

The current stopped. Ang flopped one last time. Her bowels evacuated. The monitors indicating Ang's vitals flat lined.

"You killed her, Gregg." Miles shook his head, his voice filled with reproach as the monitors hummed. "See what you did? You killed Ang."

Miles observed the horrified twist of Gregg's features, how he flung himself to the floor, now kneeling beside his poor, deceased monkey, frantically pumping at her chest, breathing into her mouth...before laying his head against the heart that no longer beat.

His shoulders began to shake.

"I know what you are doing," he sobbed. "I know what you are trying to do to my mind, what you want to rob me of."

"Then you can start writing that down." Satisfied that any remaining resistance had gone the way of Ang, Miles patted Gregg's shoulder. "You can tell me exactly what I am doing to your mind. It's just invaluable having a colleague like you here, and as long as you can keep writing we won't have to bring in your new monkey." A thought, then. Just in case. "A pregnant woman. Raises the stakes a little. You can write what you think about that, too. Again, if I like what I read, she gets the orange juice. Now go ahead and take a moment, then have a seat at your executive's desk."

LATER

Phillip looked through the glass into the interrogation lab. He had to give it to Dr. Strangelove that no one could extract information or create a desired outcome better in limited time. Only four days had passed since the meeting with Isabelle, and already Da Nang, 50 miles south of Hue, had fallen. The timing for this had to be quite precise, particularly with all he needed to accomplish before bringing Isabelle in. The speed of the North's aggression was stunning, even to him, which made his carefully timed constructs even more critical.

He was not happy, not happy at all, with the apparent disappearance of Dr. Moskowitz before he could have his agents deliver him here to keep company with Dr. Kelly. All the more reason to create some results-oriented justification of ISIC's existence, if he needed it worse-case with Command, with a video and audio of the "confession" he now had as a matter of record:

Kelly had just confessed to being a spy, a traitor to his country. He had admitted that throughout the time he had directed the in-country NGO in Nha Trang that he had aided and abetted the enemy by providing health care, medical treatment and services to known Viet Cong and North Vietnamese agents. All true. Of course, the NGO was world famous for its humanitarian work, but the VC saboteurs that Kelly had admitted treating, rather than turning in as enemies of the state, legitimately made him a fellow saboteur, guilty of treason.

Phillip shook his head at the pitiful wreck he continued to watch through the two-way glass. Kelly had actually been "cleaned up" for this audio and video confession. At this point the material was mostly for insurance with Command if need be, while an earlier video he'd had delivered to JD's little island getaway—thank you, Kate—was another kind of beast. It showed quite dramatically and clearly what Gregg Kelly was enduring, and ended with the message that the interrogation would be continuing until JD and his Poppy King brother arrived at the site—coordinates provided.

Just one thing bothered Phillip. Make that two:

JD had managed to obscure his island whereabouts for far too long before Kate had recently provided that private bit of information; and, JD had not been there when the tape delivery had been made.

Nor had he answered repeated calls to his SAT phone.

Basically, JD had been virtually untraceable since Kelly's abduction.

Phillip shook off any concerns with a smug chuckle. No doubt JD was already en route with his brother, intent on a surprise visit to ISIC to rescue his friend. What had once made JD the most valuable assassin on the face of the planet was his supreme calculating intelligence coupled with an ability to kill with surgical precision. The emotions he had acquired since Kelly and Moskowitz had befriended him, and since Kate had broken his heart, were not an assassin's friend.

Indeed, Agent J.D. Mikel was no longer at the top of the killer's game. Ambassador Phillip Jordan, however, had never been better at his.

CHAPTER 16

L eaning back in his big leather ISIC director's chair with boots
propped amidst stacks of manila folders and strategically organized
notebooks on his steer-horned desk, Miles was positively buoyant.

Between big old Texas-sized pulls from his long neck beer, he read
and reread the report that Dr. Gregg Kelly had written. Not that whole
spy business confession, no, no. This was something much better. It was
well beyond what he could have hoped for unless he had a pool of psych
post-doc students to work on, but even then they would not have this
level of experience and professionalism to lay bare the underpinnings of
their own psyches being systematically broken down.

*The agony of my guilt when I could not resuscitate Ang was beyond my
emotional and cognitive abilities to process. As a result, I tried to compartmen-
talize the fury, the absolute rage I initially felt towards Dr. Miles, but then redi-
rected at myself for losing control, which resulted in poor Ang's death. She was
my responsibility. My compatriot. All this, followed by the horror of having the
responsibility for any pain endured by the pregnant woman who was next
brought in marked the ultimate deterioration of my resistance. In clinical terms, I
reached a place of abject learned helplessness and the sense of hopelessness was
profound. I knew clearly I would always have a kind of PTSD and likely have
suffered a kind of permanent brain damage having been in a constant state of
fear and apprehension that altered my psychobiology.*

And on and on. Brilliant. The details and descriptions were really well done, walking through the scientific process of a strong man's will dissolving like an ice sculpture in broiling midday sun. "The Kelly Report" as Miles had dubbed it, was pure gold when it came to mastering the moving target of the ultimate arms race: Mind control. The Hollywood version looked easy, like in The Manchurian Candidate with Frank Sinatra—a little intense booga-booga hypnosis and bingo you have a long-term zombie doing your bidding. But that's not how it really worked. The variables were so many you could not count them, and while his groundbreaking progress with Jerry was extraordinary—my god, the latest test with his coding and the kittens, absolutely remarkable!—The Kelly Report was on another level in terms of potentially publishable research.

Miles toasted to himself and thought, *damn this beer tastes good.*

Lone Star. Just what Uncle Billy always drank and even let him have a sip while they played Texas Hold 'Em that one precious summer on Uncle Billy's ranch. It had been in New Mexico, not Texas, but that didn't lessen the authenticity of his childhood experience.

Miles eyed a leather journal that did not often grace his desk. He had lots of notebooks. Almost a library's worth, all catalogued. There were ten volumes alone on his experiment with Jerry. But this journal, it was different. A diary, really. One he occasionally still wrote in. Like he had today, about The Kelly Report, and how he might go about convincing Ambassador Jordan to let him take Gregg along with them for ongoing research when they finally evacuated. Given the rate things were going, their target date of early next year could move up as early as October.

He didn't know that for sure, of course, but those were the private sort of musings he felt free to jot down without having to justify or analyze or worry about having to eat crow. Now, if Jerry ever got hold of one of his own notebooks, especially those with the special Star Trek covers that documented his experiments with the kittens and the codes…

Miles shuddered. That would be way worse than falling off the ugly tree and hitting every branch going down. The humanity he had unearthed in Jerry would not extend to the one responsible for it, that much Miles was sure of.

Another swig of the Lone Star and Miles made a decision: He would read it. Not one of his reports or professional papers or even the research he was proudest of. Nope, it was the most personal thing he had ever written that no one else would ever see. It contained his fondest memories of Uncle Billy, the one, if not the only person, Miles could say he had honestly loved. Certainly not his brilliant, depressed, withdrawn mother, who had been impregnated by "a fellow scientist"—which summed up everything he knew about his biological father—whose disappearance brought on a postpartum depression that had sidelined her for the rest of her life. Not that they were poor or did without thanks to her sizeable inheritance. No, they were comfortably miserable together in a Connecticut mansion with equally unhappy housekeepers and nannies. It had been during his 9th year that she had a breakdown and he was sent away to spend the summer with a previously unknown relative who took him in.

With gentle hands, Miles touched the first page of his first journal. The script was small and awkward, the handwriting of an adolescent bumbling his way into the future and not wanting to forget the best part of his youth.

HAPPY TRAILS

On one blessed blue sky summer day when I was nine, I was happy. Happy my mother was in the hospital with a breakdown so I could be taken by her lawyer to Penn Station and put on a cross-country train to Santa Fe, New Mexico!

The people on the train were nice to me, especially the kid named Mikey with a little hamster in a shoebox. I liked the hamster too until it bit me, but I flushed him down the toilet later when Mikey wasn't looking, then ended up giving Mikey one of my Sugar Daddy suckers when he opened the empty box and started to cry. Because he cried so much and was eating all my Sugar Daddys I was glad when Mikey and his family got off somewhere in Oklahoma.

When I reached Santa Fe and stepped off the train, it was just like stepping into a real live cowboy movie! The man waiting for me was dressed in such fine cowboy clothes, I knew I wanted to dress just like him, right down to what I found out were his Lucchese boots. He gave me a great big smile, shook my hand like I was as grown-up as him, and the first thing he said was, "Hey, little pardner, you just call me Uncle Billy. Now let's saddle up and take you to get the best burger in the world!" And then I got to ride in a real pick-up truck that was the shiniest sky blue you've ever seen and we drove straight to what turned out to be a tiny adobe place called

"Bobcat Bite" where he greeted a nice lady at the counter and announced, loud enough for everyone to hear, "Darlin' Mitzi, meet my little pardner, the smartest boy in all of Connecticut, and we'll have two of the usual, please!" The usual turned out to be a massive hamburger smothered in green chili and cheese with a heap of fresh hot fries and a thick chocolate shake. I'd never tasted anything so good in my life, even the green chili that was so spicy hot it looked like I was crying as hard as Mikey. "Sometimes the pain is totally worth everything, pardner, especially when you can cool it down with some of that shake," Uncle Billy told me, instead of making fun of me the way some kids did back home, which made me think I never wanted to go back there again.

When we left I was so stuffed I could hardly climb back into that pretty blue pick-up truck, and from there we drove to a place called Taos where we stopped at a store and Uncle Billy got me "all gussied up" in new jeans, blue Levi shirts, t-shirts and my very own Lucchese boots! "Always buy the best for your feet, pardner, treat them right, wars were lost because of feet." I didn't know anything about wars or lost feet but because Uncle Billy said so, I swore I'd wear nothing but the best boots from there on out.

Once we got to Uncle Billy's ranch I could hardly believe my eyes. There were acres and acres with cattle everywhere and even real buffalo. Uncle Billy had a room all made up and ready for me with nice wood bunkbeds, a dresser with horseshoe shaped pulls, a desk with pens and a new spiral notebook, plus a book case filled with Zane Grey and Hardy Boys books! But just when I thought things couldn't get better, Uncle Billy pulled out a brand new Mysto Magic Magician's Set, an authentic A.C. Gilbert Erector Set, and a Chemcraft Chemistry Outfit for Boys!! His whole ranch looked like it had come straight out of Bonanza and even the horse he taught me to ride, called a "Paint," looked like it could have belonged to Little Joe (I don't think it would have been big enough for Hoss). We went trout fishing! We looked for arrowheads and old Indian pottery and panned for gold! We camped out under stars that were brighter than any stars I'd ever seen in a sky that spread out forever above us. It was all so different and exciting from anything I'd done before that sometimes I wondered if it was all a dream.

Uncle Billy and I had great talks. It turned out that he had been a nuclear scientist, a colleague of the father I'd never met, and so secretly I wondered if he was really my dad. If he was, I could see why he would not want to live with my mom and I hoped he would never make me live with her again either. Mostly though, I just wanted to live with Uncle Billy forever and ever at the ranch. He told me that he'd bought it after inventing a special instrument that made him a lot of money and quit working for the government as a scientist. Maybe it was the scientist part of him that liked science fiction so much it took up half his library. One old book he read to me was called, "Trilby" and after he read it he said, "For sure not the best science fiction book ever, but one of the very best ideas...mind control, pardner. Mind control. Somebody is going to do it really right someday, and just maybe it will be you and me!" That night he hypnotized me. I did not remember doing the silly things he said I'd done like strut like a rooster and cluck like a chicken, but we laughed and laughed about it while we were riding our horses the next day, straight into a brilliant Taos sunset. "Race ya home!" Uncle Billy called and we were still shrieking and laughing while I clucked like a chicken nearly all the way there... Until Uncle Billy's horse stepped in a hole, broke his leg, and pitched Uncle Billy high in the air, only to land on his head and break his neck and die. Right there in front of me. I still don't recall what happened after that, just one minute I was begging Uncle Billy to wake up with his neck bent at a funny angle, and then I was back in Connecticut where everything was gray again, and all I had left of Uncle Billy were the clothes he'd bought me. I threw a fit when my mother tried to get me to wear my old clothes again. I wouldn't do it. Every day I wore my cowboy outfits to school instead of the white shirt, red tie, and matching navy blazer and slacks we were all supposed to wear. I hoped the Dean would throw me out but he didn't (probably because of the extra money my mother "donated"), and I didn't care that I got called names and spitballs hit my back, I was wearing those clothes even after I outgrew them and could hardly get the boots on my feet.

It's been three years since Uncle Billy died, though it seems a lot longer than that. I still have those worn out jeans and Levi shirts and of course the boots. Sometimes when I'm alone I'll take them out and rub my nose against the fabric and think I can still smell the campfires and the sage. And then I imagine I'm still staring up into that clear night sky while Uncle Billy throws me a lasso from the stars so we can saddle up on Pegasus and ride off into the galaxy together.

Miles shut the journal and placed it in his bottom drawer where he kept a few trinkets that held some meaning. He didn't have many. After Uncle Billy he had been careful not to get too close to anyone because he never wanted to go through that again. It was a lot like scar tissue that got built up and built up until there wasn't any sensation—and maybe, just to be fairer than fair, that was what had kept him out of the UWM grad program, boasting one of the most prestigious psych departments in the entire country, if not the world, while Dr. Carl Rogers had been there.

While he would never forgive it—*middle finger to you, Carl*—the important thing was that he had found his own niche professionally, excelling where few others historically had, presently did, or probably ever would. Like Jerry, Hugo, Ambassador Jordan, he was rare in his particularly unique capacity. Even Kelly, especially Kelly, brilliant as he was, could never do this sort of work, because Kelly's greatest asset as a clinician was also his greatest flaw as a researcher: an inability to inure himself from the necessary suffering of others, whether they be rodent or human…

Hmm. Now, there was a thought:

Just as he'd helped Jerry reconnect to his humanity, could he take someone like Gregg Kelly and do the opposite? Experiment with various hypnosis-RX cocktails to see how much of Kelly's core personality could be manipulated and contrast the results to those in Jerry? If he could embed command codes that would override moral codes and turn Kelly into a *real* spy with a rare understanding of how the mind worked, minus any awareness of how much his own mind was being controlled…

Whoa, pardner! Now he HAD to get approval to bring Kelly along to their new ISIC location. Unfortunately, The Ambassador seemed to have other plans for Kelly, and while Miles knew that as Director of ISIC he was indispensable in many capacities—including his occasional assistance with Jordan's young wife—he did not have Phillip Jordan's ear. But Hugo did. And, it seemed the Commandant wasn't real happy here lately with some of their research… actually, he hadn't been supportive of bringing Kelly in for interrogation purposes to begin with. Which meant he'd be even less supportive of permanently silencing him once Kelly had served whatever purpose The Ambassador deemed necessary. Put all that together and Hugo just might be in favor of keeping Kelly around as long as he was humanely treated. Obviously, at this point, there would be no sending Kelly back to his wife.

Miles downed his last swig of Lone Star, spiked it with a microdose hit. He grabbed his Stetson just so he could tip it to the memory of Uncle Billy, and went in search of Monsieur Hugo Goulet, Commandant of ISIC.

∼

"Tchin-tchin!" Phillip toasted on the wide veranda where a fan rotated slowly overhead.

Hugo regarded the man across the table from him, impeccably dressed in a bespoke linen suit and light blue dress shirt. His tap to Phillip's raised crystal was more obligatory than from any real desire to celebrate. For what was there to celebrate? He would soon be leaving this plantation he had called home for nearly two decades, and leaving behind with it the gardens he had tended, even the cherished lychee tree that he and Jerry had planted to symbolize their trust…

But the koi. He had to find a way to transport the koi.

"Go ahead," Phillip said, settling back into his wicker chair then popping a grape into his mouth from the cheese and charcuterie board invitingly presented on the small table. "Tell me what is on your mind. Something is bothering you."

"Oui." And with that one word, Hugo tapped out a Gauloises from his cherished silver case, lit up, and steeled himself for what could be the end of a very long friendship. "Remember when we first met, at the end of The War? We were boys then, full of ideals and hopes. We had just conquered Hitler and Japan. We were kings of the world—"

"As we still are," Phillip was quick to interject.

"Non, mon ami. Non." With eyes clear and unfettered by such illusions, he met his old friend's squint. It simmered with reproach for disputing him. Did he know this man at all anymore? "We are not the kings we once believed ourselves to be. The Vietnamese humiliated and humbled first France, then your own USA. The politicians betrayed the soldiers, betrayed them absolutely. And perhaps that is what has come to divide us. You are and always will be a politician. And while I have played in your yard, in the end, I will always be a soldier."

"Oh no, Hugo, 'tis not that simple and well you know it," Phillip swiftly countered. "We are both in the business of killing. That we do it for a country that sanctions it—whether France, America, China—means very little to those we kill, does it not? If I am paying the python to kill the frog is it more righteous, more justified, to the frog? You and I, both politician and soldier, know how this works. We take small countries. We take their resources. We pay their citizens to help us do that, at least those that will, then often kill the ones who will not. It is the way of the world."

"The way of the world comes for *us* now. The North is hungry to pay us back for everything your country and mine have done to them, for all that we have done here. I cannot blame them. Were our positions reversed, I would want both your head and mine on this platter."

As Hugo indicated the charcuterie board where a knife rested amidst an assortment of sausages and cured meats, Phillip tapped the tip of his own glowing cigarette into a crystal ashtray and sniffed, "Do you have any of that disgusting absinthe you enjoy so much around here?"

"You may insult me, but not my *la fee verte*." Hugo allowed himself a small laugh, perhaps one of the last he and Phillip would share, while signaling for the bottle that his house boy quickly delivered, along with the essentials for preparation.

He did not feel his usual delight in performing the lovely time honored ritual: pouring the vivid green liquor into crystal, laying the slotted silver absinthe spoon upon its rim where he placed a sugar cube, then dripped ice water over the sugar until it dissolved.

Upon serving it without his usual flourish, Hugo returned to his Gauloises and blew out his decision on an extended puff of smoke:

"I do not think you will have need of me at your new ISIC location."

"Rubbish." Phillip made a sour face but took a second sip of the absinthe. "How do you drink this stuff?"

"Why did you ask for it?"

"Because I anticipated you wanted this meeting so you could try to distance yourself, exactly as you're trying to do, and I thought it would buy us a little more time before we had the unpleasant conversation I think we both know has been coming." Planting his glass firmly onto the table, Phillip's steely gaze locked with Hugo's unwavering own. "You don't get to decide when or if you wish to be a continuing member of our ISIC team. That is my decision, my call. And you will be continuing in your current capacity as Commandant at the new facility."

"And should I refuse?"

"I will use my considerable contacts with the French government to have you charged as a war criminal for other dirty deeds—which are plentiful enough to easily surface—and have you hunted down. I'm sorry, Hugo, but you know too much, and I can't afford to have you belatedly find your conscience and decide that confession to someone, anyone, is good for the soul."

All Hugo could do was shake his head, then throw it back and laugh.

"You find this amusing?" Phillip demanded.

"Non." Raucous laughter immediately ceasing, Hugo tossed his burning cigarette into Phillip's glass. "I find *you* drunk on your own power. An *enfant terrible* who has been too long at the top. You once told me Kennedy at least kept a naysayer, someone who would not go along with everything he thought. He relied on you sometimes to say `bullshit, you are wrong' but you imagine yourself to be greater than Kennedy now. I urged you not to bring le Docteur Kelly here, but still you did. And why? So you can destroy *your own son* and his step-brother, all because of the revenge you swore over a nose bump and broken finger you no doubt deserved."

"How—how dare you?" Phillip sputtered, rising imperiously from his chair. "It is far more complicated than that and for you to throw JD's paternity into my face after I brought you into my confidence and you swore silence—"

"SILENCE!" In one swift move Hugo surged from his chair, grabbed the sausage knife from the charcuterie board, and flung the blade razor close to Phillip's temple. The knife, whirling end-over-end, soared past the veranda and hit the trunk of his and Jerry's lychee tree. Buried to the hilt into the gray bark, Hugo silently begged forgiveness from the tree, but never, never would he ask the same from Phillip. "I could have silenced you forever just now but non, I showed the restraint that you no longer have. Now you will listen to *me* for a change. Sit. And be aware that it is a chair, not a throne."

Hugo pointed to Phillip's indicated spot and felt a rare glee in the pallor of his old friend's face, the bulge of his eyes, the unaccustomed following of someone else's order. There would be pay-back for this, but if he did not tell Phillip the truth, no one would—and any pay-back would only come if Phillip could find him.

"First, about this murder you intend to do to your son," Hugo began as he remained standing, his stare of disapproval narrowed down at the powerful adversary he had just made. "Perhaps you did not raise him. Perhaps you did not intend to impregnate a woman married to a close colleague. Perhaps you did not find out until after her death and JD was in your employ. I do not know all the perhaps. What I know is that I have done too many wrongs to others to sit in judgement, but I do sit in judgement of you for this thing that not even I could imagine doing. To kill one's own child is unnatural. It is wrong. And *non*, I cannot be a party to it."

"Then *perhaps* you should take your party elsewhere, Hugo."

There was a tingle in his palm, an itch to slap Phillip with a gauntlet, challenge him to a good, old-fashioned duel at dawn which he would win unless Phillip cheated and hired a skilled assassin to kill him first. Yes, that would be Phillip's style now. He would even take it up a notch and have Miles instruct Jerry to do it, an order fulfilled with the whisper of an implanted Code Jerry. Jerry, who never had a real father, and the closest thing he'd ever had to a son, would only spell opportunity to Phillip, a chance to orchestrate a devilish opera: While one son killed a wanted father, another father would slay an unwanted son.

Retaliating by ignoring the goad, Hugo went on, as if Phillip had not even spoken.

"In your misguided belief that you have become God, you have set loose too many demons. We began the school for a grand purpose, only for it to become Dr. Frankenstein's laboratory. While it has made me trés uncomfortable, I can understand your experimentation with Jerry—what a country would be capable of with warriors like him to command—but this business of `tweaking' your own wife with drugs and hypnosis and I suspect even codes to do your bidding, is monstrous."

"Call it what you will, but Katherine is none of your business. Are you quite finished now?"

What was finished, Hugo knew, was their decades long friendship—a liaison that had been slowly fraying, only to be so decimated in mere moments that there was nothing left to restore. He wanted to put that in Phillip's face as one would a meringue pie, rub his flared nostrils into it until he suffocated. Perhaps he should just kill him now and bury him in the garden. So tempting. Even noble…perhaps. He could spare Mikel and his brother a terrible fate, as well as le Docteur Kelly. He could intervene before Phillip could carry out his plan to bring Isabelle in to wipe this defiled toilet clean for the newspapers, the magazines, spare her whatever might come if she disappointed Phillip somehow…

But to disappear Phillip Jordan would be even more noted than disappearing Kissinger. He, Hugo, would be hunted down, eventually found, even in the far reaches of a self-imposed exile. Non, he would not kill

Phillip, at least not yet, for that reason alone. He could do more to thwart him by allowing him to hang himself.

"Oui." Hugo calmly re-seated himself, took his time lighting a final Gauloises, blew a lazy smoke ring into the still-charged air between them.

"If you attempt to leave I will find you and consequences will result."

"Of course." Hugo slightly raised a mocking eyebrow.

"I need you here when Isabelle arrives since she is expecting you. And I need you to ensure that Jerry properly distracts her if need be." A meaningful pause while Hugo blew another smoke ring. "Once you comply with these duties and assist our relocation, I will leave the door open for further discussion of your possible retirement, under certain conditions."

Certain conditions. Hugo knew exactly what that meant: He was to be at Phillip's continued beck and call, no matter where he might "retire" with Phillip's constant tracking of his whereabouts.

"So. You can still be fair."

"Of course," was Phillip's wry response, followed by a dry chuckle. "I am glad we can agree on something for a change. It has been a while."

"Oui, just as I believe we can agree that I will no longer call you `mon ami'… Monsieur Ambassador."

"As you like it," Phillip replied with a stiff removal of himself from the chair he had been ordered to sit upon.

A dismissive wave and he was gone.

As was Hugo—and every koi in his pond—when Jerry came hunting on command, well before dawn.

CHAPTER 17

"How're you doing, Izzy?" JD called from a respectful distance, if ten feet away in some bush skirting the river qualified for privacy.

"Hanging..." *Gag.* "In..." *Dry heave.* "There."

Oh man, Izzy thought, what he wouldn't give for a roll of toilet paper right now. What they'd brought from Saigon was gone before they reached Thanh Pho and his replenishment had run out long before they reached their present and completely uninhabited spot on the Mekong Delta, a good 70 miles south of Saigon. As for the easy ten pounds he must have dropped in a week, Izzy wasn't sure if that was completely a good thing when the key was speed and for the past few days he had been sicker than a dog—

An image of KO, the four legged mascot that had been the best shrink they'd had at the 99KO, burst into his mind's eye with the force of a curtain being yanked from a darkened backstage: KO nuzzled between him and Gregg while they huddled, terrified, in a bunker, watching a compatriot racing for safety get blown to bits. KO gently licking his hand as a Dear John letter shook in his grip and tears bathed his face, only for KO to gently lick those up, too.

So many things he did not want to remember. So many things he had mentally walked around with his eyes closed for the past years. Anything and everything that could remind him of when he had been a soldier in the Vietnam War had been avoided. Now, in this place, every sensory mode was a memory bomb exploding and burying him in layers of suppressed terror and grief he had spent the last five years doing everything possible to escape.

"Perhaps we should take him to our Monastery... or back to our friends in Cholon? I know he insists on coming despite the dangers, but—"

"Zhang, I can hear you!" *Gag.* "And you are not dumping me with whoever will take me after bringing me halfway across the globe in a fucking coffin! I know I'm holding us up. I feel horribly about it. But I would feel worse if you knew exactly where you were going. Like, how much can I be holding you up when the bullseye keeps moving with your best Intel?"

Mumble. Mumble. Mumble. All in Vietnamese. A lot of good that did him. He had exactly fifty-four working words and phrases in his RVN lexicon. Probably more, but he'd done his best to eradicate those from his memory, too.

"Very well." Zhang, sounding Poppy King gracious and not completely pleased.

"Izzy, we are all good to go forward and you are absolutely correct," JD assured him. "It's late enough that we'll make camp here and get an early start tomorrow."

The camp they made wasn't 5 Star Manhattan but JD and Zhang were masters at making a Vietnamese forest bordering the Mekong River as 5 Star as anyone could get.

"Thanks for the fresh coconut water." Izzy took another gulp, grateful for the settling effects on his stomach as well as his bowels. "If there's enough I could go for another piece of that grilled fish, too."

"There's plenty more where that came from, so eat up." JD extended a palm leaf that acted as a plate for some truly delicious and incredibly fresh Mandarin fish. "We'll have miles of more hiking tomorrow and you need to build up your strength. Especially if we're as close as I think we are."

Izzy nodded while silently wishing for the jeep they had ditched, or the Air America chopper they had taken before that.

Phillip is ruthless, JD had explained. *And he is totally connected to every CIA and remaining military network so he's likely watching every single movement of however many helicopters and boats are still operational at this stage of evacuation, with an eye on every major highway. We have to be completely undetected.*

It was JD's and Zhang's concern of detection that had cemented their decision not to bring additional back-up. Zhang had his own Army of trained fighters and an arsenal of weapons, but they were located a thousand miles north, and as far as the brothers were concerned the leaner, the meaner and the faster they could operate—which made his own presence more liability than asset for the equivalent of two human killing machines.

As if reading his thoughts, JD said, "There's no telling what kind of shape Gregg will be in physically or mentally when we get there, Izzy. While Zhang and I can get us in, and get Gregg out, he's going to need you for the kind of medical care we can't provide once we're out of there."

Izzy didn't miss the meaningful glance JD darted at Zhang over the small campfire they had made, where Zhang tossed another fish onto the coals and gave a short grunt of agreement.

A rustle in the near dark and Izzy nervously whispered, "What was that?"

"Not human," Zhang muttered. "Maybe a snake." Then, with a mischievous grin, "Or could be a tiger."

"Knock it off, Zhang. Izzy doesn't need that."

The brothers had a little private conversation in Vietnamese that ended with Zhang offering Izzy more fish on a palm leaf, then rising like some great Asian Zeus stretching arms to the night sky.

"After scouting the area," he said in perfect English, "I will make you a bed of leaves and ensure nothing undesirable will keep you company so you may sleep well tonight."

And in the span of a breath, without seeming to move or make a sound at all, Zhang was gone.

"I can't get used to that," Izzy blurted. "What is he, some kind of ghost?"

"The monks call him Dschung Li Kuan—one of the Eight Immortals in old Chinese fables who could fly through the air in human form. But as we both know, Zhang can be all too human at times. Sorry he hasn't been completely on board with having you along, Izzy, but I felt you were safer with us than being anywhere else. Certainly in New York, and anywhere here with the NVA swooping down like a hungry flock of vultures on half-dead road kill, though that should work hugely to our advantage."

"Our advantage? Are you kidding?" Izzy couldn't fathom things being any worse. Three days after Da Nang had fallen, the north had taken Qui Nhon 200 miles south and officially declared possession of half the country, with Nha Trang on target to be next. "We're trying to run ahead of the tanks and straight into a dark ops torture compound, while the NVA obliterates everything that's left of this poor, ravaged country, and that's a good thing?"

"It's horrible, all of it." The somber shake of JD's head was a reminder that no one felt the pain of the country's collapse more than those who called it home. Izzy knew that JD, having grown up in Vietnam, had no sympathy for the French, or the Americans, despite his beloved dead mother being French, and the equally deceased father he despised, being American. "But for our purposes," JD went on, "the chaos and panic, which is only going to get worse, means that this facility of Phillip's will literally be bleeding workers. Missing service people means missing maids, missing cooks, missing gate guards. They'll be desperate for warm bodies to fill empty positions until they have no choice but to evacuate."

"But what if they already have?"

"They're no doubt in the process of relocation but just as surprised as anyone else by the speed of the North's invasion. Besides, Phillip wants his pound of flesh first, and even this will be a game to him, seeing how long he can outlast the inevitable. Would you care to know how Margie is doing?"

JD's sudden pivot took Izzy as off guard as the country under discussion. *Margie.* There she was as close as yesterday, with the scent of honeysuckle and lemon lifting from the raven hair sifted through his fingers, the smell of her filling his senses as he buried his face against her neck and kissed his way down to the most beautiful pair of pale, full breasts that both aroused and gave solace. *Margie.* His dream girl in fatigues, turned into an absolute vision in a sundress the color of lemonade while they talked of Jung and visiting Switzerland on the mission's veranda… until the glow of bombs hitting the 8th Field Hospital could be seen across the water, where they raced back in JD's '57 Chevy to the 99KO and a nightmare unfolded: patients already out of their minds screaming, one of their fists connecting with Margie's face; watching her head rock back, blood gushing from her nose and split open lip. Her pretty lemonade yellow sundress splashed in bright red…

Would he care to know how Margie was doing? He would crawl over glass to know if she even fleetingly missed the man he had once been, if she did not hate him completely for the heartless way he had disposed of her, almost immediately after making the proposal he had no right, no right whatsoever, to make.

"Is she married?" he made himself ask, while dinner's fish swam uneasily around no longer soothing coconut water.

"No. Apparently there's some guy she never got over. What you did was really shitty, Izzy. I just have one question: Why?"

"Because..." Hand on the Torah, it was the one truth Izzy knew in a sea of lies: "Margie's the best, and that's exactly what she deserves. Not me."

"Oh?" JD raised a speculative eyebrow. "Seems to me you should have let Margie come to that conclusion instead of making such a decision for her."

While deep Jewish browns hesitantly locked with enigmatic 7-up bottle greens, Zhang reappeared on eerily silent feet.

"The area is clear. Your bed is made. My apologies for earlier, especially after all that you did for my people."

Zhang gave a short bow that Izzy interpreted as a sign of respect—one that echoed the silver Montagnard bracelet that now lay in a dark box of memorabilia that had been consigned to the bottom of a drawer he had nailed shut.

Izzy returned Zhang's bow, only lower, keenly aware that he had shat upon what little was holy about his time in Vietnam when he had removed the silver bracelet JD had formally presented on behalf of Zhang.

How much that simple but supremely meaningful bracelet had in common with the woman he never should have let go: He had thrown them both away like a common loaf of bread in the supermarket aisle of a 100 different brands of bread instead of a gift from the gods, some amazingly brilliant shining thing he would never again encounter.

No, he did not deserve them.

Even as his eyes drifted shut and he longed for sleep on the nature bed that Zhang had made, the nightmares that were his constant companions cackled from the side curtains of his psyche, whispering more truths Izzy wished he did not know:

To go back into your past, a past that you remember darkly; to go where you have very deliberately, studiously avoided at all costs, tried to switch off, ignore, blank out...it was a dangerous place filled with snakes that one must carefully consider approaching. For the mind, while a powerful tool for creation as well as for numbing and avoiding, was flawed. Because where it really counted, right down there at the bottom of its deepest well, the mind never completely forgot about The Dark Matter.

Sometimes Izzy wondered if the dark memories that could never fully be suppressed might be what dark matter was really made of, if there was so much collective darkness of the mind that it made up most of the universe, and even his own twisted black box of poisonous snakes was but a small blot upon an impervious constellation.

CHAPTER 18

The last piece of advice Hugo had given Jerry was this:

You must treat this most dangerous mission as if you are capturing a wild elephant and a tiger working together. Non, I do not like this mission but it is yours nonetheless, and what is most important to me is that you are not caught between the tiger and the elephant, so you and I may still garden together...one day again.

It was the "one day again" that was stuck on replay in Jerry's mind. As he led his personally trained, hand-picked 14 man unit deeper into the jungle, he desperately wanted to believe that Hugo had left some clue of his whereabouts and had not completely deserted him, and therefore the living trust between them. *But if you really had such trust,* came the insidious whisper, *then why did Hugo value his koi more than the friend, the protégé, the man he even once called "mon fils," why did he leave you behind?*

Mon fils. My son. No one had ever called him that. Unless he counted his step-father yelling, *you worthless sonofabitch!*

Killing that bastard, his first kill at 15, had felt So. Fucking. Good.

But for some disconcerting reason, killing just wasn't what it used to be. The hunt, the kill, the blood fever of slaughter and sheer animal pleasure of battle had once been the most powerful chemical cocktail he'd ever known: mind-blowing ecstasy wrapped in an adrenaline rush. And wasn't it ironic that the more he had become valued for his killing abilities at ISIC, the less he needed it to get his fix. Playing with Panther or debating with Hugo on Sun Tzu's The Art of War had come to provide a far deeper sense of satisfaction than the business of killing, which, given you were taking someone's life—be they enemy, stranger, or even a colleague—should provoke more emotion than this increasingly dispassionate sense of disassociation, as if he were leaving his body and watching from a distance.

There were varying levels of this disassociation between his body and mind thing. Sometimes he remembered nothing between a moment that went black, then suddenly snapping to and often having a dead person literally on his hands, ala Isabelle's playwright friend, Vuong Quan. But there were other times when he was fully cognizant of everything he said and did, such as the episode with returning the VC dad to his kid, that blurred some lines between making choices that were distinctly his own while his deadlier instincts pivoted in other directions. I.E. Let the father go; turn his killing sights against his own men if they crossed him. Those were the times he had mental rope, just not enough to hang himself with. Weird.

Maybe Doc Kelly could help him figure some of this crazy shit out if Miles wasn't around and doing such crazy shit to Doc Kelly.

It bothered him to see Gregg in such bad shape.

What bothered him more was that it bothered him at all.

They should be getting close now to the destination Phillip Jordan had pinpointed with the 24/7 arsenal of Intelligence at his command. Sometimes Jerry wondered why The Ambassador needed him at all—

And then he did not wonder anything.

Looking down at the black Rolex Submariner on his wrist, an unexpected gift from both The Ambassador and Miles for his recent promotion—which coincided with Hugo's disappearance—Jerry saw that it was exactly 1900 hours.

As if an internal switch went off he went on auto-pilot, feeling extraordinarily aware while all of his senses went into hyper-drive. The need to complete this mission went from necessary to imperative, no matter the cost.

His vision, honed to a nearly microscopic 20/10 from the last operation, cut through a tangle of dark foliage, zeroed in on a distant ember, small, calling it the last to die from what may have been…

A campfire dinner of fresh fish and tasty roots.

His nostrils quivered at the scent that he put at 91 meters away—the length of a football field.

A rustle, faint, he heard it, the whisper of familiar voices on the wind that had carried the scent of embers and food.

Just then a twig snapped behind him.

Jerry turned his laser sharp night gaze on the offender, got the message across with a throat-slicing motion: One more snap and they would be one man short, lest the rest of them suffer the consequences of his clumsiness.

Then it would be a lethal unit of 13 plus him, against 3 of them—Jordan's resources had confirmed that Izzy was now in their possession. The question that erupted from Jerry's newly sensitive and empathic dissociated self was: *Were they crazy?!*

The last time he'd seen Israel Moskowitz, nearly six years ago, Izzy was injecting him with the same curare they had dipped their spear points into for this ambush. But unless Izzy had gone through some major physical upgrades, he would be a huge liability to JD and his step-brother…

And therefore, a potential asset to him.

A momentary jolt, like internal static, stopped Jerry, and subsequently everybody following him, in their tracks.

Had he just said something, done something, signed an order?

Jerry glanced again at his watch.

Go, go, go! You have an elephant and a tiger to capture along with a weak appendage named Izzy that has no business ever being in the Vietnam bush.

Jerry signaled his patrol to creep closer quietly, quietly, pointing their drugged spears from every direction possible, every other man holding his high and low to pierce their quarry at every possible level to induce a temporary paralysis.

Had JD, Zhang heard their silent approach? Suddenly, in the shadows ahead, he perceived JD, Zhang, grabbing Izzy up from the ground, moving him away while he mumbled in his sleep. They moved incredibly fast, faster than Jerry's pitch perfect internal tracking system could track.

And so he called out: "It's stupid, don't fight, you are done, outnumbered Five to One if you can do the math!"

Silence. Except for the voice that sounded like Miles going off in his head:

ACTION REQUIRED IMMEDIATELY. MUST CAPTURE. DO NOT KILL.

In sign language Jerry gave the command *Move in now and take them alive*, and pointed in the directions he wanted his men to go.

As they moved in and he moved away toward his own target, JD and Zhang shot out of the surrounding shadows with the force of two supersonic bullets. Jerry kept moving while he had a front row seat to one of those really stupid, impossibly choreographed Kung Fu movies that take place in mind blurring speed.

JD and Zhang whirled, using his men's own strength and momentum against them, spinning a tight group like Frisbees into the air. Seconds later Jerry saw another four men go down with broken spears through their eyes and throats.

The two brothers continued to circle and spin, throwing broken stakes and spears with both hands, while flopping men screamed until the curare paralyzed them. Maybe twenty more seconds passed and Jerry only had three guys left standing. *Jesus, why hadn't he just used elephant gun tranquilizers instead, see if they could Kung Fu a bullet?*

Moving at near light speed himself, he watched Jones and Alex, his best throwers, launch their spears from a back angle to cripple their legs —only for Zhang and JD to drop to their knees, catch the spears, break them in half and fire double the missiles right back at Jones and Alex.

OK, he was now down to facing the elephant and tiger himself with precious little back up and he did not at all like the odds.

"C'mon, show yourself," JD taunted with a wicked grin and the wave of his fingertips. "Zhang, stand back. This is between me and Mr. Ghost Soldier himself."

"Not quite," Jerry called from behind them. "I have company."

Holding Izzy in a choke hold with one arm, just loose enough for him to gag out a cry for HELP, Jerry pressed the edge of a razor sharp dagger against the throat he could easily slit, oh hell, make it a decapitation.

JD stepped forward, glowering. "Let him go."

"Sorry, buddy. Game's over." Jerry nodded in the direction he and his now decimated unit had come from. "That way. I'll follow. If either of you get out of my sight or make one false move, you can say Adios to this amigo."

Show me a sane man and I will cure him for you.

— CARL JUNG

FISH SAUCE

April 5, 1975
Nha Trang, RVN

Fish Sauce surveyed the once familiar city that bore no resemblance to the place he had left to join the PAVN.

Panic ruled the streets for those who still remained. Virtually every American had fled the city they had once roamed freely, when their money flowed faster than the drinks that were poured and they could buy whatever they wanted: all the best food, clothing, entertainment, even if it included women and children to satisfy their carnal appetites.

He had known girls who sold themselves to help feed their families. His cousin Binh had been one of them. She died at the hands of an American soldier who was never punished.

The thought of it fueled the inner rage Fish Sauce kept closely controlled, making him feel like a maddened bull straining against the fraying ropes that kept him contained.

The shuttered shops and frenzied citizens of the fallen city who seemed to be running everywhere and yet nowhere reminded him of Da Nang. He had thought to outrace the flood of troops after Hue, and yet Da Nang, 50 miles south, had capitulated just a few days later—March 29. And then, *then*, Qui Nhon was captured 200 miles south of Da Nang only three days after that. THREE DAYS!

Who would ever have guessed that the Americans would simply abandon the country? Who could conceive that the RVN forces would so quickly melt away like the witch with the green face in the movie Isabelle had told him of?

Unbelievably, after Qui Nhon, just day before yesterday—April 3—their forces took command of the nearby Cam Rahn Bay Airport. That's where he had stood on top of the Flying Pig to take in the atmosphere. It was an increasingly familiar party that grew increasingly raucous with Chopsticks and his crew cheering and dancing, while other comrades sat on the wings of planes, singing with bottles of beer.

Music blared from everywhere while guns fired into the sky to join a heady celebration. And no wonder: Soldiers who had been continuously running and hiding and fighting since they were teenagers were suddenly not. They were experiencing something that their parents, grandparents, and even great-grandparents had never known:

They were free in their own country.

Now, with the official fall of Nha Trang, they had taken half of it back. But it was on the tarmac, the day before yesterday at the Cam Rahn Bay Airport, that Fish Sauce had taken something for himself:

Rows of RVN traitors, who had allied themselves with the Americans, had been tied like pigs for market, laying side-by-side.

He noticed a group near their tank wore unfamiliar uniforms, even if their wiggles and cries for mercy were the same as all the others.

"Who were they," he called to another commander. "Do you know?"

"They were guards we caught, after they decided not to stay at the despicable Yankee prison camp where they had been hired."

"Do you know the name of the camp?"

"Trường giết người, they called it. We barely kept our comrades from killing them before I could personally interrogate the traitors."

"The Killing School," Fish Sauce whispered. Then, quickly, urgently, "Did they give up the coordinates?"

"Not willingly." But the other commander's satisfied smile, the pat he gave to a sheet of paper in his pocket, was assurance he had extracted the most crucial information that had heretofore been elusive to Command. "We are finished with them now if you wish to take a turn."

In response to the courtesy, Fish Sauce had a private word before deeply bowing his thanks.

"Let's go!" he yelled to his crew.

As soon as Chopsticks, Noodlesoup and Porkrib boarded back onto the Flying Pig, Fish Sauce tersely commanded, "Drive over them."

While the tank crushed through the bodies screaming beneath their grinding wheels of steel, Fish Sauce studied the copied coordinates that Command had yet to receive.

CHAPTER 19

Grateful for the relative safety of a Saigon café booth, Isabelle knew she must smell as rank as her unwashed khaki pants, week old tee-shirt, and dirt encrusted boots. A minor consideration given the front page of The New York Times dated April 2, 1975 that a colleague had managed to smuggle in. Beneath the headline *"For Those Who Flee, Life is 'Hell On Earth,'"* was the stunning image of a U.S. official punching a desperate man in the face as he tried to board onto an overcrowded plane in Nha Trang.

It was not her photo.

With her personal darkroom turned to rubble, downed phone lines making wire photo transmission impossible, and the riskiness of entrusting a third party with undeveloped film that could be destroyed en route to an editor in a saner part of the world, her raw body of photographic work remained in the weathered backpack that protected her treasured Leica. Now more than ever, the pack carried her life. It was nondescript and invisible in its everyday way of simply being a paramilitary style backpack with the usual array of zippers and pockets and little hidden slices of places. The main two pouches, though, had even more extra sealed seams, with especially fine seals that were essentially dust proof, mud proof, water and oil proof; just not bullet proof, but close.

She carefully slid the newspaper in with the many capsules of undeveloped film that told wrenching story after story of Nha Trang's final, fateful collapse: The lawless plundering and looting of shuttered stores. Riots around the consulate with waves of bodies trying to climb over or break down the fence, desperate to throw themselves into an airport-bound helicopter since the NVA had secured all other routes out of the city. Soon, not even the runway was safe. She was there to see two Air America planes landing at Cam Rahn Bay Airport, soldiers standing on the plane's ramp, trying to control the mad rush of a crowd with guns firing over their heads. She watched, and clicked, as a fellow correspondent—French, not half Asian and blending in as she could—was dragged aboard, only for a Vietnamese child to be thrust at him just before the door could close. And as it did, she swung her camera around to capture the agonized faces of those left behind.

Nha Trang, once an important coastal resort on the South China Sea, had officially collapsed shortly thereafter: April 5, 1975.

And now, two weeks later, desperately in need of a bath and a place to sleep, she fingered the business card that Phillip Jordan had given her. It was impossible to process the whiplash metamorphosis of her homeland since toasting with Krug and dining on mussels and frites at an exquisite table overlooking the sparkling blue French Riviera with her elegant hosts.

Would the offer still be on the table if she called him now?

In hindsight, she should have immediately agreed, taken the much needed money and *RUN*—But, no. She had been in a fever to be in the midst of it all, even as a parade of North Vietnamese Army tanks rolled in.

Thinking of the last image she had shot in Nha Trang, Isabelle frowned. Some of the NVA-PAVN commanders had been waving from their tanks as if they were heroes come to save the day, not invaders intent on bending the culture of the city to their whims, brutally punishing their perceived enemies, and imposing their rigid ideals upon those who did not want them.

One of the tank commanders had looked strangely familiar, stared straight at her as she captured him with her lens, before she quickly melted into a stream of refugees, fearful her camera might be seized.

From there, packing as much paranoia as film in her pack, she chased the fighting all the way to the town of Xuân Lộc, where a population of 50,000 had mostly fled by the time she arrived. In a last ditch effort an order was issued from South Vietnam's highest command, President Thiệu, to hold Xuân Lộc no matter the cost.

Xuân Lộc had not yet fallen. But what she had witnessed, committed to film before bribing her way onto a stolen jeep just this morning, was the bloody writing on the wall:

The North would take Xuân Lộc and claim the milestone victory of possessing two-thirds of the country...

With Saigon, the capital, only 45 miles away.

"SHE IS IN SAIGON NOW?"

"Yes sir, Mr. Ambassador, since 1200 hours. She is presently three blocks northeast of the US Embassy and just paused outside a phone booth, holding what appears to be a small card in her hand, dressed in the same clothes she's been wearing for a week, backpack with the film and camera she keeps inside resting beside her feet. Do you wish for us to move in?"

"No, just keep her in your sights and be prepared for future instructions."

"Sir, yes sir."

Phillip replaced the receiver, gave Kate a hopeful glance.

"Well, at least you aren't still scowling. That's refreshing."

"She's dallying around a pay phone, holding a card. Possibly mine."

As if on cue, the phone rang.

"One ring..." Phillip examined his latest manicure.

"Two rings..." Kate admired the exquisite diamond set in platinum on her left hand.

On the third ring, Phillip picked up with a leisurely "Bonjour" as Kate lent silent applause upon Isabelle's return greeting.

"Bonjour, Ambassador Jordan...Phillip. It is Isabelle. I do not have much change to keep the telephone going so I must make this brief. Do you still wish for me to visit your facility for a photographic exposé to be made public?"

"Absolutely, my dear. But may I ask, where are you?"

"In Saigon. It is insane here... and yet, so strangely subdued, as if the entire city is holding its breath."

"Indeed." A brief pause to light up. "Everything is unraveling much faster than anticipated, even by the highest echelons of U.S. Intelligence.

Which means the opportunity we discussed likely has a curtailed window of time remaining. How does your schedule look for that visit?"

"Would tomorrow be soon enough?"

Tonight, Kate mouthed, tapping the face of her Cartier watch.

"Tomorrow would be splendid but…" Another puff, one long enough to think *you're down to a skeleton crew with too many missing personnel to get everything cleaned up and white washed in time, not to mention the situation with JD and his little entourage, and oh bloody hell Hugo would be laughing his ass off if he was still around to do it.* "Let's make that the day after tomorrow, early morning, so I can be there to greet you. Besides, that will give you time to review the materials I'll have delivered right away to wherever you're staying there in Saigon."

"Can I get back to you on that? I just arrived and haven't looked for a room."

"It's almost impossible to find one." Especially after giving almost all her money to a newly impoverished family. Stupid but admirable. Now he just needed to buy some of that loyalty for himself. "A suite will be made immediately available to you at the Rex Complex Hotel and they will see to any and all of your needs."

"Merci!"

"Also, Isabelle, per our earlier discussion, we are prepared to be generous with your compensation. I think it only fair to offer you a retainer to secure your services and tender any balance you feel is owed upon completion of the assignment. Would $25,000 USD be enough for a retainer? I can have it wired immediately to an account of your choice— though, under the circumstances, you might wish to consider a Swiss account if you do not yet have one, which I can also assist in having set up on your behalf."

"Twenty-five thousand?"

"Oh, my apologies, of course I should have offered more, given your status. Would $50,000 be agreeable with you?"

In her momentary silence he could hear her conscience working overtime.

"That's extremely generous, far more than necessary."

"Never turn down money," he admonished. "Especially from the government."

While Isabelle fed more change into the pay phone at the Operator's prompting, Kate's impatient glare only prompted him to more deeply inhale as he thought of the newest command Miles had implanted, abetted by a little rx to her tea. The doctor's assistance had involved yet another little house visit since taking her to The School had been too risky until they absolutely needed her there.

"I don't mean to offend you," Isabelle continued, "but I want to be clear that the work I do must be independent and absent of any appearances that I've been hired for propaganda purposes."

"Then let me be equally clear that the United States has a propaganda machine like none other of which I could readily avail myself, but I reached out to you for precisely the integrity that is synonymous with your work. I would say that puts us on the same page. Now moving this along before we get cut off, if there is anything else I can provide you with—"

"A darkroom."

"I could arrange for one to be made available to you there in Saigon." And then, a thought. Brilliant! "However, we do have an impressive studio dedicated to film and photography development on the ISIC campus. The equipment is the best in the industry, the newest technology available, and you could have the entirety of it all to yourself during your visit. No interruptions, develop whatever you might be hanging onto now, and have unlimited access to our UPI 16-S. That is how you transmit photos via wire, correct?"

"Oui. Oui!"

"Then I'll have everything ready for you when you arrive. As for transport…"

They traded a few more specifics to finalize the deal, but just as Isabelle asked hopefully, "And will Hugo be there as you mentioned over lunch?" the line went dead.

"Pity, looks like her change ran out," said Phillip, lifting his hand from the cradled receiver.

"Day after tomorrow?" was Kate's only response to his inspired performance. "Really, Phillip? We're all here in Saigon and could be on our collective way within the hour, and you're buying time? For *what*, pray tell? This entire business with clearing your name when the project should be over and done already? Every day counts and you act as if you have eternity."

Subduing the urge to snap, *Shut up, Katherine!* he took a leisurely last puff from his Gauloises and tried not to envision Hugo's glowing red tip landing in his glass of absinthe. Unfortunately, Katherine was right about one thing: Time was of the essence and the razor thin timing to master several orchestrations at once was shaving it dangerously close even for him.

"I'll be leaving shortly," he informed her. "And you will stay behind."

"But you told me that you would take me to the school with you before shifting it all to the new location."

"Don't pout. It doesn't become you. Besides, I need you here so you can escort Isabelle to The School. Actually, I'd like you to have dinner with her tonight. Keep an eye on her to make sure she doesn't wander."

"Oh! Well. In that case…"

As Phillip graciously accepted his wife's appreciative kiss, he made his mental list of pieces to strategize—those pieces, of course, being mostly pawns, and the pawns, his carefully selected cast of sacrificial players.

CHAPTER 20

The suite at Saigon's prestigious Rex Complex Hotel was an acute reminder to Isabelle of all she would never take for granted again: The luxury of a deep, scented bath; plush towels and fragrant, clean hair; a kimono embellished with a peony to perfectly compliment the elegantly appointed bedroom and adjoining living area.

The pink kimono, slightly wrinkled from its consigned place in her pack, was a personal treasure, a virtuoso fabric painting that was high art, exquisite silk, vibrant with deep rich colors that carried the very soul of the artist—what Buddhist monks would call Chi. She had another kimono, a blue one, painted with an iris. Although they were compact when folded, it had been an indulgence to bring them with her, but they were a pair, like sisters, not meant to be parted. A beautiful, heartbreaking story had come attached to them when her father presented them as a 16th birthday gift. There had to be ten other more practical things she should have brought instead in the pack, but the blue and pink kimonos were a touchstone she prized almost as highly as the Leica.

Lounging upon the plush couch with a Top Secret folder spread out on the teak cocktail table, she remembered a day when it would have been tempting to indulge in one of the cinemas, the library, dancehall, or eateries on the famed premises where a rooftop bar was often hopping with military officials and war correspondents.

Rumors. Tips. Spies. Intrigue. War stories, near misses, gin. They were all there at the Rex Complex, where the American military command hosted its daily conferences. Many of her journalist friends snidely called them the "Five O'clock Follies" and wasn't that an apt name now that they had ditched their command posts and thrown their vulnerable allies under the bus?

A brisk knock at the suite's door had the same effect as gunfire awakening her in a pitch dark tent.

Sweeping the documents back into the folder a Special Forces LT had delivered, Isabelle pushed it under the couch then anxiously reached for her backpack. She should have hidden it somewhere, just in case. The Leica was rare, but the film irreplaceable.

As for the Swiss knife that cozied up to a recently acquired .45 caliber pistol, an M1911 U.S. Officers Model, they were now on a par with Karl Malden advising: "Don't leave home without them."

Just as she was telling herself to stay calm, that the same sort of sudden disappearance of Vuong Quan at the Presidential Palace in this very city five years before could not happen to her—at least not in a coveted suite secured by Ambassador Phillip Jordan—another knock sounded.

"Isabelle? Are you there?" called a familiar voice. "It's Kate."

A rush of relief propelled her to the door she flung open with a cry of, "Kate! I'm *so* happy to see you. Come in, come in!" And although she wasn't usually the touchy-feely kind, Isabelle impulsively gave Kate a big, warm hug, joyous for the presence of another woman she knew, that she thought she could trust even as suspicious as she'd become of just about anyone or anything that moved—sometimes including herself—and thank God she hadn't pulled out the .45 in greeting before Kate could extricate herself to present a large bag bearing the signature logo of HALSTON on one hand, and a bottle of Krug in the other, its own gold and brown signature just out of the ice and dripping wet.

"I'm sorry, I should have called first," Kate apologized as Isabelle ushered her in, then turned back for a quick look down the hallway before shutting the door, clicking the lock.

"Non, non," Isabelle was quick to assure her. "These are strange times and your surprise visit a bright spot in what has become a very dark turn of events since our last meeting."

"Then let's see if we can brighten things up a bit more." The HALSTON bag promptly handed over, Kate wasted no time in finding two glasses to fill with the bottle of Krug she immediately uncorked. "I hope you don't mind I took the liberty of bringing a few things from my last trip to New York—a little whirlwind getaway since our lunch—not much, just an ultrasuede shirtdress that's all the rage, some amazing boots to match—hope you're a size 6 in both—and something called a kaftan that looks a little like the kimono you already have on. My God, that's gorgeous!"

"Merci. It is very old. Japanese."

"Well, it's absolutely breathtaking and maybe you don't even want what I brought, but as I was shopping I was thinking of you. And then I thought of you some more when who should show up at Halston's on Madison Avenue? Andy Warhol!"

"Andy Warhol?" Isabelle repeated while her fingertips brushed over the softest camel suede nap moving like a short, gentle wave beneath her touch. Considering how she'd spent the past few weeks she may as well have been handed a space suit from another planet—which coincided nicely with the Warhol sighting. A year before, perhaps even a year from now, it would not seem so out of touch with the reality that had painted South Vietnam blacker than black. "Was he accompanied by Mick Jagger, by chance?"

"No, actually Bianca was there with Andy, and no surprise they have the most discerning and creative eyes for fashion. They even helped me pick the kaftan out for you. Turns out that Andy is a fan of your photography. And don't be surprised if Bianca wants you to do a photo shoot. She asked for your number but obviously..." Kate gestured to Isabelle's backpack and paused.

The butt of the .45 that Isabelle had been in the process of grabbing just before Kate made herself known peeked out from its hiding place.

"I don't know how to shoot it. Reporters, photographers, all the press, we don't carry. We're non-combatants and if you become a combatant by carrying a weapon, that makes you fair game. Not that anyone firing from the other side is asking for credentials and deciding who to kill or not kill."

"If you're going to carry you should know how to use it." Kate extended a glass. "Here's to the upcoming visit to ISIC. Something tells me there's an expert on campus who could give you a few pointers."

As they tapped glasses, Isabelle confessed, "I accepted the gun for protection, and I believe I could pull the trigger if it was a matter of life or death. But I think it would always haunt me in a much worse way than all that haunts me already."

A long sip of champagne and Kate gave her a wry smile. "I think we are all capable of far more than we might ever suspect when it comes to self-preservation. The innate will to survive is enormous, whether on a battlefield or in a boardroom." Voice dipping, eyebrow arching, she added, "Bedrooms sometimes, too. It's not always easy being a woman moving in a man's world. Whether guns or other choice weapons—in your case, a camera—we use what we have in our arsenals, for personal as well as for professional purposes, *n'est ce pas?*"

Isabelle was not quite sure what to say to that. She knew there had been something of a scandal when The Ambassador had divorced his wife of nearly 30 years to marry a former pediatric nurse who had served at the Peace Mission Hospital in Nha Trang. A much younger woman who had just admitted she wasn't averse to using sex as a weapon for personal, or professional, gain.

Nonetheless, Kate's candor was refreshing, and so Isabelle told her.

"Trust me, Isabelle, it's refreshing to be candid and not have to watch every word out of my mouth for a change. As a diplomat's wife, it's something of an occupational hazard, you know?"

"No, I wouldn't know, dieu merci!"

Their joined laughter set the tone for Isabelle exclaiming over every item in the Halston bag, all of which fit perfectly, boots included.

"I'm trying to imagine wearing these into the trenches. That would be as much a travesty as throwing Jackie's pillbox hat on inauguration day to the NVA."

"You know your Halston!" Kate exclaimed, clearly more excited about Isabelle's knowledge of fashion design than the ugliness with the North they were both in the midst of.

"Why didn't you just stay in New York, Kate? Why are you really here? Surely not to bring me these beautiful things and gossip over champagne."

"Hmm. Good question," was all Kate said before calling room service for another bottle—*what, no Krug? Very well, the Moet et Chadon will do, please ensure the foil, cage, and cork are intact, and have you any foie gras to go with a double order of mussels and frites?*—then order placed, she suddenly asked, "Would you believe me if I said I didn't want to be away from my husband while he still has duties to see to as long as the US consulate remains open in Saigon?"

"No, I would not. I have the impression that as enamored as the two of you appear to be, you still enjoy your independence, which I suspect is something he appreciates about you."

"And you would be right," Kate confirmed. "So would you believe me if I said I had friends to still say goodbye to in-country?"

This was a tricky one. Kate seemed the sort who never met a stranger and could quickly engage—a quality that would be beneficial in her capacity as Phillip Jordan's wife. And yet there was something about her that struck Isabelle as guarded. Even...lonely. In need of a genuine friend she could confide in. It was a feeling a female war photographer could relate to, and not for a minute did she think that someone like Kate would return to say some goodbyes. No, she would simply go on to meet other people she could entertain who would entertain her in exchange. Surfacely intriguing but nothing you could scratch to reveal something deeper beneath the surface. Like a cover shot for Vanity Fair or Vogue.

"Frankly, Kate, I think you would be more inclined to send a postcard with a picture of yourself sunning on the French Rivera with a note saying `Wish you were here!'"

The profile of Kate's stunningly beautiful head thrown back while laughter burst from her full glossy lips made Isabelle glad she did not have the burden of being so extraordinarily physically graced herself. This woman could never disappear in a crowd, and such a level of beauty could fend off more than attract the lesser beings that made for the best photographs because of their imperfections.

"Well?" Isabelle prompted. "I can't believe you came all the way from New York because tickets are so cheap to fly in and almost impossible to be had flying out."

"Needless to say, I can fly anywhere I want and get out whenever I want, including here. But since you're so curious, I will tell you the truth: I am here, Isabelle, because I am possibly even more interested than you in touring the ISIC campus. You're going there for a job opportunity. I, on the other hand, have been relegated to the side lines for most of my husband's dealings, both nationally and internationally. I dress up. I go to dinners and galas and sparkle and pretend I don't notice the whispers behind my back. But I'm genuinely interested in the workings of the world and have always been hungry to learn more when Phillip's brought me into his confidence. Particularly concerning the Institute for the Study of International Conflict."

"But why ISIC?" The Top Secret folder she had shoved under the couch and just begun reading was no doubt instructive. However, it would be biased towards whatever point of view Phillip Jordan wanted her lens to present and she was not so naïve as to believe otherwise. It was a major reason she worked as a freelancer beholding to no one. The truth was her truth, at least as she saw it. But accept an assignment, take money up front for it, and whether professed or not, the real job you were being hired for was to make your employer look good.

A lot like Kate was intent on doing for her husband, asserting:

"Because Phillip has been a devout proponent of democratic ideals, his life's work devoted to advancing world peace and stability. ISIC was—and is—the culmination of that. Besides my husband's impeccable character, here is what I know about ISIC: Its existence was never for dark purposes in the intelligence community, but its secrecy was imperative to avoid potential contamination of the trainees that were being specially selected from often unstable countries and sent back to assist our government in establishing democratic societies from within. And now, what has been wrongfully tainted is my husband's reputation while a highly classified organization that was deeply important to him and to the world at large has been publicly and politically compromised, ensuring that its doors will be shut rather than moved elsewhere. You want to know why I'm here? There you have it."

It was impossible not to admire such an impassioned defense of a spouse. As for openly wondering why South Vietnam had been chosen over another location—say, somewhere on the same continent instead of across the world—or asking if a potential reason might be that it would be harder to trace missing dissidents, Isabelle did not think taking the conversation in that direction would benefit their evening or gain her some insights she may regret unearthing when she needed money and new doors opened for a career in freefall.

"What you said, about being so interested in touring the campus. I take it you haven't been there before?" she asked instead.

"No. Because of its highly classified nature with those brought to train needing to maintain their anonymity for obvious reasons, I didn't have the clearance for a tour. But now, with this unexpected turn of events..." An expressive shrug, before she said brightly, "At least I'm finally able to go with you and we can see it for ourselves together. Phillip's shown me pictures along the way that were quite fascinating. They should have been included with the classified documents he was having sent over. I told him I'd make sure you received them. Did you?"

As Isabelle retrieved the folder she had hastily hidden under the couch, room service arrived with the Moet and a silver domed tray that revealed a small feast that looked as divine as it smelled.

Inhaling the steaming broth of wine and shallots where delicate mussels swam in their black shells, she was further tempted by the frites, glistening with duck fat, heaped upon the mussels, and crowned with seared slices of foie gras.

Isabelle sighed deeply. "This looks last meal delicious. Should I try a frite to make sure no one's trying to poison us?"

"I think we should be safe with the food." With a mischievous grin Kate released the cork she had requested intact with a *POP*. "It's the champagne you have to watch out for."

CHAPTER 21

I sabelle had ridden in a variety of choppers. A Bell Huey, several Sikorskys, even a Jolly Green Giant Search and Rescue. None had caused her more than an adrenaline rush, but now, as she stared down from the Chinook she shared with Kate, the adrenaline felt more like an apprehensive tingle slithering along her backbone.

The early morning mists continued to lift, revealing swaths of forest, glimpses of the winding Mekong River, rice paddies, the scarred earth of nearly 8 million tons of explosives that the US had dropped in their Southeast Asian bombing campaigns. "We're going to bomb them back into the Stone Age," USAF Chief of Staff Curtis LeMay had famously proclaimed, and from her vantage point in the Chinook, the bastards had done their damndest, even if their failed goal to stop the NVA was now on global display.

"Look!" Kate pointed at the emergence of a rubber plantation, complete with a sprawling villa and color filled garden. A man in uniform was standing in its vibrant center looking up through a pair of binoculars. He waved.

CLICK. Isabelle continued to snap pictures as the Chinook slowed, skated above nearby treetops and then circled above an extensive compound. What immediately struck her was the lack of activity in a tennis court and pool, only a few vehicles driving through an organized layout of pristine cobblestone streets that appeared to be an inviting combination of quaint bungalows, lovely gardens, a town square, and professional buildings that did not look at all military.

There was a darkroom in one of those buildings with all the equipment she needed. Including a UPI 16-S and a phone line to transmit her selected images once developed. Phillip had said they had the best technology available so hopefully that meant it wouldn't be so painfully slow to send internationally—up to an hour per color photo.

But he said she could have all the time she needed. And she preferred to shoot in black and white then tone in sepia.

Within hours she could be in that darkroom. No wonder her heart was racing as they slowly dropped into the bullseye of a landing pad where Phillip, dressed for a relaxed weekend at a polo club, stood next to an impossibly interesting photographic subject: A tall, handsome man dressed for a Marlboro ad from cowboy hat to silver tipped boots, anchored by a Concho belt in a fit middle section, with a lab coat and Ray Bans to complete his inimitable look.

Click. Click. Click.

He suddenly averted his face, leaving Isabelle to wonder if he was camera shy despite inviting such attention.

"Warhol would love this guy. Who is he?" she asked over the loud *whoop, whoop, whoop* of chopper blades. The Top Secret documents had shed little light on the hierarchy of the organization and personnel, primarily focusing on ISIC objectives that were, not surprisingly, as unimpeachable as Kate's assessment of her husband's character. "Kate, do you know?"

She didn't respond, her attention riveted on Phillip. He was smiling warmly, a fingertip raised, reminding Isabelle of a conductor. A signal, perhaps, to the Special Forces LT who materialized to assist Kate out of the Chinook and escort her to Phillip's waiting embrace.

"Oh well, always the bridesmaid," Isabelle muttered while taking a couple of quick shots before returning her Leica into the pack where the two kimonos were nestled like sisters. She had even let Kate wear the blue one as they bonded over champagne and the knowledge of what a rare moment they shared because Saigon's time was running out.

After the accumulated grunge of her fieldwork and blending in with fleeing refugees, Kate's offer that morning to share her makeup and manage Isabelle's long black mane into a chic French twist felt particularly welcome. It also made Isabelle feel oddly vulnerable. She had become so accustomed to others relying on her, to having to fend for herself while watching her back, that such an act of kindness had even stirred an awful, unwanted niggle of suspicion.

Maybe that's why she was having trouble shaking this strange apprehension despite outward appearances. Dressed in the generous gift of an all-the-rage Halston shirtdress and boots, all she needed was the Chanel bag she'd bought in France before a weathered pack that carried her life became her go-to accessory.

Thanks to a little more shopping with Kate the day before, a really heavy rucksack she dreaded to lift awaited her attention since the Special Forces LT assistance had not returned upon delivering Kate to her prince. Make that Ambassador. Close enough.

The bleating of the chopper blades had slowed their rotation into silence. Squaring her shoulders and preparing to lift nearly half her weight from the floor of the Chinook before bunny hopping them both out of the chopper, a deep voice stopped her cold.

"Here. Let me help."

He intercepted her hand, just a brush, but she felt a current of electric recognition intersect with the escalating tingle of apprehension as he took possession of her pack and swung it down with the ease of blowing a feather.

His eyes, a mesmerizing, unforgettable blue hue, engaged hers, making the strange mixture of internal compounds even more impossible to sort. Rather than elegant formal attire, he wore a Special Forces uniform with an impressive array of shoulder sleeve insignias. Binoculars hung on a leather strap around his neck, suggesting he had either driven at top speed from the villa or could leap tall buildings in a single bound and not break a sweat.

She swiped both palms on new suede fabric, a soft contrast to the chiseled planes of the movie star face she'd never thought to see again, except in haunting dreams that often took an erotic turn.

He extended his hand to help her off the Chinook and onto shared ground.

When she didn't take his offering because he had to be a ghost. When she said nothing because her throat had turned to dust. When she could only shake her head in disbelief, he smiled the same smile that had undone her at their first meeting, doffed a military beret from pale blonde hair, and said:

"Colonel Jerry Jenkins at your service, Mademoiselle Chene. I owe you an apology and an explanation, and after we finish with our little group tour, I believe a private conversation is not only in order, but long overdue."

~

JERRY'S ASSIGNMENT, personally delivered by The Ambassador, was straightforward:

1. Provide escort throughout Isabelle Chene's attendance on the premises
2. Skew her perceptions to ISIC's benefit
3. Ensure she does not gain access to detained subjects in the exterior cage and/or interior basement holding facility areas
4. Provide cover for Hugo's absence
5. Distract and entertain as necessary
6. Seduce if at all possible
7. Maintain emotional detachment/report to Miles if intrusive thoughts occur
8. If she makes any incriminating discoveries, terminate her immediately

"...And here we have the library," Miles was saying in his best twang as he threw open the ponderous double doors to reveal a very different version of the library they had scrambled to reinvent for the occasion.

The Library was still a very beautiful room with deep leather chairs, beautiful teak desks and mahogany wall paneling. Missing, however, were sadistic students and nearly dead smelly bodies providing object lessons in restraint. Gone too was the impressive display of interrogation instruments from ancient Asia to the Nazis in WW2. In their place was a museum quality oversized globe around which the rest of the room orbited, punctuated by groups of elegant rattan chairs and plump couches, perfect for quiet reading or a spirited scholarly debate. Vibrant Persian rugs were selectively scattered to hide suspicious stains on the gleaming teak floors.

The remaining volumes of books, manuscripts, and even scrolls, all the resource materials that had been curated from the top CIA and NSA archives with an emphasis on human experiments and everything ever written on mind control, was all boxed up and ready to be transferred to

Thailand. In their informative place were other volumes dedicated to world history, Western Civilization, the French Revolution, an entire wall on Asian conflict, a section of major religious texts—the Bible, Torah, Quran, Vedas, Egyptian Book of the Dead, Tao Te Ching, Buddhist Sutras —and supporting literature with an emphasis on religion and war.

"...and now as you can see, Miz Chene, the study of languages also receives an impressive share of the real estate on these here shelves, the reason being we have—or, had—such a large representation of countries secretly recruited into our programs. Not only did we need to provide textbooks in multiple languages, English and French classes were mandatory for those who did not arrive with a command of them already."

"*Oui*," Jerry interjected, and pulled out the first of two volumes of Alexis de Tocqueville's 1835 classic *De La Démocratie en Amérique*. He extended the leather bound tome to Isabelle, who hazarded a quick glance directly at him after spending the last half hour avoiding eye contact. When she did not immediately accept the book, he covered the awkward exchange, saying, "*Excusez-moi, peut-être préférez-vous celui-ci,*" which was a polite "sorry, maybe you'd prefer this one instead" and traded the first offering for the English version of *Democracy in America Vol. II.*

In response she lifted the camera she had strapped around her neck—a move that counterbalanced his removal of the binoculars just before starting the tour—and gestured for him to pose in front of the impressive marching lines of bound leather against the wall.

"Can you hold up the book and stand there, please?"

Before she could *click* he positioned the book in front of his face.

Swift to intervene, The Ambassador moved to insert himself into the framework while Jerry noted Kate's attention remained on her husband. Any concerns of his being recognized as the infamous Ghost Soldier who had nearly killed her at the Peace Mission Hospital years before had clearly been unfounded.

"My apologies, Isabelle, but perhaps you could take my picture instead? While I am a public figure, discretion must be employed to protect the identities of the two gentlemen here and any other key personnel on the premises since we need to assume hostile entities will review anything that goes out in print and they could become targets after being assigned to another post. I thought I'd made that stipulation clear in the agreement we signed, but apparently not, so please forgive the unintentional oversight."

"I understand," she said agreeably enough, though Jerry noted how she scanned the room as if seeking out any other details that may have been unintentionally overlooked. Her pointed overlooking of him, however, could not have been more blatant while they continued the tour.

Next stop: The compound's infirmary, complete with a spotless surgical suite, five empty hospital beds, and absolutely no dental chairs remaining. Those had been consigned to the bowels of the basement where they now kept company with poor Gregg.

Just as Isabelle noted, "What an impressive medical facility you have," Jerry spied a stray extracted molar much too near a chic leather boot.

Maneuvering himself closer, he pointed to an adjoining room where a long white curtain divided the areas, and as he had when the moon cloaked them on a balcony and an imminent kiss was hastened by unwanted company, he swiftly considered his options: Tooth enamel, harder than steel with a 5 on the Mohs hardness scale, made any discreet grinding with his boot a no-go, along with skittering it across the floor and hopefully under a recently unoccupied hospital bed.

A handkerchief in his back pants pocket suddenly became his best friend. Dropping the square of white linen just as he announced, "Let's have a look in there, shall we? That is where the X-ray equipment is kept, isn't it, Dr. Miles?"

"Uh, why, it certainly is." Miles gave him a confused glance, but then took the hint and moved things in that direction while Jerry swept up the handkerchief along with the tooth and shoved the evidence into his back pants pocket.

What else could they have missed? Clearly another clean sweep was in order once the visitors were safely consigned to their private quarters. Kate included. While he didn't know the extent of her clearance or own clandestine functions, this was a first and only visit, coupled with The Ambassador cautioning discretion with her as well.

As they exited the medical area and passed a few Vietnamese orderlies who had yet to jump ship, Jerry could feel the nip of impatience. This "tour" could take hours once lunch was rolled in, even minus the obvious areas they needed to avoid at all costs, and his orders to "distract and entertain as necessary" were something he'd been looking forward to. He had expected Isabelle to be taken off guard to see him, but this reluctance to acknowledge his presence was not how things had played out in his mind. He'd hardly gotten any sleep, and nothing was measuring up to all the reunion scenarios in his imagination.

"You know," he suddenly said to the group, "While there is still a lot left to see, I believe there is one particular area of the compound that Mademoiselle Chene would enjoy inspecting. If the rest of you don't mind, it would be my pleasure to escort her to the film and photography labs."

For the first time she looked at him full in the face, her slightly tilted Eurasian eyes and thick sooty lashes capturing his own. Her eagerness was palpable and hopefully stronger than any aversion she might have to spending time alone with him, despite her suggested, "Why don't we all go together?"

"Actually, if you don't mind, Isabelle, I could use a little break along with a nice strong coffee." Kate covered a yawn. "We got up awfully early this morning."

"By all means, the two of you go ahead," Phillip agreed, brushing a kiss to Kate's hand.

"Dr. Miles?" Isabelle asked, "Would you care to join us?"

"Well, now, that would be mighty nice..." Miles was looking at Isabelle a little too appreciatively. A glance at Jerry and he cleared his throat. "But I do have other duties to see to while the four of you enjoy yourselves. Mr. Ambassador and Colonel Jenkins, I believe you can take it from here. Perhaps we can all meet up for a nice happy hour in the Cantina later today."

Phillip and Kate disappeared right after Miles.

And then it was just Jerry and Isabelle for the first time since he had longingly watched the small of her back retreat so she could accept a prestigious award, only for Hugo to catch him wanting what he could never have, while Isabelle would never know about the syringe in his pocket that he would stab into her playwright friend's neck.

Nodding in the direction of the photo lab, Jerry did something he hadn't anticipated needing in this situation: The 7 tap middle finger to thumb exercise to settle himself down. Just seeing her, being near her, was shaking him.

They had gone exactly five steps when he put down the backpack he had happily carted from one room to another, caught her arm, and urged her to face him.

The slight resistance he met coincided with the profile she turned.

"Isabelle, look at me."

"No."

191

"Why not?"

"Because I don't trust you. Troy."

"Understandably so, I wouldn't trust me either. But I think the real reason you won't look at me is because you don't trust yourself with me."

CHAPTER 22

I sabelle remembered a time when she was six years old. She was not quite sure how to swim but thought she could dog paddle her way to safety if she had to after another child dared her to jump in as far as she could into the pool and swim her way back.

A swimming instructor had emerged in time to drag her out of the deep end after the other children shrieked in alarm when she went under a final time and was not coming back up.

This felt a lot like that.

"Do you like cats?"

His unexpected question was enough to chance a guarded meeting of eyes. He gave her a disarming smile she would be foolish to trust.

"I once had a Burmese cat, when I was a girl."

"That's what I have. After I show you the photography lab, maybe you'd like to meet him? His name is Panther."

He said it with a boyish enthusiasm that was far from the suave Troy Donahue look alike she'd met at a black tie fine arts gala. Wait, make that Troy Hunter. Now he was Colonel Jerry Jenkins. If that was really his name.

"Are you trying to worm your way past my defenses?"

"Maybe." He wiggled a finger. "Probably." A chuckle. "Is it working?"

I can be Troy Donahue for the night. That's what he'd said when she introduced him to her friend, Vuong Quan, only for Vuong to disappear about the same time "Troy" vanished. And sandwiched in between was clearly a performance between The Ambassador, Hugo, and a smooth operator who worked in some clandestine capacity.

"A little," she admitted. "You seem to have a lot of practice at convincing people of what they need to be convinced of to suit your purposes. I'm just not sure what your purpose could have been to..." Isabelle paused. She had started to say "to seduce me that night," but he hadn't, even though she would have gladly been seduced.

"The time we spent together meant a lot to me." His smile, like his eyes, shifted dangerously. "It was completely unplanned and absolutely wonderful."

"Oh, really?" She wanted to believe him. About both parts.

"You approached me, not the other way around," he reminded her. "And when you did, I couldn't believe my luck—or the utter lack of it. I was on assignment, not there to meet a woman whose work I had admired for years. Who proved to be more engaging in person than I was prepared for." His laugh was short, self-directed. "Did I just say `engaging?' Since I'm trying to be honest here in a way I wasn't able to be with you then, let me correct that to a more accurate assessment of initial impressions: I thought you were the most intriguing, approachable, gorgeous, and yes, engaging, woman I'd ever met, with the most amazing laugh I'd ever heard, and I wanted to do a lot more than find out if you tasted as delicious as you looked."

She was here on an assignment of her own. She shouldn't ask. She absolutely shouldn't.

"And...did I?"

"No." His head descended while hers swam a little. "You tasted even better."

Fool me once, shame on you. Fool me twice, shame on me.

"Do you have any idea what happened to Quan?"

A pause.

"Excuse me?"

His breath smelled like fresh mint... with a touch of sweet black licorice. Absinthe?

"Vuong Quan. My playwright friend who joined us at the table, then disappeared for good about the same time you did."

"I'm so sorry. I had no idea."

Again, she wanted to believe him.

"Where did you go after you left me?"

"Back to work. The kind of work that didn't include being unexpectedly distracted by a most distracting woman at a highly inopportune time."

"Until recently I had a residence and a working phone. You could have found me. You could have called. You didn't."

"You're right. I could have." As he recited her now defunct Nha Trang address and phone number, she felt the brush of his fingertip tucking a stray tendril behind her ear. It was a discreet but intimate gesture that she was no more immune to than the lowering of his voice to a near whisper. "I came close, more times than you'll ever know."

"Close only counts in horseshoes and hand grenades, Colonel."

He quirked a brow. "Exactly."

Isabelle licked dry lips. His eyes followed the movement and she wished for the lip gloss Kate had given her that tasted like the melon of its tint.

There were questions she should be asking, questions about his position here, about Hugo's whereabouts, about the entire orchestration of this meeting that was by no means coincidental—*did Kate know?*—yes, so many questions she should be asking him now, and yet all that emerged was:

"Should I consider myself warned then?"

He laid two fingertips at the base of her throat. It was a light touch but she could feel the blood in her veins pumping like mad, the sound of *ba-dump-ba-dump-ba-dump* pulsing between her ears. She felt the same fight or flight instinct of a fox pursued by a pack of hounds, or a rabbit racing from the talons of a bird of prey, and yet...

The deep end beckoned.

He answered her with an enigmatic half smile, the removal of his fingertips and the cordial extension of a palm in the direction they had been walking before he'd stopped, caught her arm, and made her want to know if she looked as delicious to him now as she had nearly five years before.

"Let's pick this up later—after I take you to meet Panther. But first, I believe there's a photography lab that will be even happier to see you than the other way around. Shall we?"

∾

THEY HAD BEEN in the lab all of two minutes and Jerry was wondering if he should have checked in with Miles yesterday. He'd known this would be tough—the whole maintain emotional detachment/report intrusive thoughts impossible from the get-go—but nothing had prepared him for the one-two sucker punch to both gut and groin that one look at Isabelle had landed. And landed. And landed.

He couldn't stop looking at her.

Phillip's itemized list of his responsibilities were no doubt crucial in The Ambassador's mind, but they were edging closer and closer to go fuck yourself territory in his.

"I can't believe this place!" Isabelle exclaimed yet again. "And just look at this UPI 16S—I could kiss it! I can't wait to get to work on all the film I brought with me."

"There's more. Just wait till you see this." Jerry, jumping at his chance to impress her, strode several yards across the expansive room to produce a chunky, eight pound piece of photographic equipment that was beyond state of the art.

Isabelle's jaw literally dropped.

"What IS it?"

"You're looking at the future of photography: The world's first digital camera. It was just invented by a Kodak engineer—Steve somebody, nice guy, kind of geeky, but totally knows his sh...stuff. Anyway, The Ambassador flew him in country to bring his latest version and personally give a few of us a little tutorial. It can digitalize all the light information, record it, and in 23 minutes reproduce the photograph." Sounding smart even to himself, Jerry added, "It's still a work in progress, but..."

Isabelle was looking at him intently. Like he was someone really interesting. Maybe even more interesting than the world's first digital camera.

"Will you teach me how it works?" Her gaze remained on him, not the camera.

"Of course." His knees felt odd. Weak.

"When?"

Pretending to check the black Rolex Submariner on his wrist, he was about to reply, "Would now be soon enough?" when something that felt like the flip of a switch went off in his head. Just as immediately his acute awareness of Isabelle and their surroundings skyrocketed to a psychedelic pitch. The mission he had been assigned distilled into *Escort. Skew. Restrict. Cover. Distract/entertain. Seduce. Detach. Terminate if necessary.*

His gaze riveted onto Isabelle's expectant expression. It looked like a bullseye had been circled around her head, with her face dead center of the target.

"Colonel…?"

"Jerry," he corrected. His voice sounded normal, so why did he feel so strange looking at her, even as the bullseye dissipated with her quiet approach, so the closer she came, the more complete his focus on exotic eyes, hinting of shyness with the fan of thick lashes? The scent of jasmine from her skin infiltrated his senses and the memory of frangipani lifting from a moonlit garden wove its own kind of spell, competing with whatever else was going on in his head.

She covered his wrist, the face of the watch, with her palm. It was a tentative touch, but warm and human. Extraordinarily arousing.

"Jerry," she repeated softly. "Thank you for bringing me here. You have no idea what a gift this is to me. The past month—make that the past year…or two, three—let's just say things have been extremely difficult. Not just for me, of course, for almost everyone I know. But losing my home, even my ability to get my work out to the public, has been a particular kind of torture. I've—"

Her voice caught. Eyes glistened.

He couldn't move the hand she still touched; it felt shackled with velvet handcuffs.

With his free hand he searched his uniform until he connected with the handkerchief in his back pants pocket. Just as he was about to pull it out, do the whole knight in shining armor with a hankie routine, the unmistakable protrusion of a tooth stopped him cold.

* *If she makes any incriminating discoveries, terminate her immediately*

As clear as yesterday he was on that balcony again, a glance confirming it would be a killing distance, the sound of revelry in the background muting any last screams while she fell—if he didn't strangle her first.

He hadn't been sure at the time if he could do it.

Shoving the white linen deep into its hiding place, he touched the hint of moisture just under her right eye, traced the curve of her cheekbone with an inquisitive fingertip, then painted the bow of her upper lip with the last traces of a single tear. His gaze zeroed in on her mouth in total, lips smooth and pink, slightly parted and ripe for the tasting.

"The first kiss was rushed," he said almost to himself, "And the second one too public to do your mouth justice."

Her breathing quickened and he didn't need his senses enhanced to notice the dilation of her pupils, dark brown nearly swallowed by a turbulent sea of black.

Once more he found her pulse at the base of her throat, pressed a thumb into its center. Carefully, just so he could feel the pump of blood beneath soft flesh.

Her arms came around his neck. Her fingers plowed through his hair, insistently urging his head to hers.

"I don't know if I should trust you," she whispered. "I'm sure that I shouldn't. But I still want you to do my mouth justice and, for as long as it lasts, make this whole ugly world go away."

CHAPTER 23

Consigned to the basement beneath the sprawling facility above him, Gregg surveyed his new quarters. New, as of just yesterday... he thought. Without a clock, without a window, it was impossible to tell if it was day or night.

Concrete walls surrounded the space that was too large and well-appointed to be considered a cell. Especially after spending countless hours, days, who knew how long, in a little box resembling a coffin, where he had scratched out with his fingernails

Gregg Kelly, PhD
Pasadena, CA USA
10/1/1940 - ?

He hadn't done it in case his dead body was miraculously retrieved and sent to Shirley or his parents in California. It was so he wouldn't completely lose himself before the seemingly inevitable happened.

Comparatively speaking his new quarters, complete with a private bathroom, refrigerator filled with beer and Pepsis, and of course the requisite desk with a typewriter upgrade, qualified as the temple of Angkor Wat.

Knowing cameras were everywhere, he resisted the urge to flip off one in the right corner, moon the one in the left, and/or throw the very decent brew he was not too principled to guzzle at another camera situated beneath an overhead fan.

No, he could not be so stupid as to reveal his real thoughts, his real state of mind, or the fact that he had survived the unsurvivable, in large part by pretending to be as mentally crippled, compromised, all but destroyed, as he needed Miles and his cohorts to believe he was.

Including Jerry Prince.

And yet... *Why he wasn't angrier with Jerry?*

Jerry, who had nearly taken out the entirety of the Peace Mission Hospital back in '69 and murdered Shirley's husband.

Jerry, who had written such darkly disturbing entries about his own childhood that it made the horror novel he'd recently picked up, *Carrie*, by some new author named King, read like a moral fable.

Jerry, who had strapped him into a wheelchair, ferried them both into a secret elevator, and left something of a welcome basket behind: A stack of well-thumbed *Playboy* and *Penthouse* magazines. Bottle of Jack Daniels. A bunch of snacks including a box of Thin Mints Girl Scout cookies —*where the hell had those come from?*—and yeah, he really wanted to tear into that box.

Jerry, who had extended a dog-eared copy of *War And Peace* before back-stepping closer to the only door in or out, saying, *"Sorry, Gregg. I know I brought you in and it's been hell, but, nothing personal, okay? Just doing my job."*

Maybe he'd made a mistake by dropping the act even for a second, but when he urgently called out before Jerry could close the door, *"Is Shirley okay?"* The curt nod he'd received was even better news, way better news, than getting sprung out of a nail scratched coffin. It also suggested that maybe Jerry wasn't completely made of hate, and had some kind of humanity left somewhere inside.

"Knock-Knock!" heralded Miles's sudden entrance, accompanied by a cart draped in white linen.

Despite the delicious aroma, Gregg shuddered to think of what might be waiting under a large domed lid covering a silver tray. Besides being subjected to a variety of psychoactive chemical cocktails, suspected hypnosis while he was under the influence, isolation, sensory deprivation, assorted forms of torture including electroshocks, the element of the unknown, of the truly shocking to the mind, was not off the table.

Could there be a head on the platter, surrounded by an array of cheese, sausage, fresh fruit? Maybe a coiled snake, poised to strike upon his lift of the lid?

"Wow! I'm not sure what I did or said to deserve this, but..." Gregg hobbled over to the mini fridge, busted out a cold bottle of beer, added a Pepsi to it, then reluctantly offered his bottle of Jack too, playing the gracious host with a substantial touch of Igor thrown in. "Can you stay and join me?"

In response Miles pulled up a chair, swung it around so he straddled it, accepted the beer, and asked, "So, how are you doing, pardner? Any problems adjusting to your new room?"

"Are you kidding? With accommodations and room service like this, why would I ever want to leave?"

"Funny you should mention that since leaving's what I want to talk to you about. Amongst other things." Miles took a draw on the beer that Gregg sorely wished was laced with arsenic. "I hope you realize how much I value the association of another psychological professional. That paper you wrote for me on external object relations theory was truly remarkable. Downright inspiring."

"Really? I'm...flattered." It wasn't completely untrue. That was disturbing. "In what way did it inspire you?"

"Let's just say that the resulting experiment impressively illustrates the higher effectiveness of mind control over brainwashing." Miles made a face. "All the unpleasantness that brainwashing entails—you know, torture, coercing subjects do things against their will—is efficient when you only have limited time to achieve measurable results, but it's so common, so coarse and pedestrian. And then we have mind control: Intelligent, elegant, creative. It's the difference between getting in the mud to force someone else to drink it, and having them willingly agree to join you for whatever it is you're serving in their tea. I know which party I'd rather go to, whether as the invitee or the host. How about you?"

"Yes, yes, agreed." Somehow Gregg managed an eager nod instead of a snarl. *The motherfucker.* The difference was that the controller positioned themselves as an actual friend, or helper, to manipulate the person they wanted to control. "And even if hypnosis is employed, that's ultimately going to be far more effective than beatings or waterboarding. Certainly more elegant than..." *Rape with snakes. Mutilation. Rectal feeding.* Thank God none of that had been done to him, at least not that he recalled, or any of the other more chilling coercions Miles had ticked off in previous conversations. Although he had posited such torture techniques as distasteful and "not his thing" the underlying message had been that whatever Gregg was being subjected to could be exponentially worse if he was too resistant to getting on board with Team Miles.

"So," Gregg continued, leaning forward, "What else can you tell me about what you managed with your own, um, twist to the paper I wrote?"

"Oh, just a little something with a wearable gift."

"Like an amulet? Some kind of hocus-pocus with a magic ring?"

"Boy oh boy, do I get a kick out of you!" Miles slapped his leg and let go a big guffaw. "More like Pavlov's dog so the associative object triggers a strong suggestion that's been embedded into the ventromedial prefrontal cortex."

"Right, right. The vmPFC."

"See? See!" Miles waved a finger in the air. "That's what I'm talking about. Somebody who can talk my language around here. Nobody else is going to rattle off vmPFC like it's milk on a grocery list. But anyway, just between us, shortly before we rearranged the upstairs, I did something in the surgical center that would blow even Pavlov away. Curious?"

As much as he hated to admit it, he was.

"Well, I did a little surgery. On a dog. Make it six dogs. Obviously, I had to move them out to other surroundings—they've got a nice pen, plenty to eat and drink—and you will not believe what I accomplished with this experiment." Leaning forward, Miles whispered confidentially, "I embedded brain implants that I can operate with a remote control."

"A remote control? As in…?"

"Yep, you got it. I can make them run, turn, and stop. Not with a verbal command, but with the press of a button. A button right here, right on my watch. I simply push *that*, it sends a tiny radio signal that triggers the implant in the brain and the implant signal is paired with the response activity I want. Do you have any idea what this could mean for the future of the military?"

The beer he'd been sipping lodged in Gregg's throat.

"Wow," he managed to cough out. His eyes felt big as saucers, his head unnaturally light. "That is phenomenal! Where do you go from there?"

"On the QT, I have something even more advanced in the works. Nobel prize level. You'll see." While Gregg struggled to smile and nod, Miles burst out laughing. "Now, now. Not to worry, I need your brain for more than an experiment. And that's what brings me to my real reason for this visit. I want to take you to the new facility in Thailand with me. Not sure when that will be. Knowing The Ambassador, he'll stretch it out till the last minute before giving up the mother ship, but when the time comes? You could have a real bright future ahead. Now, if you're agreeable with that, put 'er there, pardner!"

Miles extended his hand, offered a gentleman's shake on it.

As Gregg played along, accepted the awful offering, he further pretended to drive an even harder bargain. "Okay, count me in. But, what's my new position to be?"

"I'm bringing you in as a highly valued colleague and research assistant. If you can produce some additional papers to augment my own research and help me with this big Exit Report I'm already crunching on, that will definitely up our chances to convince The Ambassador that you're much more an asset to us in a research capacity than, well, the alternative."

"Of being exposed as a spy."

Miles's sudden interest in lifting the domed lid was answer enough.

"Well now, what have we here? Looks like chateaubriand and enough for two. Please, allow me." And as Miles assumed plating duties he chatted away, until casually mentioning, "Did you know that it's possible to literally scare a person to death?"

Gregg choked down the delectably seasoned fillet of tenderloin and managed, "Literally? Like, for real? C'mon."

"It's true! I did it once. Well, actually three times to make sure it wasn't a fluke and to validate my findings."

"Did you present it in a protocol?"

"Of course! It's all there—original hypothesis, experimental design, outcome and etcetera."

"Including videotape to back your findings up?"

"Don't you know it, Old Hoss! Want to see? Oh, wait. Damn, forgot. Boxed it all up with the rest of our material from the photo lab. Wasn't ready to yet but some plans got changed, so basically here's what I did..."

After recounting how he had hooked up a subject's brain and stimulated the amygdala—the portion responsible for senses, muscles, hormones that can react to a sense of threat—Miles crowed: "Then after I stimulated it once and got the desired response, I hit it and hit it and hit it over and over again. It was just like watching a monster movie that keeps on going and going and going and getting worse and worse and worse. It just wears a body out!"

"You mean, almost like getting beaten to death from the inside out by your own biochemical responses to what your brain is perceiving?"

"Exactly! Go, go, go amygdala! Pump that heart! Pump that adrenalin, that glucose! It was like watching the fight or flight instinct with a front row view of the brain, seeing the power of internalized fear unleashed.

It's huge, the power of fear. No wonder people will do just about anything to avoid it."

As he regarded Miles savoring his chateaubriand almost as much as his macabre bragging rights, Gregg tried to imagine what could possibly frighten this mad dispenser of it. Could Miles have enough functioning human parts to have some fear of the unknown? Could even a seed of self-doubt worm its way into a vulnerable crevice that might undermine such a sick sonofabitch?

Don't do it, don't challenge him, Gregg told himself. *Don't. Go. There.*

"While what you say is true," he heard himself saying anyway, "There *are* things more powerful than fear and the limbic system is not the only thing that controls it."

"Example, please, Dr. Kelly."

"When a stranger races into a burning building to save a crying baby."

"Mmm...yes, you are correct that humans are capable of courageous acts." With a crafty grin, Miles pivoted in the anticipated direction. "Thanks to the sgACC."

"True and agreed again." *Just leave it there. Drop it now and let him preen.* "However, while the anterior cingulate cortex plays a vital role in empathy, emotion, and decision making, I would argue that there's more than biochemistry at work."

"Oh, really?" Down went the fork. Fingers steepled. "By all means, Dr. Kelly, please proceed."

"Very well. Just as dopamine, oxytocin, serotonin, adrenaline, and a flood of hormones might be the chemicals our brains release that can make usually sane people literally crazy in what we universally call love, it cannot explain why one certain person can trigger that response and a thousand others simply do not, no matter the effort expended." *He has no idea what you're talking about.* "Experimentally speaking, let's say you hit up Subjects A, B, and C with an IV full of the same chemicals—okay, give Subject C a placebo just to be fair—and I would bet the house that the subjects' attachment would be to the drug itself, and not the purveyor of it, even if there may be some associative effect."

"And from this we are to conclude...?"

"That while you may have the ability to literally scare someone to death, no one can biochemically coerce anyone to love them, which suggests to me that in terms of power, the latter is superior. It cannot be controlled and it cannot be killed."

"I wouldn't be so sure about that." Miles gave a puff to his knuckles, shined them on his shoulder. "I taught a monster to cry."

"You did what?"

"We'll save that for another discussion. Anything else?"

"Only that…" *Don't be a fool. Toss him his winning shot and tell him he got a slam dunk.* "From one clinician to another, I think it's a foregone conclusion that while one might be able to elicit a desired response in a controlled environment, real life lacks the same environmental controls, which makes the desired outcome more of a crap shoot. Even so, what you achieved was clearly a breakthrough. Something I never could have envisioned myself."

"Why, thank you for saying so. Despite the clinical nature of the study, the fact remains that my hypothesis, my protocol, and experimental outcomes are solid and could very well be duplicated in an uncontrolled environment. After all, who is to say that we have not had casualties of war who literally died of terror before a bomb or a grenade appeared to take them out? Being `scared to death' is clearly more than a hyperbolic little saying. Just ask my subjects. Oh. Wait. You can't. They're dead. And you know what? It was amazing to witness." He leaned so close Gregg could smell the beer on his breath. "I must also admit to a sensation that was almost but not quite that of being intoxicated."

"As a matter of professional curiosity, I wonder if that may be why you didn't stop short of flat lining your three subjects? Perhaps from a nice hit of dopamine being released into your own nucleus accumbens?"

Silence. Chin pulling. Enlarged pupils searching the ceiling.

Then training him into laser point focus.

"While there was no doubt activity in the pleasure center of my own brain at the time, it was primarily due to having my theory unequivocally confirmed. I am not a sadist or a sociopath, Dr. Kelly. Unfortunately, rats can only go so far. They have very small brains and are not human. I keep polite, professional protocol with my subjects, who are providing a service for the advancement of mankind. It helps, even verges on mandatory, that such subjects might be considered expendable enemies. As a physician and clinical psychologist, I'm not an anomaly at all, and I would think you would be one of the first to understand that. Doctors have been doing such things forever. Even the Incas did brain surgery and I'm fairly certain they did not practice on their friends or relatives, while enemies were, and still are, acceptable subjects. After all, they're trying to seize your power and threaten that which you're trying to protect. Nonetheless, even one's enemies deserve to be treated with respect, particularly when they are contributing to a higher purpose. When I lose a subject, I like to think that they've moved forward and aged and had their entire life span, just very quickly, not simply snuffed out like a candle flame. So, when the monitor flat lined with my first subject, then the one after him, and the one after her..."

Was she pregnant? Gregg bit so hard on his tongue he tasted blood.

It was only when Miles segued into even more troubling territory that Gregg stopped nodding and said, "Say that again?"

"I said that we can't have you being recognized if we take you to the new facility in Thailand instead of, you know, that really unpleasant alternative that won't do anyone any good before we leave here. Fortunately, I do have some credentials beyond neurosurgery in the operating room thanks to assisting with a major reconstructive procedure and perfect memory recall of it. What do you think of Jerry's new look?"

Blink. Blink. *Don't panic.* "He's... he looks like every guy wished he looked."

"Including you?"

Gregg did not remember how he answered.

He only knew that upon waking he was still in his new quarters, but something felt off. Maybe because he couldn't remember going to bed, or even how the evening ended.

Had the demi-glace been drugged?

He felt a protrusion on his left hand. A strip of surgical tape held an intravenous needle in place, on ready for a syringe or emergency IV.

Gregg checked the remainder of his person.

He was laying on a comfortable mattress. Black Vietnamese pajamas, tops and bottoms in place. *Had he been wearing them at dinner?*

Peeling a sore spine off the bed, he padded upon heels and insteps, also tender, toward an adjoining bathroom, also dimly lit. Filling his palms with cold water, he splashed his face.

His skin didn't register the bracing contact.

Gregg glanced into a mirror above the sink—

Only to urgently grab for the porcelain just before he hit the floor.

CHAPTER 24

S crub. Scrub. Scrub.

Jerry knew he didn't have a lot of time to make himself presentable before leaving the villa he had inherited from Hugo, but he just couldn't seem to get himself clean. The idea that Isabelle might catch even a whiff of the stench his pores could have absorbed was unbearable. As for his disgustingly stinky clothes, they were already washing on hot with extra Tide and Clorox. Good thing he knew how to do his own laundry since the house boy had disappeared with Hugo and the koi.

If he never had to go back to the dungeon area again, it would be too soon. Since he couldn't risk Isabelle overhearing him on a two-way radio, it was essential to make periodic checks on the guards overseeing their remaining tiger cage prisoners. They didn't have a lot but a 24/7 high alert watch was essential—even on Izzy, who wasn't faring so well despite the extra water and protein he was slipping him. It could be worse. The Ambassador seemed content to simply let his prized captives languish for the time being with limited rations but no other punishments while playing host to Isabelle.

Jerry noticed how Kate always seemed to show up about the time he needed to see to his unpleasant but necessary duties, all the while knowing that if Isabelle discovered something incriminating in his absence there was big trouble, which could only be made worse if he was the source of the incrimination due to something as simple as putrid smelling clothes.

Or, a tooth in a hankie.

Forcing himself out of the shower, Jerry buffed his backside with a big white towel, wondered what Isabelle would think of his Irezumi body art while he saw to the front, and welcomed Panther's *meow* as she did sleek circle eights around his ankles.

"I know you're crazy about her, too," he told Panther. "And because you're the best kitty in the world, I'll even let you share our date night later. Part of it anyway."

That's right, a real date. Dinner. A movie. Then more making out on his rattan couch... make that Hugo's rattan couch, but it was his now, for as long as the NVA was held at bay.

Xuân Lộc had fallen the day Isabelle arrived—just last Monday. It was Friday now. She had spent the first few days developing accumulated film, even allowing him to help her, then all of yesterday and today had been dedicated to transmitting her best shots over the UPI, so she hadn't really even started on the assignment she'd been brought in for. No argument from him! He could only hope she would take her sweet time.

Would tonight be the night? He was trying to give Isabelle something he didn't have much practice at, what might be considered a courtship. Just thinking about her created a sense of excitement that turned into near euphoria in her presence. It was very confusing. He had always had a strong need for sex which was very different from what had once been a compelling need to kill. Killing had filled an emotional need while sex was a physical outlet dictated by nature. Obviously, that made prostitutes his optimum choice: He paid, they provided, and it never got messy with expectations for emotions he was not capable of producing.

All that had changed the first time he met Isabelle. After that night at the gala he had begun fantasizing that his hookers were her. And now that she had reentered his life, every sense he possessed lit up like a pinball game with bells ringing and levers flipping and lights exploding all over the place. It reminded him of the new movie he was going to impress Isabelle with—a first run private showing of *Tommy* in a luxe private theater even The Who might envy.

Yeah. Dinner and a movie with Isabelle, the ultimate Acid Queen. All he had to do was think about her and he felt like he was tripping.

Jerry carefully selected a pressed pair of black slacks, white dress shirt, Italian silk tie. Belt and shoes, also Italian. Sport coat, Armani. The blue contacts really went well with his bleached blond hair, but a part of him wished she could see the real shades of both so he could find out if she liked the outside package just the same.

He splashed some Aramis onto the neck she had pressed her lips to the night before. A watch was essential but he chose his old Seiko over the fancier new Submariner. Miles had wondered why he wasn't constantly wearing it lately. Miles had been asking a lot of other questions, too, like what he and Isabelle talked about when they were alone, was he having secret thoughts about her, how far had they gone intimately, just all kinds of private shit that wasn't any of his GD business. Miles had even wanted to do some EEGs to get a better idea of what might be going on in his FEW's brain since he didn't seem quite himself since Isabelle had arrived.

And that much was true. Jerry wasn't sure what was happening to him, but whatever this crazy thing was, he never wanted it to end.

"I CAN'T DECIDE. The little black dress or the jeans and muslin peasant top so it doesn't look like I tried too hard. What do you think, Kate?"

"I think you should skip both and go straight to the kimono. Make it the pink one with the peonies. Guaranteed to drive him wild." Raising her hand in a claw, she growled, *"Raarrrh!"*

"Mon dieu, what is the matter with me?" Plopping on the edge of the ensemble strewn bed, in her very own bungalow that could have been copied from a luxury getaway ad, Isabelle accepted Kate's offering of what seemed to be an endless supply of Krug. "I feel like a virgin on her first date after spending nearly all week with a man who hasn't pushed for more than holding hands when no one's looking and some of the most amazing make out marathons on his couch!"

"Really?" Kate threw her gorgeous blonde head back and laughed, then clinked her crystal flute to Isabelle's. "You don't meet guys like that every day. No wonder you're nervous. Maybe he's a keeper, this Colonel Jerry Jenkins of yours."

"No, no, he is not mine. Yes, I admit he turns me on. The way he thinks, the way he talks, his intelligence and curiosity, how he listens and seems to actually see the real me…" Isabelle shook her head ferociously. It still didn't feel clear. "I know how he makes me feel, but I do not know him. Not about his past or what he actually does now. I know he works in some capacity for Phillip, for the government, the type of position where one asks no questions because all you will receive is silence, deflection, or lies. I dated a French spy once and swore never again. Subterfuge may be a requisite for intelligence agents, but it is poison for relationships."

Kate nodded sympathetically. "It can be. Unless you understand that some secrets are necessary between partners. Phillip doesn't tell me everything—not that he doesn't want to, but because he doesn't want to infiltrate our marriage with the burdens of his responsibilities outside of it. Can you imagine being married to a psychiatrist and he wants to tell you about the patient who committed suicide over the dinner you spent half a day cooking?"

"I don't think you ever spent half a day cooking anything."

And back went that exquisite blonde head again with a throaty burst of *hahahaha!!*

"No wonder I adore you, Isabelle. You tell it like it is. And my guess is that you know more about Colonel Drop Dead Dreamy than you think you do."

Isabelle considered that. *Did she?* When she had pressed Kate for details if she had them, Kate had convinced her that she had never met Colonel Jerry Jenkins before they landed at ISIC, and she'd had no idea he was the mystery man at the gala that had led to the fast bond the two women had established over cocktails and commiserations that night.

Theirs was an extension of what Isabelle had learned about forming often unlikely friendships in times of war: The odd thing about intimacy is that sometimes it does not take very long at all. You can meet and create a true friend in a single conversation. If the conversation continues, what was formed that first time is like a pearl increasing in value with the added layers of time and events creating depth and dimension. In special cases the person might even become a lover, which added another dimension to explore...

And it was that imminent dimension that had Isabelle deciding, "I will wear the Ao Dai you spotted for me that last day in Saigon."

"Excellent choice." With a grin, Kate added, "Nothing wrong with making him work for it."

As Isabelle surveyed the final results in a full-length mirror, Kate applauded her approval of the traditional Vietnamese form fitting long dress, split up the side to reveal matching red silk trousers. Kate then dusted a little more powder onto Isabelle's nose, wanded on more lip gloss and mascara, then artfully arrowed into her upswept do two exquisite lacquered chopsticks, inlayed with mother-of-pearl.

"Uh-huh," Kate pronounced. "He's a goner."

~

WHEN ISABELLE ANSWERED THE DOOR, Jerry could not have been more blown away if she had greeted him with a two-by-four and landed it straight between his eyes.

All he could see were stars.

"I picked these for you," The lilies were the same vibrant red as the killer silk she was poured into. For a moment he wondered if she had any idea what she was doing to him, only for the little giggle she hid behind her palm to assure him that she most certainly did.

"You brought me flowers! Jerry, how sweet."

As she accepted the flowers, he caught her hand, brought it to his lips.

"I'm glad you like them."

"I like you even more than the flowers."

"Are you flirting with me, Mademoiselle Chene?"

"Maybe. Probably. Is it working?"

Without regard for the lilies, he bent her back and completely demolished what looked like a carefully applied lip job. The flowers, crushed between their chests, did not fare much better, the petals falling to the floor once he let her up for air.

Isabelle pressed her ear to his chest, whispered, "I can hear your heart beating."

He wanted to say, "You make it beat too fast." And he wanted her to know the truth about him; that most people would say he had no heart, at least not one that was human. There was always so much he wanted to say to Isabelle that would forever go unsaid.

"What does it sound like?"

"Ba-dump. Ba-dump. Strong and steady. It sounds like life."

Then she looked up at him and in that singular moment he realized that he had never been in such clear and present danger of a situation outside his control. Which, in turn, put Isabelle in a dangerously unpredictable, precarious position.

He offered his arm. "Ready for dinner?"

Their dinner, complete with a cozy candlelit table for two, was served on the same palatial veranda filled with vases of white jasmine and red geraniums where he had enjoyed his first breakfast at ISIC almost exactly six years before.

The tropical call of night birds could be heard in the distance. Nearby was the soothing trickle of a fountain. Wind chimes tinkling.

All so familiar now. And yet, with Isabelle, laughing that amazing laugh of hers over a silly joke he had told her, it was as if the space they shared had been imbued with some magical effervescence.

Isabelle reached across the table and grasped his hand.

"Jerry, if you had a wish, what would it be?"

"That's easy." At least this much he could be honest about. "I would wish for an endless supply of nights just like this."

"Then we would share the same wish. Except…"

"Except, what?"

"My family," she confided. "I feel guilty being so happy right now, knowing how much they are all struggling to adjust. When those you love are struggling, it is much harder to accept one's own happiness, n'est-ce pas?"

"I would not personally know that," he admitted. "I didn't have much of a family growing up…" A little *blip*, almost like a tiny electrical shock, made him involuntarily twitch. Jerry ignored it. "But I hope your family appreciates how fortunate they are to have you."

"Merci, but I am the fortunate one. Although…" again she laughed and he just wanted to eat it up. "They can be real pains in the ass sometimes! Maybe you will get to meet them one day and see." She squeezed his hand; it had begun to hum from the inside out. "They would like you."

The girl who made him see stars wanted him to meet her cherished family.

Careful, came the internal whisper, *Don't forget what you do or who you are. This is make believe.*

And if this was make believe, with Isabelle blowing him a kiss then teasing his lips with a shrimp from her plate, just sign him up.

SOMEWHERE BETWEEN ERIC CLAPTON parading down a church aisle in a white robe and offering "Eyesight to the Blind" and Tina Turner dragging Roger Daltry around to hit him up as the Acid Queen, Jerry, ever so slowly, let his hand drift from Isabelle's shoulder to the rise of her right breast, encased in red silk.

When she leaned her head on his shoulder, it was all he could do not to fondle her in full, but with the light projecting from the screen, he had no intentions of giving Miles or anyone else a cheap thrill in the event they were being observed.

By the time Elton John was pounding a keyboard to slap down that deaf, dumb and blind kid, Isabelle had decided to do a little hand drifting herself, up from his knee to a tensed thigh that couldn't bear the suspense.

"Ready to get out of here?" he quietly suggested.

"I thought you'd never ask."

It was a bit of a walk from the intimate theater to Jerry's private villa, and a little cool so he took off his jacket, draped it over her shoulders. They passed a few military personnel who saluted him. A night cleaning crew bobbed their heads as they passed. Once beyond the main group of buildings, an unruly tropical swath of ferns and palms loomed on either side of a dimly lit path filled with the scent of wild jasmine. The sound of vegetation moving in the wind, of wildlife and skittering insects whispering in ominous tones, was joined by a faint, eerie howling.

"What *is* that?"

Jerry's jaw clenched. "We're close enough to the jungle that a lot of night sounds carry. And once you get outside the compound's perimeters we're not too far from some rice paddies." Deciding to speed the pace to what was now his villa, he scooped her up and strode purposefully ahead, when an answering howl had him suggesting, "My guess is that we're hearing someone else's date night out there."

"If that's the case, I wish they'd keep it down!"

Although he chuckled along with her, Jerry silently seethed. *Goddam JD and his brother.* Trying to freak out the guards with their creepy communications. However many precious days he and Isabelle had left, he did not need anyone or anything taking that from him. From *them.*

It was only a single word in a private thought, but it caught him off-guard. *Them.*

Having reached the veranda where a rattan fan eternally turned overhead, he could still hear Hugo saying, *Another drink? How do you like the absinthe, our lovely la fee verte? You know the little green fairy. She is magic, no? We will become good friends you and I... Tomorrow we will begin our classes. French. War. Gardening.*

Their trust tree had given root to a deep friendship, where they spoke in terms of "we" and "us." But it was not a romantic relationship and he had never thought to entangle his singularity with that of a woman to produce the coupling of him/her to *they/them.*

He should not take her inside. The couch would no longer be enough.

He would take her to his bed, and she would open her arms, open her thighs, and—

Nearly choking on his own groan, his feet were heedless of the inner command to *Wait! Stop!* as he carried her ever closer to the point of no return and back kicked the front door behind them.

"Would you care for some wine," he made himself say, "Or—"

"No." She put a fingertip to his lips. "Just you."

"Oh god," he breathed, and he knew he was in so much trouble. *They* were in trouble. And there was no will, no wherewithal, at his command to stop it.

At the side of the bed, he slid her down his length, their silhouettes angled in jagged lines upon the floor from a brilliant moon slashing through wide plantation blinds.

He pushed his much too large coat off her shoulders, let it fall.

The ferocious urgency that gripped him met an equally compelling mandate to make this experience last, to commit to memory every tic of the toc with her under his hands. He watched how his fingertips slid from the base of her throat to the rise of both breasts, still bound in rich scarlet silk, before he fully cupped her within his palms.

If she knew what your hands have done, the blood you've bathed them in, would she want them on her now?

As he paused on that hateful thought, Isabelle hastily undid his tie, tossed it the way of his coat. She slipped free the buttons on his shirt, all the way down to his belt.

There, he caught her fevered hands.

"Wait." His voice didn't sound like his own.

"For what?"

"For..." He had no idea what to say, or how to say it; all he knew was that this rare intimacy, with this rare woman, was too important to be a complete fraud.

"Isabelle, there's something that you need to know. I..." Bending low, into the shell of a delicate ear he whispered, "I'm not like other men."

Their lower clothing still in place, she pressed her belly against his straining groin and breathed into his seeking mouth, *"I know."*

MILES SWIPED HIS BROW, took off his headphones. If Jerry ever found out about this, he would be *furious.* And a furious Jerry Prince, even with all his tweaks and clinical reforming, was not something Miles ever wanted to deal with first hand.

Still, in many ways Jerry was his ultimate creation, and with creation came its own set of responsibilities for playing God: Jerry needed to be tracked for recent changes in behavior that Miles found disturbing. They had worked very hard to get his impulses firmly under control, even while the kitten—the one still alive—had been instrumental in restoring his humanity. How completely, Miles was not yet sure. And should Jerry's impulse control begin to slip, would other regressions follow? Another unknown.

The codes and commands that had been deeply embedded, and reinforced again and again, were imperative to maintain his hold over Jerry—who had begun to avoid him in direct proportion to time spent hovering over that woman. His posture, his voice, every nuance of expression indicated that the more Jerry was around her, the more he was acting on instinct.

The primal chest beating kind.

Another listen into the headphones assured Miles of that. Good. God.

Isabelle Chene was trouble. Miles had known it the second Jerry gave him that "don't even think about it" look of possession in the infirmary that had been scrubbed down at least three times since Jerry had gotten so worked up about finding that damn tooth.

I would argue that there's more than biochemistry at work. Just as the chemicals our brains release, that can make usually sane people literally crazy in what we call love, can't explain why one certain person can trigger that response and a thousand others simply do not. You may have the ability to literally scare someone to death, but you cannot biochemically coerce anyone to love you, which suggests to me that in terms of power, the latter is superior. It cannot be controlled and it cannot be killed.

Shit. Could Kelly have been onto something?

Six years of intensive work with Jerry and volumes of paper to document it. He could not afford to throw it all into the incinerator… Wait.

The incinerator wasn't the only thing keeping company in the basement with Kelly.

Having heard enough of the post-coital music Jerry and his little problem photographer were making, Miles pulled out his newest notebook. And he began to write.

CHAPTER 25

I sabelle glanced around the photography lab and felt an unexpected pang of loss as the inevitable closed in. After a week of its high-tech use, she was going to miss the trays filled with developing chemicals, the necessary darkness to process her light-sensitive photographic materials. She would miss experimenting with the Worlds' First Digital Camera and having such immediate access to the best UPI transmitter she had ever used.

But most of all she would miss the real reason she had not yet left.

So odd how she had arrived with an inexplicable unease, intent to leave as quickly as possible, only to have that unease slam into reverse when she confronted the appointment calendar in her backpack that had pronounced it Tuesday, April 29 this morning. In looking at the mostly empty pages going forward, she had wondered at her lack of urgency to rush back to Saigon where things were heating up even faster than anticipated.

Yesterday a mortar round had exploded at the Newport Bridge outside of Saigon, sending South Vietnamese troops running. The Ambassador, her primary news source, had indicated that journalists had been running with them. *But,* he had hastened to add, *please stay to finish up your work here and I'll get you out in plenty of time.*

The work she did was time sensitive. It was risky. And highly addictive. Getting that once in a lifetime shot, the blast of adrenaline, the way the sky looked at sunset and the taste of gin and tonic while the stars came out and you knew you were still alive after a near miss and would never feel so alive as this...

She had not realized her own ignorance.

Who knew there could be an adrenaline rush from the mere glimpse of a man who sipped Krug from her navel to set off an explosion of fireworks at dawn, beating the hell out of G&Ts still getting kicked back at midnight with the backdrop of exploding bombs?

The result was thrilling and yet disconcerting: Saigon was being threatened by nearby mortar rounds and her focus had never been so compromised. She had lost track of precious time, kept having to remind herself of where she was and why she was there in the first place: To grab a breaking story that could stir controversy, confront disturbing rumors in such venerable media as the BBC after one of their own had made shocking allegations he was unable to substantiate—and she had to do it in a rapidly shrinking window of time with the added incentive of getting a solid leg up on a golden ladder just when everything else was falling apart.

There was nothing sensational to find here; had there been, The Ambassador never would have invited her in. She was here to exonerate his pet secret project as it was being dismantled. But... could she have missed something? She had always prided herself on clear, independent thinking while opening others' eyes with the lens of her camera, so why was her relief so enormous that the most revealing discoveries she had made were private?

How did you get this scar on your knee? The fingertip that traced the long, thin white line had been light, curious, and carnally knowledgeable after that first night of alternately ferocious and tender... something more than sex.

Earlier in my career I was photographing a very beautiful tiger. It was supposed to be tame and I let down my guard. When it flexed its claws, all I received was a suggestion of the lethality it was still capable of, but the scar was a lesson to keep: Practice caution lest your subject not only be beautiful but deadly.

Horseshoes and hand grenades, he had softly reminded her. *Tigers aren't the only predators you have to watch out for.*

And he had proceeded to prove how entirely he could devour what safeguards she had left, leaving her shaken and shaking from the intensity of a hunger that she had never encountered, nor shared, before. Even so, there was still a sense that this man, who indeed was not like any other man she had known, was exercising restraint, merely flexing his claws while she scratched at the surface of something incomprehensively complex and deep. As for what the eye could readily see, even his movie star face had not prepared her for the magnificence of an unclothed physique with sinew, muscle, skin and bones so anatomically perfect as to be a marvel of human engineering. And while she had never cared much for body art before, the distinctive style of Japanese Irezumi cloaking his chest and sweeping up to the base of his neck was worthy of the canvas of flesh upon which the intricate spread of wings, outstretched claws, and a mythical raven's head with knowing eyes were inked.

The photograph she had begged to take had been denied, but in all else he was exceedingly generous.

And just as demanding.

A little involuntary shiver went through her as she hit the PLAY button of the portable cassette deck that would soon be sharing space with pink and blue kimonos in her backpack. The tape was a mix of her favorite R&B artists: Marvin Gaye, Stevie Wonder, Earth Wind & Fire, Barry White, Al Green, and best of all, Joe Simon. It was his voice that spilled out from the cassette Jerry had made just for her, and she felt all tingly all over again at Jerry's choice of the tape's opening number.

While "Drowning in a Sea of Love" played, she assembled her materials by rote, her thoughts returning yet again to how he had warned her and then invited her to join him in what felt closer to the middle of the South China Sea without a raft than a nice concrete pool with plenty of company to scream for help when she'd gone down one time, gone down two times, then wasn't coming back up.

She had been reckless then and she was being reckless now. There would be a price to pay for this, surely. No words had been spoken as to where they might go from here, if anywhere. But she had to believe he wouldn't just let her walk.

Well. It was time to find out before she got her heart completely broken. As soon as she was finished with today's work, she would request transport for…Saigon? Of course, Saigon. Since she hadn't seen a chopper parked on the helipad she would see if one could be brought in for her first thing in the morning. That would give her one last night to be reckless before she paid the piper for it.

Feeling more love zombie than human, Isabelle was grateful she could do the remaining work in the sleep she hadn't been getting:

Take the negatives and put on print paper to make a contact sheet.

Turn on the light in the enlarger. Once exposed to the light, time to develop, fix, and finally wash the photo paper in a stop bath and no, she was not going to bother with a sepia treatment for her present purposes.

It was a soothing process, almost like doing dishes while Barry White crooned, "You're the First, the Last, My Everything" while she relived in celluloid the practice range where Jerry had provided more than expert lessons in shooting her recently acquired .45 caliber officers pistol. Next were a series of shots of the deserted barracks where they had tested out the springs on a top bunk that ended up on the bottom while they laughed uproariously before things turned serious. It had been an indulgence to take a picture of the demolished results; not for public consumption, a memory shot just for them. As was the commissary wiped out of chocolate bars after he had bought what remained for her.

After that, a series of various garden shots. Her fave was where he had clipped a dozen pink peonies before she shot the swath remaining with concertina wire and guard posts in the distance.

Oh yes, the BBC would be yawning about now. Maybe TIME might be interested?

And here was that perfectly lovely shot of Ambassador Jordan in the library after Jerry had covered his face with the *Democracy in America Vol. II* tome she hadn't wanted to accept since she didn't trust herself if he touched her.

Next up, several shots of the impressive surgical facility and empty infirmary... beds?

Al Green was singing "Let's Stay Together" when Isabelle went very still.

She blinked. Closed her eyes tight then opened them again.

Her hands went numb as she lifted the contact sheet.

There was no air in the room, in her lungs. She couldn't breathe. The high pitch of bees filled her ears.

It couldn't be.

She looked again. Wanted to jab her eyes out.

This can't be real. You're having a nightmare. You need to wake up. WAKE UP! WAKE UP!!

"Isabelle?"

She jumped at the sound of his voice directly behind her, tried so very hard to wake up.

At his touch to her shoulder she nearly leaped out of her own skin. It felt like a thousand maggots were slithering through her pores when he insistently turned her to face him.

"Isabelle, is something wrong?"

His fingertips lifted her chin. Her teeth were chattering. She tried to look normal but she immediately knew... he knew. Eyes that had simmered hours before suddenly sharpened, turned an icy blue. Lips that knew every secret of her body, her mouth, hardened.

"Let's see what you have there, *ma chérie.*"

She tried to shake her head, but he had it locked in place. He suddenly had all of her locked in place, including the photographic contact sheet that was worse than a venomous, deadly snake.

Just as she tried to jerk a knee up to connect with his groin, she felt his hand on her throat, pressing into a point that had her eyes rolling into the back of her head.

As the world went black she heard his hypnotic whisper, "I'm so sorry I had to do this. I...I think I love you, Isabelle."

CHAPTER 26

Escort. *Skew. Restrict. Cover. Distract/entertain. Seduce. Detach.*
TERMINATE IF NECESSARY. TERMINATE. TERMINATE.
TERMINATE.

The orders he'd been given continued to echo in Jerry's brain, the final one growing louder, LOUDER until he slapped both sides of his head hard enough to blow out his eardrums and internally roared back:

SHUT UP! SHUT UP! DID YOU HEAR ME? I SAID SHUT THE FUCK UP!!!!

Silence. Except for Al Green continuing to sing *loving you forever...* while he stared at the soft heap on the darkroom floor that was Isabelle and resisted the urge to puke.

There was surveillance everywhere. Bugs. Cameras.

He pretended to kick at her crumbled little body before hunching down and putting two fingers to her jugular, then his mouth over hers, inhaling the wisp of her breathing.

While careful not to apply any pressure to her windpipe, he had resorted to a carotid artery strangling, rendering her completely unconscious in a matter of seconds.

Knowing they could have company any minute, he examined the contact sheet in her lax grip to ascertain the damage.

Fuck. There was her friend Vuong Quan. In the infirmary, strapped to a dental chair. And there he was, standing over Quan with a #10 blade raised in his surgically gloved hand, dripping blood, compliments of Quan's slit wide open throat.

Quan's eyes were open in terror, as was his wired-open mouth. A horror show, only worse because it was so obviously real.

Jerry took a second he didn't have to examine himself in the still frames. There was a sequence of them, capturing the deed being done. It was odd to see his own eyes looking straight ahead, looking both clear and glazed, mouth posed as if he were speaking...

To Miles, that's who he had been speaking to. Miles who had assured him he was acting on his humanity to put Quan out of his misery after he had no recollection of doing it.

Miles, who was constantly recording, documenting, either with film or on paper, his findings and experiments... and would be the one with access to the negatives that Isabelle had ended up with on the contact sheet.

Fuck.

Did Miles actually think he wouldn't figure this out—that he would either just kill her as instructed or urgently seek help with some of his pharmaceuticals and memory tweaks and beg him not to mention it to The Ambassador—make him an accessory to getting her out alive and be eternally beholding to him for it?

Miles. He had to be behind this. A set-up. No, something much worse. *Betrayal.* Taking the most priceless thing he'd ever had, just to try to control and destroy it.

A vision of whipping the scalpel across Miles's throat sparked a thrilling sort of joy—the kind of blood ecstasy that had been missing for years.

Jerry realized he was grinning. He felt like an abusive alcoholic guzzling a fifth of 100 proof after years of staying dry. And it was just at that moment that the door opened, closed, and who should stop just a few feet away in cowboy boots and a lab coat?

"Whoa, pardner! What seems to be going on here?"

Jerry crumbled the evidence in his fist.

Rising quickly while shoving the paper into his fatigues, he shook his head.

"I'm not sure. I came in to let Isabelle know she needs to wrap things up and start packing since the latest intel indicates Saigon is under attack. She'd told me earlier she wasn't feeling well and then, she just fainted."

"Oh? Well, that's sure bad timing, needing to get things finished up here and passing out like that. Why don't we bring her into the infirmary? Doctor Miles will have a look, make sure nothing's wrong—and meanwhile you can have a look around here, make sure nothing's amiss with the work she's been doing before she closes shop."

For a moment Jerry considered killing Miles right there. But that would create a worse clusterfuck than the one he already had on his hands: The Ambassador would not easily forgive the loss of his genius director who he needed to run things at the new facility, and tattling about the incriminating evidence Miles had planted would only ensure Isabelle's termination. Not by him, someone else would be brought in, but his refusal would smack of disloyalty and he'd be a walking bullseye.

"I know you haven't liked her being here." Jerry placed a cool palm on Mile's shoulder, good buddy-like. "But she's leaving as soon as Jordan can get a chopper in. I know he's estimating we'll need at least a couple to lift the most essential personnel out, and you and I will probably be some of the last to go."

"And Panther," Miles reminded him. "Can't forget your kitty."

"Right, Panther comes with me. With us. But her?" Jerry shook his head, leaned in closer, and wished beyond wishing that it wasn't the bitter truth. "I'll never see her again after this. So I'd appreciate you stepping aside while I steal what time I can with my lady friend—not to worry, a little mouth-to-mouth should resuscitate her—and I'll make sure nothing's leaving with her that The Ambassador wouldn't approve of."

AT FIRST SHE thought she was waking from an obscene nightmare in Jerry's villa while their song, "Drowning in a Sea of Love," played nearby. But when she tried to move her hands and they were restrained above her head, tried to move her legs and they were trussed at the ankles, then tried to open her mouth only to realize she had been gagged...

Isabelle knew the macabre was real and the man sitting stone-still by the side of the bed, his gaze transfixed on her face, was a monster.

Did he intend to kill her quick or torture her first? Had he brought his surgical gloves to do it?

The monster she had thought she was falling in love with put a finger to his lips. He left his post and laid beside her bound form. Recoiling, she tried to roll away, only for him to strap an arm over her torso, clamp a thigh over her legs, shackling her in place.

Terrified she was about to heave and choke on her own bile, Isabelle commanded herself: *Calm. Stay calm. Maybe you can convince him to let you go and then you can run for help—*

"It's very important that you listen to me," he whispered next to her ear. "If you understand, nod."

She could barely hear him he spoke so quietly, but she understood plenty. The butcher who had slit Vuong Quan's throat and choked her in the darkroom before stringing her up in his remote quarters had to be humored.

Somehow she managed a nod.

"I apologize for the restraints. And I'm sorry I had to render you unconscious—three times, you almost woke up twice. It was necessary. So is our proximity." He indicated some indiscernible point in the bedroom where shadows lengthened through slitted plantation blinds. "We're not alone. Someone is listening. If you cry for help, it will not be the kind you want. You have every reason to fear me but right here, right now, I am your greatest ally and the only hope you have of escaping. The negatives were planted to compromise your security." He shifted to stare her straight in the eyes. Shook his head at what he saw then returned his lips to her ear. "Of course you don't believe me. No more than you would if I said the pictures were doctored—which, most unfortunately, they were not. I was responsible for your friend's abduction and ultimately for his death. Now that I have hopefully assured you that not everything I am saying is a lie, let me ask you this: Who took the pictures? And who would want you to find them? *Me?*"

Again he searched her skittish gaze and she noticed something wasn't right...His eyes.

WHILE JERRY REMAINED SILENT, letting everything sink in for either her acceptance or rejection or some of both—after all, there was no disputing the gory evidence of his role in Quan's death, but at least he'd owned it— he felt almost queasy from the risk he had to take. They were finished. But that didn't stop him from still loving what he could never have and he would kill anyone who threatened her safety—unless someone killed him first.

At least she had stopped moving and become very still, as if digesting the possibility she had not just been seduced by one viper but could be in the heart of the nest.

"Isabelle." He whispered her name into the ear she surely loathed his ever touching, but he stole the contact while he still could and knew it wasn't just because of the miniscule bug he had belatedly discovered. "The more you know, the more expendable you become, and the second you saw those pictures, you became expendable. I've done my best to cover up what happened in the lab, but you will not be out of danger until you're anywhere but here. Even then, you won't be safe if you are *ever* considered a threat to something that is much bigger than either of us. Did you notice my eyes aren't really blue?"

He felt her slight nod. Heard her tight swallow.

"Do you remember our first night together, here in this room, when I told you I'm not like other men?"

Hesitance, as if she did not want to remember. Then, another nod.

"When I came here, in '69, I was someone very different. And not in a good way. I know it's hard to believe I could have been an even worse version of who you see me as now, but I was. And I was considered valuable for research, for experimentation. I'm not going to burden you with the extent of it all, but let us just say I've been... modified. On nearly every level. This face? It's not mine. It belongs to the vision of a reconstructive surgeon. And it's the least of what's been changed about a man once known as Jerry Prince. My real name. For all intents and purposes he is as deceased as official records show."

Jerry pulled back to judge the reaction he might be getting, expecting eyes clenched shut. Amazingly, they weren't. And while he still saw the shadow of fear, a healthy wariness that would surely always be there, her eyes were open, unblinking. Maybe she was really listening. He could only hope. Pray...? If it was like meditation, maybe he could learn how to do it. For now, hope was enough to continue.

"It wasn't too long after the plastic surgery that you and I met at the awards ceremony. Actually, we'd met once before when you were doing a piece on the Special Forces during the Siege of Hue. We didn't talk much and I looked a lot different, but while you were busy taking pictures of me and my men, I was developing what you might call a `crush' on you and ended up collecting a large body of your photographic work. It was confiscated about the time I arrived here, and you can fill in the blanks on that. When our paths crossed again, I'd been here about a year and a half. Those

I answered to—Dr. Miles, Ambassador Jordan, and Hugo—were pleased with the progress I had made. Enough to promote me within the organization and see how well I could do on assignment in such a venue. I told you our meeting that night was completely coincidental and ill-timed, which it was. What I did not tell you was that…was that…" *Tell her. Forget the bread-crumbs, just say it.* "Was that I had been extremely stunted emotionally and didn't know how to handle normal feelings. It was like having the body of an adult with all its grown up needs and desires and responses but the emotional maturity of a big mixed up kid. Hugo offered to let me stay. My answer was that I liked you too much to do that. But I couldn't forget you. And when I returned here, I had some incentive to work on those areas that made me… unnatural. Unequipped to have any normal sort of relationship. Obviously that will never happen now, but I was foolish enough, delusional enough, to imagine we could have a future together."

She made a noise, a guttural sound. It could have been disgust. It could have been a question. He was tempted to remove the gag.

Not yet.

"I think you may be asking me about what else happened that night?"

A hard nod.

"I was there to abduct your friend. I wasn't expecting him to join us at the bar and wished he hadn't since then I had to associate him with you. However, it was my assignment. I'm not sure where it originated but it was clearly politically motivated. As for what happened after he arrived here… that's an area of information you're better off not having access to. I did not want to see him suffer. It was an early indication that I was starting to develop what most people take for granted. A conscience." At her snort, he was glad he'd left the gag in place. "I realize how ridiculous that must sound. Listen, I take responsibility for all the inhuman things I've done, and I can promise you there are too many to count, but… Not all of them have been with my conscious consent. About the time I began to exhibit feelings like concern or remorse, I started having episodes of blacking out. And just as you saw, usually bad things happened when I did…"

Justlikethat, something clicked. The first time was the broken glass of juice on the terrace with Miles. One moment they were talking over breakfast, then *snap,* there was the broken glass. Dozens of similar events raced in blurring speed across his memory path, and returned to the still frames planted for Isabelle to find, ending in the moment he had blinked and stood there with the #10 blade dripping Quan's blood. He had been performing the interrogation techniques in front of students while Miles pontificated about AIQP: Accurate Information as Quickly as Possible, but because he kept remembering the moment Isabelle had introduced them while Quan made awful noises, it was proving too disturbing and…

Snap. One instant he was asking Miles if they could take a break, and the next he was standing over a very deceased Quan with Miles patting his shoulder.

All of the blackouts, at least those he could remember, had one thing in common: Miles. Miles was always there.

He thought of the little boy, of the father he had let go and the threat he had issued to the men reporting to him. He thought of how he'd let Shirley go, warning her to get out and take a gun with her. Those were all actions he had taken on his own, aberrant behaviors in their own way, but no blackouts, no Miles around.

And then he thought of the escaped BBC journalist that had set in motion all the events since: Bumping into Gregg in Saigon. Spotting JD. The subsequent abductions, detainments, tortures and experiments. But that BBC journalist. The first domino that had set everything else into motion. A journalist somehow escaping when JD and his brother, Buddhist Houdinis of the first order, were still consigned to their tiger cages along with Izzy…

Isabelle made another sound. A little mewling that coincided with Panther jumping on the bed. While Panther stroked Isabelle's cheek with his own, then flicked his rough little tongue on Jerry's furrowed brow, Jerry continued to think back.

He and Miles had been having one of their sessions. Like after Happy Hour in the cantina with Hugo. It wasn't one of their controlled LSD experiments, more like Miles casually asking, "If there's something you really wished you could do, but believe the people around you wouldn't approve of, what would it be?"

And then *Snap.*

The next thing he knew Miles was shaking him awake in the bed he had no recollection of turning into, while sirens were blaring in the background.

Get up, get up! Dad-gummit, we've got an escapee you need to track!

At that groggy moment Miles had reminded him of Yosemite Sam firing pistols he didn't know how fire while shooting off at the mouth. It had not occurred to him until now that maybe *he* was the one responsible, that it was possibly the result of one of Miles's experiments going off the rails.

Isabelle made some more muffled noises.

"I'll take it off soon," he quietly promised. "Just a little more business to finish before you do whatever you decide to do, and hopefully not to your own detriment. You asked me before about Hugo and I conveniently changed the subject. Here is what I know: Other than you, Hugo is the best thing that ever happened to me. He was—is—the closest thing I ever had to a father. This was his house until he recently disappeared. Vanished. Took his koi and his house boy. To where, I have no idea. But he'll find me when he's ready, I have to believe that. I think that's called faith. Something I don't have a lot of experience with but I hope despite every reason not to, you can find some in me."

Knowing how deeply she must despise him, it almost felt like rape to put his hungry lips to her forehead while undoing the restraints binding her wrists. If she slapped him, tried to gouge his eyes out, he wouldn't stop her. He'd even help her do it.

And so he told her as he unbound her ankles, then paused just before removing the gag, fully knowing it may very well be the last thing he could honestly relay to the woman who had given him every reason to grow from a deeply troubled boy into a deeply in love man:

"And now that you know all this, you're even more compromised than before. I just didn't know any other way to convince you to let me help you. There's so much and yet nothing left to say, Isabelle, except that proceeding from here, it all comes down to whether you'd rather trust the Devil you know, or the ones that you don't."

CHAPTER 27

THE FALL OF SAIGON

"Where ARE MY choppers!" Phillip bellowed into the crackling phone.

"They shot them right out of the sky, sir."

"Bloody hell, then send more!" he snapped. "We've been waiting since yesterday!"

"Yes sir, I understand, sir. And...yes, sir, I understand exactly who you are and that you ordered three choppers, but believe me when I say there are no more choppers to be sent. None, zero, sir, we sent you all that we had within range—the Huey and a Bell 205, but they were shot down trying to get to you. Sir, they are gone, no survivors."

No survivors. Well, wasn't that rich. No choppers or pilots to fly them. As soon as he'd gotten word of the 150 rockets smashing into the Tan Son Nhut air base before dawn the previous morning, terminating fixed wing evacuation plans along with two marines guarding thousands of evacuees, he'd been kept apprised in fits and spurts of Operation Frequent Wind. Since yesterday, in the course of 19 messy hours, well over 5,000 Vietnamese and 1,300 Americans had been evacuated from rooftops and even the rear parking lot of the US Embassy by helicopter—81 helicopters to be exact, AND NOT ONE HAD ARRIVED FOR HIM AS PROMISED.

He'd kept the most daunting details to himself, barely sleeping, knowing how much he needed Hugo right now, Hugo who was no doubt laughing into his absinthe somewhere. Still, he had been certain his own evacuation would be prioritized, even if Air America had to be called in to do it—until he'd learned the latest details: The US Ambassador to South Vietnam, Graham Martin, who had refused to leave, had brought his personal cook and a security detail carrying his luggage along with his poodle, Nitnoy, to the Embassy. After sending load after load of evacuees ahead, Martin had finally climbed to the roof of the sixth floor to depart—depart, so much better than *flee*—and was choppered out to the USS Blue Ridge, one of 40 US warships waiting offshore.

That was just before sunrise, a little over half an hour ago, and now telecommunications had become so compromised that he was consigned to speaking to some little peon officer painfully explaining, "...I am talking to you from a Navy ship, sir. We evacuated the base and were lucky to get out. Aerial surveillance of your own coordinates indicates—hang on, sir, the Admiral, he has news."

"Ambassador Jordon. We were just able to locate a single chopper that can still get to you and any necessary personnel who can fit on the last Sikorsky, the last anything, leaving Vietnam via airlift. There will be room for 16 max, no cargo, and arrive at the coordinates you provided in exactly 27 minutes—at 0600 hours. Be ready to jump on and fly with those you deem most valuable. Anyone left behind will be in immediate jeopardy as surveillance shows an aggressive NVA tank campaign continues in your direction. It will be a race between us and them. I hope to see you aboard ship within the next hour."

Phillip didn't wait for "Over and out" or some other decorous nicety before lighting up as one might before facing a firing squad, though what he presently faced was even worse:

His own shockingly obliterated chess board.

He was not just moving chess pieces now, negotiating war and peace over a table in Paris. If they did not get out, the NVA would viciously destroy them on sight. If they made a run for it in their jeeps, they would be plunged into the midst of an apocalyptic nightmare, identifiable targets of blind rage by the people from both South and North who would immediately see them for who they were—Americans who had either abandoned them to slaughter or had been bombing them into hell's oblivion for years. It was a certainty that on every road, every panicked street and trembling alley, in every hamlet, village and town, dire events were playing out. The airports had already staged dramatic, deadly endings. In every harbor, every marina, overloaded boats were desperately seeking sanctuary anywhere to escape bloody surrenders and pleadings for mercy that would not be granted.

Always strange how dying in the final moment of a war's end somehow seemed worse than being one of the uncounted thousands in the middle of it all.

Phillip ground out his half-smoked Gauloises in his make-shift war room. Such a cozy, lovely study, *and bloody hell if he was going to die here!* It was time to get a new chess board.

He had one chopper on its way and minutes to assemble those most valuable. They would be short space, even as scaled down as they were. Miles would simply have to accept that he could not bring Dr. Kelly along, even though he had won a reluctant agreement when their separate departures were on track. As for the remaining prisoners, they would need to be disposed of, which was all fine and good, except for JD. He'd had special plans for JD and now those had to be reconsidered.

As did the essential equipment and files stowed out of Isabelle's sight, all of it far better destroyed than left behind. They had an arsenal of munitions. He just needed someone to torch the facility as soon as they were air bound, then conveniently blame it on the NVA—

"Phillip?" It was Kate, rubbing tired eyes. "You look upset. What's wrong?"

"Except for eleven Marines, who are packing up the flag, the Embassy has evacuated. Saigon's fall is imminent. One of the very last choppers leaving the country will be here shortly."

"What can I do to help?"

"Get Isabelle." A thought then. He had brought her here to clear his name. Now she could do one better—show the world what a hero he was, helping her to narrowly escape the NVA. "She can put that Leica to good use."

THE PINK KIMONO was the closest thing she had to home, and so she had been wearing its comfort when Kate rushed into the bungalow Jerry had returned her to deep in the night.

Still wearing the kimono, Isabelle continued clicking away at the helipad where quiet pandemonium reigned. She had been in war zones, had colleagues abducted, seen men killed in action and come close to joining them. But never had she experienced such a rush of relief riding the back of raw fear as chopper blades sounded in the distance and Jerry emerged with a familiar figure in Ray Bans, boots, and a lab coat from the main facility.

Jerry was pushing a wheelchair. A man's slack body, dressed in black pajamas, was strapped into the chair with an IV bag hooked above it. Other than a patch of sandy hair at the top, he resembled a mummy with surgical gauze wrapped around his head, nothing showing other than slits for his eyes, nose, and mouth.

She automatically adjusted the lens to capture their fast approach but when The Ambassador stopped his authoritative shouting to the assemblage, and she thought she heard the hiss of an expletive, she cautiously swept her camera skyward to capture first sight of the chopper, then returned her focus to the man clearly in charge, who now had his eyes on her.

Click. Click. She gave The Ambassador a thumbs up—let him know he looked good—and made sure she didn't snap anything or anyone that could be construed as a threat to the image he clearly wanted to project.

This was not the time to be reckless. This was the chance to get out alive and onto a Navy vessel, along with the backpack that carried her life —a generous concession considering no one else was allowed to bring so much as a toothbrush. Then again, the pack also carried all the innocuous photos she hadn't been able to develop or wire out due to their emergency evacuation.

While all heads pivoted skyward to their means of narrow escape there was no mistaking the *Boom! Boom!* of heavy artillery coming their way.

Just as the helicopter began its loud descent, Jerry parked the mummy next to Miles, and came to her, wrapped her in what appeared to be a fierce hug.

"Plans have changed," he said in her ear with noise blasting the air all around them. "I've been given orders to stay behind to destroy evidence. I won't be there to watch out for you, so you keep your head down. Don't say anything, don't do anything to call attention to yourself. Don't ask any questions. Just give him what he wants and watch your back."

And then he kissed her. It was only her forehead but she felt as if years were condensed into that last, momentary connection that she was both hungry for and repelled by. But it was the squint of Mile's attention, making her feel like a butterfly, with wings spread and pinned alive into a scientific display, that caused her to shiver when Jerry extended the music cassette she didn't think she could ever listen to again.

Everything happened so quickly then: The chopper's ramp opening, The Ambassador making a show of getting Kate on first, then gesturing for Miles to take what appeared to be an unexpected addition—"one of the guards, injured last night"—followed by assorted personnel before Jordan insisted, "Isabelle, quick get on and Jerry, you join her, and...I will stay behind, we've hit maximum occupancy!" as if he were the proverbial captain going down with the ship.

"Sir, I ask permission to stay," Jerry shouted above the bleating blades while the pilot, flying solo, frantically gestured to lift off. "I consider it my duty and an honor. Sir!"

Jerry's sharp salute was met with what appeared to be a moment's hesitation before The Ambassador saluted him back, and Jerry took off at top speed in the direction Isabelle thought the artillery fire had come from.

The door still open, the chopper immediately began to lift, seeming to struggle with the weight of capacity as it very slowly, incrementally rose higher, higher...

A cheer went up on board but Isabelle hardly registered it, her attention riveted on Jerry's racing form cutting in and out on a partially obscured path below, moving so fast he looked more cheetah than human while she wrestled with too many emotions to sort. *Click click. Click click.*

And on she clicked as they continued to lift, skirting over treetops that gave way to a partial clearing with what might have been...cages? She thought she saw hands or arms sticking out of bamboo at the top and sides; thought she saw Jerry reach the outskirts, pointing a rifle.

The hair on her nape turned electric. Some instinct made her pause, glance over where Miles was stationed, standing about five feet away with the mummy parked to one side, and the backpack Jerry had pitched in for her, open at Miles's feet.

Kate was staring at the mummy, shaking its arm, and shouting what sounded like, "Gregg? GREGG?" while her husband was suddenly trying to calm her down, and at that point Miles appeared to be lifting something out of Isabelle's backpack—

A canister of film, large enough for a movie reel.

"Look! Look!" he shouted above Kate, "I told you she couldn't be trusted!"

As if in slow motion Isabelle saw the mute faces of the ISIC personnel look away.

Click.

She saw The Ambassador's attention move from the canister to settle coldly on her face.

Click.

Kate had stopped shaking the mummy to press a fist to her chest, lower her beautiful head.

Click.

And as Miles stepped forward, looking like he meant to grab her, Isabelle felt him give her a discreet push instead. For a moment she was enveloped by the sensation of hanging suspended in air. And then she was falling, falling backwards, in a freefall as stunning as Saigon's while Miles smiled down as she plummeted.

CLICK.

CHAPTER 28

"**G**et out! Get out!" Jerry shouted, flinging open the door to Izzy's cage, then jamming a key into the iron cuff that kept him dangling by one wrist.

He didn't wait to see if Izzy managed to pick himself off the bottom and crawl out before firing at the locks of the cages he raced past until he blasted the lock off JD's cage door.

Working at a blurring speed, he released JD's shackled wrists, stretched from side to side. He was about to assist with the remaining iron restraints that ran from midsection to feet, when the NVA announced their breach of the compound with another explosive *BOOM! BOOM!*

Jerry looked up, expecting to see tanks rolling in, only for his mouth to open in a huge *O* of horror as something—a small body in pink—sailed out of the chopper.

"NOOOOO!"

He dropped the keys at JD's feet while his own legs turned into pistons, his nearly superhuman body pushing past all previous limits. Surgically enhanced vision registered peripheral streaks of green while all he could see were his arms wide open to catch what had to be Isabelle falling from the sky...

He arrived just in time to see her go *splat.*

The primal, mournful cry that ripped from his lungs began with his first wild leap into wet, verdant green and did not stop until he fell to his knees in the middle of the rice paddy where Isabelle floated on black paddy water, a lotus wrapped in a pink kimono with long silky hair and arms splayed out, sooty lashes fanned shut.

Ever so carefully he scooped her up. She was so still in his arms, her beloved camera lying like a rosary around her neck.

She couldn't possibly have survived the impact, but...

Both neck and camera appeared to be intact.

Her body looked to be just as miraculously unbroken, but...

Internal ruptures and injuries were far more fatal than fractured bones and—

He thought he felt her twitch.

Jerry learned how to pray on the spot.

Loping as fast as possible in the direction of squalor it had been his duty to oversee, and ultimately, to obliterate, he thought of The Ambassador's final order:

Kill them all, including JD.

He had blatantly defied the direct order of his superior's superior. And he wasn't through defying orders yet.

Use every short range rocket, every grenade, every sparkler from the last Fourth of July if necessary to incinerate the entire compound. Keep a single jeep for yourself but destroy the rest. You know where to find us. A handsome reward will await.

Indeed, he did know where to find them. As for a handsome reward, all he could ask for was the life of the woman who had trusted him when she had every reason not to.

Reaching the edge of the rice paddy field, Jerry laid her down, did the whole desperate CPR procedure with water gushing from her lungs and out of her mouth, but even after a cough, two, her eyes were closed, breathing labored.

There was a surgical facility he had no intention of torching and a New York doctor he'd just released from a cage, a top notch surgeon in need of some serious care himself.

BOOM! BOOM! BOOM!

And then there was that.

Holding Isabelle close, Jerry returned the way he had come, all the way chanting:

Izzy can fix you...Izzy can fix you...Izzy can fix you...

~

IZZY WONDERED if he was hallucinating. He thought he had been hallucinating for some time, where days no longer counted and nights bled into sounds and sensations that were either distorted nightmares, or something much worse: Real. Guards that hit him in the back, in the head, in the stomach with sticks and rifle butts, then retreating at the "Stand down!" order of the man who had brought him there, the Ghost Soldier known as Jerry Prince who poured precious water down his parched throat, slid food through the bars and into his mouth, and even occasionally let him out to relieve himself so he didn't have to crouch in his own bodily waste...

Or maybe he had hallucinated all of that, too. Just as he must be in some kind of delirium, imagining his cage door was open, his numb hand attached to a raw, bleeding wrist was no longer shackled, and the command to "Get out! Get out!" was replaced by a different voice, JD's voice, urging, "Izzy, Izzy, c'mon, bro, wake the fuck up!" while he thought he felt his cheek being lightly smacked and JD's haggard face blended with the palm trees shifting in a slight breeze above him, making that sound like rain, while blue slits of sky played hide and seek with puffy white clouds that were making loud sounds, like farts. No... like artillery.

"Zhang, help me get him up!"

Zhang yelled something back about helping "Bao" who may have been the next voice, weakly responding in Vietnamese, then broken by the frantic shout:

"I've got her, I've got her! Isabelle's hurt and needs Izzy's help—"

A thunderous roll shook the ground, so visceral that Izzy wondered if maybe he wasn't hallucinating the lumbering tank plowing into their midst with an NVA flag flying out of the top, its commander perched like a hood ornament out of the center and shouting, "BAO! BAO!" while the tank's big gun veered to point directly at Jerry Prince, who dropped to the ground and protectively covered a splotch of pink.

It all seemed too real to pass off as a hallucination, and yet so surreal that they all could have been 3-D figures spun into a diorama, or actors trapped into a movie scene, reminding him of a darkened smoky theatre that smelled like popcorn and tasted like Good N Plentys, where he was a boy transported by wagon trains, mesquite campfires, and dusty trails, and the good guys always won. Only now, instead of horses and 6-shooters, the "bad guys" had a tank and several AK-47s trained on the rest of them—and, really, as far as "good guys" went, he would have to be delusional to believe he could ever qualify as being one again.

CHAPTER 29

F ish Sauce had dared to imagine many great things, but even he was stunned by all that had happened in no more than a blink:

Being one of the first to roll into the Tan Son Nhut airbase to lend fire power and clip the last wings of the invaders, while the capitol of Saigon found itself surrounded with no way out but rooftops and makeshift landing pads. So swiftly had the city dissolved into chaos, he had moved ahead on his mission, full of confidence that Saigon's fate was sealed, and all too aware that his initial orders—to race ahead to the ISIC death camp and recover any prisoners, capture the war criminals, and retrieve documentation of the CIA's monstrous experiments for leverage against the all-powerful US—had shifted with the light speed capitulation of an entire country that had shocked the conquerors as much as those being conquered.

Which meant he was arriving late instead of early and full of terror that if Bao still lived, retribution would be swift before his captors fled themselves.

Remembering how he had beat his chest, like Tarzan, and let out a blood-curdling yell of *Chiến thắng! Chiến thắng!* just last month upon proclaiming victory in the Central Highlands, Fish Sauce told himself anything was possible. And so he'd held on to hope as they approached the wall of the compound his superior had called "Trường giết người," and taken charge as the consummate warrior riding his steel horse, commanding "FIRE! FIRE!" from the 85mm main gun until the Flying Pig plunged past the final barrier and into the Yankee death camp known as The Killing School.

He had imagined killing every remaining Yankee, their last cries owed to an excruciating death he would exact for any harm done to Bao. But that imagining did not include his own racing heart plummeting at the sight of the American helicopter making its escape overhead.

Nor had he imagined that after all the agony of wondering what his brother was going through, surely worse than the whispered conditions at Hoa Lo Prison, what the American POWs had dubbed The Hanoi Hilton, that the Flying Pig's destination would end here:

In a small town center with pleasant cottages, a tennis court, tidy gardens, various buildings wearing white stucco and red tiled roofs that looked to belong more to an exclusive campus, the sort that Isabelle had been sent to, than the darker than dark Killing School.

It was eerie, like a ghost town, no white flags or guns firing out of the windows. Except for them, the grounds, the buildings, everything seemed deserted, abandoned. But he knew how the VC worked. All would *appear* to be deserted when the French, and then the US GI's would sometimes come to actually help the villagers; many other times to torch humble homes, rape the women, kill the men who may, or may not be, secretly working for the North, just like him:

Fish Sauce. A boy of humble beginnings on a plantation near Nha Trang where his mother was a servant to a wealthy French/Vietnamese family that while, overall kind, would be answering to the likes of him now.

Surveying their surroundings with wary eyes, Fish Sauce ordered a round of machine gun fire into the closest bungalow.

No response. Except, what had he just heard in the distance, coming from the opposite direction they had plowed through?

There it was again. *Gunfire.*

And where there was gunfire, there was either an ally, an enemy, or even possibly Bao being shot while they wasted precious time ripping holes into an empty building.

Shouting directional orders to Chopsticks and the rest of his crew, Fish Sauce remained at his post, surveying all that they passed at top speed, AK-47 positioned on his shoulder and ready to fire at anything or anyone whose eyes or skin did not match his own.

They came to a plantation, a beautiful French masterpiece surrounded by exquisite gardens reminiscent of where his mother had served and Isabelle had befriended him and Bao, and for that reason alone he did not unload the 600 rounds in a minute the AK 47 was capable of delivering. Besides, except for a black kitten perched on the veranda's banister and licking its paws, there were no other signs of life.

The gunfire he'd been following ceased. Fish Sauce was urgently scanning for a trail when he heard a man's excruciating cry.

"That way!" he called to Chopsticks, helming the tank's controls, while Porkrib stood on ready with the big gun and Noodlesoup stroked his own AK-47, poised to spring into action.

They tore up the beautiful garden with tread prints, uprooting everything in their path and shattering an old fountain that showered them with water. They didn't bother opening the large gate on a stucco garden wall but blew it out with streaking tracer rounds that revealed a trail just wide enough for a jeep.

Clearly designed to remain as hidden as possible, they rammed the Flying Pig through dense jungle green on either side while Fish Sauce's gaze darted in every direction, his heart pounding hard, then harder still when an opening came into sight.

As they burst into the clearing, Fish Sauce rapidly assessed the immediate area: It stank of death, disease, and human waste. A number of concrete cages, each made to hold 5 or 6 prisoners, were partially built into trenches with bars on top. They appeared to be empty.

But there had to be 20 much smaller bamboo cages, made for an animal the size of a tiger, with gates flapping open to reveal wretched looking prisoners crawling out of several, while what had to be a Yankee was being tended by another prisoner in tattered clothes who did not look Asian either, and near to them was a fierce looking man, much larger than most native countrymen, with another man in his arms, as if he had just pulled out—

"BAO! BAO!" Scrambling from the tank, Fish Sauce barely noticed the blonde man in a US military uniform hunched over something on the ground.

Racing past him while his crew piled out with their weapons, Fish Sauce ran to his twin brother, fell to his knees.

"Liem," Bao weakly greeted him, appearing so frail that Fish Sauce was afraid he might break if he held him as tight as he longed to.

The fierce looking man who had given Bao up said in Vietnamese, "You are Liem, Bao's brother. He said you would come even if you had to fight dragons to save him—as I would my brother. That is him. His name is JD." He gestured to the one who did not look like him at all, who continued to examine the Yankee.

Chopsticks was fast approaching, aiming his AK-47 at the one named JD and the Yankee. Sensing the brother who had spoken was about to intervene, Fish Sauce held up his hand before more blood was spilled than was already evident on the grounds surrounding them.

"Speak quickly. Tell me what you know."

"I know your man will make a terrible mistake if he tries to kill my brother. I also know the American JD is helping is not your enemy. That man is not a soldier, he is a doctor who came here with us to find a friend. As you can see, he has been punished, we have all been punished, by the same enemy. And even if the doctor is a Yankee, he is the best hope you have now to save your brother. He can help Bao. He can help anyone else who needs medical attention."

Fish Sauce glanced at Chopsticks. He was grinding his teeth, looking like he wanted to hurt someone. Chopsticks had not been happy about leaving Saigon before the same flag on their tank was raised high above the city. Chopsticks was loyal, but if he had a failing, it was his quick temper and a tendency to act on impulse.

"Stand down," he ordered Chopsticks. "Do not shoot unless ordered."

In response Chopsticks made a grunting sound, then marched over to the man in a US military uniform, with many stripes and insignias on the sleeves. He remained hunched over something dressed in pink... a woman?

Chopsticks smashed the butt of his rifle into the officer's blonde head. As blood gushed out of a gaping wound, Chopsticks turned a big, satisfied smile on Fish Sauce and announced, "Toi da khong ban!"

I didn't shoot. Fish Sauce did not find the humor in it that Chopsticks apparently did as he snickered and lifted his rifle butt to strike again.

Fish Sauce shouted for him to stop, which Chopsticks did—only to give his target several hard kicks in the side.

Still, the officer with many stripes did not move, except for a slight shifting of his hand and fingers, possibly a signal to the others. But he uttered no sound, not even a whimper, as if made of the same stuff as their tank.

"No," Bao protested, "No."

Returning his attention to his twin, Fish Sauce gleaned what he could from Bao's broken explanation, with interjections from the one named JD and the brother he called Zhang, all of them speaking in rapid Vietnamese.

Bao: *Do not kill him.*

Zhang: *We would all be dead if he had followed orders. He set us loose.*

Bao: *He gave me water. Food.*

JD: *He has information we need.*

Zhang: *And he knows where any supplies are stored once we get Bao to the medical facility. Just look at him. What are we waiting for?*

Glancing from Bao, who had fallen unconscious, to the doctor, Fish Sauce decided if the doctor couldn't stand then everyone could take turns holding him up while he did his job.

Reluctantly letting Bao go, Fish Sauce let his displeasure be known with a rare glower at Chopsticks, gestured for all his men to go check on the few other remaining prisoners who had crawled out of their cages.

Standing a prudent distance from the officer his brother did not want him to kill, who was possibly too valuable right now to kill anyway, Fish Sauce said in his best English, "I am Commander Nguyen Liem, 2nd Corps of the Perfume River from the 203rd Tank Brigade. In accordance with the Geneva Conventions, state your name, rank, and serial number."

And in perfect Vietnamese, his head still down, he responded, "Jerry Prince. Captain, Special Forces," then quoted his service number before adding, "Previous Assistant Director of ISIC. Rank of Colonel."

"The Killing School."

"Yes. Previous."

The Practice Wisdom that had guided Fish Sauce through many close calls told him that the man who had set the cages free and kept his brother alive, even if barely, who also had information and quick access to the resources they needed, could have torn out Chopsticks' throat, grabbed the AK47 and left them all dead by now if he wasn't so concerned about whatever he was protecting being harmed in the process.

A woman. It had to be a woman, small enough to be gathered beneath him like she was knitted into a pink silk cocoon.

"Stand, Colonel," he ordered. "Stand up and show us what you have there."

The head that slowly rose with a gash bleeding freely from his skull momentarily froze Fish Sauce in place. He had looked death in the eye too many times before not to recognize its imminent threat. But these eyes, they were not like any human's he had seen before.

With incalculable speed they went from gaze lock to Fish Sauce gasping for breath with an iron hand lifting him up by the throat while the little pink cocoon remained shielded by the stance of her warrior guard that was now using him as a human shield.

"No one has to get hurt," said the very scary maybe human, maybe not, in the language everyone understood—except for perhaps the Yankee doctor who was struggling to get to his feet while the other brothers just as immediately turned into Shaolin Temple Kung Fu monks. In mere seconds his entire crew was writhing on the ground with their AK47's in such deadly bare hands the weapons were no more than tooth picks after a hearty meal.

"We need to work together here," said the Colonel with strange eyes who abruptly put him down so his feet were no longer dangling in the air and the air trapped in his throat was just as suddenly free to move into his lungs. "My apologies, Commander, for resorting to force to speed things along. You see, what I have is someone very dear to me, as your brother is to you, and I need to ensure that she receives treatment first. Your brother can go next. If you can agree with that, and can keep your crew in line whether they like the pecking order or not, then let's get the hell out of here and into a hospital—where I can assist Dr. Moskowitz."

It wasn't as if he had a lot of choices with Bao desperately in need of medical attention and his men rendered as ineffective as wrung out tea bags. But still, something in Fish Sauce demanded to know who or what could possibly hold such sway over this man, if that's what he actually was, and therefore, over them all.

No sooner had the Previous Assistant Director of ISIC gently lifted the woman in a pink kimono, revealing a camera around her neck, than Fish Sauce understood completely:

Isabelle.

CHAPTER 30

"Isabelle," Jerry said gently beside the hospital bed where he had placed her. "You had a bad fall but you're safe now and a doctor is here to help you. His name is Izzy. You can trust him."

"It's going to be okay," Izzy reassured her in a wan voice while Jerry literally held him up. He'd already done a quick wrap job on Izzy's wounds and started an IV of antibiotics and glucose to keep him hydrated. If a two minute shower, fresh surgical gown and gloves counted, he had gotten Izzy cleaned up and dressed, too. Miles had always insisted on the importance of maintaining a sterile environment.

Miles. He was a walking dead man now.

Isabelle's eyelashes fluttered. One of her hands moved. She whispered something.

Jerry nearly dropped Izzy to get to her. *Shit.* Where were JD and Zhang when he needed them? Oh. Right. After field dressing his head gash, their job was to make sure Mr. Trigger Happy and the rest of the group stayed in line while the Commander kept vigil beside his brother, already prepped, IV'd up, and on a stretcher in a waiting room.

"Okay, this is going to make things a lot easier," Izzy said, seeming to come half back to life himself. "Isabelle, we're going to do some tests. If you can hear me, squeeze my hand. Good. Very good. Now I think you whispered something. Can you say it again?"

"Camera," she said faintly.

"I've got it, Isabelle," Jerry assured her, "I've got your Leica."

When she winced he wondered if it was from hearing his voice. Or maybe she had glimpsed the surgical gloves he was wearing.

Izzy quickly ascertained she had several broken ribs and a ruptured eardrum but no evidence of a spinal injury or resulting paralysis. She wasn't vomiting or exhibiting other indicators of internal bleeding from her chest or abdomen although she had multiple contusions around the back area. Their state of the art CT scanner, just recently invented, was something Jerry actually had more experience with than Izzy. A grainy 128x128 matrix image indicated some bruising of surrounding tissues in the skull but no evidence of swelling or bleeding from the brain.

By the time they were finished Isabelle was still disoriented but responsive, able to take several steps without falling, and could touch her finger to her nose.

Final diagnosis?

"You have a concussion, and not a minor one, but between the scan and tests, I don't see evidence of a TBI—that's a Traumatic Brain Injury— which is the best news I could possibly give you. Actually, landing in that paddy no doubt saved your life by dissipating the impact of what Jerry estimated to be a 70 foot fall. If it had been water, you may as well hit concrete from that distance, but fortunately it was a muddy paddy and not the South China Sea. Nonetheless, we need to keep you awake and monitor your condition for at least the next few hours, and after that, plenty of bed rest and nothing too stressful or strenuous that could create complications."

Jerry was still giving thanks to the rice paddy angels that had saved her when he wheeled Isabelle out while Izzy collapsed into a surgical chair.

More than anything he wanted to be the one to sit with Isabelle and monitor her condition, but one look at the NVA tank commander quietly reassuring his unconscious brother—god, he hoped he wasn't already dead—and Jerry knew what he had to do. He thought it was what normal people simply called "the right thing."

"Commander, I'll take your brother in now. Would you mind making sure…" *the first, the last, my everything,* "making sure our first patient stays awake and if she starts complaining of a headache or nausea, hit this buzzer and I'll be right here. Her name is—"

"Isabelle." The NVA tank commander went from grasping his brother's hand to softly touching hers. "Isabelle, it is me. Liem. Do you remember?"

"Liem? Liem!"

And Jerry left Isabelle in the NVA tank commander's embrace.

Two hours later Jerry was thinking of all the letters he had written to the bereaved of the men he had lost—whose blood was on his hands—and how he had said all of the things he was supposed to say but didn't really mean it. After all, Ghost Soldier psycho-sociopaths did not come equipped with normal feelings or a conscience. They were just very good at emulating the appearance of actually having them.

But now, here he was, knowing that no matter the language—whether *Desole* in French; *Toi xin loi* in Vietnamese; or I'm sorry in English—the news he had to deliver was going to devastate a brother...and in the end, as he pulled down his surgical mask and met a hopeful gaze, all it took was a sad shake of his head.

The Commander, Nguyen Liem, openly wept and Isabelle right along with him. Jerry heard her say, "Liem, you were always my favorite, but you know how much I loved Bao, too." And she called him her brother.

The room was so thick with emotion that Jerry felt like a claustrophobic eavesdropper who desperately wanted to strip down naked and run as fast and furious and as far away from here as he could.

Instead he checked on Izzy who was taking a rest, cleaned up the surgical mess, made Bao presentable for visitation and any rituals his brother would naturally wish for.

He found JD and Zhang sizzling up something that smelled awfully good from a huge wok in the mess hall while the tank crew guzzled beer and the remaining few prisoners, who he knew were part of the group that Bao had been captured with—a suspected intelligence team—had fared amply better to be medicating themselves with something stronger than beer.

It was an odd feeling being here on the campus that had been his only real home and knowing he was the last bit of ISIC remaining—almost like being a dorm mother and watching out for everyone else now that the president and professors and even the janitors were gone.

He knew every inch of the campus he had been ordered to obliterate.

He knew every nook and cranny of each and every house, garden, and medicine cabinet.

He knew the cantina a little too well.

And he knew enough to realize there were some things, important things, that he didn't know.

Miles had thrown Isabelle out of the chopper, picking up where he had left off in the photography lab. Why exactly he wanted her dead, Jerry wasn't sure. And why exactly Miles thought his dear FEW would be so malleable and forgiving and willing to do whatever his "superior" bidding might be, Jerry wasn't sure of that either.

However, if there were answers to be had, he knew exactly where they would be. Especially since Miles had seemed so torn between taking Gregg Kelly or salvaging some personal belongings with only a minute to choose. And perhaps that choice was already made for him since no personal belongings were allowed, only actual people, and while he was sure Miles's most important belongings had already been shipped, whatever was left behind should have been torched by now.

If that torching included unshipped notebooks/research papers, given Miles's photographic memory, that wasn't such a big deal since he could duplicate anything he'd already written down anyway.

Having assured himself that all the "guests" were taken care of in what was now his "house"—at least until the NVA, which he was presently hosting, decided otherwise—Jerry went hunting, only this time for answers.

THE PROFESSOR'S NOTEBOOK

Well, pardner, we're going to do something a little bit different for a change. I mean, you can only write so many entries with scientific protocols, date/time/hour, TX/RX/All That Shit. The clock is ticking and I think there's a good chance this could be my last post before the last boxes are shipped and we giddy on up out of here.

In that vein I feel a need to summarize particular accomplishments during my lengthy tenure on this campus, with a look to the future as well.

I have spent quite a bit of time on progress reports for my Future Elite Modern Warrior, and indeed Jerry is my most supreme accomplishment to date, but by no means am I finished with him yet. I believe my initial reference to building my Code Purple Jerry originated in Entry #102, stating "While still an engrossing work-in-progress Code Purple Jerry is the assassin I can soon trigger into operation with just those words: *Code Purple Jerry*. Let me be clear that this is a whole other level of consciousness that is under *my* control and not Jerry's conscious control… I have to say I feel a bit like Dr. Frankenstein, creating my own entity inside of Jerry's psyche so a portion of his mind belongs to me, and can be controlled only by me." And then I go on to discuss early commands such as dropping the juice glasses then building up to rendering my notebook virtually invisible to him so it could be sitting right there on the table and he doesn't even see it, blah, blah, blah, and I go on to say "To wield this much control over anyone, particularly an elite warrior I foresee as the prototype for this and future wars—highly skilled killers following commands without question or remembrance of their actions—is mind blowing, even to me."

Ah yes, that photographic memory does come in handy.

In subsequent entries I have also discussed certain limitations such as not being able to make all notebooks invisible since that would impede Jerry's ability to function day-to-day. I.E. "Jerry, could you please grab that notebook over there for me…" or "Jerry, have you seen that notebook with a list of…" etc. and he just says, "Notebook? What notebook? I don't see any notebooks." So it gets very specific with these sorts of commands, the notebook just being a particularly sensitive one for obvious reasons. Which means he has specific notebooks with recognizable qualities—ex: the Star Trek notebook with Spock on the cover (and wipe codes inside) —that have been hypnotically erased, while, say, this run of the mill black spiral would be readily seen.

No biggie. The rest are all shipped or crated/shipping asap, and he won't have access to this one.

While the escalation of our need to evacuate has been frustrating, my far larger and most immediate concern is Isabelle Chene. She's pleasant enough, obviously talented, and wrapped in a very attractive package, but, end of day? THAT BITCH HAS GOT TO GO. Period. I have far too much invested in Jerry for him to start acting on primordial instinct like a rutting pit bull after a bitch in heat. Clearly he is experiencing sensations and emotions I am not personally familiar with, while unfortunately giving credence to Dr. Kelly's observations about love being greater than fear and all that shit. I don't have the time for it or the patience for such nonsense if I did. Miss Chene presents an immediate danger to under-mining everything I have achieved with Jerry over the past six years and she has done so in a matter of days. I dare not contemplate how much more progress she might undo if a serious intervention is not employed. I am still contemplating what interventions might be most expeditiously effective in removing her from a very complicated equation. Permanently.

Adding to this complication, and no doubt related to it, is Jerry's recent removal of the Rolex Submariner watch. As recorded in Entry #342 the watch was meant to serve these primary three purposes:

#1 Serving as a gift from me and The Ambassador after Hugo took his koi and boogied to who knows where, it would create additional loyalty to us in Hugo's sudden absence. The jury is still out on that, no thanks to Miss Chene.

#2 The object relationship I have creatively layered into Jerry's subconscious with embedded commands allows the watch to serve as a trigger. When Jerry checks the watch, the commands I have placed in my voice are akin to electrical brain waves, like going to a Sonic burger speaker and placing the order: "I'll have a foot long hot dog, two chili cheese fries, and a Sonic Burger, hold the onions please, and the biggest chocolate shake you've got!" Only he looks at the watch and hears me say, "ACTION REQUIRED/DO NOT KILL" for example when he was hunting The Three Musketeers here recently that are now consigned to cages in the dungeon area. I'm sure he would have performed just as successfully without the watch in that situation, but it was a trial run before Miss Chene's arrival during my last deep drug/hypnosis session with Jerry. The results in this case have been less than remarkable. Hopefully this is not a negative indicator for the most important purpose of all:

#3 The watch is an early stepping stone for the big procedure in the works that it is my intent to execute within the next year: Code Purple Jerry will be substantially upgraded to eclipse the experimental dogs. Obviously, controlling Jerry will be much more complex than "Here Boy! Sit! Roll over! Speak!" but the surgical implantation of a controlling device into Jerry's brain will work much the same as it has for the six Rovers. While I am still working out the details, the model I envision is with matching watches. In simplest terms there will be a button on mine that communicates with his, even at long distances, like two people talking on phone lines across continents. The proximity of his watch can then send a tiny radio signal that triggers the implant into his brain and the implant signal is paired with the response activity I want.

For now, however, the CODES are god, even if rudimentary in comparison to an actual brain implant. At this point I have used the deep drug and hypnosis sessions to create Code Purple Jerry; Code Blue Jerry; and more recently Code Orange Jerry. While I know Code Purple works, Code Blue (to self-destruct) and Code Orange (to self-destruct at a given day/time) have only been briefly tested, with Jerry instructed to drink a vial clearly marked POISON, which he did, without knowing I had filled it with sugar water. The one other code—Code Green Jerry—is a recent addition due to the escalating developments with the NVA. That is more like a homing code, ensuring that Jerry returns to me in the event we somehow get split up.

Obviously it has been just as essential for me to have a "Wipe" system (See Star Trek/Spock Vol. 4) to override/erase the codes in the event something goes awry and reprogramming is required. So if his brain is basically a chalk board and I have formulas written all over it, only to discover I made even a minor mistake that results in an undesired outcome, then out comes the eraser. Hopefully the implant will eventually do away with any need for Codes whatsoever and Jerry won't end up with a crayon box for a brain.

There is just one more thing—actually two—that bear mention regarding my iron-clad control over Code Purple (Blue/Orange/Green) Jerry. In referencing back to Entry #330 (Star Trek/ Captain Kirk, also rendered invisible), I provided extensive detail on how I taught Jerry's inner monster to cry, with the two kittens as essential triggers to peel the onion of consciousness and memory back, layer by layer. They, along with the MDMA drug cocktail, allowed him to reconnect to the pivotal emotional events which shaped the very core of his personality and subsequent world perception, and ultimately return to that original place where he could feel the full spectrum of his emotions again (mine obviously would be a different set; one size does not fit all). Consequently, he became deeply attached to the two kittens I had given him. The black one with most of the personality and curiosity was his initial favorite, but then the shy calico brought out his protective instincts and seemed to become even more dear to him.

This is when I decided to perform the ultimate test of my hold over Jerry, which I deemed imperative given his increasing humanization over the years, only to fully realize that humanity with the kittens. After all, while it was an extraordinary accomplishment to fully humanize a psychopathic serial killer, the ultimate goal is to create the most formidable military on earth with "highly skilled killers following commands without question or remembrance of their actions." The lack of remembrance being key since it would torture anyone with a conscience and while we want the most formidable military on earth, what we don't want is a bunch of psychopaths on the loose (which is why Jerry was brought here in the first place—he had to be contained *and* controlled; now that he is self-contained, he just has to be controlled).

To that end, I persuaded him to agree to a follow up session designed for his "personal growth," but upon blending the drug cocktail and deep hypnosis, I commanded him to strangle his favorite of the two kittens. Without hesitation he snapped the neck of the calico. I then told him we needed to take a walk to his favorite place so he could bury it. Jerry went directly to that tree he planted with Hugo (fortunately not around) and shoveled a deep hole, about 3 feet down, and buried the kitten under the lychee tree. I told him to be sure to get the grass placed just right on top so it would look undisturbed, which he did. Then we returned to the SET and I erased any memory of that kitten completely. It was as if the beloved kitten had never existed in his mind or memory after the event.

I did find myself wondering if creating a second wounding within the original wound would result in an ultimate psychological devastation that could cause a subconscious rupturing. Thus far there is no evidence of such. If Miss Chene has contributed anything, I suppose it is that she has in many ways duplicated his responses to the calico. Now, if I could just duplicate the same neck snapping and have him bury her along with the kitten.

Hugo would not be around to raise a stink about that, which now brings me to a "foot" note to wrap all this up. After The Ambassador's big blow up with the Commandant, he had me tweak Code Purple Jerry to hunt down, but not kill, Hugo. His specific order was to "CUT OFF HIS RIGHT FOOT" to hobble any efforts to leave. This did not go as planned with Hugo giving us the old slipperoo and Jerry returning with an envelope with his name on it instead of Hugo's foot. After I read the contents, I repeated the earlier experiment and had him go bury it near the calico. Obviously, I have not attempted to wipe Hugo from Jerry's memory (or Miss Chene *yet*), but one thing's for certain: You NEVER want to piss off Phillip Jordan. He and Hugo were friends for decades. I do what I need to for science and can feel good about my outcomes, but The Ambassador? That is one cold hombre.

And with that, I can only say that I'm glad I don't believe in ghosts. Because pardner, this place would be full of them.

As the final words continued to assault his eyes, the black letters swirling into a bottomless well of darkness, Jerry could only stand there at the desk, fronted by a set of longhorns, he had pulled a chair up to countless times before.

His hands were trembling, cold. He dropped the plain black spiral notebook next to the bottom drawer he had blown open upon finding it locked, and reached in again, wondering if there was another notebook he had not seen, but could detect by touch.

Nothing. Only wood.

He examined his hands, turning them up, then down, then palms up again. Had he used only one, or both, to kill the kitten? Would he have used both to amputate Hugo?

God. What kind of freak show was he?

Jerry heard the crack before he felt the impact of his foot connect with a curvy steer horn. He watched a large chunk sail through the air—

And caught it before it hit ground.

He thought he passed JD as he tore past the dining hall and hit the cobblestone street at top speed, never stopping, just running, running, running until he came to the lychee tree. The Trust Tree.

The garden was torn up with tank treads, the stucco fence and gate leading to hell blown to bits, the exquisite old fountain near the koi pond shattered with water still gushing out from the pump. The area around the Trust Tree was soggy mud.

And that is where he started digging with the steer horn, slinging mud and grass at a torrential velocity, all around the tree, careful not to go over 3 feet deep until...

He saw the first small sliver of white. A tiny bone.

Jerry thrust away the horn, sank to his knees.

Carefully, ever so carefully, he extracted each tiny bone until he had the skeletal remains of the calico, even a few tufts of fur not yet decomposed.

"Oh god," he cried, cradling the remains in his palms, seeing exactly where the neck was snapped, and stroking the severed white notch. "I'm so sorry...so sorry. I didn't mean it. I promise I didn't mean it..."

After he was able to pull himself together, he placed the bones on the veranda table where Hugo would have been sitting, then returned to dig, and dig, all around where he had buried the kitten.

He had almost completely rounded the tree, coming full circle, when he saw a hint of white. Jerry crouched down to delicately part paper from dirt, blessedly far enough away and buried deep enough to be spared ruin from the spewing fountain.

With hands that he wished belonged to someone else, and on knees that kissed the ground that was the most sacred place he knew on earth, Jerry extracted a sheet of paper from the envelope.

After hungrily scanning the message several times, he re-folded the paper, returned it to the envelope with his name on it, and cast a grateful glance at the veranda…

Even knowing that where Hugo should be sitting, there was only a sad, small pile of bones.

Your vision will become clear only when you can look into your
   own heart.
Who looks outside, dreams; who looks inside, awakes.

— CARL JUNG

FISH SAUCE

Nguyen Liem sat on the front of the T-54 tank he had commanded, legs dangling on either side of the big gun. His war weary gaze searched left, swung right, then darted skyward in search of elusive answers.

He and his crew—Porkrib, Noodlesoup, and Chopsticks—had survived longer than any other crew that he'd had. They had been like family, fighting the same fight, sharing the same hunger, relishing the same joy upon hearing jubilant shouts of *"Chiến thắng! Chiến thắng!"* as they cruised down Route 7, then Hwy 1, as heroes.

And yet, that absolute joy of claiming victory, of reclaiming the country that belonged to them and their ancestors, had been much too short lived. Nothing was as it should be.

Yes, he was deeply grateful to have embraced his twin once more, to have the memory of their last words, to have given Bao a funeral their parents would have approved of, were they still alive. But to be reunited only to be torn apart again, without hope now that he was truly dead, it had brought him more grief than closure. He felt adrift, without the mooring of the emotional anchor his brother had always been. Even his search for Bao had been a constant, something unwavering to keep him set on a solid path. All their lives they had turned to each other for help, direction, knowing no matter the crisis or uncertainty, they would always be there for one another.

The loss he felt was worse than he had ever allowed himself to imagine. Seeing the other two brothers together—JD and Zhang—was a piercing reminder of what he no longer had.

It did not help that the loss extended beyond Bao.

Just that morning he had sent Porkrib and Noodlesoup away with the freed NVA officers who had fared better than Bao. They had each been given a jeep to drive to Saigon, part of a nice fleet of abandoned vehicles. A small arsenal of weapons had also been loaded in, mostly for show since THEY were the ones who were feared now that the Americans had vanished like ghosts and left most of what they had brought with them behind.

There was no enemy left to fight. Those who had worn RVN uniforms would be hiding like rats waiting for the exterminator, lest they join the traitors who had already been executed for fighting alongside the Americans.

And this is what had brought him to the Flying Pig, a true dilemma he had never envisioned facing. Bao's final words to him had been a plea to spare those he had come to know: the American doctor, who had tried so hard to save him; the French-American monk named JD who called Vietnam home and his step-brother, a fierce Chinaman named Zhang. And most troubling of all, the one named Jerry, the ex-assistant director of "Trường giết người," The Killing School, who would die to protect the girl that had always treated him, and Bao, like her brothers, not the sons of a servant.

The fact that the three warrior-men could have killed him and his crew instead of trying to save Bao and even extending their hands in friendship over the past week, weighed heavily upon Fish Sauce. But it was the resulting distance between him and Chopsticks, the unraveling of what he'd thought was an unbreakable bond, that made this truly distressful.

Chopsticks wanted to kill them all, except for Isabelle, who he probably wanted to kill too but suggested she could be consigned to an internment camp in a show of leniency. Chopsticks had argued that by helping them they were at risk of being considered traitors too, instead of the war heroes they were. They deserved glory and honor and pretty girls and celebrations! Not another day at the Yankee death camp that would soon be running out of pho and dumplings, even worse, beer and booze.

Subduing a groan, Fish Sauce thought he could smell the alcohol Chopsticks had apparently imbibed before noon, given his unbalanced weaving in the Flying Pig's direction, and the AK-47 he was waving around in the air.

Too late, Fish Sauce wished he had parked the tank at the French villa where Isabelle was recovering instead of in the middle of the little town square.

"*Nuoc Mam*," yelled Chopsticks, clumsily fumbling for one of his prized steel possessions while he waved around the AK-47 some more. "*BẠN là anh hùng CỦA CHÚNG TÔI!!*"

There had been a time when he, Liem, had glowed inside, wanting to believe "*Fish Sauce. YOU are OUR hero!!*" was true, even if was too much praise for a PAVN tank commander who would be nothing without his crew.

But the way Chopsticks said it now hinted of sarcasm. His uniform was no longer soiled from diesel oil and battle, but from a spilled bottle or a bowl, and if ill-fitting it was not from a lack of nourishment or the sauce he no longer needed to lay on.

As if the answer had dropped from the sky as surely as Isabelle—he had seen the pictures she had taken of those who did deserve punishment —he knew what he needed to do.

"Get in the tank," he ordered Chopsticks. "We are leaving."

"Okay," Chopsticks slurred. "After I kill the Yankees and their friends!"

"No," Fish Sauce barked with all the authority he had earned and Chopsticks was not respecting. "We are returning to Saigon so I can report to command and see if they have interest in coming to see this deserted place for themselves."

"But the Yankees could be gone by then."

Precisely, Fish Sauce thought.

"That is not your concern," he countered instead. "Once we are there you can keep your mouth silent, clean yourself up, and get sober. It shames me to say that you have become an embarrassment to our uniform and as your commanding officer, I am ordering you to—"

Fish Sauce heard the *rat-a-tat-tat* of the AK-47 unloading its rounds at the same time he felt the bullets slice across his midsection. He put a hand where a profuse wetness seeped through his uniform. A dizzying pain spread from his weeping gut to his head.

It was only as he slumped forward, his cheek connecting with the big gun, eyes open in an endless stare, that the pain slid up and up into an unspeakable agony.

For the last thing he heard was Chopsticks scream, *"Nuoc Mam!"* as the AK-47 dropped to the ground. And the last thing he saw were two steel chopsticks that had pierced an enemy heart before being turned to a precious goat's liver, but would never play in what the Americans called a band.

They were gripped in the hands that Chopsticks used to stab himself between his temples.

CHAPTER 31

Two Weeks after the Fall of Saigon
Thailand, near Kho Yao Island
Classified Location

It had been a week since Jerry found Mr. Trigger Happy's head looking like a speared olive in a martini glass. No loss there, though it really was a pity tank Commander Nguyen Liem had been a casualty in the process.

Isabelle had been devastated.

Before blowing up most of The Killing School they raided the considerable coffers of CIA make-up, wigs, facial prosthetics, costumes—NVA uniforms to be exact for the major part of the trip.

What had been the hardest for him was not the raw self-exposure of sharing Miles's notebook entry that had sent him racing to dig up a dead kitten and a letter, or asking for help to open every goddam box in the basement in search of Star Trek notebooks that he could not see even if they were amongst the items yet to ship.

No, the hardest part was watching Isabelle grab a pair of scissors and chop off her beautiful mane of silky black hair to better disguise herself as a young male officer in their midst. *"It will grow back,"* she had assured him while he pretended a stray eyelash had caused his eyes to well.

Everyone could speak fluent Vietnamese except for Izzy so he just kept his mouth shut and held onto Panther as they passed themselves off as a little caravan of jubilant victors who cheered at the sight of piles of bodies rotting in "enemy" uniforms while they made their way north on the most heavily traveled roads, hiding in plain sight.

Like Panther, Isabelle's Leica was too important to leave behind. They had stored it in a special compartment until they were "safely" in Thailand.

It still wasn't safe enough for Isabelle to risk going home to family. Not safe enough for her and Izzy to appear in public. Not safe enough to leave them without additional protection, as in Zhang and some of his best men also in disguise, to beef up Shirley's muscle at the new Peace Mission Hospital in case all did not go according to plan to eviscerate the Powers That Sill Be at the new ISIC Thailand.

Enter him and JD.

It helped that the new ISIC was an almost exact duplicate of the one he—the CIA's Future Elite Modern Warrior—had destroyed. And it certainly helped that JD had not long ago been the CIA's most deadly assassin and a master of disguise. But to lay odds they would be the new A-Team going in to retrieve Gregg while divvying up the duties to deal with Miles and Ambassador Phillip Jordan fell into the category of go figure or get a new bookie. As for Kate, she was off limits and, per an old associate of JD's, sited shopping in Paris as of yesterday.

"Ready?" he asked JD, just outside the perimeters where a sniper laid with a dart in his neck, a wad of gauze stuffed into his mouth, and the rest of him trussed up tighter than a Thanksgiving turkey.

"Got my mop." Hunched over and looking like an elderly janitor with an ISIC badge, JD muttered, "See you at 20:00 hours as planned."

While JD went in search of Gregg, Jerry knew exactly where he would find Miles.

Miles, who had called "CODE…" something, something upon getting into the chopper he had thrown Isabelle from. Isabelle being the reason Jerry had his eyes elsewhere while the bleating chopper blades drowned out everything but the thud of his heart as he watched her go.

Knowing what he now knew, Jerry could only presume it was Code Green Jerry, to bring him back to Miles like a homing pigeon.

MILES WAS GETTING A LITTLE WORRIED. Okay, more than a little. Jerry, his greatest achievement, his FEW, should have arrived by now, make that a week ago.

He had embedded into Code Green Jerry that after destroying all evidence of ISIC's original existence, any leftover prisoners included, Green Jerry would do anything and everything necessary to return to the new ISIC nest.

That new nest was still somewhat bare of inhabitants—including Jerry. Which either meant his Code hadn't worked or Jerry could have fallen victim to the NVA en route to home.

The former would be worse than the latter, putting his protocol and findings in jeopardy.

And yet… maybe not. Codes could be re-embedded. Jerry was one of a kind.

"Howdy, pardner!" said the familiar voice as the new office door flew open, then shut with a neat kick of a combat boot. He was dressed in his ISIC best—even his Submariner Rolex was back on his wrist! "Ready to get back in the saddle again?"

"Jerry, where have you been?" Miles exclaimed with genuine concern. "I was afraid the NVA may have gotten to you before you could get to them first."

"Nope, nope, the NVA turned out to be the least of my worries," Jerry assured him with a big, friendly grin. "I was just a bit delayed due to some unforeseen complications."

"Sure hope that didn't include any problems in decimating things as ordered. That would not please The Ambassador and we both know which side of the bread our butter is on. Right, Old Hoss?"

"You are right as rain on that, and… Say!" He nodded at the new notebook Miles had opened on his new desk. A duplicate of the other, right down to the longhorns. "What's that you have there?"

Just then Miles realized his hands were placed on either side of the notebook—one that would be clearly visible to Jerry. Almost as immediately he saw Jerry whip out a familiar knife from his back pocket—the same combat knife Miles had given him at their first meeting, during breakfast on the veranda, with four snipers having their guns trained on the infamous Ghost Soldier, Jerry Prince.

In disbelief Miles watched Jerry's combat knife slam through the flesh, muscle and bone of his right hand, his primary surgical and writing hand, securing a not-going-anywhere embedment through paper and wood.

"That's for my calico," Jerry informed him over Mile's shrill howl of pain. "And this is for Isabelle."

Before Miles could yank away his left hand, two silver steel chopsticks crucified that much of him to the desk as well.

"CODE PURPLE JERRY!"

Jerry suddenly jerked rigid, like he had been electrocuted.

Hardly able to think past the excruciating impalement, the shock of seeing his blood leech out on his latest journal entry, Miles realized his mistake—purple to kill; blue to self-destruct—and screeched, "JERRY CODE BLUE!! CODE BLUE JERRY!! Withdraw the knife and cut your throat with it now! NOW!!"

Jerry went very, very still, a mannequin's preternatural pose. Then another rigid jerk before he went full-on possessed: Jerry's head shook back and forth. His feet danced. He went "MEOW-MEOW" so loud it hurt the ears, until—

He gave Miles a grin as big as Texas, pulled a familiar Star Trek notebook from under his special ISIC highly decorated military shirt, and slapped it between them on the blood stained desk.

"And now, let us return to the sponsor of this show. Your journals have been most instructive, Dr. Miles. It is rather shocking to realize one is considered no more than an insect, a lab animal, no different than the kittens were to you. But, I must say that despite some serious character flaws, you are an excellent teacher. And, being a highly motivated student, I have taken detailed notes. First we'll hit you up with a little pharmaceutical MDMA before we get to work on a new protocol going forward. Since we don't have enough time to binge on Roy Rodgers or Howdy Doody, how about some Willie Nelson while I gather additional information and we lay down a few tracks for you?"

IT WAS 20:00 hours—8:00 pm and dark—when they rendezvoused, just as planned.

JD had their rescued cargo in the janitor's push cart, albeit unconscious, nicely trussed, and ready for a ride back to his wife in the jeep they had arrived in. Other than Gregg having been subjected to some reconstructive surgery that came as something of a shock, plus his reluctance to leave thanks to some codes needing to be wiped from his subconscious—

"Not a problem" said Jerry, extending a blood stained notebook—the first two objectives of their infiltration had succeeded without a hitch.

If anything bothered JD, it was that things had gone a little *too* smoothly.

"And you were able to set the good doctor up for what will be going down next?"

"Affirmative. Sure you don't want me to come with you?" Jerry produced a couple of syringes from the new ISIC pharmaceutical cabinet. "Happy to help close shop."

"Thanks, but you stay with Gregg." JD twirled the tiny dart he had specially prepared for the occasion. "This is personal. Phillip is mine."

CHAPTER 32

"I'm sick of seeing you in that ridiculous kimono, Katherine. Wear your Halston, wear your Dior, wear what you just brought back from your latest spree in France, wear any damn thing you want—nothing, preferably—but would you just get rid of that thing?"

"Why?" she snapped. "Because you don't like to be reminded of where it came from, who it belonged to, before your stupid Dr. Miles killed her?"

"She slipped. He was reaching for her and she backed up. And why? Because she had been found out. She went where she should not have gone and was going to damage us. It's just as well that we didn't have to deal with her ourselves. As far as I'm concerned, he saved us the trouble."

"She was my friend, Phillip."

"You'll find another one."

"Like Gregg?" She gave a short, bitter laugh. "Like Shirley? You have systematically ensured I have no friends."

"When you signed on for the position you coveted—both positions—as an agent under my direction and as my wife—"

"Neither being what I thought I was signing up for!"

"Oh, please. Cry me the entire Mekong, Katherine. You followed your ambitions and desires to end up precisely where you are, only to cry foul for the price attached to your own decisions. You remind me of a petulant child who got exactly what she wanted yet lives in a perpetual state of discontent because no matter how much you have, it's never enough."

"Like the other women you keep on the side? As for a child—"

"Do not you *dare* throw that into my face again. I had nothing to do with that fall."

"But you were glad when I had the miscarriage, weren't you? *Weren't you?*"

JD frowned from the shadows where he lurked and listened near an open window. Kate had told him she couldn't have children. Only later had he learned from Gregg, who had known her since childhood, that it was because of a botched abortion when she was an exchange student in France—which happened to be when she had first met Phillip.

Tucking this newest miscarriage revelation away for later contemplation, JD continued to listen to the bickering between the biological father who wanted him dead and the only woman he had ever truly loved, except for his beloved French mother. *Maman.* So exquisite, yet cursed with the twin demons of a crippling depression and incredibly flawed taste in men with much in common: Rich, powerful diplomats from prestigious American families who were Ivy League classmates and served together in the OSS before it became the CIA. Both having cause to permanently silence her once she became too unstable to trust further than the mattress he had been conceived upon. But his suspicions that the charming brute she was married to may have orchestrated her "suicide" had expanded in recent years.

It was right after he had put together the pieces about his true paternity. Which was in the same pocket of time that Kate had inexplicably turned against him, aligning herself with the man who was seething, "For the love of God, Katherine, would you just please take yourself out of my sight, along with that little Beretta you like to brandish around like a snippy Chihuahua on a rhinestone leash, and get some fresh air? Much more of this and I am finished with you. With us. And you most definitely do *not* want to end up on the short side of my wrath. Now, be gone with you. And the next time I say stay in Paris? Stay there!"

JD further blended into the shadows of the French estate that was eerily similar to what Jerry had called "Hugo's house," only this one had an impressive gated entry with two guards—both recipients of the syringes he had accepted—and an electric fence that could no longer fry so much as an egg. The surveillance cameras had been similarly addressed, also compliments of Mr. Prince.

The door slammed with a *bang!* He watched Kate kick a porch swing, then take a healthy swig from a bottle of Krug before she threw it into the air. The glass shattered with a well-aimed shot from the Beretta and he tried not to envy the gun too much when she kissed the still smoking barrel.

JD considered the CZ75 that he'd brought along, a very fine 9mm advance production pistol. There were always options. He could go forward with the plan or he could retreat and return once she was gone. Only, when would that be? And there was still the Dr. Miles set up to consider. Step back now, the rest could easily, if not immediately, fall apart.

A familiar, unwelcome hunger stirred as his gaze lingered on Kate, roaming the gardens. Forcing his attention where it belonged, he expertly positioned the tiny dart under his tongue. The tip had a thin, protective coating that would disintegrate on impact with its intended target, and was far more dangerous than the CZ75 which he slid into the chest holster beneath the loose fitting janitor's shirt.

He slipped the surgical booties over his shoes. Next, the surgical gloves. Hairnet. Swiftly, silently, he entered through the front door Kate had slammed shut.

Just for a moment he watched the man he had once admired and trusted, even loved in his own way, puff on a Gauloises while he paced around and swore. Softly, of course. Phillip was too refined and too reptilian to do otherwise.

"Did you kill her?"

Phillip whirled around, cast a shaking finger at JD.

"How the hell did you get in here? Guards! Guards!'

"Please, spare me. Spare us both. What guards you had went nighty-night. Kate is trolling the garden grounds while she wonders whatever possessed her to marry you. As for me? Well, here I am despite your every effort to erase the mistake you made after you possibly erased my mother. Which leaves me with this burning question—Did you ever really love her, and if you were incapable of that, did you at least love Kate before you took her from me, too?"

"No to your mother and yes to the other—at least at the time. Anything else?"

"Were you responsible for my mother's death?"

"You were the one who found her hanging. Did you see me there?"

"You have quite a talent for making things happen even half a world away," JD pointed out, only to receive a slight bow, as if he had bestowed an accolade. "I wonder. Do you still have the coin I tossed in your lap at our last meeting—the one you could make appear and disappear when I was a little boy? Or did you toss it into a fountain and wish me as dead as Maman?"

"I've always admired your deductive reasoning skills, JD. Actually, I wished you and your step-brother both dead. You never should have humiliated me like that." Phillip touched his destroyed little finger to his no longer perfect Patrician nose.

That's when it struck JD that his own nose was a duplicate of what Phillip's had been before he and Zhang had rearranged a few body parts. And the hands, except for the destroyed little finger, he had inherited those, too. His eyes, his hair, olive complexion, they were all Maman's. But in much else he saw himself in Philip now. He had tried so very hard to erase Phillip from every nook and cranny of his existence, that he had not allowed his mind to roam where it was presently, unexpectedly, going.

He had come here not to kill Phillip, but to do something much worse. To his father. *His own father.* The man he continued to stare at, to look at somehow differently than before, was toxic. He considered life a grand game, people mere pawns for his strategies and amusement. Phillip certainly would not hesitate to kill him on the spot if he could. But they were two very different men despite their genetic link and a very long professional liaison, and suddenly JD was unsure if he could go forward with ensuring that Phillip would be consigned to the living hell he absolutely deserved.

JD disguised his hesitation with, "When did Kate have a miscarriage?"

"A very good question. Especially since there was the possibility you were the father, not me." In JD's stunned silence, Phillip smiled as he looked past him and casually suggested, "But why don't you ask Katherine instead?"

There was an unnatural high pitched whistle in his ears; his stomach was flopping somewhere on the floor. While his mouth moved but no words emerged, JD turned to see Kate standing behind him. For the first time in five years she was almost close enough to touch, and despite it all, he longed for her as intensely as the moment she had returned the silver bracelet that was attached to the hand that should be reaching beneath his shirt.

She had her Beretta pointed at him.

"Katherine Lynn Morningside," Phillip said very distinctly. "Code Pink. Shoot him."

She fired twice and down went JD.

His eyes fixed disbelievingly on Kate while he clasped both hands over the chest area that had taken two hits, as if from a great distance he heard Phillip say, "Well, my little bastard son, how Freudian this all seems to end. And actually poetic. Your lovely mother was also susceptible to suggestions while vacationing at the French Rivera, which we all know was a polite way of saying she was in what had to be her favorite mental institution, given her number of visits. Shock treatments. Pharmaceuticals. Hypnosis. It all became just a bit much for her, you understand. And that brings us to the final act in the play: Katherine Lynn Morningside, Code Blue. Now. With the pistol."

The shot rang out. In horror, JD watched her fall.

Phillip came to lean over JD, his satisfied face only a few feet away, filling JD's vision.

"I did love her, Katherine, you know. Only, she always loved you more. Obviously, I couldn't have your brat remind me of that, any more than .your father by name could bear your apparent resemblance to me and shuttled you away to that monastery he paid handsomely to raise you. I was quite fond of you, JD. Actually, I do still have the coin you landed in my lap on our last, most unpleasant visit. I kept it as a reminder that we did not always have bad blood between us. But alas, you claimed something I could never fully have. Katherine's heart. How fitting that's where she's bleeding out."

JD whispered, too faint for Phillip to hear.

"Are you fading dear boy?" he asked, leaning down. "Or perhaps you're thanking me for having the two women you most loved ready to greet you on the other side? No competition between us anymore, they're both yours now. And good luck with that hellcat Katherine. I should have just let you keep her to begin with. Who knows? If I had, perhaps we could have avoided all the things that came between us. But how boring would that have been? More like playing tiddlywinks between toddlers than dueling masters at a game of GO."

Another whisper, inducing Phillip to lean even closer...closer. "What was that? I can't quite hear you. And your last words are—"

"You lost the game."

It was through long practice that JD brought the tiny dart lodged under his tongue to his lips and blew it directly into Phillip's neck. The

270

needle point released the neurotoxin upon shock of impact. Phillip jolted upright, staggered back, tried to walk, only his legs looked like rubber bands with the elastic yanked to the point of breaking.

He fell inches from Kate. His beached fish gasping for air, the lips parted in shock and the tongue that wagged out, would remain exactly so, as would the wide open eyes that could no longer close without assistance.

JD took his turn leaning over Phillip and considered doing something very kind—pulling out the CZ75 that was strapped against the thin Kevlar combat vest beneath his shirt. *Bang-bang* and this whole sorry, horrific soap opera would be over. It would go the way of a mysterious double homicide, or suicide, as impossible to solve as JFK's assassination and the conspiracy theories surrounding Marilyn Monroe's death.

Kate would love the company she would be keeping.

But the wrenching sight of her unspeakably beautiful face, frozen in the sort of surprise one might express with an unintentional self-inflicted bullet through the heart, and JD knew he would not be humane.

As he cut off the emotions that would interfere with his speed and accuracy, JD went about the necessary forensic crime scene staging of where each body would fall, with Kate the victim, all her fingerprints wiped from the Beretta perfectly gripped in Phillip's possession.

In the process, JD explained, "The very, very bad news, Phillip, is you are unlikely to die. Bad news because with your wealth and fame and background you will have the best of medical care despite the over-whelming evidence that you murdered your wife. Speculation will swirl for decades to come, your impeccable reputation tarnished, and yet you will be unable to fight back, to plead your innocence, due to your own deplorable, helpless condition. After a multitude of tests, the best doctors in existence will concur that you have Locked-In Syndrome, for which there is no cure. If that diagnosis escapes them, you will likely receive great pity nonetheless, being rendered into an apparent vegetative state after what must have been a terrible stroke that possibly contributed to your mishandling of the gun that ultimately killed your wife. You see where I am going with this?"

JD did not allow himself to glance again at Kate, not just yet. If he did, Phillip would have the consolation prize of knowing just how close he was to utter emotional devastation, which was a luxury no agent could afford at the top of his even shakiest game.

"Just so you know what to expect," he went on, blinking several times against moist eyes that could weep in private, while Phillip's had to be painfully dry already, "You will continue to feel pain, hurt, anger, loneliness. You can even feel an ant crawling across your face but won't be able to speak or move. Perhaps worst of all for you will be the ability to mentally calculate, strategize, think, and have an endless supply of time to do it with the end result being that you will drive yourself far madder than Maman ever was. You had a monstrous game going, Phillip. A dream of owning the world with elite warriors that would be yours to control, their minds and actions completely at your command. And don't you agree..."—he reached down to grip a thick shock of gray hair and nodded Phillips immobilized face up and down—"how beautifully ironic that you will retain your mind but have absolutely no control over anyone else, or anything, not even your own body, ever again."

JD gently patted Phillip's stately head.

He then wiped down every surface he had touched in the event even a partial fingerprint had been transmitted past the surgical gloves; the booties would be burned off premises.

Once everything was ready for company, he concluded his nightbird's tour into the future abyss.

"Dr. Miles will be coming on call soon. He will be the one to discover this little horror show and contact Command to tell them a tragedy has occurred. As you know, they will send a 'cleaning team' and scramble to create whatever scenario will best whitewash 'a bloody mess,' as you would say. Oh. Dr. Miles will have some rather odd, severe injuries to his hands to explain, which will be one of those tasty bits that are just too rich not to eventually leak out. The media and tabloids will have a field day. Dr. Miles will, of course, be implicated even further once some very damning journals fall into the possession of the US government. What a surprise it will be for many, though clearly not all, to learn of a dark ops program that has flourished without any oversight. I think it safe to predict a plea bargain may be struck but some quality incarceration will still be in the cards for Dr. Miles—unless he makes a run for it. However, I would say his chances of a successful escape will be on a par with yours."

JD expertly removed the dart. Smiled. And they were done.

Saying goodbye to Kate was infinitely more difficult. He gently touched his lips to hers and remembered how warm and generous and pliable they had once been. The urge to cover her up, to keep her warm and protect her from the indignities soon to come was so great...

But it would change nothing, only indicate someone else may have been involved, someone who cared for the victim. All he had left to offer was contained in the promise he breathed into her ear:

"You brought so much light into my life before things went so wrong. Next time, we'll get it right. Sweet dreams, shining star. Meet you on the dark side of the moon."

CHAPTER 33

Peace Mission Hospital
Thailand

Izzy was so nervous he was queasy trudging down the tropical flowered path leading to what Gregg called his "beach shack."

"Gregg, I told you that I'm just not up to seeing Margie."

"Sorry, buddy, but she is on her way and will be here by this time tomorrow. Which means—"

"I need to get a ticket back to New York."

Gregg grabbed his arm as he pivoted to avoid the destination they neared—a small, artfully crafted building made of bamboo with polished teak steps leading to French Doors. Palm trees waved above the porch decorated with lush plants that slightly blew with a cool breeze off the Andaman Sea.

"C'mon, Iz. You agreed."

"I shouldn't have had that last shot of Jack last night."

"Actually, I think it was the weed." A pat on Izzy's shoulder and Gregg said, "Look at me."

Izzy mentally braced himself. He was still the same Gregg underneath, but it was just downright creepy what the director of ISIC had done to him. The mind molestation was bad enough, just truly horrible, but to use the techniques he had memorized during the one facial reconstruction he had assisted with, and to apply them *exactly* to another patient to receive almost identical results, was beyond jarring. The fact that Gregg already had sun bleached hair and sky blue eyes, while Jerry Prince had stopped wearing his blue contacts and dying his hair, had created a perverse sort of irony: Gregg looked more like Jerry Prince now than Jerry Prince did.

"I'm really sorry he did that to you, Gregg."

"Hey, a little identity crises is just an opportunity to grow in disguise." Another reassuring pat to the shoulder and Gregg nodded to the so-called beach shack. "I've got an old friend of yours waiting in there."

"It's not—not—"

"No, it's not Margie. I'd never spring something like that on you. Besides, we need to get you in better shape before she shows up. And it just so happens the old friend who's waiting in there is an even better shrink than me."

That's all Izzy had to hear to nearly beat Gregg to the French doors that revealed a private office with teak paneling and bamboo floors, a carved bookcase, wide desk, two big, inviting leather chairs facing each other, and—

"KO!" Izzy shouted.

The old girl struggled and heaved to her feet from a tatami mat between the two oversized chairs. She mustered an enthusiastic yelp and a tail that wagged a sweet, familiar greeting as he dropped to his knees and cradled her head next to his.

"KO, I can't believe you're here," and if it sounded like he was choking up that's because he was and who the fuck cared. KO sure didn't. Gregg would say he was making progress.

"She's always been our best shrink for the nonverbal PTSD kids. But she's still damn good with us grownups, too." A scratch behind KO's ears and Gregg headed for the door they had just entered. "I'm going for a walk along the beach. Dr. KO is with you, no one I trust more. You know the drill, Izzy. Tell her everything, hold nothing back, take all the time you need."

At the sound of Gregg's retreating footsteps, Izzy told her, "Man, is he good. But none better than you, girl."

KO tilted her head, looking at him attentively. Her dear familiar face was now white with age, but those soft brown eyes were the same as ever and Izzy couldn't help it, his chest just started to shake while every awful thing he'd had pent up for years erupted to the surface.

"Maybe Gregg was right, KO. Of course he was right. It's not like he's said anything I haven't known all along myself, that what I've stuffed down, tried to ignore, hide from, deny, it never goes away, and the longer it sits there the stronger it gets and the more it eats me alive. I've just become this cesspool of poison I can't even stand to be around but I'm trapped in my own body with my own twisted thoughts that play over and over and over again..."

He saw it then. The thing that he could not erase, that no one knew of, that had plagued him in his every waking hour, stalked him in his sleep. So much worse than anything they endured in the cages. Physical pain could be excruciating; psychic scars more painful than death.

"I've thought of killing myself," Izzy confessed. KO seemed to nod before she licked his cheek. It was only then that Izzy realized he was crying. He never cried. Never. After all, crying took emotion and his best defense had been to have no emotion, to go through every word, deed, every day, like an automaton programmed to give the appropriate responses while remaining safely removed from any genuine interaction with others.

"The past five years have been so excruciating; I've lost count of how many times I've envisioned throwing myself in front of an oncoming subway. I came really close several times because it just seemed the only way to make the agony end, but I always stopped at the last second because I knew it would be so horribly selfish to heap that kind of pain onto my mother, my family, to Gregg and JD. But just in case, I have a note of apology at my apartment, in the top of my desk where I know it can be found. No real explanation, of course. Every now and then I'll take it out and read it, and I think of other ways to kill myself that would be more discreet, less violent, or might look like an accident instead. And then my mind goes other places that makes me wonder if it's worse or if it's better that I know as much as I do about these things... "

KO whined, sounding as if she wanted him to move on and away from that awful place his mind knew by rote, so often had he gone there.

"Funny, but not really," he admitted, "How I would rather think about dying than the reason I want to. Talk about avoidance."

KO agreed with a yip.

"Okay then. I can lie to myself and I can lie to Gregg, and, let's face it, my whole life is one big fat lie at this point, but I won't lie to you. I have a story to tell you, KO, and we'll start with me taking an oath to `First, do no harm' before I was landed on a steaming tarmac in Nha Trang in '69 and the Army didn't care that I was a children's specialist. That's—that's an important part for you to remember. My life was going to be dedicated to working with traumatized kids, and I just took for granted that's what I would go back to once my time was up. I had gotten through the worst of it, I thought, when I was down to 82 days and a wake-up. That's when Gregg came back because JD had pulled us in after Kate went missing..."

And there he was, where he never let himself go, on the overcast late afternoon when he and JD and Gregg were traipsing through the bush where only JD was at home. They had barely escaped some VC and JD had the radio, trying to make contact to send in air and get them out of there. Gregg and JD were racing ahead for the river where a chopper could land, but as usual his stomach was acting up and his bowels were turning to water and he was wondering what in god's name he was doing with the gun JD had insisted he keep for protection.

He could still hear himself yelling for them to keep going, that he would catch up as soon as he relieved himself. He could still feel the slap of palmetto leaves and sandy soil mixed with giving earth under his feet in the tropical brush, the fear of some large and poisonous insect connecting with his exposed backside as he crouched down to evacuate before he soiled his pants. Then just as he was frantically searching for a wad of toilet paper in his pocket, just as he heard the bleating of chopper blades, up rose a figure maybe eight feet in front of him, pointing an AK-47 at the beach.

"It was hard to tell how he was dressed but it didn't matter," he whispered to KO. "Even from my vantage point near the ground, he looked short, scrawny. But it didn't matter. I pulled out the pistol. I had always been nervous shooting it when JD made me practice, but right in that moment, while my heart was racing, my hands were surprisingly steady, and all I could think was that I could not miss and I had to act quickly. I released the safety and just as the chopper got so loud it had to be landing shortly, I pulled the trigger and—and I heard it go off and watched the sniper drop."

Deep breath. Another. And another. *Just finish it, finally finish it.*

"I stood up and mostly I felt relief. Relief I had been there, relief I hadn't shat my pants. Relief that I could just make out Gregg and JD waving for me like crazy while the chopper descended. I felt so much relief I almost didn't go check on the target I'd shot, that I really didn't want to look at anyway, but I thought I should make sure he wasn't just faking it and we could all end up taking a hit before making it onto the chopper. So I... I pushed through the palmettos, the vegetation that had separated us and kept him from noticing me and...and...and—"

The serrated breath he drew felt like notches of glass climbing up his throat only to shatter out on a sob, "*It was a child.* A CHILD. *Oh. God.* A little boy. He couldn't have been more than ten and I saw the blood coming out of his stomach, his eyes glazing over and I tried to pick him up and he coughed and said 'Me. Me.' And I knew that meant mother, that he was calling for his mother just before his eyes rolled back and he died in my arms. And then I...I was just so horrified and I knew I couldn't save him and I thought I heard more VC coming, maybe more child soldiers, and I knew Gregg or JD would be coming after me any second and I...for some reason I looked in his front pocket and there was a picture of him, with what had to be his family, and I..." Unable to bear the weight of his sacrilege any longer, he cried out, "I took it!"

As KO whined and lapped at his face, Izzy told her again and again, "I killed the little boy and then I took his picture... I killed the little boy and then I took his picture..."

When Gregg's hand came to rest on his shaking shoulder, Izzy forced himself to release KO and look Gregg in the face while tears continued to stream down his own.

"I killed a little boy," he made himself confess. "And then I took the picture of him and his family."

"Do you still have it?" Gregg asked softly.

"I keep it in my wallet so I never forget him."

"That's good. That's good," Gregg assured him.

"I'm a monster. I don't deserve to live."

"That's not true. You know it's not."

"I feel like a leper and want to stay away from everyone. Especially the people I love the most, so I don't infect them with all the darkness that's in me, the disease that I embody."

"Well, that may be how you feel, but it's not true, either. It is so not true."

"Margie deserved the best, not a murderer and a liar and a fraud. I tried to fake it. I tried to act like it never happened. I tried but inside I knew I was going to run and hide."

"I think it's safe to say that as of now, your running and hiding are over, my friend. You are braver than you know, Izzy. Fearless?" Gregg shook his head, extended a handkerchief that Izzy took and blew into. "No, you're not fearless. You're something much tougher: Courageous.

You're afraid but you do it anyway. Like today. And tomorrow. And the day after that. You've got your work cut out for you, but this was a milestone and now you can start to heal. For what it's worth, there's more than a little help to be had from your friends."

KO barked her agreement.

"Margie's coming tomorrow." Izzy scrubbed at his wet cheeks, knew his eyes had to be swollen to the size of golf balls. It was a wonder he could still see through his black horn rims. "I don't want her to see me like this. Look at me, I'm a mess."

"Quite the contrary, I think you're in better shape now than you've been in years. And as far as Margie is concerned, you'll be the best thing she's seen since…well, the last time she saw you."

"Must your glass always be three-quarters full, not one quarter empty?"

"It wasn't always that way," Gregg reminded him. "But moving back to Viet-fucking-nam and marrying my dream girl just took that frown and turned it upside down. Maybe something for you to consider, too. Lots of room at the mission. Especially for doctors of psychiatry who specialize in children, when we have so many child victims of the war. Including child soldiers struggling with PTSD. It could be a very effective form of self-therapy for you, substantial payback, and a godsend to the kids in need. Just something to think about."

Izzy knew he had a lot to think about, but there was one thing he didn't have to think about at all as he rose from the floor and clasped Gregg on both shoulders with steady palms.

"Thank you Gregg. You and JD are so much more than friends. You are my brothers."

With a nod, Gregg slipped the silver Montagnard bracelet from his wrist and placed it on Izzy's. "Absolutely."

CHAPTER 34

August, 1975
On a train to Ang Thong
60 miles north of Bangkok

Jerry was nervous. He tried to calm himself by stroking the little calico kitten he had found in a Bangkok alley and promised not to ever, ever harm. She was nice and plump now, purring contentedly in his lap. He had named her Butter.

Panther had not wanted to leave the Mission since arriving, and Jerry could understand why. His doppelganger, Gregg Kelly, doled out kitty treats as frequently as the cigars he was still handing out a month after his and Shirley's baby girl had arrived on—send up the fireworks!—the 4th of July.

They named her Katherine.

Izzy and Margie were re-engaged and already making plans for a honeymoon in Switzerland.

"Homeland of the famous psychiatrist Carl Jung," Izzy had told him.

"And the C.G. Jung Institute in Zurich," Jerry had pointed out. He had not been at the top of his class in mind control for nothing...not to mention the time he'd done in psych wards.

"I want to go skiing and build snowmen," Margie had told them both.

"Don't forget ice skating." The way Izzy said it and received a private smile that could melt the whole Swiss Alps before they got there was cue enough to give them their space.

Margie, he really had to give it to her. Not only had she accepted his profuse regrets for nearly killing her all those troubled years ago, she had chosen to retire early since relations between Washington and Bangkok had literally gone South, with the Royal Thai Government telling their once good buddy to get all their combat forces out no later than the next year. With 27,000 troops and 300 aircraft, that was no small U-Haul move between now and then.

For Margie to give up her cushy post as an Army Major in Hawaii after so heavily investing in her military career, just walking away with whatever benefits she had accrued to sign on as Head Psychiatric Nurse at the mission with an engagement ring from its new Psychiatric Director on her hand...

Jerry took a deep breath. Did that thumb to middle finger exercise that Miles had taught him, before reaching into his front pocket for two items of hope:

A small velvet box and Hugo's dirt stained envelope.

Carefully removing the letter inside he re-read the well memorized lines:

Jerry, mon ami. It is with deep regret that I travel without you, but it is necessary for now. Do not lose faith in our Trust. Do not lose faith in Yourself. Garden when you can. We will find each other again when you least expect it. Till then, guard yourself well, mon fils. Hugo

How many times had he gone over each word, each letter, trying to find some embedded clue as to Hugo's whereabouts? But... nothing to suggest a clandestine meeting. No invisible ink. Chances were that Hugo presumed the letter would be taken and investigated and never reach its intended recipient, so he had simply resorted to saying what he had to say.

There were other letters, not from Hugo but just as cherished, that he had been receiving at a new monastery that was heavily supported by Zhang and JD. As for how he'd gotten there...

"What are you going to do now, Jerry?" JD had asked after delivering Gregg back to his wife and they passed a joint under a full, watery moon with the lap of waves washing in from the Andaman Sea.

"Lay low. Let the dust settle. See what happens after the `cleaning crew'

sweeps through ISIC like a tornado of fire ants. Thanks for helping me make sure all the film footage and written records concerning me are goner than gone."

"You never existed," was JD's assurance. "That leaves you with a clean slate to be whoever you want to be now. If you need any help with new fingerprints, falsified documentation—"

"Appreciate the offer, but I can handle that. Besides, I've been thinking it may be a good time for me to take a little break, figure out what I want to be when I grow up. I'm trying not to be too impulsive or reactive, you know?"

"Good idea. I did that for a while, maybe a little too long. Actually, if you're interested, the monastery I grew up in and taught at for a while has been relocated not too far from here. Say, a day on foot if you know where you're going. I could take you there if you want to check it out and see if you'd like to stay as a guest at the monk hotel."

"Hmm. Sounds interesting. But..."

"Isabelle should be safe to go home soon. I would just advise her to keep her pictures under wraps until one of us gives her the signal to go public."

"Does that mean you'll have access to classified information? Obviously, my own major resources are going to be severely limited now that they're either destined for a nursing home or a secret government prison." Hugo did not bear mention. Jerry knew he would be hiding somewhere in the Shadowlands. Or, possibly tending a garden down the road in disguise. With Phillip Jordan out of the way, Hugo could go undetected indefinitely... especially if there was someone planted in the system with access to Top Secret information and informants. "I don't guess there's any chance you're thinking of going back to your old job?"

"Let's put it this way. Word has it that a certain George H.W. Bush will be stepping in for William Colby to head the CIA next year. Impressive resume: Previous Ambassador to the United Nations, more recently Chief of the Liaison Office to the People's Republic of China. He's someone I think I could work for."

"In that case...about this monk hotel. Do they have mail service?"

"I'm sure that's something that Zhang or I could arrange."

Jerry thought of the latest letter he had received, one that simply said, "Will you, please? They want to meet you." Enclosed was the train ticket. The envelope had a familiar lipstick imprint on the seal.

The train was slowing, the lush verdant greenery on either side giving way to a station just up ahead.

He had the address. He could catch a car or a cyclo. Or, he could walk and hopefully shake off his nerves.

And then...

All thought left him at the unexpected sight of her standing at the station, wearing a red silk Ao Dai, a flower in her chin-length hair, and a small bag or purse with its leather strap riding her shoulder.

He barely remembered to grab the piece of luggage he'd brought, filled with gifts for the very large family he would be meeting.

Bounding from the train, Jerry had no idea what he was going to say until he stood there, his luggage hitting the ground, Butter curiously sniffing at Isabelle before he put the kitten down, tethered to her little leash.

"You look beautiful." He touched her cheek, testing the waters.

"I'm nervous." Ever so slightly she moved her head, deposited a small, soft kiss into his palm, then turned back with a shy smile. "After all of our letters, it feels like a first date."

"Maybe we should toast to new beginnings."

"Please don't tell me you brought a bottle of Krug." Her small laugh was a little dark, as was the look that crossed her exquisite Eurasian face. "That wasn't funny."

"Actually, it was. In a macabre kind of way."

"There's no getting around that, is there?"

And there they were, facing the elephant their letters had skirted around.

"Can you ever look at me without seeing those pictures, or knowing what I had to resort to in the darkroom to keep you quiet?"

"And that is the million dollar question, isn't it?" Isabelle picked up Butter, hooked her arm through his. "Come, let us walk to my family's house. It will give us some time to sort things out. By the way, I like your natural hair and eyes even better than I did your Troy Donahue look."

"Maybe that helps you see me differently?"

"What I see is pleasing to the eye, but it is what exists beneath that carries one's true substance." Suddenly, she stopped, let go of his arm, and withdrew a Polaroid instant camera from the small bag she had been carrying. "I asked you in an intimate moment if I might take your picture. You said no. I tried to take your picture that first day at ISIC and you put a copy of a big, boring book in front of your face. And now, I will ask you, may I take your picture?"

"Isabelle, I can only hope you realize that I am incapable of denying you anything."

"Then let us put this camera to good use."

She handed him Butter, instructed him to put his arms around her with Butter in the middle, and held out the camera, the lens facing them.

Click.

As the camera spit out its instant negative and immediately began to develop, Isabelle hooked her arm through his again. "We will arrive at my parent's house soon. It is not nearly as extravagant as our villa where I grew up, but it is just as warm and hospitable as our more impressive surroundings. Only the heart is what counts, whether in a home or inside of us. No?"

"*Oui.*" Unable to withhold the urgings that had been shouting since spying her at the station, Jerry turned her in his arms. He kissed her without regard to the unseemliness of such public shows of affection within the culture, and if Isabelle had a problem with that, she was not making it known by kissing him back just as fiercely.

It was only when Jerry heard a loud clearing of a masculine throat that he reluctantly pulled back. He did *not* need to give her father reason to throw him out before he even took off his shoes and entered their house.

"Jerry, mon ami. It makes my heart full to see you harvest such precious fruit from the garden you have tended without me. My old neighbors asked me to join them for your much anticipated visit. Your friend JD and Isabelle did not think you would mind."

Looking from Isabelle to Hugo, to the doors that opened for assorted relatives to pour out, Jerry wondered, could a man literally die from the rush of too much joy?

If so, he had to be a dead man walking when Isabelle produced the Polaroid shot she had taken. Fully developed and without special lighting, effects, pretense, she told him just as simply:

"And this is how I see you now. How I see us looking forward, not back. Happy ending."

EPILOGUE

Twenty Years Later
Washington, D.C.

After concluding yet another meeting with some of the top brass at the FBI regarding his profiling of a new Most Wanted, Jerry headed for his private practice. It was one of several offices he kept, the others spread from New York to LA to Bangkok.

So it went when you weren't just any doctor. That's right, he was a Doctor-Doctor with a Ph.D. in Forensic Psychology and two MDs in Forensic Psychiatry and Neurology. It amused him to think of how he had been hailed a wunderkind who whizzed through medical school and blew his professors away with his level of expertise in such areas as where the mind and criminology intersected, as well as cutting edge experimentation with hallucinogens in treating mental illness that the government had since banned. His enthusiastic endorsements by such renowned International experts as Dr. Israel Moskowitz and Dr. Gregg Kelly—not surprisingly often mistaken for his brother—had only added to demand for his highly sought after services.

But Jerry knew it was his marriage to a famous photographer whose last name he had taken, and rumors that he kept company with spies, might even be a CIA secret agent himself, that generated the most speculation in do-tell circles.

Hell, he wasn't a CIA agent. He didn't want anything to do with that shit! JD could have all the fun. Besides, with the number of kids that he and Isabelle had adopted from the mission, there wasn't time to dabble in the cloak and dagger business. Grandpere Hugo was a lot of help for sure, even in his advancing years, but he liked to disappear every now and then. Usually when JD suggested it might be a good time for him to take a little vacation, which usually coincided with some overly ambitious FNG wanting to dig up old dirt on unsolved cases.

The Ambassador Phillip Jordan Affair, as it had been dubbed by the tabloids, had never been solved, only ensuring that it retained a sensational mystique—especially after Jordan's death just a few years ago, with any secrets to be had taken to his grave.

Jerry wasn't sure but he had a hunch that JD or Hugo or maybe the two of them in concert had decided to show some compassion and set The Ambassador free from his living hell prison.

Which naturally brought his thoughts to the monstrous genius indefinitely detained at a top-secret holding facility after the "cleaning crew" descended upon ISIC. Miles had yet to resurface. Similarly, Isabelle's pictures had never seen the light of day. Would they have provided the story of a lifetime, something important, risky, controversial that would have kept viewers awake at night? Oh, you bet. The Ambassador had not gipped her on the goods she had asked for—or the generous deposit he had made into a Swiss account from funds the government apparently had no knowledge of, and that's how Isabelle wanted to keep it. The tradeoff of her safety, of his, of their privacy, just wasn't worth it, she had insisted. The dainty foot she put down subsequently ascended to a Pulitzer prize for an album of photography dedicated to children of war.

Jerry's cell phone buzzed.

"He's out," JD said without preamble. "Delivered to an undisclosed location."

"Were you able to make sure the sleep aid is where he can find it?"

"Of course. It won't disturb any neighbors."

"Nice touch."

"Would you like his just acquired, unlisted cell number?"

"Of course."

They laughed together quietly.

"How's Isabelle?"

"Wonderful as always and getting us packed for our trip next week to see her folks and all our extended family at the mission. Will you be there?"

"Absolutely," said the voice that transformed to sound exactly like Izzy's.

Another good laugh, a few more opaque details transmitted, and Jerry went about his usual business.

It was only after activities, homework, and dinner were over, their children of various ages finally giving it up for the night, that Isabelle wrapped her arms around his neck in their bedroom.

"Whew. What a day. Ready to snuggle, Dr. Chene?"

"Actually, Mrs. Chene, I have a few things to see to before I join you. Get the bed warm for me?"

"Sure. But I'll probably be asleep before my head hits the pillow."

It was her head he kissed, softly, lingering, before he retreated into his private study.

Jerry set the mood with lights dimmed, Hovhaness's Mysterious Mountain playing in the background. He lit some incense and said a Buddhist prayer he had learned at the monastery.

Next, he poured himself a snifter of some very fine Cognac, an excellent Hennessey he saved for special occasions. It had been an anniversary gift from Isabelle's father, which made it all the more meaningful.

As he sat at his expansive teak desk with every indication he was a highly successful forensic specialist, a master of dissecting the criminal mind, Jerry reminded himself of some important truths:

He had worked very hard to keep a tight rein on his impulses, to exercise the sort of kindness and compassion that wasn't often shown to him growing up. He strove to be a good and loving father who taught by example what it meant to be a person defined by their character, perseverance, and moral substance. That included the ability to forgive.

Uncountable times over the past twenty years had he imagined this moment. Twenty years to reflect on the positive behavioral changes that Miles had been responsible for. Twenty years to wonder what might have become of him without Dr. Ronald Miles to heavily lobby to bring him to ISIC in the first place. Twenty years to be grateful for the private tutorship of a brilliant scientist since it had allowed him to escalate his own education and career at a remarkable speed.

Jerry unlocked the bottom drawer of his desk where exactly six items resided. One by one he lifted them from their hiding place and laid them on his desk.

A combat knife.

A pair of silver chopsticks.

A Star Trek notebook with Spock on the cover

Another Star Trek notebook with Captain Kirk

A copy of the picture Isabelle thought was no longer in existence. It was the shot she had taken with Miles smiling down as she plummeted backwards from the chopper he had pushed her from.

And a small, intricately carved teak box.

Jerry opened it. A tiny white neck bone lay nestled in a bed of warm, gold velvet.

A moment of reflection and *Snap* went the box.

He returned his gruesome treasures to their hiding place, locked the drawer, and went to an expansive bookcase where an untraceable cell phone was waiting.

Enough of Hovhaness. The music was all wrong.

Resisting the urge to crank it up, he hit the perfect selection: Blue Oyster Cult.

As "Don't Fear the Reaper" played on loop, he swirled the amber liquid that reminded him of the Mekong doing laps around the crystal, until he made his decision.

"Needs more cowbell."

Jerry punched in the number that JD had provided.

The other end picked up with an uncertain, "Howdy?"

"Robert Frost had a poem I need you to remember, Dr. Miles. It's called Stopping By Woods on a Snowy Evening. So much more poetic than `Code Blue,' don't you agree?"

"What...who? Jerry, is that—"

"Look in the cutlery drawer beside the stove."

"Look in the cutlery drawer..."

"Yes. Because *I have promises to keep. And Miles to go before I sleep.*"

There was a pause, then the muttering of "Promises to keep... promises to keep..." accompanied by the scrape of boot steps until the phone clanked on a countertop just before a cutlery drawer rattled open.

Whock! Whock! was followed by the distinctive sound of a body drop.

Jerry disconnected. He lingered over his Hennessey.

Then turned out the lights.

"We are not what happened to us, we are what we wish to become."

— CARL JUNG

ACKNOWLEDGMENTS

From John Hart

What a long, strange, interesting journey it has been to create and craft the Murder on the Mekong trilogy—*Unbreakable, Unknowable,* and finally, *Unspeakable: The Killing School.* Because of the subject matter of mind control and torture, *Unspeakable* proved to be the most emotionally difficult and painful to research and to write of the three novels. We thank our readers for taking on this emotionally and psychologically challenging story and subject.

A big shout out to co-author Olivia Rupprecht for her steadfast belief in these stories that have not been easy to tell but resonated with her in terms of historical importance and their unique, sometimes aberrant, entertainment value. Without her guidance, good humor and tireless spirit these books would not have been fully realized. Over the near decade we have worked together to complete the *Murder on the Mekong* series, her brilliant writing, creative insights, ideas for character development, and consummate editing are evident on every page of every book. Along the way she has become a dear friend who has enriched my life.

Olivia and I want to acknowledge with real gratitude our publishers Nina and Brian Paules at ePublishingWorks!

We thank again our early readers Nuala Vermeiren, Nick Torokvei, Nancy Gold, Peter Spear, Annie Figi, and my lifelong friends Steven Smith and Charley Bensley. A special thanks again to the esteemed Tai Ji master Chungliang Huang who inspired various aspects of this book.

Thanks to Professor Alfred W. McCoy whose books and writings informed, inspired, and provided important source and reference materials.

We are again grateful to our medical consultants Dr. G.S. and Dr. N.S. for their expert advice and acknowledge that any medical and pharmaceutical errors are our own, not theirs. We also thank Sue Elle for her guidance and expertise and Steele Clayton, Vietnam War veteran and helicopter pilot for his invaluable help.

Aloha Scott Rupprecht and Andrea Hart for all you did once again in getting us both through another Murder on the Mekong. Only you know what it takes.

And finally, a word about my late brother Joseph Truman Hart. Brotherhood has been a central theme running throughout the entire series, whether we be brothers by blood, by shared cause, military affiliation, accident or choice. My brother Joe was considered among the best and brightest of his generation in the field of psychology. He was my protector as the older sibling, a larger than life persona I always looked up to; and yet, he never made me feel diminished in his shadow, only elevated by his belief in me and nurtured by the warmth of his heart. May all who read this find that same sweet place with a loved one to stand by, for as my brother's teacher, the great poet William Stafford, wrote: "The darkness around us is deep."

ABOUT THE AUTHORS

Hart Rivers is the pen name for bestselling co-authors John L. Hart and Olivia Rupprecht. John, Creator of the Murder On The Mekong series, has been a practicing psychotherapist for over 40 years, starting in Vietnam where he was a psychology specialist. He received his doctorate from the University of Southern California, is an internationally respected lecturer, has been a consultant to the nation of Norway for their Fathering Project, and maintained a private practice in Los Angeles for twenty years. His time is divided between Hawaii—where he enjoys snorkeling, stand up paddle boarding, and is a featured artist at the Mauna Kea Hotel—and Vancouver Island, B.C., where he is an adjunct associate professor at the University of Victoria in British Columbia.

Olivia is an award-winning author whose novels have sold worldwide, and Series Developer of True Vows, the groundbreaking series of reality-based novels from HCI Books. She lives in a historic tavern on a lake in Wisconsin.

We love to hear from our readers. Please visit us at:
www.MurderOnTheMekong.com.

www.ingramcontent.com/pod-product-compliance
Lightning Source LLC
Chambersburg PA
CBHW050924030726
47503CB00007BB/2461